SILENT SCARS

B. J. MEEHAN

Thanks to my wife Shelly for her insight and patience.
And to my daughter Deanna for her review.

PART I

THE SCARS FORM

1

SUMMER OF 1956 – REVERE BEACH

The stalker stared at Shirley and her companion from his perch overlooking the beach. His stomach growled. The smell of fried clams and hot dogs from across the street at the Howard Johnson's concession blended with the pungent smell of Atlantic seaweed stewing on the beach, buried mussels and oysters, and salt air. In the background, people were screaming as the Cyclone rollercoaster raced down the first drop, and they distracted him for a second. Carousel calliope music playing in the distance danced in his head. An old Ford convertible drove by with the radio blasting "Tutti-Frutti" by Little Richard.

A bead of sweat dripped into his left eye. It was hot today, but the weather could change quickly. Several strands of his hair were already lifting and pointing to the south. There was a coolness shifting from the north. He pulled his arms into his body and looked up at the sky. It had ever so subtly darkened. He smiled.

His car was parked about one hundred feet from the ramp on the beach side of the road. He had arrived half an hour before the women showed up. He first waited in a little coffee shop until he spotted them walking down the ramp onto the beach. Then, after they had been at the beach for a while, he walked across the street and gazed out and tried not to stare at the women. But every so often, his eyes darted to them. They were about halfway from the street to the ocean. He was straining to hear. While the crashing of the waves somewhat drowned out the voices of the two women, he nodded to himself as if he understood what they were saying. Then he rubbed his elbow over and over again.

Shirley's companion, Edie, stood up.

The man's posture straightened, and he raced to the coffee shop.

Edie slipped on her sandals, strolled up the ramp to the sidewalk, walked past the coffee shop, and stood at the Howard Johnson's food stand. After a few minutes, the clerk handed her a white bag and two paper drink cups. She returned to the beach, down the ramp, and sat back onto the beach blanket.

The man's facial muscles relaxed. He returned to his perch overlooking the beach.

The girls juggled the napkins while they munched on their hamburgers.

The man's hair moved a bit more. The sky was changing, and the wind was ever so slightly picking up. He wrapped his arms around himself, looked up and his forehead wrinkled. Then his eyes blinked, his eyebrows moved up and down, he opened and closed his mouth, and clicked his tongue. This sequence of facial movements lasted about thirty seconds. It started slowly, then accelerated. Finally, it tapered and eventually stopped.

He looked impatient and stared into different directions more frequently while still trying to seem like he wasn't paying attention. Then, finally, he turned his head, straining to hear what the women were saying.

"I'm getting a chill," said Edie, Shirley's cousin, and best friend. "It looks like we might get a storm. So I'm going to split."

"Yeah," Shirley said. "They always say the beach is the worst place in the world to be during a thunderstorm."

Edie laughed, "Who's they?"

"You know who '*they*' are," Shirley paused. "Ma!"

Edie broke into a laugh. "She is rather a worrywart."

"Me too." Shirley's facial expression shifted from the lighthearted look to a somber one.

Edie's laughing abruptly stopped and paused for a few seconds. "I know."

"You go ahead first," Shirley said. "I'll stick around for a few more minutes. This is the first time I've been to the beach all summer."

"How did you escape work?"

"Slow day at the store. Mr. Means assumed the weather would turn sour tonight and that it wouldn't get any busier, so he gave me the afternoon off."

The stalker stiffened as if he had learned something. As he did, a gentle wind began to blow some sand, giving the beach a light-yellow hue.

"What's the plan for tonight?" Shirley said. "Want to chill at my place?"

"No way, Jose. I promised I would babysit Bobby. Why don't you come on over?" said Edie.

"I wish I could. But unfortunately, Dad has to work a double shift. I hate leaving Ma alone, especially if it storms," said Shirley.

"How is she?"

"You know."

"Yeah,"

A chilly wind started to whip up. Edie packed up her towel, put on her shirt, then shuffled through the sand. "Don't hang around too long. Just look at those clouds." They both looked up.

As Edie walked up the concrete ramp and stepped on the sidewalk, she passed by the stalker whose face was now making that twitching motion. She tried not to stare, but he looked at her. She had a strange expression on her face. He turned away. Edie seemed like she had an inexplicable desire to stop and say something, but she didn't.

The man took another deep breath. Then, he smiled while continuing to rub his reddened elbow back and forth.

The wind was bringing a storm, and the incoming smell of rain was getting stronger, overtaking the fried food smell.

Edie turned to Shirley and yelled, "See you tomorrow, Shirl. Be careful." Then she looked up at the sky, picked up her pace, and crossed the street.

The man's expression turned worried.

Edie turned toward him. As the young woman leaving her cousin passed the Howard Johnson concession stand one last time, she looked back at the bizarre-looking man standing and watching the beach.

The twitching man's body stiffened. As Edie continued to walk away, his shoulders lowered slightly. She kept walking. The beach was on one side of the road, and all the amusements and concessions were on the other. An old metal green fence separated the beach from the sidewalk. He stood leaning on the fence, one foot on the berm and one elbow on the top bar. He stared at the ocean with his head lowered. A large wave crashed on the shore. Then his head jerked up as if he had just remembered something. He walked to his car, a maroon, 1951 Mercury four-door sedan, and opened the rear door. The metal hinges creaked. He coaxed a cowering beagle out of the vehicle, grabbed the leash, and pulled the panting dog back to where he was standing.

Shirley had only eaten half her hamburger. The dog focused on the burger while pulling on the leash. "What luck," the man muttered under his breath. He released the leash and kicked the dog in the backside. The dog raced down the ramp, across the sand, down the beach, and snatched the burger.

Shirley seemed startled. Then just laughed.

The man ran across the beach, stumbled on the sand, and almost fell. He took hold of the leash and pulled the dog away.

In one split second, the dog gobbled the left-over burger whole.

"Heck, I am so sorry. I was walking him along the sidewalk, then I changed hands on the leash. Then the pooch bolted. Gosh, he then saw you and the hamburger. Couldn't stop him."

The man held up his arms in a shrug.

Shirley leaned over from her sitting position on the blanket to pet the dog. It licked her mouth.

"Buster. Hey. Leave the pretty lady alone. I don't know if I'm walking him or he's walking me. Bad boy. Could've scratched the lady or ruined her gorgeous bathing suit."

Shirley's expression turned serious. It went from laughter to caution. She moved away from him.

"Could've scared her." His voice was one of reassurance.

Shirley seemed to relax a bit. "Oh, I love dogs. I can't imagine he'd hurt anyone." She continued to pet the dog. "Say, don't I know you! I think I've seen you a couple of times at the firehouse. Don't you work on the trucks?"

Now on one knee, the man petted the dog, Then the man stood. "Sure, I'm a mechanic. I come over to the firehouse every other week." He paused. "So, what brings you there?"

"My dad is the captain. I work around the corner at Mean's drugstore. Pop in now and again and bring him a frappe from the soda fountain." She glanced at her watch, then put on a shirt over her wet bathing suit.

The sky was getting dark. The storm was on its way.

"No problem about the dog. So maybe I'll see you at the firehouse sometime. I gotta get crackin'." She pulled her beach towel into a ball and headed up the ramp toward the sidewalk.

"Wait. Look at her," yelled the man from behind.

"Who?"

"Not who. It. My new car. Like the one in the movie, you know, *Rebel Without a Cause?* With that cool cat, James Dean."

Shirley continued to walk away.

"Hey, got to swing by Hennessey's Garage. You know, where I work. Not far from where you work. Give you a lift home, don't mind. It gives me a chance to show the car off. What do you say?"

Shirley continued to walk away, picking up the pace a bit.

He stumbled from behind, yanked the dog, who was now not cooperating.

"No. I shouldn't. I don't even know you. Know what they say?"

"What?"

She picked up her speed. She turned, and half yelled. "Never accept a ride from a stranger?"

"Yeah. But see, I'm not a stranger. I work at your father's firehouse. That makes me an acquaintance, not a stranger." The man picked up the pace and was now panting. "Besides, Fido here needs some company. C'mon, no big deal." He gestured toward Shirley to take the leash.

"I thought you said the dog's name was Buster?"

"Oh yeah, Fido was my old dog. Sure, it's Buster, no wonder he doesn't obey me."

He raced up the concrete ramp to catch up with Shirley, picking up speed. Finally, he caught up with her and handed her the leash.

She didn't take it at first. Then she took hold of the leash. "How come he doesn't have a dog tag?" Shirley rubbed her fingers on the dog's collar.

"Oh. Umm. Must have fallen off."

Shirley wrinkled her brow.

A solid breeze blew off the water while sand blew in their faces.

The man wiped his eyes.

"How are you getting home?"

"The MTA."

Most people took the MTA train to Revere Beach. MTA stood for the Metropolitan Transit Authority. It was the public transit system that served the greater Boston area. The man knew Shirley would have taken the MTA to the beach. The closest train station was the brand-new Wonderland Station, about a mile from where they were standing. "No big deal, right. Look, you gotta walk to Wonderland Station. That will take, what, fifteen, twenty minutes? Then you wait for the train. Probably another ten minutes. Then you change trains at Park Street Station, right?"

"No, Devonshire. But yes, I have to change trains."

"Then to Sullivan, where you hop a bus. It will take you over an hour. It will only take me fifteen minutes to get you back to

Somerville. Just have to stop by the garage. I'll only be a minute. I'll save you probably an hour."

"No. It's okay. I don't mind the rain."

"What about the lightning? I hate thunder and lightning. How about you? It could start any minute. C'mon, I work with your father. But if you would rather dodge the lightning."

She handed the leash back to the man.

"Sorry. But thanks anyway. Maybe I'll see you at the firehouse sometime."

She jogged across the street, diagonally toward the Howard Johnson's stand.

The first raindrops appeared. The wind now was blowing at about five miles an hour.

As she headed toward the Howard Johnson's stand, the clerk dressed in a red and white uniform stood still for a few seconds. He had his hand on the handle of the metal door about to pull it down. A storm was coming fast. He peered out toward the sky.

The stalker pulled the dog toward the car. It was parked in the opposite direction from Shirley. He pushed the dog into the back seat, jumped into the driver's seat, started the engine, drove a few feet, then did an abrupt U-turn and pulled over.

The Howard Johnson clerk glanced at Shirley rushing by. He also looked down the street at the Mercury idling a few hundred feet to his left. It was almost as if he noticed something off, something not right.

The stalker's eyes focused on the Howard Johnson guy, then Shirley. He waited.

The clerk did two movements with his head, one towards Shirley and the other towards the Mercury as it lurked, rumbling, pouring smoke from its exhaust. Then, finally, the clerk shrugged and pulled the metal door down with a screeching clang.

The Mercury peeled off toward Shirley.

A bolt of lightning lit up the sky. Crack. It was followed within seconds by earsplitting thunder. The stalker made a jumping motion. The dog barked.

"Nice." The man said out loud with a smile. He rubbed his elbow faster.

Now the rain was beating steadily on the car roof. It was like the sound of rapid gunfire.

Another burst of lightning flashed across the sky. Boom! A crack of thunder followed within seconds. The lightning was close.

Shirley glanced up at the sky and picked up her pace.

The Mercury caught up to the nearly running Shirley. The man pulled the car to the sidewalk, beeped the horn, leaned over to the passenger side, and opened the door.

"C'mon. It's getting really bad. I'm no stranger."

Shirley stopped. Her long brown hair was dangling in soaked strings. She jumped into the car and closed the door. "Yeah, I guess it will be okay. No, no big deal."

"Nope. It's bad out there." The man cracked an ever-so-subtle smile.

2

EARLIER THAT DAY...

"I told you so." Shirley giggled as Al Means climbed the stairs from the cellar of the dusty old drug store carrying a case of Coke-a-Cola six-ounce bottles. It was hard to explain how the store smelled. On the one hand, it had a sweet scent of various concoctions made from peppermint, spearmint, and vanilla. But it was mixed with oldness and maybe even mold. Next to the soda fountain was a water-cooled metal chest. He lumbered to the soda chest, opened the chest cover, and placed the bottles into the chest one at a time.

Shirley took a deep breath. She loved the smell of the inside of that chest. It was like cool, humid air. It reminded her of the "Air-Conditioned Somerville Theater" scent in Davis Square during the double-feature matinee. Today the store was hot and humid.

Shirley felt that Al Means made a mistake that hurt his soda fountain business. He told her that the soda fountain attracted the Somerville riff-raff teenagers. Al muttered that kids hanging around the store would scare off high-paying customers. He had just put in a new line of women's cosmetics. So rather than have those boys buy five-cent cokes, the ladies would spend 2 or 3 dollars on that new Max Factor lipstick. Shirley didn't believe it.

The mistake she had told him was, pulling out all the soda fountain stools. So now the punks, as he would routinely call any boy who hung around the store, would have to stand at the fountain. This action, he figured, would deter the juvenile delinquents from hanging around.

"Told me what?" Al asked.

"You know. Pull out the stools from the soda fountain. I told you that the kids wouldn't come in unless you had stools."

"They were more trouble than they were worth! They scare off the ladies."

"Where are the ladies?"

"Don't be such a smart aleck. I don't like a young, basically part-time employee telling me how to run my business. If you were anyone else, I would fire you."

"No, you won't." She laughed a sassy laugh, "Didn't you know I am your main attraction?" She twirled around, her long dark brown hair swinging across her face.

She never failed to speak her mind. She had argued that the stools gave the store a welcoming feel. She had told the grumpy old man that now, it felt like it just inconvenienced customers with no seats. They both were right. The punks stopped coming in. But women didn't flock to the store either. On this day, it was just slow. No punks, no ladies.

"Business will pick up. You know, word of mouth. Those ladies will come in. It's just too damn hot today. Why don't you take the rest of the day off? You aren't attracting any customers anyway."

While Al Means was a bit of a crank, Shirley knew he liked her spunk.

"Git." Al cracked the slightest of a smile.

"Just as soon as I make Dad a frappe. I'll pay."

"You never pay, and I don't expect you to. Free frappes are one of the fringe benefits of working here," said Al. He continued to load up the Coke-a-Cola bottles in the rusty old cooler.

"Fringe benefits? You mean the only benefit. But seriously, I do appreciate it," And despite Al Means cranky nature, she liked him.

Making a frappe for her father was a regular ritual for Shirley. However, the frappe was a special thing between her and her father.

Al Means would coach Shirley on the fine points of the difference between a frappe and a milkshake. A frappe was so much better than a milkshake. You would make a milkshake with whole milk, a squirt of vanilla, chocolate, or strawberry syrup. Then you placed the metal cup on the mixer machine and whipped it. The frappe was made like a milkshake, except you added a scoop of ice cream. Whenever Shirley made a frappe for her father, she added a little extra scoop. Al would never know, nor probably care. She liked the intrigue.

With frappe in hand, she had laughed a cute laugh and left, then called her cousin Edie from the phone booth right outside the drug store. "Let's go to the beach. I'm going to see my father, get my stuff at home, then I'll head over. Let's meet across the street from the Virginia Reel at around two o'clock." To get to the beach, each would have to take different buses and trains. That meant that they would leave the beach separately. Edie would take the bus to the Rapid Transit Line and Lechmere Station from Highland Ave to get to the beach. Shirley's bus ran to the Sullivan Station's Mainline from Broadway.

Shirley walked briskly to the Central Firehouse since she didn't want the frappe ice cream to melt.

Her heart leaped, approaching the firehouse. Even though giving her father a frappe was a regular occurrence, it was always special. She walked through the big garage doors of the firehouse, which were always open. All the guys stopped what they were doing and gawked at her. She knew it too. Brad, her father, raced to greet her.

"Hey, sweetie. What's in that white paper bag?" asked Brad. But, of course, Shirley knew that her father knew exactly what was in the bag.

She thought her father always looked so handsome in that fire captain uniform. He had spent his whole career working up to the rank of captain. She was proud of him and loved him dearly. "You know what it is," gushed Shirley. "Now get it into the fridge before it melts completely. Boy, it's hot outside!"

Brad grabbed the bag. Peeked inside. "Ummm." He rushed to the firehouse kitchen and carefully placed his treat in the fridge. "I'll beat the living shit out of any of you bums who even looks at that bag." He raced back to Shirley. They hugged tightly.

Shirley was worried about her father. He was under a lot of pressure. Being the fire captain at the firehouse, he had a lot of responsibility. Her mother was dying. Her terminal breast cancer weighed so heavily on both. The frappes were special to him. It was just a little thing. But it meant a lot to Shirley to do it. She could sense that her father had a newfound sadness about him. When she delivered the frappe, joy sprouted upon his wrinkled face even for a few minutes. That had made her so happy.

"Back to work?"

"Nope. Heading to the beach. Meeting Edie there." Shirley waved goodbye and hurried through the big garage doors.

"Brad had waved to her as she left. "Have fun. I'm jealous. Don't forget to get those special Howard Johnson's French-fried potatoes. Same spot?"

She turned back to her father. "Yeah. Right across from the Virginia Reel. I'll eat some for you." Shirley had laughed as she hurried out of the firehouse. She headed home to gather up her beach clothes and then catch the bus to the train station. Her journey would take about an hour.

Shirley hadn't paid much attention to the man at the rear of the firehouse.

Several days ago, the man had left one of his tools behind. A few minutes before Shirley had arrived today, he had returned to pick it up. Once he spotted her, he strained to hear everything she said to her father. "Revere Beach. Across from the Virginia Reel." The MTA would take at least an hour to get to Revere Beach. But it was just a

15-minute drive in his Mercury to the exact spot where Shirley and a companion would be sunning themselves.

He added the tool he left behind to his toolbox. He glared at the firefighters as they walked around the building in their uniforms. "Pricks." He muttered.

On the same day he had left his tool behind, he was changing the oil on the big hook and ladder. Shirley had been standing not ten feet from him. When he finished the job, he had walked past Shirley. Shirley nodded to him and smiled for just a second. He smiled too but held it well past the time she walked by him.

The night after the encounter, the man told his mother about Shirley. He called his mother, Mother, not Mom, or Ma, but simply Mother.

"Her name is Shirley. I'm going to show off my new car," said the man to his mother.

"Oh. That's great."

"She'll love my car."

"You are so proud of that car. Isn't it just like the one James Dean drove in that movie? What was that?"

When he was 17, he snuck out of the house at midnight, walked all the way to Davis Square, which was about a mile from the run-down tenement. *Rebel Without a Cause* was playing at the Somerville Theater for a five-day run. On each side of the movie theater's front entrance were two locked glass frames that housed movie posters. He was able to pick the lock on the frame and carefully peel the poster. He rolled it into a tube, then ran all the way home and snuck back into his bedroom. He didn't even wait until morning. He hung the poster over his bed. The poster displayed Jim Stark, played by James Dean. In the movie, Natalie Wood played Judy. She was the one that Jim Stark wanted as his girl.

"*Rebel Without a Cause*," the man answered. "It is the exact car that James Dean drove in the movie."

Yet, it wasn't the same car. James Dean drove a customized two-door 1949 Mercury. The man's car was a 1951 Mercury four-door sedan. Pure stock. The base version of the car.

Brad had caught sight of him as he walked back from saying goodbye to Shirley.

"How you doin, son? Today is not a scheduled maintenance day, right,"

"Fine. Sir. No, I realized that I left one of my rachets here. I was just picking it up. Left it on the workbench," said the man.

"You looked a little concerned just a few minutes ago. Everything alright?"

"Well, my boss Mr. Hennessey would be mad if I lost one of the tools. So, I was a little concerned. But I found it, so everything is just fine. Today, everything is perfect, just perfect. Everything is falling into place." The man forced a grin.

"Great." As Brad turned around, the man's eyes blinked quickly. Next, his eyebrows moved up and down. Then, finally, he opened and closed his mouth rapidly and clicked his tongue.

The man left the firehouse. Driving from there, he passed a house on Walnut Street when he saw a beagle tied up in a front yard. So, he stopped in at the Pearl Street Market for a small batch of raw hamburger and then returned to the house with the dog. He pulled over in his car, jumped out, waived the bait in front of the dog, opened the gate, and cut the leash with his jackknife. Then he coaxed the poor unsuspecting animal into the car.

~

"How come the worried look, honey?" asked Edie's mother, Doris. In addition to being Shirley's cousin, she was also her best friend. Doris had seen that look before. There was something about Edie that had bothered Doris ever since she was a little girl. She had seen that look on Edie just before Jerry, Edie's grandfather was going into the hospital for a gall bladder operation. Edie was seven at the time. Jerry died on the operating table. When Doris broke the news to the family, Edie said that she had known that it would happen.

"Nothing. You know, I get these feelings every so often." Edie lied. She got those feelings more than every so often, more like every day.

Mostly, Edie ignored them. If every time she got those feelings and acted on them, she would stay tucked away in bed and never move. But there were times that there were more than just feelings. Although she never heard voices, she felt the presence of people that had died. To her, it was almost as though people were telling her things. Yet, they were just thoughts. She had a hard time differentiating her thoughts. Were those thoughts something she made up in her head? She didn't know. It happened often enough that she merely lived with the curse. Many times, she just blocked them out. Today though, the messages were quite strong.

She had promised Shirley that she would meet her at the beach. And she was determined to go. Probably nothing would happen. Edie had learned to live with these feelings at twenty years old ever since she could remember.

"Is this about Auntie Ethel? Do you feel something bad will happen to her?" asked Doris. Ethel was Shirley's mother and Doris's older sister.

"No, Ma. It's nothing. Nothing bad is going to happen. Besides, Shirley would never leave her mother alone if she thought she was close to... you know." Dying. She was pretty sure that her feelings had nothing to do with Shirley's mother. She would just have to deal with it. Going to the beach would help. While she and Shirley were close, she never confided to her about those feelings. Her mother and her boyfriend Buddy were the only ones who had the slightest clue. Edie took a deep breath. "Stop worrying. It's nothing." She kissed her mother goodbye, walked the quarter mile to the bus stop and waited for the Highland Ave bus to Lechmere Station.

She still could not shake the feeling.

3

Glancing back at the dog in the back seat, it had a sad look, almost resigned. Despite the destructive storm, Shirley toyed with changing her mind for a second. However, that thought disappeared once the car door closed, and the Mercury peeled out with its rear tires sliding in the rain-soaked streets.

Too late. Shirley got one of those odd sensations when you think you shouldn't do something for a few seconds. It just flashes across your brain for the shortest period. Then the thought, the feeling, goes away. She slammed the idea of not getting in the car as they drove down the boulevard, passed the Cyclone, the dodgem cars, and the funhouse, heading for Somerville. The rain was now steadily bouncing off the windshield. It highlighted how dirty the windshield was. As the raindrops carried with them the grime that had been there for a while, Shirley mused that for someone who wanted to impress a girl, she would have thought the man would have cleaned the car. The car also didn't smell right. If it indeed was a new car, how come it had this sort of stale smell, almost like sheets that needed changing? She could put up with this smell since it would only be a fifteen-minute drive home.

Hennessey's Garage on Vernon Street was right off Central Street, a hilly street lined with worn-down three-deckers and corner stores in the very crowded urban Somerville. Hennessey's was a converted red-brick factory building from the 19th century. It backed up to the Boston and Maine railroad track right-of-way. The right-of-way was about twenty feet below the back of the building down a steep embankment. Separating the railroad tracks and the back of the building was a high old wooden stockade fence. It provided a private alleyway hidden from the railroad and the street.

There were several parking spaces lined up in front of the building. Instead of pulling into one of those, the man drove around to the back of the building. Then, he headed for the alleyway behind the building and backed the car into the narrow space. This maneuver didn't leave more than three feet from the passenger door to the old fence. Shirley's first thought when the man pulled the car around back was that this place was not safe. It was dark and way too secluded, adding to her apprehension.

There were all kinds of junk piled everywhere. A small door barely accessible between the rubbish barrels and the junk car parts was almost hidden. A bug-stained old light bulb lit the back door to the garage.

It was still raining heavily.

The car radio had just started playing "Are You Lonesome Tonight" by Elvis when the man stopped the engine and took the keys. He jumped out of the car. He peaked his head back into the car. "I'll be just a couple of minutes." If he was only going to be in the garage for a minute, wouldn't it make sense to keep the car running? It wasn't like they were strangers. Right?

Shirley thought his mood shifted as the man raced toward the old door. First, he had seemed happy to her, then he seemed to look, what was it? Nervous, upset. For the second time, she felt a sense of, well, it wasn't precisely dread, just that she had made a mistake. Then he disappeared into the creepy building.

"Please don't be any longer," she said out loud to no one. Shirley didn't like this. There was no one around. While the garage was in the middle of the city, it was still isolated. She toyed with the idea of getting out of the car and walking to Central Street. Then she could walk to Broadway, where she lived. It would probably take thirty-five minutes. Not too bad.

The thunder and lightning made things even more upsetting. But Shirley thought to herself. It would be fine. He'll be out in a minute, and I will be home in ten, maybe fifteen minutes. The rain was steady, and the wind was blowing heavily. She even wondered if that creaky old fence separating the alley and the railroad tracks might fall.

But he wasn't out in a minute.

As he entered the old garage, the man paced. The plan had worked flawlessly. He had stashed a bottle of Old Granddad bourbon, in his locker, just in case he needed a bit of courage. Now he wasn't sure what to do. Shirley had seemed pleasant enough but certainly not engaging. She hardly said a word during the ride from the beach to Hennessey's. He was sure that she had looked at him at the firehouse. He thought it was a smile. Now he wasn't so sure. Maybe she was playing him along? Like many people in his life, she would make fun of him.

He opened his locker. The bottle of whiskey beckoned him. He knew that if he started drinking, his courage would increase. But he also knew that the whiskey would also make him lose control. He grabbed the bottle and took a large swig. Then another. Then another. The alcohol gave him more courage but built a small fire of resentment. He took several more mouthfuls. Hurt blended with his excitement. Why wasn't she more friendly to him? After all, he gave her a fucking ride home. She should have been grateful unless she was using him. Why was it that people always used him? See, the bourbon was giving him more courage. The anger was growing. She was like all the others.

He knew that the longer he stayed in the garage, the more Shirley would be unnerved.

"I thought you were going to be different." He spoke out loud. "Mother, you told me that girls would like me. Right? You told me to dress nice and be polite that they would fall for me. Why did you lie like that?"

He knew he had two choices. The first was to make up some excuse that he got caught in some paperwork at the garage, apologize and take Shirley home. Or he could encourage her to drink with him. Maybe even force her?

Then he surprised himself and began to cry. "I've been a good person. Shirley, you will be able to see that, right?" He then realized that he had been in the garage for a while, not just a few minutes. He even thought that maybe Shirley would have left the car and walked home. He gathered his wits, wiped his eyes, took another swallow of alcohol. And another. His mood turned dark. Now he was furious. Not just at Shirley, but at his father, the firemen, his boss. The years of rejection and hurt had conditioned him to expect rejection. He thought about what his mother had told him. "Fuck you, Mother. You are so full of shit. This girl had better not reject me. I won't stand for it." He had made his choice.

It was now more like twenty minutes. Shirley glanced back at the sad-looking dog. "Hey, boy, why so sad? I know, I'm getting pretty concerned myself." It was dark. Another flash of lightning made her jump. Then the boom of thunder followed. She was now convinced she had made the wrong choice.

The man burst through the garage door.

Shirley jumped.

Buster barked.

He had a big smile on his face and a bottle of whiskey in his hand. He slammed the creepy door to the garage shut with his foot. He jumped into the car. "Wow. The rain is really coming down."

"You told me it would only be a couple of minutes. You were in there for at least half an hour. Take me home now."

"Half an hour?"

The man did not start the car. "It was only a couple of minutes." He took a swig and offered her the bottle. "Here." He slid to the middle of the front seat up close to her.

A Boston and Maine commuter train lumbered by in the railroad right-of-way below.

"You left me here. It's dark and scary," said Shirley.

"Ah, don't worry. No one ever comes by here." He pushed the bottle almost into her face.

"No! Take me home."

"Okay, suit yourself. See what you are missing." He pulled back the bottle, took another long swig, and spilled a bit on his shirt in the process. "See what you made me do?" He tugged on his shirt. "This is a good shirt.' He wiped off the liquid. "Your turn." He pushed the bottle toward her face.

She shook her head. "No. I want to go home right now. My mother's alone, and she'll be worried." She took hold of the car door handle. "I'm not going to sit here and drink with you."

"Mom's alone, huh?" He took another long messy drink and wiped his mouth with his sleeve. "Where's dear old Mister Hero, Fire Captain dad in his fancy uniform?"

"None of your business." Shirley's eyes grew wider. Finally, she pressed hard up against the car door. "C'mon, you don't want to get in trouble. Now please take me home right now."

"I am not going to get into any trouble. I saw you showing off your stuff at the beach. You wouldn't do that if you didn't want it. You want it. You all do."

Shirley slapped him. She pulled the car door handle and opened the door. The rain poured in. Thunder cracked.

Buster barked and growled.

The man pulled Shirley back toward him. He grabbed onto the car door handle and closed the door, hitting her shoulder hard. He then hit her across the head. This action knocked her off the seat and into the dashboard with a hard crack. Blood poured out of her nose. "You hit me! Now you will drink with me or ..." He jumped on her, straddled her between his legs, forced his hand over her chin, pried her mouth open, and poured the whiskey into her gaping mouth.

She coughed and choked on the liquor and spat it out into the man's face.

"You shouldn't have done that. Whatever happens next will be your fault. It will all be your fault."

She wanted desperately to cry. Then, finally, she began to understand what was happening in her head. But in that split second, she decided that she would refuse to let that bastard see her cry.

"Just a little kiss, that's all. You teased me, now you pay. Then I will let you go."

"Go to hell."

He forced his mouth to hers.

She shook her head back and forth. She shut her lips tight as he tried to kiss her.

He pulled her face back, still straddling her. She couldn't move.

"What's the matter? You think I'm ugly. Offensive? Do I make you sick?" He pounded his hand on her chest hard.

The rain pounded on the car roof.

The dog barked wildly.

The man ripped her shirt off.

She had heard of women getting raped. But she never, ever thought it could happen to her. So, when he ripped her shirt off and just before he started to untie her bathing suit, it was as if she went into a sort of trance. She thought back to the several times she had casually seen whatever-his-name-was in the firehouse. While all the violence was happening at that minute, the man who would surely rape her never told her his name. During the ride from the beach to the garage, all the man could talk about was his job and car. She thought about her mother, who would probably die in a couple of months. She thought about her mother's cancer. Incurable, they had told us.

During this what couldn't have been more than a couple of

seconds, she hoped he wouldn't kill her, not for her, but her mother and, of course, her father. She knew that both needed her more than ever during the next couple of months.

Shirley's bathing suit consisted of a single-piece suit tied around the back of the neck. However, Shirley always made sure she tied a double knot. The last thing she wanted was the knot to come loose when she came out of the water at the beach.

The man pulled her from her sitting position to a laying position across the front seat. He laid on top of her. While keeping Shirley trapped under him, he worked on her bathing suit knot. It was still wet. He was trying to use only one hand, so he couldn't get it undone.

Shirley considered screaming, but she thought better of it. That would just enrage him even more. She decided to stay still, stay quiet, and hope that he would do what he would do then go away. Please, dear God, just go away.

"Shit." He yelled very loud. Shirley could see that he was getting more frustrated with the bathing suit knot. Her level of concern accelerated.

Buster leaped out of the back seat and landed on the man's back. He pushed the dog off him, then jammed him under the seat. The dog persisted and leaped back onto him, now biting his neck. "Fuck, fuck, get off me." This time he pulled the dog off him by the dog's skin and threw him at the windshield. Not to be deterred, the poor mutt returned to his back and continued to bite aggressively. "Goddam you." The man's blood dripped onto Shirley's face. He struggled to reach into his pants pocket and pulled out a jackknife. It was still closed. Since he had one hand holding Shirley down and now one hand trying to pull the biting dog off him, his actions were erratic. He put the jackknife handle in his mouth and, with his teeth, opened the blade.

Shirley gasped.

He grabbed the dog off his neck and stabbed him repeatedly.

Dog blood, Shirley blood, and the man's blood were all over the place.

"You ruined my car."

The dog was now dead on the floor next to the gas, brake, and clutch pedals. The man took a deep breath. He held the knife blade to Shirley's neck. "Don't move." He reached back and grabbed the dead dog and threw him in the back seat, blood dripping from its body. Then the facial movements kicked in. His face was not more than a couple of inches from hers.

She smelled his stale, boozy breath and could still taste the alcohol and his spit. The eyes blinked quickly.

The man's eyebrows moved up and down, opened and closed his mouth rapidly, and clicked his tongue.

If she wasn't so terrified, she might have laughed out loud.

The rain continued to make a rhythmic pounding on the roof of the car.

The enraged man kept her pinned down for a couple of minutes. The facial movements slowed down and then stopped. He cut her bathing suit strap with the knife. He then slowly pulled the bathing suit down to her midsection. He slowly moved off her and menacingly kept the knife in plain view. "You better stay still, or you'll end up like that mangy mutt. You better not say a word." Finally, he ripped her bathing suit entirely off, exposing her naked body.

Lightning flashed across the sky, illuminating her.

In her head, she thought that this was it. This was how women get raped. But, even in her panic and fear, she would not give him the satisfaction of saying anything. She decided at this point to close her eyes.

Thunder rumbled in the distance.

The man unzipped his fly.

She felt the cold, wet blood on the back of her head and neck. The car seat soaked up all that blood like a sponge.

He then mounted her. He plunged himself into her.

It just hurt. No, she wouldn't even move nor yell in pain. She just kept her eyes tightly shut.

It didn't take long for the man to ejaculate. He rolled off her into the space under the dashboard, almost hitting his head on the glove box. "You loved it, didn't you? You can sit up now." The man moved into a sitting position in the middle of the seat.

Shirley sat up without opening her eyes.

The man reached over and opened the passenger side door.

Now Shirley smelled his body odor and, of course, his semen. She felt like throwing up but did not want to give him the satisfaction. She was still afraid that he might kill her.

"Get the fuck out. You are a lousy lover."

He kicked her hard, pushing her out of the car.

Her naked body hit the ground with a loud thud. She landed into a puddle and rolled toward the rickety fence. The force of her body moved the fence toward the railroad tracks. It didn't fall. The rain wiped much of the blood off her head. Unfortunately, it didn't do much for the semen. She wanted so, so badly to moan in pain.

She would not.

The man threw the bathing suit, her towels, and her shirt on top of her.

He reached into the back seat, grabbed the dog, and pitched the dead body right on top of her. The poor thing rolled off Shirley's chest and landed limply into the puddle next to her. Again, she stifled a cry. In her shocked mind, all she could think about was that no, he was not going to kill her. She would be able to be with her mother before she died. For some odd reason, this calmed her.

"Gotta get rid of the witnesses, don't I? You like dogs, right? Well, you can keep him. Oh, by the way, the same thing will happen to you if you tell anyone. If I find out you told anyone, I will kill you and your father too."

Shirley stayed quiet.

"Understand?"

Shirley stayed quiet.

"Silence is acceptance." He nodded. Then the facial movement happened again as he looked at her. She would remember that look, that movement. Finally, he closed the car door and started the engine. He then peeled out of the back alley behind the garage, showering her with muddy gravel. She would remember the smell of the engine oil from the old garage and exhaust mixed with his scent for a long time. As the car sped around the corner of the alley, she stared at the maroon Mercury's red taillights. It was as if they stared back at her. As if they mocked her.

4

The man was gone. Shirley was alive. Now it was okay to cry. She heaved and heaved, terrified, horrified, angry, and somehow grateful to be alive. Then the crying slowly stopped. She sat up. Her whole body quivered. She was cold and had nothing with which to dry herself. Her beach towel was soaked. Everything was wet.

Then she tried to stand. She turned her body from the sitting position and braced herself with her hand on the wet, sharp gravel. "Ouch." Her arm and now her hand hurt as she tried to get herself up. Everything hurt. As she rolled to one side, her knees dug into the gravel. Then she pushed herself up to a standing position. She was woozy and hoped that she would not fall over. Steadying herself, she looked up. The storm had passed. The sky was now brightening. Thank God for small favors. The shower had cleaned the air. She took a deep breath. She had always liked the smell of the air right after it had rained. The air was moist and humid but refreshing. It was sort of like the smell of the old Coke-a-Cola chest at the drug store. It seemed to give her the courage to get moving. She wasn't afraid that the man would come back for some reason.

She jerry-rigged her ripped shirt and bathing suit back on herself.

Even though they were wet, it didn't matter. She just needed to cover herself for the walk home. The walk home? No, she couldn't go home. Not like this. She would have to go to Edie's and make up some story about why she couldn't go home. She knew that Edie was babysitting Bobby and that her parents would not be home for a while. It was still early enough. Luckily the walk to Edie's was shorter than the walk home. As she took her first step, she almost stumbled on the dead dog. She took a second or so to stare at the poor animal. "Thanks, Buster or whatever your real name is. You tried to save me." She wished that she could do something. Bury him? No, she couldn't. And she certainly couldn't carry him anywhere. She resigned herself to leaving the poor thing there. She would have liked to pat his head, but she was afraid that if she bent over, she would fall. As she took her first step, she felt unsteady, probably from when she cracked her head on the dashboard. She edged toward the fence and used it as a crutch as she walked toward the end of the building. Then she let go and was now on her own to walk. She entered the parking lot. She was okay, she told herself.

It was quite a walk from Vernon Street to Central Street to High-land Ave, where Edie lived. Thankfully there were very few people hanging around the front stoops of the two and three-deckers. She never realized how much of a hill Central Street was. She was exhausted by the time she arrived at Edie's apartment.

After leaving Hennessy's garage, the man decided not to go straight home. Instead, he pulled over into the parking lot of an abandoned meat packing plant. He was shaking badly. Why couldn't she have been nice? He wasn't sure he would have hurt her if she hadn't talked so mean to him. He banged his hand on the dashboard of his beloved Mercury. He glanced over at the passenger seat. Bloodstains. And that dog. Blood in the back seat too. It was horrible. The back of his neck was still bleeding a bit from the dog bites. How was he going to explain this to Mother? He would have to sneak into his room.

He was angry about the car. Both the front and the back seats were blood-stained. "Son of a bitch. It was her fault! Damn. And that stupid dog." He knew that they had ruined the mohair cloth seats. By the time he would get home, it would be dark. Too dark to clean them. Besides, Mother would be asking why he was cleaning his car that late. She would ask too many questions.

Then it hit him hard. As he pulled out of the parking lot, he began to panic badly. What if the girl told her father? How could he show up at the firehouse again? What if she accuses him of rape? Would he go to prison? He thought maybe he should see if she was still there. She had ruined everything. Maybe he should figure out a way to shut her up. He pulled out of the parking lot and headed back to the garage. The route took him from Pearl Street to Medford Street, then left onto Central. What he didn't know was that just before he turned left on Central Street, Shirley had walked right from Central Street onto Highland Ave. He had just missed her.

He pulled into Hennessey's parking lot, parked in the front of the building, and ambled around the side of the building toward the back alleyway. His heart raced. What if she was still lying on the ground where he had left her? What was he going to do? He slowly approached the corner of the building. A commuter train rolled by on the tracks below. The lights from the train forced him to turn away automatically. Then he eased around the corner to the back of the garage. She was gone. Was he relieved? He wasn't sure. As he walked toward the back door, he nearly stumbled on the body of the dead dog.

He knew he had to get rid of it. There were a bunch of old oily rags in a barrel just inside the garage. He cracked open the door just big enough to see the barrel. He reached in, grabbed a handful, and wrapped the dog body in the rags. He then threw the dog and the rags over the fence down the embankment. The body rolled and settled a few feet from the railroad tracks. He reasoned that it would look like a stray dog had been hit by a passing train. No one would notice or care that the dog had been stabbed. If he had left the body in the parking lot of Hennessey's, it would have raised all kinds of questions about why a dog was stabbed. Maybe even Doug Hennessey would call the police.

He now felt better. But he still worried as he headed home.

~

His apartment was on the first floor of a run-down two-family house deep on the city's east side. He knew his mother would be sitting in the front room just off the hallway, so he would have to hurry past her. So, he raced through the door down the hall passed his mother.

"Hello, honey. I've made you a nice tuna sandwich. It's in the fridge." Mother turned abruptly in her worn-out recliner. But she was too late to see him.

"Thanks, Mother. I'm filthy. Going to jump into the tub for a bath. Is the water hot?" he yelled from down the hall.

"Yeah. It should still be hot. Are you okay? You sound funny." She didn't move out of the chair.

"I'm in the bathroom. I'm fine." He wasn't fine.

The steam from the hot water in the tub cleared his head, which was pounding. He stepped into the bathtub. As he sat down in the soothing water, he realized his body was aching all over. When he had fallen in front of the car seat, he had moved awkwardly. His back ached. His neck was burning from the dog bites and scratches. He now realized that the alcohol and the shock of the incident numbed the pain. Now it was fully present.

The girl deserved it. Now he wished that he hadn't left so quickly.

"Enjoy your bath." Mother yelled through the closed bathroom door. "I'm going to bed early tonight."

"Okay. Me too. I'm going to soak for a while here. I'll be heading to my room after my bath." He was relieved that his mother wouldn't see him. She knew him well enough to know when something was bothering him. He needed some separation from her. Usually, he would kiss her goodnight. Not tonight. He would not be able to fake his emotions to his mother. He was never very good at lying to her. He would never be able to hide this intense emotional state. At least not tonight. To be sure, he decided to tell Doug Hennessey that he no longer wanted the assignment at Central Firehouse. He would make up some story that some of the firemen made fun of him. It was partially true, at least in his mind.

~

"We won't be late." Edie's parents, Doris, and George, were leaving for a night out.

Her mother was right, she thought. Nothing terrible has happened. It was a nice quiet day at the beach with an uneventful transit ride back home. No drunks approached her. No derailment. Her parents were fine. Auntie Ethel hadn't died. It was nothing. Nothing at all. By now, Shirley would be home. If something terrible had happened, she would have heard by now. And yet.

She couldn't help but think about that man who was hanging around the beach. She had looked at the guy. There was something about him. Then there was that strange movement of his face. As Edie had walked up the concrete ramp and stepped on the sidewalk, she had passed by him. He had looked away. She had a pang of fear. That's what it was. Fear? All too many times in her young life, she had the feeling. But, mostly, her fears came true. For a second, she had thought about going back to Shirley to warn her to stay away from that guy. But Edie was late. It looked like the thunderstorm was on its way. She lived halfway between bus stops on Highland Ave. She had a quarter mile walk to her apartment from the bus stop. She hated lightning and didn't want to get caught outside during a storm.

Her thoughts were suddenly interrupted. Bang. Bang on the door. Her fear accelerated. She wasn't expecting anyone. What if something had happened to her parents? For an instant, she couldn't move. Something horrible had happened. She knew it like always.

"Who is it?"

"It's me." Shirley could barely speak.

"Shirley?" Edie opened the door.

Edie was shocked when she saw Shirley. "What happened?"

"I need to take a bath."

"You're shivering."

"And borrow some clothes."

Edie knew not to probe. At least not right now.

"I'll call my mother and tell her that I decided to spend the night here. Okay?"

Edie nodded. She knew something had happened after she left the beach.

Shirley stood in the middle of the living room. Waiting. "I need to take a bath. Now."

Edie raced into her bedroom. She scurried through her drawers and found a top and a pair of shorts.

"I'll need a long sleeve top."

Edie ran back into her bedroom. She handed Shirley a couple of tops and pants. And a towel.

Taking the clothes and towel without saying a word, Shirley walked slowly into the bathroom. She shut the door

Edie just stood there watching the bathroom door shut. Her heart ached for her cousin. Looking at the torn shirt, what appeared to her a ripped bathing suit, she imagined the worse. She had the strongest feeling that someone had violated Shirley without really seeing anything. She even pictured the car that stood near where the man was standing in her mind. Something about that car. Shirley didn't have to provide the details. Edie knew.

In the tub, Shirley surveyed her bruises. Her right arm had a horrible black and blue covering about five inches. She could easily hide that with a long sleeve blouse. While her nose had been bloody, nothing had been broken, and the bleeding had long stopped during her trek up Central Street. She could explain away the bump on her head. But let's see. She had slipped on the concrete ramp leading from the beach to the sidewalk and fell, conking her head. The other stuff, no one would ever see. The water washed away the stink of that man.

What would happen when she visited her father at the firehouse? Her thoughts ranged from, what if that man was there? Would she panic? Would she cry? No, she would not. Never. Maybe the best thing was not to go anymore. She could say she was busy or something. Yeah, that was the best way. Stay away from the firehouse. Shirley emerged from the bathroom at least half an hour later.

"I don't want to talk about it." She was still a bit shaky even after the bath. She dialed the phone. It was hard. Shirley wasn't sure she could even speak to her mother over the phone, let alone be with her. She took a deep, deep breath while the phone was ringing. She tried desperately to sound cheery. "Hi, Ma. Yeah, I had a nice time at the beach. Yes, I used plenty of lotion. No. Didn't get any burns. She's good. She's right here." Shirley looked over at Edie, pleading.

"Hi, Auntie. We had a nice day." Edie's expression was grim.

"We are going to the Rosebud to meet some friends. It will be a little late. So, I decided to sleep over. I know, Dad's told me. He's on the night shift. But it will be late, and I don't want to walk home that late. So, I'll go to work from here. It will be fine. I'll borrow some from Edie." Shirley pulled on her shirt and motioned to Edie.

"Just did the laundry. Don't worry. I won't have her looking like a ragamuffin." Edie nearly choked as she attempted a fake laugh.

"Gotta go, Ma. See you after work tomorrow. You'll be okay?" There was a pause. "I know. Bye. Love you." She hung up. Shirley slumped into a chair. She hated to leave her mother alone, but she had no choice. Shirley looked deeply over at Edie with solid determination. She was hurt physically, but she was angry.

They both sat for at least twenty minutes in silence.

"It was the guy with the funny way he blinked his eyes and moved his eyebrows, wasn't it?" Edie leaned over and looked squarely into Shirley's eyes.

"Yeah."

"Bad, huh?"

"Yeah."

"Do you know the guy?"

"I've seen him at Dad's firehouse. He services the trucks."

"I know who you mean. Yeah. I've seen him there. You need to go to the police," pleaded Edie.

"I need to focus on the wedding. Two weeks Edie. Two goddam weeks. You can't tell anyone about this. Please?"

Edie nodded. "I won't. I promise." Edie would break her promise.

5

TWO WEEKS LATER

Edie fluffed Shirley's wedding dress. They waited in the back of the vast Saint Ann's Catholic Church, not that far from Hennessey's Garage. The wedding would start in a few minutes. There was enough space in the back of the church for a huge wedding party. The wedding party consisted only of the bride, Shirley, Edie, the bridesmaid, Bobby, Edie's brother, the ring bearer, and the flower girl, Mary O'Connell, Willy's five-year-old niece.

Brad stood a few feet away from the girls, consumed in thought. And nervous as hell.

Edie walked over to Brad. "Unc, you okay?"

"Me? Sure." His thoughts were interrupted for a few seconds. He wasn't okay. He was nervous, joyful, and sad all at the same time. He looked at his watch. It was getting close. He had been pacing between the girls and the church's front door, waiting for the organ to play that song. What was it? Something about a canon. There would be no mother of the bride being escorted down the aisle. Ethel, his wife of thirty-five years, was too sick to attend. The doctors had told him the cancer was incurable when they first diagnosed her three years ago.

Now he missed her more than ever. Ethel would have given anything to see their only child, their precious and frankly sometimes hard-headed daughter, Shirley, get married and have a gaggle of grandkids to dote over.

Brad was proud to have Willy as his son-in-law. Having only one child, a girl, meant that he could not continue having a fireman in the family. Brad's father, James, was a fireman too. So, Willy was nearly as good as having a son as a fireman. Willy was a decent, honest, and terrific fireman. Brad knew that Willy had a penchant for drinking and gambling, but so did most of the guys. Brad himself was no teeto-taler. There were many nights Brad would come home drunk. Ethel never complained much about it. Brad knew that Ethel had heard about those stories of mean drunks. Ethel would wait up, have a cup of coffee and a piece of brown bread slathered with butter waiting for him. Then she would go to bed. They never discussed it. Brad thought about stupid things, little things, like the brown bread. Focus on this wedding.

"I miss her. She should be here," said Brad.

"I know," replied a solemn Edie.

Brad motioned for Edie to walk away from Shirley closer to the door. "Is she okay? She has been a bit distant these last couple of weeks."

"Yeah, just a lot on her mind. That's all." Edie did not make eye contact with Brad.

"You know, we tend to drink. Probably more than we should. I've always been a sloppy drunk. Willy drinks, like all of us. I believe he will be a sloppy drunk, too. Do you think Shirley is worried about the drinking?"

"Not at all. She would have said something to me. Nope. It's all good."

"She seemed to have a sort of, I don't know how to put it, a melancholy. I know this is stupid, but she always brought me frappes at the firehouse. Then, all of a sudden, she decides to bring them home."

"She probably just got too busy at the store. But, you know, old man Means can be a bit of a grouch. Didn't want her to leave the store."

"Yeah, maybe. I miss her coming. The job can be a bear, so seeing her bounce in with that white bag with my frappe. It was so special. Suddenly, she changed her routine. Our old Philco fridge just doesn't keep the frappes cold like the new fridge at the firehouse."

"Gotta get back to Shirley. You hang in there." Edie walked back to Shirley, who was staring blankly toward the front of the church.

Brad was glad that Shirley chose Willy over Buddy McBride, Willy's best man. Buddy was excitable, sometimes erratic. A good guy, sure and a good fireman as well, but he wasn't convinced that Buddy would behave as he did with a couple of beers under his belt. He thanked God that Edie and Buddy had started dating. Brad thought Shirley, a rebel, would be attracted to Buddy, more so than Willy. After all, Shirley hung around the firehouse a lot and watched all the guys. Buddy was the flirt, the guy with the Elvis hairstyle, the rebel type. Willy was so serious. He never flirted or drew attention to himself.

Brad took in the smells of the candles, the incense, and the old church waxed pews. As he listened to the vast pipe organ playing some lead-up music, he thought, it turned out all right. Shirley went for Willy and Edie for Buddy.

There it was, that wedding tune that Brad couldn't quite remember. It was Pachelbel's Canon. He wished they would have played that song, *Here Comes the Bride*. Every other wedding, he had ever experienced played that song. But he didn't have the heart to complain to Shirley. No, he laughed to himself. Shirley had to be different.

Her husband-to-be, Willy Duffy, and his friend and co-worker Buddy were also waiting at the altar. Then, the music started: Pachelbel's Canon.

"Here we go. Nervous?" asked Buddy.

"Yup."

"Compared to rushing to a fire?" pressed Buddy.

"Worse."

Buddy laughed too loud. Several guests looked up.

"Jesus, Buddy."

"The wedding, or you know? Tonight?"

"Both."

Buddy stifled a laugh.

As Edie lifted Shirley's train during the walk to the altar, she wondered how their wedding night would be.

"Nervous?" asked Edie, who repeated Buddy's question to Willy.

"Nope."

"Liar."

She whispered to Shirley. "Everything will be wonderful. Even tonight." Edie didn't have any of her usual feelings. Even so, she continued to worry. Shirley had been distant and would have agreed with Brad that she now had this sadness about her. Edie fully understood. Edie so desperately wanted to tell Brad that Shirley didn't bring him his frappe because of that mechanic that might be at the firehouse. But, instead, she tried not to give him any clue as to what was wrong.

"I know."

Edie knew that Shirley was a virgin like herself. Well, except maybe for that awful night. Shirley indeed would have told her if she and Willy had sexual relations. She didn't mind telling Shirley about how forward sometimes Buddy was. Buddy was a tease, and occasionally, he tried to push the limits on Edie. But Edie knew that he respected her and wouldn't do anything to harm their relationship. Edie didn't think it would be too long before she would be the bride and Shirley, her matron of honor.

If Willy had expected Shirley to be a virgin, Edie wondered what Willy would do. Would he reject her? Stop thinking about it! She had to make sure that this wedding was perfect. She told herself to focus on the wedding. After all, *I'm the bride's maid.*

She wished she hadn't alluded to the wedding night.

Shirley just lifted her head. "I'm ready."

She and Brad walked majestically down the aisle. They faced Willy and Buddy.

Edie gave Buddy an approving glance.

Brad was crying as he handed Shirley over to Willy.

"Take care of my baby."

Willy nodded. His eyes were wide, lips pursed, and hands shaking.

The wedding was outstanding. Small but perfect. The reception in the back room of the Mount Vernon restaurant on lower Broadway was exceptional. The only downside was that the restaurant's name might have reminded Shirley only briefly that Hennessey's Garage was on Vernon Street.

People clanged their glasses. They toasted. They did the bride feeds the groom, and the groom feeds the bride ritual. Shirley had warned Willy not to even think about pushing cake into her face. Willy gave only the slightest nudge of the cake into Shirley's mouth. She gave him the dirtiest look. Willy held back.

The reception was a success except for Edie. She had caught the bouquet and danced every dance with everyone but Buddy. She got drunk then threw up in the men's room. Buddy was embarrassed. He had to carry her outside. Buddy was so busy with Edie he almost forgot about decorating Willy's old Nash with beer cans and toilet paper. Instead, he had to sit her on the curb on Broadway while he painted the back window with shaving cream.

The guys at the firehouse had chipped in for a one-night stay at the Park Plaza Hotel in Boston for the couple's wedding night.

That night sex was just fine. In the back of Willy's mind, he thought that the first entry into Shirley would be difficult and that the guys had told him to expect bleeding. Everything Willy knew about having sex he had heard from the older guys at the firehouse. His father never spoke to him about sex, foreplay, women, or their sensitive parts.

There had been no bleeding. It crossed his mind that maybe Shirley was not a virgin, but he could not have imagined it being the case. While he filed it away in some deep recesses of his mind, he never brought it up to Shirley. Ever.

As they laid together in post-sex pleasure, Shirley held on to Willy tight, almost too tight. "Hold me."

He pulled her close to him. "I will. Always. I will always hold you this tight. It was wonderful. I love you so much." Willy then dozed off to a gentle sleep.

Shirley shed a single tear. Sleep did not come quickly or easily. She felt the silent scar of shame deep within her.

Later that week, Edie and Buddy spent the night at the Meadow Glen Drive-In in Medford.

Playing was a double feature, *I Was a Teenage Werewolf* and *The Pajama Game*. Buddy liked horror movies, so he planned to spend most of the kissing time during *the Pajama Game*. Yet Buddy sensed something was bothering Edie on the drive to the movie. He loved Edie. Ever since he lost his mother, Buddy had felt an emptiness. Edie helped fill that. He settled himself into the idea that this was not the night for any heavy-duty petting.

While Buddy was forward, he was a good guy like Willy. He grew up in a twelve-family tenement building across from the Kemps Nut Factory on Somerville's shabby east side. He worked hard, saved his money, and wanted to do only one thing for his life work. Be a fireman.

Now he was. His best friend, Willy, was a fireman. Most of his friends were firemen. He was determined to honor Edie. He didn't want to mess up the second-best thing in life. He wanted to be a good husband and a father to boys, who would grow up to be firemen, just like their father.

"You're quiet," said Buddy.

"I'm just not in the mood. It's not you."

"It's alright. I've heard that *I Am a Teenage Werewolf* is pretty scary. We can watch it." Buddy used a creepy, scary voice when he said the movie's name.

Edie chuckled. "The wedding was nice, wasn't it?" She paused for a moment. Did Willy say anything about, you know, the wedding night?"

Buddy was surprised. "What? You mean?"

"Don't guys talk about it?"

"Do girls?"

"Sure, sometimes."

"No. We were busy at the firehouse. We had a couple of small fires and another false alarm at the Winter Hill Rest Home."

"Oh. So, nothing."

"Okay. I punched him on the shoulder and said something like, good night, huh?" Buddy was getting uncomfortable. "Then he just smiled. I guess everything went fine."

"Good. That's good." Edie was biting her lip.

"What is it? What's wrong?" Buddy focused.

"Yesterday, when I came by the firehouse to see you, there was this guy there." Edie kept looking down at her hands. She rubbed them together.

"What guy? You know all the guys there."

"Not one of your guys. A guy in a mechanic suit," answered Edie.

"We have a contract with Hennessey's Garage. Oil changes, grease jobs, tire rotations, stuff like that. What about him?"

"I've never seen him before."

"Me neither. The regular guy must have been out sick or something. So why are you interested in the mechanic guy?"

"Not him. The guy who is usually there. He does this funny thing with his face."

"Oh. He's an odd duck. So weird. He's always giving us dirty looks. So, what's this all about?"

"Nothing. Forget it. Nothing."

Now Buddy was irritated. "Edie, you can't ask me about Willy and Shirley's wedding night, then some unrelated question about the mechanic. What is it? Is this one of your feelings?" Buddy was not fully aware of Edie's special gift, but he caught glimpses of it. Occasionally Edie would slip and tell him just a little.

"Nothing like that. I promised never to tell." Edie was on the verge of tears.

"Edie, tell me."

"I promised." She burst into a full-blown cry.

Buddy just held her. "It's okay. Take your time."

"Me and Shirley were at the beach. It was getting late. I had to leave. Dammit, I should have stayed with her. But, Buddy, why didn't I stay?"

"What happened?"

Edie took a deep breath. "As I was walking up the ramp from the beach, I noticed this big guy, the same guy, that weird mechanic guy, just standing with one foot on the fence. He was making this odd expression with his face. It seemed like his eyes were blinking, and his eyebrows moved up and down. Buddy, it was scary. See, I should have gone back."

"You mean kinda like this." Buddy moved his ears and blinked his eyes.

"Sort of, but even more exaggerated."

"A real odd character. We just figured he has some kind of palsy."

"It gives me the creeps every time I think of him." She grabbed onto herself and shuddered.

"Did he have a car?" Buddy probed

"I don't know. There was a car parked right behind where he was standing."

"Do you remember what kind of car it was or what color?"

"I think it was a dark red."

She turned sharply toward Buddy. "You know when you have a bad feeling? I had this awful sense that that guy was not right. Why was he even there? What if he was waiting for Shirley to leave?"

"Edie, you have these sensations a lot. Right? Are you guessing, or was this one of your feelings?"

"Yes."

"Jesus, Edie."

"How could he show up at the exact spot where we were on the beach? I mean, the beach is huge."

"Maybe the bastard was at the firehouse and overheard Shirley talking to Brad. She goes there all the time. So maybe he was there too," said Buddy.

"Shirley would never take a ride from a stranger, much less a creep like that."

"Well, she probably figured he knew her father, so he wasn't a stranger."

"Yeah, and it looked like it was going to thunder and lightning," added Edie.

"So, how do you know anything happened aside from your special feelings?"

"Shirley wanted to get together at her house later that night. She didn't want to leave her mother alone. But, you know, Ethel was getting real bad. I couldn't go cause I had to babysit Bobby. Mom and Dad weren't gone more than, I don't know, half-hour when someone was banging on the door. It was Shirley." Edie took a breath and sobbed. "Buddy, I should have stayed!"

Buddy just held her tight. "Not your fault. Whatever happened, it was his fault."

Edie collected herself, "I opened the door, and she nearly fell in. She was soaked, her shirt was torn, and she had a big bump on her head. Buddy, she was raped. All she wanted to do was to go into the bathroom. She said she needed a bath and needed to borrow some of my clothes. I handed her some of my clothes, including some undies.

Her bathing suit was on the floor. I could tell that the strap had been cut."

"She told you the guy raped her?" Buddy's neck was bright red. "I'll beat the living shit out of that guy."

"No. She didn't say he raped her. I just know. Buddy, you can't tell anyone. Shirley pleaded with me not to ask questions about what happened and not tell anyone. I shouldn't have even told you."

"Okay.

Edie cried and cried.

Buddy just held her.

"When Shirley stood at the door, I pictured that man in his car, you know - forcing himself on her. She was terrified. You can never tell Willy. Ever. I promised Shirley."

"I won't."

"I was worried on their wedding night that Willy would think she, you know, was with someone else."

"I promise I won't tell anyone."

"Buddy, repeat it. Promise! Swear to God." Edie was frantic.

"I swear to God. I promise."

Like Edie, Buddy would also break his promise.

6

The next day, all Buddy could think about was that secret Edie had told him. He thought about how Shirley hadn't been at the firehouse in the last two weeks. Up until then, he never thought much about it. Now he understood why Shirley would not want to run into that mechanic. He was trying to figure out how to get the guy reassigned or fired from Hennessy's, but he hardly even knew Doug Hennessey. If Buddy did tell Hennessey, someone at the garage would surely tell Willy. If he took matters into his own hands and confronted the mechanic, what proof would he have? It just wouldn't have worked. He figured that Willy should know. That was the only way.

Buddy decided to tell Willy.

It would be at the Paddock Tavern, the local bar, not two blocks from Hennessey's garage.

"Another false alarm at the rest home. I'm surprised that place hasn't burned down by now." Buddy was trying to ease into the conversation. The knowledge of the attack on Shirley was agonizing for Buddy. He was trying to be calm with Willy, but he was going back and forth about whether or how to tell his best friend that someone had assaulted his new wife. He loved Willy like a brother. His first instinct was to protect him from pain. Even while fighting the fires, Buddy often would make sure that Willy was safe. Now he knew what he was going to say would hurt Willy.

"Someone ought to shut that place down. Rest home, my ass. What rest do those poor people ever get? The place stinks. Everyone looks like they're in a daze. But, hey Buddy, shoot me first if anyone ever tries to put me in one of those places," said Willy as he wiped the foam off his mouth from the Pickwick Ale. "And if for some reason, I die before Shirley, don't ever let anyone ever put her in one of those places. Promise?"

"Who do you think keeps pulling the alarm? "Asked Buddy. He was barely paying attention to the conversation about the old rest home.

"Who knows? Maybe some of those poor old people just want someone to pay attention to them. Maybe they just want company," said Willy.

"Jesus."

Buddy took a long gulp of his beer. He tapped his hands on the bar. "Can I tell you something, and you promise to listen and not go crazy?"

"I never go crazy."

"Yes, you do. You gotta promise?"

"Depends."

"Okay. Forget it. Unless you promise," insisted Buddy.

"What's this all about?"

"Shirley."

Willy turned deadly serious. "What about Shirley?" Willy turned sharply toward Buddy.

"Hang on. You promised not to go crazy, and you are almost crazy right now."

"Stop double-talking."

Buddy, of course, violated Edie's promise, which broke Shirley's promise. So now Buddy had to hope that Willy wouldn't violate his.

Buddy told Willy what Edie had told him. Buddy had promised not to tell a single soul. So now he told the only soul that mattered, Willy.

"I don't even know his name. But it's the guy that blinks his eyes all the time," said Buddy

"I'll kill that son of a bitch."

"You promised not to go crazy."

"We can't have him come near the firehouse anymore. That's the most we can do. We can never tell Brad. He would kill him, and I certainly don't want that on my conscience."

"I'm gonna kill him myself first."

Buddy wished he had kept his promise with all his heart. "I'll figure out a way of getting that guy reassigned, so he never shows up at the firehouse again. I'll talk to Brad. I'll make up some story."

Willy just kept sipping his beer. For Buddy, the night just dragged on. They hardly talked. They just listened to the Red Sox game on the radio. Shortstop Don Buddin just made a great play in the field. The sparse crowd cheered. Not Willy.

"Too bad he stinks as a hitter." Buddy was just trying to make a feeble attempt at conversation.

They finished their drinks and left.

～

Willy didn't wait long. The next day, he decided to pay Hennessey's Garage a visit.

He looked around. The thought had occurred to him that this might be the place where he did what he did to Shirley. Based on the second-hand story that Buddy had told him based on Edie's story, he assumed that he had somehow conned Shirley into driving her home from the beach. He peered around the building. There were plenty of secluded areas where he could have taken her, probably in his car.

Then he spotted the car. He had seen it parked on the street outside the firehouse.

In the front yard of Hennessey's parking lot was the same maroon '51 Mercury he had seen at the firehouse. It was the only car backed into the parking spot. The vehicle was unlocked with the windows open. He didn't care if someone thought he was stealing it; he was going to look inside. People would probably think he was a policeman anyway. Most people wouldn't know the difference between a fireman and a police uniform. He stuck his head into the passenger front door window and opened the passenger side door. "Jesus," he said out loud. The car smelled terrible. The smell was a symphony of odors, from stale cigarette smoke to unwashed underwear to body odor.

Willy held his breath.

The top-of-the-line '51 Mercury's came with a leather interior. This model was the base version. The seat covers were a mohair-type material. Willy figured the longer that guy sat into the mohair, the more the cloth took on his smell. What Willy did notice was what seemed like bloodstains. Based on what Buddy had told him, he thought that if that mechanic guy had bloodied, never mind assaulted Shirley, it would have been about two weeks ago. He was convinced that there were bloodstains on the seats. He closed the door and took a deep breath.

The sight of the bloodstains began to boil Willy's blood. He could feel his temples pounding. What was he going to do?

The garage had two areas, the office, and the main garage. Willy entered the front door into Doug Hennessey's office. Unfortunately, when the big garage door was closed, customers had to enter Doug's cluttered office to get to the garage. Stacks of invoices and papers were everywhere. The first thing Willy noticed was an outdated calendar stuck in November of 1955.

"Can I help you?" Doug was busy with paperwork. Doug did a lot of work on the vehicles himself, so his hands were permanently greasy. The paperwork had Doug's fingerprints everywhere.

"Your shop does work on fire engines, right?"

"Sure. We have a deal with the city for maintenance services at Central Union Fire Station. We also do work for some of the fireman's cars too. We give a 10% discount. Which firehouse is yours?"

Willy lied. "Davis Square."

"It's okay. Any of the city's firemen can get a discount. What's wrong with your car?"

"Nothing. I need to talk to one of your mechanics."

"Who?" Doug was getting a bit nervous.

"Ah. I forgot his name. He does this funny kind of thing with his face."

"I know who you mean. What do you want with him?"

"Where is he?

Doug peeked into the garage area. "He's under the Hood's milk truck. What do you want with him?" Doug knew the man under the milk truck was very odd. He had toyed with simply firing him, but he could never come up with a good excuse. None of the mechanics had much to do with him. In fact, on the days he was servicing in the field, the rest of the gang made fun of him. He had to stop himself from joining in. Despite the jokes on the odd man's behalf, he worried that someday he was going to snap. Doug noticed that this fireman had rage in his eyes. Usually, customers didn't just walk in. Most of the work for the garage was fleet vehicles.

He glanced at the fireman's bulging veins in his neck. Doug had seen his share of fights in the shop. Only last week, he had to separate two of his men who were pushing each other around. But this guy looked like trouble. Real trouble. Given how odd the man he was looking for was, it flashed through Doug's mind that a firefighter wouldn't have anything to do with him. So why would he come to the garage to meet with him? It just meant trouble. Now Doug was very concerned.

"Look, he's busy working on a truck. If you want to meet with him, wait for his shift to be over. We're busy here and..."

Willy barged out of the office into the garage area, pushing Doug aside.

Doug fell into his office chair, "What the hell?" Doug's fears were justified. His first thought was that this wasn't going to go well. Doug quickly followed Willy into the garage. "Hey, I don't want trouble." He stepped in front of Willy.

Willy pushed Doug out of the way. The milk truck had the front end jacked up. All he could see were two work boots placed on a mechanic creeper.

Willy raced to the truck. First, he pulled the creeper out from under the truck. Then, the man's head cracked on something.

"Jeez. What's going on?"

Now the man was fully exposed, lying flat on the creeper. Then his facial motion began. His eyes blinked rapidly, and his eyebrows moved up and down.

First, Willy picked him up by the overalls. Then, in one quick motion, he twirled him around and pushed him up against the old brick wall. Stunned, the victim was now standing facing Willy. Willy pushed his face right into his. Then his facial motions accelerated.

"Who are you?" The terrified man's eyes grew large, making his facial movements even more bizarre.

Doug noticed that everyone in the garage seemed in shock. No one moved. Doug stood still at the door to his office.

"What did you do to Shirley?" He then punched him hard in the solar plexus. The man groaned.

The rest of the mechanics watched. No one said a word.

"I don't know what you are..."

Willy gave him another shot in the stomach. "Tell me, or I will kill you right here, right now."

"Don't hurt me. I don't know nothing."

Willy gave him another shot into his neck.

"Tell me, now."

Doug raced over to the two men.

"This man violated my wife," screamed Willy. "This is between the two of us." Doug backed off.

"I never hurt her. She wanted to be with me. I saw her smile at me at the firehouse. She made believe she didn't want it, but I know she did. It was her fault. She hit me."

Willy punched him, ten, maybe fifteen times in the ribs. He then bloodied his face with sharp lefts and rights. It was hard to tell if the motion of his face stopped. The man's eyes were closed. His nose was bleeding. He slid down the wall to a sitting position on the floor. Willy kicked him repeatedly in the ribs and the groin.

Doug had seen enough. He motioned to three of his mechanics. They grabbed Willy and pulled him away from the bloody mess. Willy nearly got away, but two more mechanics joined Doug and the others and held him back. Finally, Doug realized that fireman would surely kill that oddball mechanic, now barely conscious. Then, slowly, Willy calmed down and gave in.

"He assaulted my wife."

Doug jumped in, "We could call the cops. But the best thing for you to do is get the hell out of here. Now!"

"Okay." The mechanics released him. "I'll go. But first, I have to tell him something."

"Don't touch him," said Doug.

The man was barely conscious.

Willy dropped to his knees and faced the bloody wreck. "Here's how it goes. This is my city. All my friends live here. If I ever see you here in Somerville, or if any of my friends see you, I can't even say what will happen to you. Hennessey, see this piece of garbage. He just gave you his notice. He no longer works here or lives here." Willy turned to the barely alive man. "Right?"

The man said nothing. He just groaned.

"Let me hear you say it. Right?

The facial rhythm was now gone. Under his breath, he said, "Yes."

Willy straightened himself out, walked through Doug's office, and left. The bleeding hulk just laid on the garage floor, breathing heavily.

"I'm calling for an ambulance. In my office. Now."

All the workers except the wounded man, still lying on the floor, jammed into Doug's tiny office. Doug called the police station. "There has been a fight. Please send an ambulance here. We have an injured worker."

"Okay. My business and your job depend on the contract with the city. Right. So, none of you remember the guy was a fireman. Just some guy. Got it?"

The group just nodded.

The wounded man ended up at the Somerville Hospital with multiple broken ribs, a broken nose, and internal bleeding. To no one's surprise, the man with the odd facial movements never gave Doug his notice. He never heard from him again. Doug didn't care.

Unlike Edie and then Buddy, who each could not keep a secret, Willy kept this encounter with the man who had raped Shirley a solemn secret. Since none of Hennessey's mechanics knew who this mystery fireman was, they also kept the secret.

7

Today was Marjorie Kowalski's twenty-ninth birthday.

She had asked her boss if she could leave a little early since it was her birthday after all. He had agreed. She raced to get the subway train at Boylston Station to Lechmere, where she would pick up the Clarendon Hill bus via Highland Ave. to Central Street, then hike up the hill to her house.

When she opened the door, she was greeted with, "Surprise!"

Neighbors, old friends from the projects, and a few high school girlfriends packed the place. Even some co-workers from the phone company had managed to leave work even earlier than Marjorie. The group immediately brought out the cake that read, *Happy Birthday, Marjorie – May you be 29 forever.* Twenty-nine candles adorned the cake. The crowd then struck up an out-of-tune version of *Happy Birthday*.

She was so touched. She hugged and hugged her husband, Phil, for his kindness and thoughtfulness.

"Hey, Marjorie. Look what I got for you." Then Phil brought out a bottle of champagne. Marjorie knew it wasn't real champagne. It didn't matter to her. Phil popped the cork, which hit the ceiling. Everyone cheered. They drank and laughed. Phil gave her a beautiful necklace. She had always loved jewelry.

Her mother, Magna, was there as well, beaming with pride. "Stay proud, my daughter." Marjorie Kowalski was one of five children. Most of the families that grew up in the projects were Irish. The Kowalski's were the only Polish family. The projects were a group of several hundred apartments that the government created to provide housing to poor and older adults. Too often, however, the flats were occupied by the families of local mobsters. The poor and the crooks filled the place. There was no in-between. It was not a great combination. The kids of the gangsters routinely harassed the poor kids.

The family had one of the three-bedroom units that viewed worn-down Mystic Avenue and the upscale Ten Hill section of the city.

Life wasn't easy for Marjorie growing up.

The problem for a twelve-year-old at Southern Junior High School, which was a tough place to begin with, was that you were looked down upon if you came from the projects. The irony was that the kids who looked down on Marjorie were just a hair above social status than the Kowalski's. Add to that her father had gone off to work to the New England Dressed Meat and Wool Company on a Tuesday when Marjorie was seven and never returned.

Marjorie's mother, who had immigrated from Poland when Marjorie was a baby, was the epitome of tolerance. She tried to raise her five kids with kindness and discipline. Magda's only genuine fault was pride. She refused to let the world knock her or her family down. Instead, she told all her children that they were proud paupers. She would tell the kids just because they are poor does not mean you must hold your head in shame. So, Marjorie grew up with her head held high, even though her hand-me-down clothes smelled funny.

She did well in school, graduated from Somerville High, class of 1950. Then promptly got a job at New England Telephone and Telegraph as a receptionist at the main building on Boston's Tremont Street. She graduated as an operator four years later and married Phil Dodds, a phone company repairman. They had one son. When they got married, she finally left the projects forever and moved into their second-floor apartment of a decent two-family on Central Street, two blocks from Hennessey's garage.

Magda's mother had taken ill when Marjorie got promoted to operator supervisor. After a long stint in the hospital, her grandmother entered the Winter Hill Rest Home. Marjorie, true to form, felt a need to visit her grandmother, who she affectionately called Gramma, nearly every day after work.

Marjorie announced to the group, "I plan to stay twenty-nine forever. If Bob Hope can stay twenty-nine, so can I." Everyone laughed. Phil gently reminded Marjorie, "Bob Hope wants to stay thirty-nine, not twenty-nine. But if you want to stay twenty-nine, that's just fine." Marjorie, a bit embarrassed, said, "I knew that!"

Everyone left by nine o'clock. "What a wonderful time. A perfect birthday. A perfect party!" As Marjorie, a bit drunk, headed into the bedroom to get changed, the glow of the evening washed over her. Then it hit her. The glow faded. She poked Phil. "I never got to see Gramma. Dammit."

Phil brushed it off, "You'll see her tomorrow. Stop worrying. It was a great night, wasn't it?" It was, but the glow from the party faded fast. Her silent scar started to form.

The Winter Hill Rest Home building started as a secretarial school for women, called the Reynolds School and was built in 1895. One of the most stunning structures on Broadway, it was complete with ornate woodwork and fancy dormers on the third-floor attic area. Most homes and even businesses in the Winter Hill section of Somerville in the late 1890s and early 1900s were built on tiny lots. However, the Reynolds family bought five standard lots for their masterpiece. It even had a garage for the horse carriages. Later, the Reynolds family used the garage for the headmaster's Auburn and Cord automobiles collection.

The depression ultimately killed the business. By 1939, the building stood empty. In the spring of 1949, the Somerville building department considered it a fire hazard and was on the verge of condemning it. However, the Somerville Historical Commission intervened. The Commission got its way. The one condition was that someone would have to occupy the building within two years.

Finally, in 1952, the owners of the crowded decrepit old rest home around the corner on Evergreen Street agreed to buy and occupy the building. However, the old Reynolds building was almost as bad a shape as their old building was now. The only good thing about the new building was more space and a decent parking lot. Since the Reynolds building was still in Winter Hill, they didn't even have to change the name. They even reused the old sign. While the Historical Commission hoped for a tenant to bring the old building back to its former glory, the new occupants didn't.

The owners of the new location took advantage of the enlarged space by cramming even more patients into the building. As a result, conditions inside the Reynolds structure were no better, if not worse, than the old Evergreen Street building, which the city quickly tore down once the owners moved out.

The fire alarm system was the only renovation the owners performed on the Reynolds building. It got used a lot, but not for the right reasons. The residents routinely pulled the fire alarm box, conveniently located right outside the main bathroom. For many of them, it was to relieve the boredom of the dreary place. Some just pulled it for no apparent reason.

As always, the fire department dispatched the standard number of firetrucks to the scene, even though the department was certain the alarm was false or, at the very least, the fire alarm was for a small rubbish fire.

Tonight, Edie had looked forward to a quiet night at home. Her favorite TV show was *Sugarfoot*. It was a western about a lawyer from the east who settled in Oklahoma. She liked most about it because the star of the show, Will Hutchins, reminded her of

Buddy. Not that they looked that much alike, but the character of Sugarfoot, Tom Brewster, played by Hutchins, was a wise-cracker, like Buddy. She settled on the sofa at nine o'clock. Buddy had to work the night shift at the firehouse, so tonight, she would curl up and think of Buddy as the lawyer in the wild west.

Edie's mother, Doris, sat next to Edie. "He doesn't look a bit like Buddy. Plus, Buddy's shorter." Doris looked over at Edie. "Honey, what's the matter? You're white as a ghost. Did you get one of your feelings?"

"Yes. It's strong."

"What is it?"

"Buddy. I know it's about Buddy. Something bad," said Edie.

"Do you have any idea why you should be worried about him?" asked Doris.

"Well, I told him something I shouldn't have. It was a secret I was supposed to keep but didn't. I promised not to tell, but I did."

"Sometimes, you have to break promises. Try not to worry. Call Buddy in the morning. I'm sure it will be fine." Edie knew that Doris was just trying to calm her down. It wasn't working.

"I don't think it was about the promise. It's something else. I think it is about his work. I think he is in danger."

"He's at the firehouse. Go see him if you are that worried. Call the firehouse first."

"I hate calling there. Buddy will get harassed by the guys if girl-friends call."

"Too bad. I've seen that look. Trust your feelings."

Edie called. The dispatcher told Edie that they had received an alarm from the Winter Hill Rest Home. Buddy was unavailable.

"He's getting ready to go to a possible fire at the old rest home. They get calls there all the time, mostly false alarms. The dispatcher told me it was probably nothing, and Buddy would probably be back at the firehouse in an hour or so." Edie was not convinced.

"So, call back in an hour," said Doris.

"No. I'm going to the rest home. I've got to see Buddy."

Edie knew that her mother would not try to stop her. "Just be careful."

~

Tommy Swartz was one of the few Jewish kids in the Somerville school system. For some reason, the tough kids gave the Jewish kids a pass when picking on them or stealing their lunch money. Maybe they were concerned that it would come back to haunt them later in life since the rumor was that Jewish kids tended to own all the businesses in town, and they might have to get a job. There was also the impression that the Jewish kids were the smartest ones.

Tommy Swartz was the exception to the rule, at least in Somerville. Tommy was, at best, a C+ student. It wasn't that Tommy was dumb. He just hated to study. Instead, Tommy was consumed with building model airplanes, cars, and boats. This behavior started when he was ten and continued through high school. As he got older, Tommy loved to work on real cars.

Tommy liked girls too. He was a decent-looking kid, except for the goofy glasses, which he hated. However, seeing was more important. Luckily there were plenty of decent-looking girls to date who, like him, wore goofy-looking glasses.

At Somerville High, he was going steady with Lucille Beaumont by senior year.

Tommy got work at Bellotti Oldsmobile as a mechanic. Working on cars was the only skill that he had. The new 1955 and 1956 Olds were the prettiest yet. Sleek and modern. The used vehicles all seemed old-fashioned compared to the new ones. The dealership had just too many used cars. Revenues were down, so Tommy was relegated to work on the used cars in the back lot part-time. He did the best he could keeping the old clunkers running.

Meanwhile, Lucille had a full-time job at the Winter Hill Rest Home. Her aunt was part owner. She got a good job as a nurses' aide. Because she was related to the owners, she made more money than even some nurses. Luckily for Lucille, they never found out.

While she knew that Tommy liked to work on cars, she also knew that there was no way she could even think about staying with a boy, never mind marrying him, if he only had a part-time job at the Olds dealership. So, she spoke to her aunt about getting Tommy a full-time job.

The deal was struck. Tommy and Lucille would be working at the Winter Hill Rest Home, Lucille, as a nurses' aide, and Tommy, well, no one was quite sure what his job was, as a handyman, a helper, and sometimes cook. Whatever was needed.

What Tommy enjoyed the most was talking to the patients. He loved them. And they loved him. He felt as though he was their protector, their guard. He would organize their belongings, play cards with them, and spend individual time with them. So, it was clear to management, who didn't like to spend money on anything other than the essentials, that Tommy did provide value to the rest home. Besides, they were paying Tommy very little.

Tommy loved his job. He felt loved and cared for by Lucille. For her part, she felt closer and closer to Tommy because she saw a different side of this rather unmotivated and frankly uncharacteristically unbrilliant Jewish kid. Tommy would make a great father and husband in her mind. So, what if he didn't have much ambition? The more Tommy catered and loved the old folks, the more she cared for him.

Tommy loved them all. But his favorite was the Polish Mrs. Novak. Being Jewish and an absolute minority in this primarily Irish Catholic city, he related easily to her since he felt that Poland was the home to many Jewish people, maybe even some of his ancestors. So even though she wasn't Jewish, he could relate to her. She would tell him stories about growing up in Warsaw, about how her family fled during the war. He ate up all of it. She was also one of the lucky ones. Rarely would anyone ever come to visit any of his beloved patients, who he called clients. That was except Mrs. Novak. Instead, her granddaughter, Marjorie, saw her nearly every day. The same Marjorie, who was celebrating her 29th birthday.

Except she did not come today.

It was late. Usually, Tommy left at about seven-thirty. It was after eight o'clock. For some reason, something told him to linger a bit. Lucille was scheduled to work the night shift, so there wasn't any compelling reason to go home. He made one more walk-round the building. He usually started on the third floor. The third floor was smaller than the others due to the roof angles. The dormers took up a lot of space. He figured that the third floor was once an attic. There were only twelve beds on the floor. When he walked by Mrs. Novak, he could sense something was wrong. She was sad.

"Mrs. Novak, what's wrong?" asked Tommy.

"Oh, it's nothing." She handed Tommy a piece of paper.

"What's this?"

"I made a birthday card for my dear granddaughter, Marjorie. Well, it's not a card, just a piece of paper. But I made up the birthday wish myself. I even drew a little picture of me holding hands with her when she was little. We were always close. You know, I had a place in the projects. Marjorie would visit with me all the time."

"What happened? She comes every day." Tommy sat on the side of her bed. He so much wanted to cheer her up.

"She didn't come today. I shouldn't expect her to come. She's got a husband and a son, Benny. I'm sure she will come tomorrow. This is the first day she hasn't visited. I feel awful being like this. I'm the only one here that gets visitors regularly. I shouldn't be sad. It's only one day."

Tommy wanted so much to hug her. He knew that was against the rules, plus the other patients would notice. He would never want them to feel bad. "You told me a lot about her. How she's a wonderful lady. Works for the phone company. Probably got caught up on the subway, or maybe there was a problem at work. She always comes after I leave. Someday, I'd like to meet her. She will come tomorrow, for sure. I'll stay late and meet her. Don't worry."

"You're right. I'll give her my birthday card, well, not card. I guess you could call this a birthday letter. I'll give it to her tomorrow and you can meet her."

"Deal. Look, I'm supposed to leave now. Lucille has to work

tonight. So, I'll grab a chair and sit by the stairs. I've got my catalog of Revell model cars to read. I'll be on guard tonight. I'll guard the floor until everyone is asleep. If you need me, just call me." Tommy looked around to make sure no one was looking and planted a little kiss on her cheek.

"That would be nice."

He sat down by the stairs and pulled out his catalog.

Then he smelled smoke. Well, it sure smelled like smoke. Not very strong. Even though smoking in the rest home was frowned upon, many patients smoked regularly. But this didn't smell like cigarette smoke. It was more like a rubber smell. He had been focusing on the latest model car kit in the catalog. While he was a bit old to be building model cars, he still did. The model in the catalog was a 1956 Ford Fairlane Convertible. You could make it stock, custom, or in between. He took out his pencil and circled that one. Maybe tomorrow, he would head to Fuchs Hobby shop on Tremont Street in Boston and pick one up. Fuchs had the best selection in town. He could spend hours there. Tommy always laughed to himself when he said the name. He wondered if people would think of the "f" word whenever they would pass Fuchs store and double take. He wondered why whoever owned Fuchs wouldn't have changed the name. Who knows? Maybe it brought more business? Anyway. Yeah, tomorrow he would go to Fuchs and pick up that model Ford.

That smell. It was getting stronger. Tommy stuffed the catalog into his back pocket. He had decided to investigate. First, though, he would check to make sure the patients were asleep. He walked over to Mrs. Novak.

"Tommy. Do you smell something?"

"Yeah. Smells like burning rubber. Don't worry for a minute. I'll check it out and be right back." Tommy patted Mrs. Novak on the shoulder. He walked by the other patients. They all appeared to be asleep.

Lucille would be on the second floor during her shift. They had a little desk which they called the nursing station, stuffed over into the corner near the bathroom. It was hardly a station at all, just a desk.

He walked down the stairs. Lucille was not at the desk. The other patients looked asleep. The smell was not as strong on the second floor. He shrugged. He walked down the stairway to the first floor.

There was Lucille.

"Hi, Tommy. You still here?" asked Lucille.

"Yeah. Nothing to do tonight. Mrs. Novak was a bit upset, so I thought I would keep her company until she fell asleep."

"Everything is quiet here. Why don't you keep me company? "

"Where is everyone?" asked Tommy.

"Betty went to the White Tower to grab a hamburger and some French-fried potatoes. I don't know where Louis is. He was supposed to be the guard on duty tonight, but he never showed up. He drinks, you know. I smell it on him all the time. So, it looks like it is you and me." She gave Tommy a devilish smile. She put her arm around his waist and pulled him to her.

"Let's go into the supply closet." Tommy completely forgot why he had gone downstairs.

Lucille took his hand. They hurried into the supply closet and closed the door. After a few preliminary kisses, Tommy unbuttoned Lucille's uniform and massaged her. She moaned and moaned.

The moment she slipped her hand into Tommy's pants, they both heard something terrifying.

It was a scream. No, not just one scream. Several.

"Shit. I forgot about the smell of smoke."

Tommy immediately pulled his hand out from Lucille's shirt.

Lucille quickly buttoned her shirt.

8

As soon as Tommy opened the supply closet door, the smell of burning rubber hit him. It was now extreme. He raced up to the second floor. People were awake and coughing. He ran up to the third floor, skipping steps along the way. Then he saw the flames.

The wall opposite Mrs. Novak was gone entirely. Instead, wires that used to be behind the wall were glowing and flaming.

The fire had a unique way of growing. At first, it seemed manageable. Maybe you threw a blanket on top of it, and that's it. The fire was confined to that one wall.

Tommy's mind was racing. Okay. I can put this out. The only water available was from the bathroom. He ran into it, grabbed a bedpan, and quickly filled it with water. Of course, it couldn't have been more than a couple of quarts at the most. The fire beast would laugh at the tiny little spray that poor Tommy threw at it. It just sizzled a little. It was an electrical fire. Electrical fires don't like water anyway.

"Tommy. Thank God. Where were you? What were you doing?" Mrs. Novak had been the first one screaming. Now all the patients were yelling. None of the patients could make it down the stairway on their own.

At that second, what flashed into Tommy's mind was that he had his hands full of Lucille's breasts. Tommy yelled to Lucille. "Pull the fire alarm box."

Tommy heard the alarm sound. The fire alarm box was directly linked to the fire department's Central Station.

Lucille appeared on the third floor. "Oh no! The whole wall is on fire. I pulled the alarm. The firemen will be here soon."

"Grab the blankets. Let's wet them down." Lucille pulled the blankets off one of the beds, leaving a poor terrified Mrs. Doucette uncovered. Lucille raced into the bathroom to soak the blanket. It was taking too long.

"Hurry." Tommy was panicked.

"Tommy. Protect us. You are our protector!" Mrs. Novak cried out.

"I will. I will put the fire out. I promise." Tommy would not make good on his promise.

The ceiling next to the wall seemed to disappear, exposing the roof. A large box stored in the attic of the old building crashed to the floor. It was engulfed in flames. It fell on top of Elenore Gilmore, one of the first patients to die in the fire. The box seemed to be full of papers, probably old bank receipts. That missile set the bedding on fire. Tommy blocked his ears from the screaming.

By the time Lucille emerged from the bathroom with the wet blanket, the fire had turned the corner on the adjacent wall. The blanket was almost too heavy for her to carry. Tommy saw her about to throw the blanket on Mrs. Gilmore. Before she could make that move or any other, a piece of the ceiling crashed in on top of her. It wasn't the blow that killed her. She fell to the floor. The heat from the burning material set her blouse on fire, the very same blouse that Tommy had unbuttoned not moments before.

Tommy was now wholly disoriented. The smoke was now getting so thick that he wasn't sure what part of the floor he was on.

The roof was now on fire.

Then in an instant, things got quiet. Well, except for the turbulence of the fire. All screaming had stopped. Even Mrs. Novak was silent. Lucille, of course, was also silent. Then, finally, it occurred to Tommy that he was probably the only one alive on the third floor. That's when he started to cry.

~

Buddy and Willy were on the second shift at the firehouse. The shift started at 3:00 PM, and it would end at midnight.

Willy noticed that Buddy kept looking at his hands.

"You didn't kill him, did you?" asked Buddy.

"No. Deal the cards."

"Cuz if you did, it would be my fault. I couldn't live with that."

"He'll never come back to the firehouse. Now deal and drop it."

At 8:25 PM, the fire alarm blasted. No matter how often Willy had heard that alarm, each time it rang, he jumped. Then his stomach went into his throat.

One of the guys in the central part of the firehouse yelled, "It's the Winter Hill Rest Home again."

Willy settled down since this would have been the fourth time an alarm sounded from that old place this week.

The Winter Hill Rest Home was less than half a mile from the Central Fire Station so that they could get there in a matter of minutes. They would take the then-brand-new McGrath Highway to Broadway and the Winter Hill Rest Home.

The fire alarm system was a hard-wired system that looped around the city of Somerville. Pull boxes were mounted on power and telephone poles throughout the city. If someone sees a fire, they could go to the nearest pull box, break the glass with the provided little hammer, and pull the lever. Then the alarm would sound at the nearest firehouse. Aside from the pull boxes on poles, several pull boxes were installed at critical facilities like rest homes and hospitals. The problem with pull boxes was it was too easy for wise-ass kids to pull them and watch in hysterics as the fire engines drove up near the pull box only to see no fire.

There were no wise-ass kids at the Winter Hill Rest Home.

However, several of the patients believed in their hearts that a fire was about to begin, so they made a habit of pulling the pull box.

When Buddy and Willy heard that someone had pulled an alarm at the Winter Hill Rest Home, they just figured it was yet another false alarm. Did that slow them down and the rest of the crew? Their training would not allow it, of course. But maybe their response was not quite as crisp.

Willy and Buddy would have to pick up their conversation later.

By the time that Willy and Buddy arrived at the Winter Hill Rest Home, flames were shooting out of the roof of the building.

"Holy shit," was all Willy could say. The team connected the hoses to the fire hydrants on Broadway and Sycamore Street.

Brad raised the alarm level to three.

Both Buddy and Willy had been in that building dozens of times, and they knew full well how many people were trapped inside.

It appeared that the second and third floors were hopeless. The flames were pouring out of every window.

Willy and Buddy were on hose duty.

"I only see about ten people out on the street. The rest must be in there. We gotta go in," said Willy. He looked toward Brad. Brad gave Willy and Buddy a knowing nod.

They raced inside. Willy couldn't quite tell which was worse, the screaming or the smell. It appeared to Willy that the patients on the first floor, who were ambulatory, managed to escape.

Willy and Buddy split up.

Buddy bounded up the creaky stairway to the third floor.

Willy found two people still alive in the kitchen area and dragged them to safety outside. There were four people in beds that he quickly determined were dead. Willy had to decide to rescue the bodies or search for some still alive. He went back in.

There was screaming on the second floor.

Tommy turned and turned, not knowing where he was. His lungs were shot. He tried to scream, but nothing came out of his mouth. Then he saw a shadow through the thick smoke. It was a fireman.

"Quick. You got to get out of here. Fast." Buddy raced toward the disoriented Tommy.

Buddy grabbed on to Tommy and yanked him to the stairway. A piece of the roof fell right beside him. Tommy opened his mouth again. Nothing came out.

"Now. Move." Buddy grabbed on to Tommy's arm and pushed him toward the stairway. Tommy slipped and fell backward down the stairway.

Buddy looked around. All he saw were corpses, all lying silently, most still with what was left of blankets covering them. He heard the screaming from the second floor.

So did Willy.

Willy raced up to the second floor. He quickly determined this was a lost cause. Then suddenly, a body appeared at his feet. It was Tommy. He was alive but badly injured.

Buddy realized that whoever he was holding on to ended up on the second floor. Now he was disoriented. His lungs were giving out. His sense of direction was excellent, so he knew he was within only a few feet from the stairway to the second floor. But time wasn't on his side.

He heard creaking wood. He looked up and saw the roof coming down on him. He knew that there was no time to escape. The roof material was on fire, and he knew from even his few years as a fireman that it was damn heavy and would crush his skull, never mind burn him immediately. The temperature was just too hot.

At that point, time seemed to stand still. This was it. Buddy would die in the fire. There would be no sons growing up to be firemen. Edie would be devastated. Willy would probably feel guilty as hell. The burning roof material was about a foot from his head when he ran the discussion with Willy in his head. The one about his wife, Shirley. He thought in that instant the promise he had made to Edie not to tell Willy about that crazy guy at the beach. He was glad he told Willy. In the last second of his life, he reasoned that if he had not told Willy or that if he had waited until say tomorrow, Willy would never have known. Yeah, breaking Edie's promise was a good move. His last thought was about Edie. She would be sad for a while, then move on. She was young. They had talked about getting married, but nothing definite. He was glad about that. That would have been tougher for her.

Then the roof crashed down on him. He thought it was going to hurt more than it did. He worried more about the burning. There was no burning. He died instantly when the main roof beam crushed his skull.

Willy dragged Tommy down the stairs and out the door. Brad raced to him.

"Jesus, Mary, and Joseph. This place is going up fast. Thank God you got out."

Willy then dropped to his knees. Too much smoke. He spat up blood and coughed uncontrollably for several seconds. Then Brad and Willy heard the old building groan. Willy's first reaction was that it was a human or large animal voice. But, no, it was the building. Then the second and third floors crashed down into the first floor.

Willy looked up at his father-in-law, Brad. "Where's Buddy?"

Edie pulled up to the fire scene in her father's old Lasalle. She leaped out of the car, still leaving the car door open, and the car running. She ran to Brad and Willy.

"I don't know. I didn't see him come out." Brad was panting.

"Is he in there?" Edie cried. Without getting an answer, she ran toward the burning building. Willy raced after her.

"Edie. You can't go near there. It's collapsing."

Edie stopped. "Buddy's dead. I know it now. I felt his heart stop." She fell to her knees.

Willy jumped up. Then he tried to race to what was left of the front door of the building. "Buddy. No. No. No. Goddamit. No." He joined Edie on the ground, held her hands, and sobbed.

Buddy was gone. Only thirteen people survived of the fifty or so patients at the Winter Hill Rest Home. Tommy was among them. Most of those were on the first floor. At the time of the fire, no one knew for sure how many employees were in the building when it caught on fire. By the time the on-call nurse had made it back from the White Tower, the Winter Hill Rest Home was a total loss. No one even knew what happened to the night guard.

Buddy was Willy's best friend. Buddy and Willy had made a pact. Willy asked Buddy never to let his beloved Shirley ever get locked away in a place like the Winter Hill Rest Home. The problem was that Willy never told Shirley about their agreement.

Later, every so often at night, when Willy couldn't sleep, he would sit up in bed, Shirley next to him. He would light up a cigarette and think about the fire. What he couldn't get out of his head were the screams. He remembered a chorus of "get me out of here." But of course, he couldn't save them. Or Buddy.

9

Tonight was a particularly long night at the Paddock Tavern for Willy.

On Paddock nights, Shirley would customarily crawl into bed about ten o'clock. She would read a magazine or a book for a while. Then fall off to sleep.

On drinking nights or poker nights, Willy did the drill. He would open the front door slowly. Then carefully undress in the bathroom. He avoided sitting on any of the squeaky kitchen chairs. He then would silently slip onto his side of the bed. Most nights, he would be snoring by the time his head hit the pillow.

Willy and Shirley had told each other that having a child would be easy. Most of their married friends had two, three, and sometimes four kids. Willy often mentioned to Shirley that their boy would be a fireman. Yet no boy had come. No girl either. They rarely mentioned their lack of children to each other. Though childless on their twentieth wedding anniversary, Willy and Shirley were happy for the most part. They got used to the way things were. Willy had progressed to Deputy Captain. Shirley had a decent job at the local discount department store, Bradlees, as an assistant manager. They made enough money to make ends meet. They bought a lovely two-family house on Bartlett Street in Somerville, right near the bus stop. Their 75 Dodge Dart ran like a top. Yet, they only had two thousand dollars in their savings. The savings wasn't growing either.

Willy told everyone he worshiped Shirley, and he did. Yet, he loved his job and the camaraderie of the firefighters. That included regular nights at the Paddock Tavern hauling down Pickwick Ale's or Narragansett beers and an occasional shot of Old Grandad. Each night at the Paddack, Willy smoked at least a pack of Marlboro cigarettes. Two nights a week, Willy and five of his buddies played poker. He consumed at least two giant imperial quarts of Narragansett each poker night and a pack of cigarettes. Often, Willy lost a couple of hundred bucks.

Tonight, as he quietly opened the door, he knew something was different. Shirley was sitting on the sofa in the living room, smoking a cigarette. The ashtray was full. He smelled freshly brewed coffee.

"You, okay?" Willy knew he was pretty drunk. He tried to steady himself as he walked toward Shirley.

"It's real late. After two. You shoulda called." Shirley lit up another cigarette. "Do you want some coffee?"

"No. I figured you would be asleep. I'm sorry. I'll call next time." He sat down next to Shirley. He put his arm around her.

She stiffened.

This situation was new for Willy. While he had understood that staying out late was not great for a marriage, it was just what he did. Shirley never complained.

"I'm pregnant." Shirley crushed out the newly lit cigarette. "I was late for my period for the first time since I can remember. So I bought a test kit at the drug store. It was positive." She stood up wrapped her robe tight around her waist. The bedroom was at the end of a long hall. As she walked to the bedroom, Willy watched her movements. He wondered if she was unsure of her feelings. Was she just mad at him for being late, or was it something else? He wasn't sure. Willy thought about chasing after her, giving her a big hug, and telling her how happy he was.

He didn't move. He was not sure about his feelings. What he did know was that one of his feelings was not happiness. He noticed that Shirley hesitated for a second at the door, then it closed. No slam. She just closed the door, as she would typically do. Willy would rather that she had slammed the door. Then, at least, he would have exactly understood where she stood.

Shirley still felt the pangs of guilt from the rape. While it didn't change their lives on a day-to-day basis, it was a barrier to intimacy. Each time they had sex, somewhere in the back of Shirley's mind, the image of that awful man seemed to be lurking. Shirley thought that maybe that had something to do with their inability to conceive a child. This condition just added a tinge more guilt.

In all other affairs, Shirley was outspoken. Yet with Willy's night out, she held her tongue. Shirley felt that he had an unspoken advantage over her in her heart. Even after all those years, she knew that the rape was not her fault in her head. Had she brought it on? Was it at least partially her fault? In her distorted sense of responsibility, she figured that she could tolerate Willy's absence as a penance for her sin. Tonight, was different. Edie was the only one she could talk to about it. While she did on rare occasions, Edie would tell Shirley that it was like a scar on her emotions – a silent scar. Tonight, she thought about that scar.

At exactly forty-two years old, Shirley had long since abandoned any form of birth control. She missed her period for the first time in her post-puberty life. She was undoubtedly pregnant. The answer to a prayer? A decade ago, it would have been a blessing. Now it was an issue. Willy had wanted a son to carry on his name and his profession. Shirley had wanted a boy or a girl. It hadn't mattered to her. People change. The baby would change all that.

She climbed into bed with mixed emotions. A deep, not cleansing breath was the last thing she remembered doing before falling asleep.

It took a while for Shirley and Willy to talk about it. There was no big hug or "wow", or "I'm thrilled!" from Willy. Willy treated the news like any other unexpected event. He was used to fires taking wrong turns. So, he planned out the response. They needed to make room for the baby. They would buy furniture. Make appointments. Do what was necessary. Willy would handle everything. Calmly. Methodically. Emotionless. Efficiency would make up for his lack of feeling.

Unlike most things in life for Shirley, Sean Michael Duffy's delivery was relatively easy. Of course, Edie would be Sean's godmother. Buddy would have been the natural godfather, but that was not possible. Buddy's younger brother Ken was the stand-in godfather for Buddy at the baptism. The baptism was a stark reminder of the absence of Buddy.

Sean turned out to be Willy and Shirley's only child.

The poker games all but stopped. Even the Paddock Tavern nights grew less frequent.

Money was now tight. Willy would have to make choices. Choices he hadn't even thought about a year before. Shirley had taken a leave from her job two months before the baby was born. She now needed to be with the baby full time. So, their collective income was cut, and their costs grew. There just was no room in the budget for the gambling or the long nights of drinking. Except for an occasional night out with his firemen buddies, cigarettes were Willy's only real vice.

The other problem was he had to share Shirley's affection. He did what he could for Sean, like take him to a Red Sox game now and then. But both Willy and Sean knew that a solid father-son bond was not in the cards. It was okay with Sean. Willy could be a hardass now and then, especially after drinking. Luckily for Sean, Willy worked a lot of nights. Their relationship was respectful but primarily tolerant.

For Shirley, Sean provided comfort and fun during the nights Willy was away.

Like his father, Willy's dream was for his only son to be a fireman. Shirley dreamt that Sean would become a doctor. Sean's dream was to play for the Red Sox. None of those dreams would come true. Sean was a pretty good pitcher in high school. He even pitched a one-hitter for the Somerville Highlanders, his high school baseball team. Shirley cheered him on at every game she could. Willy hardly ever saw his son play. There were no college scouts, no scholarships, no baseball future. His second-best dream was to be a cop. He went to Northeastern University and graduated with a bachelor's degree in Criminal Justice.

Willy missed the graduation ceremony at the old Boston Garden. He was working the night shift. Could he have had someone cover for him on this important day for Sean and Shirley? Of course. Willy never offered. Shirley didn't ask. She knew if it was important enough, Willy could find a replacement. She had thought back to a Saturday night in October 1986. Willy was supposed to work the night shift. This situation occurred on the night the Red Sox were positioned to win the World Series for the first time since 1908. She thought back to that night. Willy came bouncing into the old apartment. He had gotten the night off. His buddies would spend the night at the Paddock Tavern cheering on the star starting pitcher, Roger Clemens. But, she thought, was that game more important than their son graduating from college in her head? Of course, the Red Sox did not win the world series in 1986. Willy had been crushed. He had moped around for days after the Mets took the series in seven games. Shirley had measured Willy's emotions about that loss against the lack of feelings of her only son graduating from college, a feat neither Willy nor Shirley would have ever accomplished.

After the graduation ceremony, Shirley, Edie, and Sean had a celebratory dinner at Polcari's restaurant in the North End of Boston.

"I'm so proud of you. Imagine my son with a college degree—Criminal Justice. You can get a job in the mayor's office. How about the legislature? Some staff job to a big-shot politician. Hey, maybe run for office. You could work for the...."

"I'm gonna be a cop. I've been accepted at the police academy. Medford, Somerville, and Boston PD's assured me that I could start in any of the PD's if I make it through. Boston would be my first choice."

"A cop? You have a degree. And Boston is dangerous. You could..."

"You're worried about Dad. Right?" said Sean.

"Sean. Your father will be proud of you."

Edie rolled her eyes.

Shirley glared back at Edie. She knew that Edie didn't believe it. Shirley was much more worried about Willy's reaction than some punk Sean might run into Southie or Dorchester.

"Dad wasn't crazy about me going to college. You know his dream was for me to join him at the firehouse. Carrying on his name. You know, Ma. I've always wanted to be a cop."

"He'll be fine. It might take him a bit of time to get used to it. Maybe someday, you'll have kids of your own. One will be a fireman."

"Sure, Ma. Gotta go the bathroom." Shirley figured this was his way of stopping the painful conversation.

"I know Willy too well," said Shirley. "Becoming a cop was the last straw."

"There was just too much time having so much freedom to do what he wanted," said Edie.

"We never stopped loving and caring for each other, but yeah, things did change." Shirley teared up.

"Well, now that Sean will be leaving home, you and Willy can have more time for yourself." Edie grabbed Shirley's hand.

"Edie, that's bullshit, and you know it. You know me. I'm a worrywart. I'll be waiting for something to happen to Sean. You know what I want?"

"What?" asked Edie.

Shirley suspected Edie already knew.

"I just want one goddam day of complete peace. I'm tired of the tension. And the guilt."

"Guilt? You have nothing to feel guilty for." Edie looked away.

Sean returned to the table. "Okay, ladies. Now I'm starting a brand-new career! Let's drink up!"

All three chugged their beers. They laughed and toasted.

Shirley held in her fears. She knew Willy all too well. This cop thing was just another stressor that tugged at her soul. She loved Willy with everything in her. But she also loved Sean in a completely different way. She had hoped that with Sean out of college, the unspoken stress between Sean and Willy would fade out on its own.

But now she feared that it would just move to a different phase.

"You'll be a great cop. Maybe make detective, then chief, "said Shirley.

"Just for you, Ma."

Edie chipped in, "Then you can run for mayor!"

Shirley got up from the table, hugged Sean so hard, kissed him on the side of the head, and took his face into her hands. "I am so proud of you." She grinned. Behind the grin was a deep sadness.

"You'll be a great cop," added Edie.

Sean joined the Boston Police. That was the bad news for Willy. The only good news was that he didn't become a Somerville cop. That would have been a terrible blow to his pride. Willy never verbalized his disappointment. For a firefighter to have his only son, a policeman was hard to take. There was no love lost between the police and the fire departments, especially in Somerville. Willy and his union buddies felt the police union always got better contracts and favors from the Board of Aldermen. Willy thought that the police believed that firefighters just hung around the firehouse and played cards most of the time. He knew better.

10

Shirley witnessed that Willy barely tolerated Sean. This situation created an undue burden on Shirley. She loved both husband and son and wanted so much for the two most influential people in her life to love each other. If there was an upside for Shirley, it was Sean's absence from Willy. Sean had his place and his own life. His job was all-encompassing. As a result, the visits were rarer and rarer.

This tolerance ended on New Year's Eve as 1999 turned into 2000.

Willy and Shirley had invited some friends over to their house for their annual New Year's Eve party. The friends mainly were the fire department personnel and some employees from the phone company, where Shirley now worked as a customer service agent. Shirley, as usual, invited Sean, and as usual, Sean declined. But Sean showed up anyway. Shirley dreadfully wondered if it was out of guilt, curiosity, or to spite his father.

Shirley greeted Sean at the door and smelled alcohol on his breath. Her heart sank.

"What have you been doing all afternoon." She could guess.

"Oh, there was a get-together at the Olde Time Pub in Dorchester. You know, the famous cop hangout on Blue Hill Ave."

Shirley knew that no respectable firefighter would ever be caught dead in that bar.

Sean spent most of the evening avoiding Willy's fireman buddies. Except for Brad. While Brad didn't like police officers any more than Willy, he loved his grandson. Shirley watched her father and figured he didn't want to show his grandson too much affection for fear of creating an issue with Willy.

Willy and Sean were equally drunk.

Before the ball dropped in Times Square ushering in 2000, Willy approached Sean.

"Hey Sean, what's it like being a cop?"

"Great, Dad. Real busy. You know, spending every minute chasing bad guys. Busy at the firehouse?"

"So, you don't think I'm just as busy at the firehouse?" Willy walked closer to Sean.

"I never said that. I just haven't heard about many fires in the city. You know, with smoke detectors and all. Things seem pretty quiet."

Shirley had been paying close attention to Dick Clark's countdown. People were cheering. As her custom over the last twenty years, Willy was to be the first person she hugged and kissed to usher in the new year. But, instead, she glanced around the room and saw what she feared the most. Her two most beloved people in the world, nose to nose, are ready to usher in the new year in the worse possible way. Shirley raced to them. She pushed herself between them.

"I'm sure that you guys are very busy," said Sean.

"What's that supposed to mean?"

"C'mon. The ball is ready to drop," Shirley tried to pry them apart.

"Nothing. I just don't think there are that many fires. That's all. You guys must play a lot of cards, waiting for the bell."

Shirley wished with all her heart that Sean hadn't said that.

Shirley begged, "Willy. It's almost time. The ball. C'mon."

"You became a cop just to spite me. Why?"

"Dad. Drop it. I didn't mean to say that about playing cards."

"You did. Didn't you?"

Meanwhile, the room filled with the countdown. Ten, Nine, Eight, Seven, Six, Five, Four.

Between the count of four and three, Sean turned around and raced out the door. No Happy New Year. No kissing his mother.

Three, Two, One. Happy New Year. Most of the people at the party did not notice how disappointment turned into acrimony between father and son.

Shirley just turned away. No kiss or hug for Willy either. This situation was the first New Year's minute since they had begun dating that there was no kiss. Instead, she joined the rest of the party. With just a tiny drop of tears on her cheek, she glanced over at Edie. She understood that probably only Edie had noticed the tears in Shirley's eyes.

"I saw. I could feel the tension." Edie grabbed Shirley's hand.

"You know. It was bound to happen. I dreaded this. It's been coming for some time. Willy resents Sean. For being born. For being a cop. Sean resents Willy," said Shirley.

"They'll work it out."

"No. I don't think so."

That morning Willy never brought up the argument with Sean. Neither did Shirley.

On New Year's Day, 2000, Shirley's father, Brad, died of a massive heart attack. Shirley felt she lost a father and a son on that same day.

That was that. Shirley had spent the rest of their marriage futilely attempting to reconcile Sean and Willy. Shirley's general disappointment of never having a close-knit family now turned into an awful pain of devastation. She loved both Willy and Sean unconditionally. She felt that both men deeply regretted the incident but could never rise above their stupid Irish pride. She knew that both were hurt. But for the second time in her life, Shirley was the devastated victim. Again, she blamed herself. It was yet another silent scar.

∽

Edie never married and never recovered from the loss of Buddy. She wasn't sure that Buddy kept the secret about Shirley that she hadn't kept. Many times she concentrated on that, though. But she never had a clear picture. Never once since the attack at Hennessey's garage had Edie ever brought up that awful night when Shirley appeared at her door, wet, bloodied, and terrified. Nor did Shirley ever mention it to Edie. Also, Edie never spoke about her trips to the scene of that awful fire. Instead, every Wednesday at dusk, she ventured to the vacant lot on the corner of Thurston Street and Broadway, the former site of the Winter Hill Rest Home. It was a comfort to her since she believed that she felt the presence of Buddy, still lingering there.

On this particularly cold Wednesday, January evening, two weeks after the disastrous encounter with Sean and Willy on New Year's Eve, Edie walked onto the pathway on the site of the old rest home. Kids would regularly cut across the vacant lot from Sycamore Street onto Broadway, creating a diagonal dirt path across the weed-infested lot. However, most of the people who had lived nearby during the fire avoided it. Some thought they heard voices.

She got about halfway to the middle of the lot and noticed something was different. For the first time, she had company. A young woman followed her. There was also a new sign facing Broadway on the lot. The old 'For Sale' sign had long since withered. She slowly walked toward the middle of the lot. Before she got to it, the woman following her spoke out.

"Hello," said the woman.

Edie, startled, turned around. "Hello?" and stopped walking.

"I've watched you every Wednesday come here for a few minutes, then leave. I live right there." She pointed to the house adjacent to the lot. "That's my kitchen window. We've lived here for the last five years. For the last several months, we've been fighting the city about this lot. We think it would be perfect for a park, some needed green space. I mean, the city is so crowded."

"I'd like that," said Edie.

"Not going to happen. Sorry. Well, at the Planning Board meeting last night, the plans were approved for a new building. Some kind of nursing home and rehab center. We are pretty upset about it. I wondered if you knew."

"Sort of. Not the details."

"I've seen you walk to the center of the lot, then stop for several minutes. It's none of my business, but, of course, the construction and building will make that harder. Just thought you would want to know. Is there something special about this spot?"

"Thank you, and yes, this location is special to me." Edie turned and walked to her usual spot in the center of the lot. She whispered, "Oh Buddy, I miss you so much." After a few minutes of silence, she slowly walked to the sign. It said, "Site of the new Winter Hill Nursing and Rehabilitation Center."

"I've heard that some people think this lot is haunted. My neighbor across the street told me about a bad fire here." She pointed to a rather worn-down two-family house across the street. "She believes she hears voices. She was here when the building burned down and heard the screams from the fire. It was some kind of old age home."

"Yes, I know. No. It's not haunted. It's just that some of us are more in tune with the energy that surrounds us," answered Edie.

"Energy? You mean from dead people?"

"We all have the gift. It's just that the world is too distracting."

"Well. I hope you find whatever you are looking for." The neighbor shuddered a bit and briskly walked back to her house.

Edie always knew that she had, as her mother would say privately to her, "the gift." She just knew things. There was a time she thought maybe she could become a professional medium. But then she was afraid that maybe there was something wrong with her. So instead, she would simply have her feelings and leave it at that.

The lot of the former Reynolds Building stood vacant for nearly twenty years. Winter Hill had been an upscale neighborhood during the glory years of the Reynolds School for Women. By the late sixties, the neighborhood became more known for underworld activities. Property values stagnated.

Within two years of Edie's visit, a family-owned company called Prospect Hill, LLC built the modern but bland Winter Hill Nursing and Rehabilitation Center on the site. It was a two-story wood-framed building, with a nice lobby but with stark rooms and services. In the back overlooking the parking lot was a big wooden deck. The owners thought the deck would be an excellent place for the residents to congregate and get some air. In addition, they had planted some trees along the border of the parking lot, so it provided a relatively nice view. While the owners were frugal, the nursing home had a good reputation.

11

TEN YEARS LATER

Since New Year's Eve 2000, contact between Sean and his mother lessened. Instead, he would visit on his shift here and there, calling beforehand asking the question, "Is he home?" Only if the answer was "no, he's working" would Sean visit his mother. On those occasions, Shirley would make sure there was never a sign that Sean had visited and of course, never mentioned the visit to Willy.

Willy got sicker and sicker from the emphysema. The smoke from the fires, the toxic fumes, and the two-pack-a-day habit of cigarettes was just too much for his fragile lungs. It had become more apparent to Willy that he would die soon. He knew that he would never return home this day. So, he plotted in his mind how he could somehow reconcile with his son.

Today, in the hospital, he was barely able to breathe. Shirley, now herself having suffered severe headaches, was still loyally at his side.

"I need..." Willy coughed up a load of phlegm and spat it into a tissue. "A cigarette. It's been a week." He continued to cough. "God-damit. Shirley, get me a cigarette."

"You know you can't smoke in here," Shirley said with intense compassion.

"Then take me…" Willy wheezed.

"Take you where?"

"The hell out of here. Gimme. Gimme a goddamn cigarette."

"I can't, Willy. You are too sick to move. Besides, you're hooked up to all kinds of tubes, including oxygen. Imagine lighting a cigarette in here. I'll have one for you when I leave.

"Don't rub it in." He grabbed hold of Shirley's arm. "How are they?" Willy struggled to get the words out.

"What?"

"Headaches."

"Getting better." Shirley turned her head away from Willy.

Willy picked up on it. "Worse, huh?" He turned away. He waved his hand as if to dismiss her comment. "Liar."

"No, about the same. "Shirley stood up. "I'll see you tomorrow. Love you." She leaned over the bed and kissed him gently on the lips.

"Love…" Willy strained to speak. "too." He could barely get the words out, watched her leave the room and wondered if he would ever see her again.

She decided to go back as she left the room and walked down the hospital corridor. She would finally tell Willy about the rape. Ever since Willy had been in the hospital and it was clear that he was never coming home, she needed to tell him. It was a burden that she desperately wanted to lift.

She walked back into the hospital room.

Willy was half asleep.

"Willy. There is something I need to tell you."

Willy barely moved. "Umm?"

"Never mind. We'll talk tomorrow." She had thought that maybe earlier in the day would be better. Perhaps she would also have more courage. Plus, she needed to figure out exactly how to tell the story. She would have to think about it more.

By the time she got home, the headache was unbearable. It was just stress, she had hoped. She called Sean.

"Dad's not doing well. I wish you would at least go to see him."

"How are you doing?" asked Sean.

"Go see your father."

They continued to speak about nothing for a short time. Shirley never answered Sean, and Sean didn't agree to see his father.

But he did go. Not long after the call, he drove to the Somerville Hospital. After visiting hours, he just walked in because he was a police officer in uniform. Even though Sean was a Boston policeman and had no jurisdiction in Somerville, nobody would dare question him. His father's room was dark. He could hear his father laboring to breathe. He had not seen his father for many years. He looked old and frail. He cried for the first time since he was a child. It wasn't a loud cry but a muted and inward. He thought back to that New Year's Eve night. That awful night.

He walked to the bed.

Willy's eyes opened. "Sean. Sean. I've been thinking a lot about you. There is so much..." Willy coughed uncontrollably for a few minutes. Then said, "Gimme a Kleenex."

Sean handed it to him.

Willy spat into it. "So much I need to tell you. But I don't think I have time. I've wanted to reach out to you, but I was afraid to."

"Afraid of what, Dad?"

"I don't know. Afraid that you wouldn't talk to me."

"Me too. I was afraid of the same thing." Sean was now holding back a burst of tears.

"Son. I am so sorry for the way I treated you. I have been a selfish and stubborn Irish bastard. Can you forgive me?"

"I do. I've been a stubborn bastard myself. I take after my old man."
Sean chuckled a bit.

Willy smiled. He grabbed his son's hand. "I don't think I am going to last much longer. I need to tell you a secret that I have held for a long time." He choked and spit and his face turned red.

"Jeez, Dad. Let me get a nurse."

"No. I need to tell you this now. Before I go."

"No. No. You can't go now. We need to spend time together."

"No time. Now listen. Don't go anywhere." Willy held Sean's hand in a tight grip.

"What is it?

"There was this guy." Then, Willy started into an intense coughing fit.

"What guy?

Willy's face got redder. He shook his head. "I beat the living…" The coughing got worse.

"Okay. I get it. You beat the living shit out of him. So what?"

"I. I." Willy nearly choked on his phlegm. "Killed him."

Sean's eyes widened, "You killed someone? Dad, who?"

In the middle of his fit, he violently shook his head. Then, finally, he just got out the word, "Almost."

"Who was it?"

Willy shrugged, suggesting he didn't know. He pointed to his eyes and then his eyebrows."

"Something about his eyes?"

In between the coughs and the labored breathing, he nodded. He barely got these words out, "Your mother."

"He did something to Ma?"

Willy again nodded.

"What?"

With all the strength he could muster, Willy pulled his son to himself. Then, amidst the wires and tubes, He grabbed onto Sean. But it was only for a few seconds.

"What?" said Sean, the tears now pouring down his cheeks landing on Willy's face.

Willy's eyes closed. He gasped. The heart monitor then alarmed.

Within seconds several nurses rushed in and then stopped. They slowly walked to the monitor. They turned off all the electrical equipment. "I'm so sorry, officer. Are you related?" one of the nurses asked. She disconnected the tubes and the wires. She pulled the sheet over his face.

"He's, my father."

Sean had agreed with the hospital staff that he would tell his mother since he didn't want her to get a call from some stranger. Sean dragged himself from the room. He sat in his car in the parking lot of the Somerville Hospital for what seemed like a long time. It was only a few minutes. Finally, he started his car and pulled out of the parking lot onto the main street. Police sirens howled in the background. He headed for his mother's house. The light at Highland Ave and Central Street was red. He stopped. His heart was heavy. Then he was angry.

Angry at himself for being such a stubborn jerk. Sure, his father was to blame too. But he could have made things better. He now knew that Willy wanted to heal things between them too. That made him even angrier. In the meantime, who suffered the most, he thought. His mother. He peeled through the red light onto Central Street. Thankfully, no one was in his way. Central Street is a narrow cross street, and Sean was going sixty miles an hour. He needed to see his mother that minute. Sean took a left onto Broadway without waiting for the green light. Then he took a left on Bartlett Street nearly on two wheels, jammed the car into park, and ran up the stairs to Shirley's apartment. It was almost 9 PM when he opened the door.

Shirley was sitting in her recliner watching TV. She loved to hold the controller tightly to her chest. When she saw Sean, she looked curiously at him. It would be very unusual for Sean to show up this late at night.

Sean knelt in front of his mother.

She didn't speak.

"Ma. Dad just died. I was able to say a few words about..."

The TV controller dropped to the floor with a loud crack. Sean's heart jumped.

Shirley's left side of her face drooped. She tried to speak, but all that came out were mumbled sounds. Her left arm fell to her side.

"Ma. Are you alright? Talk to me." Sean raced to the kitchen. He poured a glass of water. He was afraid Shirley was going to faint. He tried to get her to drink.

She could not control her movements, now her mouth was completely crooked, and her right eye widened in fear, while the left eye was stationary.

His first reaction was to get her up and maybe walk her around. He reached around her to lift her. Then he knew. His mother was having a stroke. He should have known from the symptoms. Drooping face muscles. Loss or weakening of the limbs. Slurred speech. His thought was now, why did he get the water, why was he trying to get her up. While he was screwing around, the blood in her brain was killing millions of neurons. Fuck, he thought. Should he take her to the hospital now or call 911? He had just left there.

He called 911. The EMTs came within five minutes. One was Timmy O'Shea. He was one of the New Year's Eve party guests ten years earlier. Now Sean needed him to save his mother's life.

"Timmy. My Dad died tonight. Am I going to lose my mother too?"

"She's having a stroke. The sooner we get her to the ER, the less damage will be done. They will get her on an IV. It will break up the clot and get the blood flowing. She will get better." Timmy paused and put his hand on Sean's shoulder. "So sorry about your Dad. He was a good man."

"Yeah."

Timmy rolled Shirley into the ambulance. Sean looked around the living room. The TV was still on, the ashtray was full of dead cigarette butts, and the controller was on the floor. Willy was gone. Maybe his mother would be gone too. Regardless, life would never be the same for Shirley and Sean.

He immediately returned to the same hospital where he had raced less than an hour. Why had he not seen the symptoms? Shirley had been complaining about headaches for a while. He should have known.

≈

The damage was permanent. Shirley would never regain the use of her left side.

She spent months in physical therapy. Finally, she was able to learn to eat and to speak reasonably well. She worked on increasing the strength in her right side. However, she could never master walking. The left leg had no feeling, nor was she ever able to support herself. After months in the rehab hospital, Sean placed her at the Winter Hill Nursing and Rehabilitation Center in Somerville. It was clear to Sean that it would be home for her until she died.

The Winter Hill Nursing and Rehabilitation Center was only several blocks from Shirley and Willy's house. It had a good reputation. So, it was a natural place for Sean to place his mother. Unfortunately, the decent reputation built by the original owners, Prospect Hill, LLC, eroded. Ernie and Janis Owens managed the facility. Running a single nursing facility and making a profit was challenging for the Owens. In 2011 Redwood Ventures offered the Owen's to buy the property and the business. While the Owen's loved and cared for their residents, the offer was too good to refuse. They were getting older and barely made ends meet. Redwood had been buying up small nursing homes over the last several years. Its business strategy was to run a facility strictly for profit, avoiding as many expenses as possible.

PART II

SCARS COME TO A HEAD

12

EIGHT YEARS LATER - WINTER HILL NURSING AND
REHABILITATION CENTER

MONDAY – MIDDAY

The last time that anyone maintained the sign facing the main
street was in 2013. Since Redwood Ventures bought the business, they stopped doing even the simplest repairs. So what if the sign
read Winter Hill Nursing and Rehabilitation Cente. Who cares about
a missing r was the attitude of the new owners? They might argue that
people in New England dropped their r's all the time. It would be
apparent to the people that needed to go there it was a place to die.
There wasn't much rehabilitation going on. One could even argue that
there wasn't even much nursing happening.

Redwood Ventures invested money in a company called Enstat.
One of Enstat's divisions bought privately held and family-owned
nursing homes. Then they cut the staff, cut back on maintenance, and
let the facilities deteriorate while collecting the lucrative state
payments. The business model was since the population was aging,

the source of customers was unlimited. The older the people, the more money Enstat got.

Aside from the missing "r" on the sign, the outside of the building was still in decent condition since the former owners took pride in the facility. The one major issue was the roof. The prior owners repaired the roof in 1987 after an excessive buildup of snow, and then a bitter freeze occurred, then a quick melt. This situation created significant issues. In the purchase and sales agreement with Redwood Venture and Enstat, the former owners faithfully disclosed that they had been doing roof repair for leaks but determined that the entire roof needed to be replaced. As a result, Enstat negotiated a twenty thousand dollar decrease in the selling price for roof repairs.

After the purchase, Enstat ignored the roof. The impact was predictable. After a rainstorm, water dripped onto the floor. Rather than fix the roof correctly, they patched the most severe sections. While that helped for a while, it was not uncommon for rain to drip onto the second-floor corridors.

Today, it was drizzling a bit. Metal buckets that caught the slow drip from the snow-stained suspended ceiling littered the second floor. The drip, drip of the water blended with a mix of sounds, some from the patients and others from the beeps of computers, printers, and call buzzers from the rooms, created an eerie sensation. The facility smelled like a combination of urine, antiseptic cleaner, and mildewed clothing. There was also an underlying smell of mold from above the stained suspended ceilings.

Both patients and staff had to watch their steps along the corridor. They could and occasionally would stumble into the buckets, then slip on the splashed water. Unfortunately, while the staff was aware of the issue, the patients often would walk right into the buckets.

The nursing station was at the corner of two long over-lit corridors, the A and B wing. The elevator was just several feet from the nursing station. A sign next to the elevator read: Floor 2. The last time anyone had painted the walls was ten years ago. Nearly all the walls were now worn and stained. Patients in wheelchairs would regularly rub up against the corner of the nursing station and the elevator enclosure. Thus, the edges of any corner were even more worn. The prior owners had attempted to brighten the corridors by hanging pictures of historic Boston scenes. By now, however, those prints were gloomy with grime. As a result, the overall impression of the corridors was of woeful neglect.

The floors were made of a yellowish ceramic tile material that was bright and cheery when the material was first installed. Now, the edges near the walls were stained with dirt and the once white caulking between the tiles was black. Several tiles were cracked. Patients often noticed cockroaches roaming the floor once the lights were turned low. These images would be a proxy for the staff's actual negligence of the patients. Any newly initiated rare visitor would get a visual image of neglect.

Healthier patients would gather at this intersection of the elevator, the two corridors, and the nursing station. Some were in wheelchairs, while others used walkers to get around. Several patients could walk with the aid of neither. The sound coming from the collection of residents could be an actual conversation, but mostly it was muttering, wheezing, and regular complaining.

There was never a sound out of Tommy Swartz, one of the Winter Hill Rest Home fire survivors. Tommy was the unofficial greeter on the second floor. He was confined to a wheelchair. Tommy's left leg was stiff and stuck out straight like a battering ram. When Tommy got upset, he would charge like a bull into something or even someone with the one leg sticking straight out. Even the patients who were unaware of their situation instinctively got out of the way when Tommy started charging down the corridor.

Tommy behaved like he was aware of danger ahead for anyone who exited the elevator. Tommy stopped whoever came out. He would warn the visitor or worker that something terrible had happened inside the nursing home. Tommy would first put his index finger up to his mouth, with a shushing motion, as if to tell the unsuspecting visitor not to disclose his warning. Then he would point to the nursing station with a warning glance. Since he couldn't talk nor write down anything, no one ever knew what dangers Tommy was aware of. Since there were no visitors today, Tommy lingered about six feet from the elevator door in a trance. Tommy also had a habit of listening to the walls. It was as if he heard something from behind the walls, particularly near the elevator lobby.

∾

Caroline was well into her nineties and unaware of her situation. Today as always, she just sat in room 208, like she did every day. Her head slumped downward, as was her position nearly every hour of every day. She was wheezing and gurgling. The TV flashed an eerie light across the dimly lit room when a shadow of a figure enveloped her wheelchair.

Smash. A glass fell on the floor and broke into pieces.

Caroline barely stirred.

The shadowy figure stopped and waited for a second. Then it moved closer to the ancient woman. Now it stood over her. Its hands reached out to her neck and slowly moved to surround it, closer and closer. Finally, they were within inches of clenching the woman's neck.

The figure grunted. But a squeaky noise broke the silence. The grunting stopped, and the figure looked around. The light shined on his grotesque face highlighting that he had only one eye. Half the face was just a mass of skin. The blue veins in his neck popped out. The figure was ancient, perhaps as old as Caroline.

Suddenly Shirley, in a wheelchair, entered the room. One of her arms dangled lifelessly by her side. "Nelson. Leave her alone!"

Nelson jumped. He pulled his hands away from oblivious Caroline. Then he rushed toward Shirley.

In a soothing, loving voice, Shirley took hold of his hand. She displayed no fear, just compassion. "It's okay, Nelson, now just go to your room."

Nelson's single eye lit up. He smiled. Shirley motioned to the door. "That's right. This way. Good. Very good." She continued to rub his hand tenderly. She finally slowly and lovingly squeezed it.

Nelson then wandered out of the door. This situation was not the first time that Nelson tried to bother Caroline. His attack was harmless each time. It seemed to everyone that Nelson just liked to touch the old woman's neck. No one knew why.

Since Shirley's room was next to Caroline's, she was always first on the scene. She wheeled over to Caroline and rubbed her shoulder. "Rest well. It won't be long."

The fire alarm softly sounded in the background. Shirley looked up at the red fire alarm speaker on the wall of Caroline's room. "What now?" Shirley whipped her wheelchair around and hurried out the door. "Why only one alarm went off?"

The patients loitering around the nursing station panicked. Wheelchairs began to dart, like when electric cars at the old Dodgem ride at Revere Beach started up. They turned in a random fashion and crashed into each other. Tommy woke up from his trance. He turned in circles in front of the elevator.

Someone yelled out, "Help! Help! Oh! Fire. Fire. Run for your lives."

From her wheelchair, Ruthie warned, "Repent, you sinners. The Lord's wrath is upon you. The fire is coming from hell. Repent. Repent." Ruthie was the official Bible thumper of the group. She was not pleased about being critical of anyone who violated her interpretation of the Bible.

Marjorie Dodds, formerly Kowalski, leaned on her walker and was on the verge of tears, "I dropped my necklace. Everyone just stop. Stop. Where is it? Don't run over it." Marjorie, unlike most the patients, dressed properly. She dressed the same way she did when she had worked at the phone company. Marjorie's grandmother had perished in the fire at the old rest home.

Colleen, one of the nurses in her early thirties, and Lauren, an older charge nurse, bolted from behind the nursing station.

Marjorie's necklace slid across the floor. "There it is. Someone get it, please."

Smoke appeared from one of the rooms down the corridor.

Colleen picked up the necklace. She quickly handed it to a nerved-up Marjorie, who then clutched it with loving care. "Thank God!"

"Don't you take the Lord's name in vain," yelled Ruthie.

"I didn't. I just thanked him."

Bill Bennett casually emerged from his smoke-filled room. He was in his late seventies, alert, and in good physical shape. He walked without the aid of a cane or walker. His dark, leathery face had guilt written all over it. The scuttlebutt from those patients who still had functioning minds was that Bill was not sick but somehow managed to use the nursing home as his private homeless shelter. Rumors were rampant here. Bill blew the smoke away with his hand. His old dog, Rudy, ran out of Bill's room barking.

"He's smoking in his room again. He thinks the wastebasket is an ashtray," said Lauren.

Bill glared at Lauren as he watched her pass.

"Smoke outside or on the deck. How many times do we have to tell you? I swear you will be banned from smoking. We will confiscate all smoking materials! And another thing, tie up that mangy mutt, or we'll have it put to sleep."

Bill's expression turned angry. "Bitch."

The other rumor had to do with the dog. How did Bill get permission to have a dog in a nursing home? Some believed that he had incriminating evidence against Paul Batty, the administrator. Some speculated that Bill was blackmailing him. Other less rational people believed that Bill was a spy for the government. In any case, Bill commanded a lot of respect or at least some wariness. He knew this too and used it to his advantage. Bill never referred to Paul Batty by his given name. Whenever he spoke about him, he only used the term sleazebag.

Lauren turned back to Colleen, "Keep the inmates calm."

Out of nowhere, Shirley raced down the corridor and crashed into a pail of water, sending it and its contents flying.

On seeing Shirley moving so quickly, Rudy ran alongside, barking like crazy, as he used to on the outside when he regularly chased cars.

The patients gathered around the nursing station immediately made a pathway for her and the dog.

Shirley sped through the newly created path.

Colleen raced after her, slipping on the spilled water.

The patients yelled and cheered for their hero, savior, and spokesperson, Shirley.

"Son of a bitchin, bastards. You people don't give a god-damn shit about any of us. Where's the Fire Department! How come the smoke detector didn't go off?"

She made a beeline for the administrator's office. "Paul, you fat bastard. I'll give you a piece of my mind. After that, I'll turn you into the state."

Colleen raced after her. She caught up and stepped in front of the rapidly moving wheelchair, stopping its forward progress. Not ten feet away, Colleen looked over at the sign on a door that read, Mr. Paul Batty, Administrator. Batty's office was directly across Shirley's room at the end of the A-wing.

Once Shirley's forward progress was stunted, the dog, Rudy, walked off, seemingly now bored.

"Out of my way!" Shirley pushed with her good arm to move the stopped wheelchair.

"Wait, Mrs. Duffy."

Shirley tried to get her wheelchair to move, but Colleen had wedged her foot under one of the wheels. Shirley was stuck.

"Where are you going?" asked Colleen.

"I'm going to see Paul." Shirley continued to push ahead with no luck.

"Hold on!"

"This place is gone to shit. You know it." On this point, she was correct. As she had said on numerous occasions, it had indeed gone to shit.

Colleen now had a firm grip on the wheelchair. "It's tough running a place like ..."

"If I could, I'd punch him right in the nose. That prick."

Colleen stopped the urge to laugh out loud. "Mrs. Duffy! You don't have to see Paul. I can help you. That's my job. Stop here a minute and tell me what's wrong."

Shirley rocked the wheelchair in a futile attempt to run by Colleen. Colleen didn't budge.

Lauren placed the fire extinguisher on the floor. She wiped her hands and frowned.

Colleen looked over at her and rolled her eyes. "Crap."

Lauren yelled toward Colleen, "Nurse McCarthy. I need you here. Is that one settled down yet?"

"I'll be right there." Colleen turned her attention back to Shirley, "Why are you so upset? It was just a small wastebasket fire. Nothing to worry about."

"Call me Shirley. I've seen you around for a week or so. So you're new, huh?"

Shirley grabbed Colleen's uniform to get a better look at her name tag. "Colleen? Nice Irish name. Willy, my husband, was Irish, well, not actually Irish. His grandparents were from Ireland."

"This is my second week. Still learning the ropes."

Shirley had softened her expression with the mention of her husband, but now she shook her head back and forth and was seeming mad again. "Well, don't learn them too well. The ropes around here are tied to our necks."

"I gotta get back to the nursing station."

Shirley motioned to Colleen to come closer to her.

Colleen leaned up to Shirley's face, which was firm and determined.

"My husband, Willy, was a fireman for forty years. So I learned a little about fires myself. The smoke alarms are supposed to go off in the entire building and if the heat gets high enough, the sprinkler activates. Bill used to set off the smoke alarms all the time. Creates so much noise. Bill is so careless with his butts. Paul got so pissed. But now, most don't go off anymore. The only one that alarmed was outside Bill's room. Someone has messed up the system, I swear." Shirley stopped pushing on Colleen's foot.

"They can't, I'm sure ..."

"He is cutting back on everything. The food sucks. The ceiling leaks. It's dirty. I hear bugs crawling around my bed at night. I hear voices in the middle of the night. It's..."

Lauren craned her neck down the corridor. "Nurse McCarthy. I need you here. Now. If she's giving you a tough time, I'll get an aide and have her put to bed."

Colleen straightened up and hurried toward the nursing station.

"Coming. She's fine," said Colleen as she turned back toward Shirley. "Look, we'll talk later. Try to settle down. I'll talk to maintenance." Colleen rushed back to the nursing station.

"Like that will help." Shirley shook her head.

Now that the crisis had ended, the patients gathered again into their usual places around the nursing station. Tommy returned to his location outside the elevator. Lauren and Colleen stood behind the station, busy with paperwork.

Shirley didn't move. She stayed right outside of Paul Batty, the administrator's office. She glanced back at the nursing station and said to no one in particular. "Sure, you people always have paperwork. Just a goddam excuse to ignore the people who need help. Bastards."

13

The residents who regularly gathered at the nursing station were back in position. Wheelchairs were lined up neatly in a row, led by Phyllis, a tiny, very old woman. She looked at least ninety years old. By now, she was missing most of her teeth. It would seem she didn't care because she always seemed to have a smiling expression. Her devilish eyes were still bright. Phyllis was the little group's eldest, who spent much of their time together at the nursing station.

Next in line was Millie, a shriveled up, sour woman. In contrast to Phyllis, she continuously wore a frown broadly across her face. Occasionally, her son and one of her grandchildren would visit. The problem was that every time they came, Millie would berate her son, telling him he was stupid and lazy. The son would simply take it, saying nothing in his defense. Millie's visitors never stayed more than a few minutes.

Unfortunately for Shirley, Millie was her roommate. While Millie used a wheelchair, she could manage to get in and out of her bed without help. That was to her advantage since she often wandered the corridors late into the night.

Ruthie was third in line. She was a hefty, stern-looking woman and was what some of the patients called her, the Bible thumper.

Ruthie was the one that warned that Bill's wastebasket fire was from hell. She constantly held on to a Bible. No one had ever witnessed Ruthie reading it. She just held it. While Millie was just plain mean, Ruthie could be pleasant at times.

Tommy brought up the rear, nearest the elevator. The talk amongst the group was that Tommy thought he had a real job, that of guarding the rest of the patients against harm.

The rest of the group that gathered around the nursing station used walkers:

Marjorie, who had lost her beloved grandmother during the horrible rest house fire, years earlier, had lost her necklace during the wastebasket fire. As she had been her entire adult life, she never had a hair out of place and also complained about the foul language, particularly when Shirley would swear and call Paul various vulgar words. Marjorie had never used offensive language that anyone had ever heard. Some of the patients avoided her since she did not get too close to anyone. Millie would often tell anyone who would listen that Marjorie thought she was better than everyone else.

Bones McGraw lined up on the opposite side of the corridor. His most notable feature was an old-fashioned crew cut. Shirley would tease him about it regularly. She called his hairstyle a whiffle. Whiffle was an urban term for a crew cut. He had a Marine look, but not a drill sergeant type because of his kind face. No one knew why he was called Bones. It certainly wasn't because he was all skin and bones. He had broad shoulders and a pronounced midsection. There were rumors he had been a gravedigger at Mt. Auburn Cemetery. He just smiled, never agreeing, or denying the rumor whenever someone asked him about it. Shirley had mentioned to the other patients that Bones liked the story. He still wore a wedding ring, although he never mentioned anything about a wife or children. There were times when Bones seemed mentally perfect. Too often, though, he just stared blankly.

Bill Bennett, who had just recently created the wastebasket fire, joined the group. Unlike the others, he didn't have a usual spot. He roamed since he was the most mobile of the patients that gathered at the second-floor nursing station. Bill called Lauren, the charge nurse, simply the bitch.

Today, the group had to accommodate Vinny, the maintenance man, cleaning up the spilled water from the bucket tipped over by Shirley's racing wheelchair. Once finished, he returned the bucket to its usual location.

"These charts are all out of order. Please sort them by head, then by date," barked Lauren to Colleen.

"I thought you needed me right away. I can sort the charts tonight when everyone is in bed. By head, I suppose you mean by person?"

Lauren sighed. "Yes, by name." Lauren stopped the paperwork and turned to Colleen. "Look, let me give you some advice. You get too close to them, and they take advantage of you."

Colleen started to say something.

"You are not here to make friends. You're here to do a job. Period. They will use you. If every time one of them gets an urge to pee, and you jump to toilet them, you're screwed. That's all you'll be doing."

"But they are ..."

"One by one, on and off the toilet. Half the time, they won't go. They learn to hold it. Just like a dog. It just takes training."

Colleen's face grew tight and flushed. She took a deep breath and began to sort the charts.

Lauren continued, "Don't spoil them. It just makes it harder on the rest of us. Get it?" Lauren hurried off.

Colleen's eyes grew wide, and her face reddened. She took a deep, deep breath.

Paul Batty's office was the same size as a patient room. Since the original owners also ran the nursing home, they put a lot of money into the administrator's office. It was, in effect, the owner's office. It was also sort of a conference room for patients' family meetings. The owners had it nicely appointed. There once was an attractive, cherry-wood desk with a matching file cabinet. To the left of the desk used to be cherry wood built-in cabinets. Between the desk and the window once stood a matching credenza. There also used to be a fancy coffee table surrounded by four nicely upholstered chairs. When Enstat took over, they sold off the big desk, the credenza, and the coffee tables. A grey metal desk half the size of the cherry-wood desk stood in its place. The credenza now was a single metal table. Enstat replaced the upholstered chairs with Home Depot folding chairs. The only remnant of the once plush owner's office was the cherry-wood coffee table.

Year old People, Motor Trend, and Arthritis Today Magazines littered the coffee table. The new owners replaced the built-in shelves with grey metal file cabinets. When Paul sat behind his now industrial-style desk, he seemed too big for it. He looked like a parent at a 2nd grade meet the teacher meeting, sitting in one of the children's chairs. It wasn't clear what Enstat did with the expensive furniture or why they bothered to refurbish the office. Paul had told Lauren that he suspected they wanted to message the employees that they valued economy over comfort. This message was communicated to everyone in the building.

Today, Butch Donovan, a local loan shark was paying his tardy customer, Paul Batty, a visit to not so gently remind him of his obligation to pay his debt. His payback was due today. "Paul. I hope the fuck you have our money. We've been more than patient. If it was up to me, I'd give you more time." While Butch was a tough guy himself, his bosses were brutal. When he didn't collect, the bosses put the same pressure on him that Butch planned to put on Paul. Paul owed the loan sharks a hefty sum.

Butch had given Paul today as the final day for payment.

Suddenly, Shirley stormed into Paul's office. She hit the coffee table head-on, knocking off half of the magazines.

"Jesus Christ. I am in the middle of a very important meeting."

Paul's face immediately turned red. Butch jumped out of the way of the charging Shirley.

Butch mouthed to Paul, with his back to Shirley, "Who the fuck is that?"

"Mrs. Duffy is one of our patients." Batty gave Butch a look, like, 'please don't say anything to her'.

"I didn't know you had company. You must be from headquarters. I'm Shirley Duffy, one of the inmates. I mean guests here," said Shirley.

Butch looked away. "No. I'm Mr. Batty's financial advisor. We are in the middle of some personal business. Come back later."

"You should make an appointment. I really don't appreciate you barging in on me. I'm a very busy man. Can't you see I'm in the middle of something?"

"Personal matter on company business?"

"I can't speak to you now. Please see your charge nurse," insisted Batty.

She pulled closer to his desk, banging it with her wheelchair. "More interested in your personal finances than figuring out how to make this place work better?"

"Mrs. Duffy. We do the best we can with the money we take in and please be careful of the desk. For your information, I had been working on the budget. It's a challenge to continue to operate this facility with so many freeloaders not carrying their weight. Get my point? Now, what's so very important that the nurses or aides can't handle?"

Shirley banged up against the desk.

"I'll come back tomorrow. Tend to your, whatever you call them," said Butch as he walked around Shirley.

She glared back at the loan shark. "People! Goddamit! People, we are all people."

"Jesus. See you later." Butch walked out.

Shirley banged into Paul's desk again. "Financial advisor, huh."

"Watch the desk! None of your business who he is." Paul stuttered his response.

"Freeloader? Well, this freeloader is reporting to you that you violate all kinds of health and safety codes. The smoke alarm system didn't operate properly. It was supposed to alarm the whole building. The Fire Department didn't show up. Someone locked the fire doors the other day. Bugs, I see bugs all the time! I hear rats scurrying around at night. Nobody ever fixes the leaks in the ceiling and sounds, people talking all night. People walk around at all hours. You people don't know what you are doing."

Paul waved his arms and shook his head. "Would you like to run this place? You know, I called the Fire Department and told them that we had everything under control. We have rigorous management over pests. There are no bugs and certainly no rats. I'm here late at night, and it's very, very quiet."

Shirley shook her head.

"Mrs. Duffy, there was a tiny wastebasket fire that was out in a matter of seconds. We service and test the smoke alarms per fire code. Please don't insult me. Everything is done by the book around here. Now is there anything else?"

She pointed her finger at him with her good hand. "What about the fire doors? Who locked them?"

"They are never locked. Probably something got stuck in them."

"Bullshit."

"Maintenance checks them every day. They are fine." Paul's hands shook as he picked up a pen to write.

"What about the overflowing crap in the toilets and ..."

"Enough. If you have a complaint, talk to your charge nurse. Now please return to your room." He slammed the pen down.

"There are laws. Just because you want to save a few bucks so that you can look good to your bosses doesn't mean you can break the law."

"Go to your room, Mrs. Duffy. Next time you have a complaint, see the nurse."

Paul turned around and stared at the computer, which sat on his plain metal back table.

Shirley crashed into the coffee table again, knocking the

remaining magazines on the floor and running over them. She backed up wrinkled them badly. Then, with her wheelchair to Batty's back, she smiled. As Shirley moved out of Paul's office, she yelled back. "I'm calling the state and reporting you."

"Have a lovely day, Mrs. Duffy." Batty's jaw was set tightly. His temples were pulsating.

Paul muttered under his breath, "Fuck," as he picked up the phone. "Lauren, keep that Duffy woman away from me." He hung up the phone with a loud bang.

Paul had never stolen anything in his life before he started working at Winter Hill. He studied accounting and could have become a certified public accountant if he had wanted to. But instead, he got a job at the Central Hospital as a supervisor in the accounting department. He worked there for eight years, then applied for and got the job at Winter Hill as an administrator, which meant he was a glorified book-keeper. But unfortunately, what he did know how to do was embezzle.

Paul was married to Emily, a woman who loved to buy things. Paul and Emily when there were first married, used their credit cards to set up housekeeping like most young couples. Unfortunately, their credit card bills were high in the first several years of marriage. So instead of cutting back, Emily discovered what First Bank of Boston called their customer First checking account. Their promotional material read, "If you write a check that you just don't have the funds for right now, no problem. Just write the checks. We put you, the customer, first and cover the shortage. Then whenever you get the money, pay it off, at your convenience, or if that's inconvenient, First Bank of Boston will simply roll it over and let you pay it off, whenever."

The problem for Paul and Emily was that they owed more to First Bank of Boston than they did on their mortgage for their three-bedroom ranch-style house in Melrose. They had re-mortgaged in 2007 and taken out several home-equity loans, just before the housing market collapse. As a result, the value of their house was lower than the balance on their mortgage and equity loans. Even after the housing crisis, their house value never exceeded their housing debt. So that ended that source of cash to pay the growing debt habit to the bank on their credit cards.

When Paul got the administrator job at Winter Hill in 2012, Emily had shared with Paul that the hundred thousand dollars a year salary would finally pull them out of their financial woes. So rather than take the raise and pay off the debt, Emily continued her spending ways.

Paul and Emily were in a deep financial hole. There was no way they could make the payments required of First Bank of Boston on Paul's administrator salary and Emily's minimum wage job as a receptionist at the Melrose High School principal's office. Adding to their financial woes in addition to the mortgage, the equity loans, and the lease payment on the Mercedes was Emily's habit to eat out at expensive restaurants at least twice a week.

The only way to keep financially afloat was to embezzle funds from the nursing home. But, since even that didn't quite make ends meet, Batty resorted to borrowing money from a local loan shark. Of course, no one knew about his plan.

Except for Vinny, the maintenance man.

14

A fter the excitement of the wastebasket fire wore off, the residents gathered in the dining room for the daily bingo game after dinner. Luckily for them, this bingo service was not provided by the nursing home, since according to most patient accounts, the staff was incapable of doing anything right. The local YMCA sent over one of their volunteers to run the game. Sadly, this little exercise in humanity was the day's highlight for many patients. The irony was that the stranger from the Y was one of the few outsiders seen at the facility.

Each person had a couple of bingo cards in front of them on one of the worn dining room tables. Some just stared blankly at the cards and didn't understand what to do. They each had a batch of blue bingo chips.

Shirley, Bill, Ruthie, Phyllis, Bones, Marjorie, and Millie sat together. They were the most active in the competition since they were not nearly as trapped into the prison of dementia or Alzheimer's. Tommy at least moved from his usual position guarding the elevator to his alternate location guarding the door to the dining room. Nonetheless, he continued his routine of warning everyone that something terrible was about to happen. Usually, the YMCA bingo volunteer had to force her way into the dining room to get by Tommy. Tommy had never failed to motion to her his secret and pointed toward the nursing station. The new volunteers stopped and tried to figure out what Tommy was trying to say. The repeat volunteers just played along with Tommy.

Today the volunteer was Mary Beth McCabe or, as her friends called her simply, "MB."

"B-10. I-17." MB's dream was to be an actress on stage. Instead, she married Ralph Tulane, a pipe fitter for the gas company. She used a kind of English accent to pronounce the letters and numbers. It was a far cry from the nasal Somerville accent that she used during the rest of her life.

While the group that normally gathered at the nursing station was focused on the game, they used this time to tell their stories.

"I don't have much time to play. My son is picking me up in a limo. He lives in California, you know. Hollywood. He's taking me there. Oh, look, all I need is O-72. Josh, my son, he's very famous. He wrote songs, made movies." Phyllis grinned through her missing teeth.

Bones delivered an expression of scorn. "Really?"

"Yes, he wrote the song, *Wind Beneath My Wings*. It goes like this." Phyllis started singing the song's words, but to the tune of *You Are the Sunshine of My Life*.

"You are the wind beneath my wings."

"Please, Phyllis. I can't concentrate," said Shirley.

Unfazed, Phyllis continued, "Remember the song *Feelings*? He wrote that one too."

Millie chimed in, "Don't sing it."

Phyllis continued, "He's going to introduce me to all the famous people in Hollywood. He also made the movie *Star Wars*."

"Phyllis, you're full of shit. Spielberg or Lucas made *Star Wars*."

Bones looked for support from the group. "Right?"

Shirley winked at the crowd, making sure Phyllis didn't see. "No. I think it was Phyllis's son, Josh."

Bones decided to change the subject. "Hey, Millie. Did your strip-tease again, huh? So, who wants to look at that ugly bod?"

All the folks at the table burst out in laughter, except Millie, who just continued her usual frown. Not only did Millie like to roam the corridors late at night, but she also occasionally wanted to do it naked. Last night was one of those times.

Bill giggled and whispered to Shirley. "I walked out of my room this morning, and there she was stark naked. Damn near choked."

Millie's hearing was good enough to pick up the conversation.

Bill continued, barely able to contain his laughter. "Why do you suppose she strips?"

"For attention," Millie replied with a complete lack of emotion.

Marjorie perked up. "Have you ladies noticed the new guy? See over there. The big guy. Ruthie says he's the Anti-Christ. I think he's kinda cute in a creepy sort of way."

The ladies all strained to get a good look.

Phyllis jumped in. "Marjorie, anyone know his name?"

Bill rolled his eyes. "Yeah, he's my new roommate, Theodore something. Strange character. My luck."

"N fifty-two," MB announced in her fake English accent.

"Bingo!" Bill bellowed.

Shirley tossed her bingo chips in mock anger.

The new guy, Theodore, hurled his bingo card at MB. Then he ran across the room, showering the residents with bingo chips. He crashed into Tommy's stuck-out leg and spun him around in a circle until his leg crashed into the dining room door jam. All Tommy could do was make a large silent O with his mouth. The new guy then crashed into MB and the cage holding all the bingo balls. The balls went flying all over the floor. The bingo players yelled and screamed.

Then the new guy screeched, "Cheaters. Cheaters. Ahhhhhhhh."

The new guy was in an uproar.

Two of the nursing aides raced into the dining room and restrained him. Bingo balls rolled everywhere. As they held him steady, his eyes blinked quickly. His eyebrows moved up and down.

Finally, he opened and closed his mouth rapidly and clicked his tongue.

The color drained from Shirley's face. Her body shook. "Oh my God. God, no."

"What's the matter? You alright?" said Bill.

"I gotta get out of here!" yelled Shirley. She spun away from the table, pushed through the residents standing near her, and sobbed hard as she moved toward the door.

As Shirley approached the door, Tommy created a clear pathway by moving people out of the way.

Shirley raced out of the dining room. She drove immediately into her room, while shaking badly. Bill, Marjorie, Phyllis, and Bones rushed to her room. Even her roommate Millie rolled in.

"What was that all about?" asked Bill.

"He terrified me. That new guy reminded me of someone I once knew."

"Do you want to be alone?" asked Marjorie.

"I'm fine. Go back to the game."

"He creeps me out. I gotta share a room with that asshole," said Bill

Bones chimed in, "Hey Shirley, if that guy bothers you, I'll pound him out. Don't worry."

"I appreciate it, Bones. Go back to the game. I'm tired anyway."

They paraded out of Shirley's room in a single file.

Shirley was still shaking. "Willy, Willy. I miss you so bad. I need you to hold me. I so want to tell you about that horrible man, that horrible time in my life."

Colleen had been on her dinner break during the bingo game chaos. Lauren didn't mention it to her at all. It was Bones who filled her in. Colleen sat alone behind the nursing station. This was a tough day for her. She disagreed vehemently with Lauren about treating the patients. She didn't know how long Lauren had worked at Winter Hill, but she supposed it was more than a decade. She wondered what it would be like in ten years for her. Would she view the poor patients as barely human? Would she, like Lauren, get tired of them soiling themselves, always having to urinate, and their endless complaints. She didn't think so. Like Shirley, these were real people with real feelings, like her father. She wasn't much of a Catholic, but she always remembered the phrase from mass or the dreaded catechism about treating the least of my brothers as they would treat me or something like that. So she thought of that phrase. But, no, she wouldn't turn out like Lauren.

She was what was called a "practical nurse" as opposed to a registered nurse. A registered nurse, which she supposed Lauren was, meant you had to pass all kinds of tests, have a full Bachelor of Science degree, and who knows what else? In effect, Colleen was a glorified nurse's aide. Nurse's aides at Winter Hill did most of the dirty work, like changing the beds and the diapers. Christ, she mused. How humiliating. Fortunately, if she would examine her thoughts, many patients were not all that aware of their situation. For many, though, it must be tough. She thought about the more lucid ones, like Shirley and Bill. What must they be thinking? When would their minds finally go?

She shuddered at her dark thoughts. She needed this job badly and was desperately trying to dig herself out of the mess she had made of her life. She had met Serj Sarkissian in her junior year at Somerville High. Serj was a real charmer. Oddly enough, he had bright red hair. Serj lived on the other side of the Winter Hill section of Somerville, on the city border in a tiny Armenian enclave.

It didn't take Serj long to convince Colleen that having sex was pretty much the same as kissing or getting and giving oral sex. By the second semester of her senior year, she was pregnant, and Serj was having sex with Julie Bavokian, his former girlfriend from the old neighborhood.

Colleen's father forced her to finish high school even though she was getting close to a full term of pregnancy by graduation. "What the hell? Most of the girls at the high school were screwing around anyway. Getting pregnant was not that big a deal." Her father had told her.

Colleen's mother had been mortified and skipped the high school graduation ceremonies at the high school football field. Not dad, Sonny McCarthy. He hooted and hollered when poor Colleen shuffled down the aisle to receive her diploma. Colleen bet that half the people in the stands were holding their collective breaths waiting for her to deliver right there on the fifty-yard line while the Somerville High School band played the graduation march. That didn't happen. Cassidy Marie McCarthy was born three weeks later with a shock of bright red hair. That wasn't so bad. She mused since the Irish are supposed to have red hair.

There were two periods in her life, before Serj and after. She would never be the same. She despised the thought of Serj. Maybe that's why her relationship with Cassidy today was so… How would she have put it? Complex.

She started her adult life as a single mother at barely eighteen years old. Luckily Marie and Sonny supported her while she scrounged for a job. Thankfully, Somerville was a short bus ride to Lechmere Station. Then she would ride the Green Line Rapid line trolleys to Park Street Station in Boston. Not so rapid, by the way. Finally, she got a respectable job at the John Hancock Insurance company in the mailroom. Then graduated as a clerk in the accounting department. A high school graduate with a B-minus average was probably the highest she would ever get at the insurance company. But she persisted. She enrolled at the Powder House Community college and received a certificate in nursing technology. That brought her to the Winter Hill Nursing and Rehabilitation Center.

Things were quiet on the second floor. Colleen was still furious at Lauren for what she had said earlier. Lauren's shift was over and now was gone. Now Colleen could unwind a bit. Her mood was interrupted by the elevator opening. Usually, when an elevator door opens, a light goes on, and there is a sound, a chime, telling people the elevator door was opening. No such sound. She speculated that the chime stopped working sometime years ago. Since there were very few visitors, she craned her neck to see who was arriving on floor two of the Winter Hill Nursing and Rehabilitation Center or, as the locals would have pronounced, Centah. Good thing because the "r" was missing on the front sign anyway.

Tommy was right on the spot, waiting to warn the visitor.

15

Sean Duffy walked out of the elevator. "What's up. Tommy?"
Tommy blocked his passage. Tommy motioned for Sean to come closer to him. He put his index figure to his lips. If Tommy could speak, he would have said, "Shush."

Sean nodded. "Won't say a word." He understood that Tommy was a seriously damaged person.

Tommy nodded back. Sean leaned in close to Tommy. He could tell Tommy liked that. Tommy glanced sideways in the direction of the nursing station. He lifted his good hand slightly. Then with his hand just lifted off his lap, he pointed to the nursing station. He did this so that only Sean could see his motion. He often wondered why Tommy was so concerned about what was going on. But he just figured that Tommy had delusions and simply was seriously mentally ill.

"I'll be careful. I won't tell anyone," Whispered Sean.

Tommy nodded and let him pass. Tommy had repeated this little ritual for Sean dozens of times. Sean knew the drill and understood that if he didn't appease Tommy, it would delay his visit to see his mother.

Sean was now a sergeant in the Domestic Violence Unit of the Family Justice Division of the Boston Police Department. Technically, Sean was a detective, but detective was more of a function than a rank at Boston PD. But like most police officers in the union, he worked overtime on various situations, rarely involving detective work.

Like his mother and father, guilt played a dominant role in his life. Now the only thing Sean could do to ease his guilt was to make somehow things a bit easier for his mother. He was the only consistent visitor to the nursing home. On the elevator ride from the first floor to the second floor on his way to see his mother today, Sean had felt the pangs of guilt again, thinking of how he could have made things so much easier on his mother. He knew that he was at least equally responsible for the schism between his father and him. While he finally reconciled with his father, it was too late to do anything meaningful. He also knew that his father would have accepted him if he had taken an early step at reconciliation. He also wondered if he had been able to build a relationship earlier with his father, he would have been able to figure out what his father was trying to tell him on his death bed. Instead, his pride had prevented that. His mother suffered the most.

These were common feelings entering the building. That smell, that combination of institutional food, urine, and flowers, constantly reminded him of the nursing home.

Sean and Colleen hadn't crossed paths or at least not seen each other. This would be the first time.

Sean offered his hand to Colleen. "Hi, I'm Sean Duffy, Shirley Duffy's son. I haven't seen you before. You new?"

"Won't tell what?" asked Colleen.

"What? Oh, you mean about Tommy. I have no idea. Every time I visit, he warns me about something. I feel sorry for the poor guy, so I just play along and it gets me in and out of here a lot faster."

"Yes, new. I've been here only a week."

Sean thought that she was going to cry. "You, okay?" asked Sean.

"I feel so bad for them." She took his hand firmly. "Colleen McCarthy, LPN. Today I had a run-in with my boss, the charge nurse.

She urged me not to get emotionally involved with the residents." She said the word, emotionally, sarcastically. "I mean, they are people, right."

"Well, I can see her point to a degree. But, like Tommy, some of the residents are just not right mentally. So, I suppose you have to be compassionate, but you have to put your emotions aside. I'm a police officer. They trained me to deal with emotionally crippled people. They say reach out, but with your hands, meaning put your feelings behind your back."

"I suppose. I like how you put it. You can be compassionate but not let their condition drag you down. I'll think about that," answered Colleen.

Sean thought that Colleen brightened up a bit.

"Have you run into my mother, Shirley Duffy? She's a stroke victim, but other than some physical handicap, her mental abilities are still very sharp."

"I did for the first time today. I'm afraid it wasn't very pretty. We had a small fire, and your mother raised a bit of a fuss," answered Colleen.

Sean chuckled, "That doesn't surprise me. She's sort of the ring-leader of her cast of misfits. She'll settle down."

"Well, your mother has been complaining a lot. Had a nasty run-in with the administrator. He believes she is in the early stages of senile dementia and progressing rapidly. Maybe even Alzheimer's disease. She acted very strange at Bingo."

"What? I don't believe it for a second. I see her almost every week. She seems as sharp as any of us. Frankly, I don't blame her. Please don't take offense, but this place is shabby."

"She got a bit violent. I heard her say she was going to punch the administrator in the nose." She giggled.

Sean smiled back. "She can be feisty for sure. But can you picture an old woman, a stroke victim, for Christ's sake, getting into a fight with a man half her age? I bet that would get a million YouTube views."

"Frankly, I didn't take it seriously. Talk to your mother and try to settle her down."

"Right. My goal is to move her to a better facility. She's been on the waiting list for St. Joseph's in Quincy. It's got a great ocean view. Her cousin, who is her best friend, is there. Her cousin's niece is one of the nurses. It would be ideal. My mother has been dreaming of going there. They have an opening in a week, and she's next in line to get it. But they don't take people with serious mental problems. They will need a positive report from this place. If there is some indication she has advanced dementia, that would change things. No one has ever mentioned that before. Maybe you could keep an eye..."

"Look, I'm new here. I need this job. I'm a single parent. I can't afford to mess this up."

Sean was startled a bit, "I didn't want you to..."

Colleen leaned toward Sean.

"If I tell you something, please promise not to say anything."

"You don't have to."

"This place isn't just shabby. It's awful. They're always short an aide or two. There isn't enough help to even begin to service the patients. It makes me sick the way they treat people here."

Sean wondered why she was so open, so honest.

"You okay?"

"Your mother deserves to be in a better place. They all deserve to be in better places. Nobody ever visits. Well, except you. It's like they've been abandoned. Since your mother is so vocal about the conditions, she's going to create problems."

"What kind of problems?" Sean was getting concerned.

"I don't know. Problems. I shouldn't have said anything."

Sean said, "In a week, if we get a good report, she'll be out of here. There better not be any bad reports."

Colleen continued, "She angered the administrator, Mr. Batty. I didn't know anything about her being moved. She needs to be careful around him. Please tell her to back off."

Sean, not thinking, "What's your phone number?"

Colleen's expression sharply changed, "What?"

"I will text you with my cell phone number. Then, if you don't mind, you can let me know if she's misbehaving."

She read off the phone number.

Sean recorded it on his phone.

"Thanks." He smiled widely at Colleen.

Sean walked toward Shirley's room. He stopped and looked back toward Colleen. He caught her looking at him. He smiled to himself. Then quickly turned around. It had been six months since he broke up with Jessica. She had wanted too much commitment, just like most of the women he had dated. Relationships were complex for Sean. But, of course, he liked the physical aspects and the companionship.

Sean entered Shirley's room. He made an expression like he smelled something terrible. He opened the door to the bathroom. He flicked on the light. Something scurried behind the toilet.

The bathroom toilet hadn't been flushed. There was toilet paper all over the floor. Trash overflowed the trash bucket. Sean said under his breath, "What a fucking mess."

Two aides were putting Shirley into her bed. Their motions were mechanical as if they were lifting a heavy object, not a person.

The older aide said, "My stupid sister borrowed my car again."

The younger aide replied, "You are such a pussy. Tell her to get her own fucking car."

"She's too cheap, married to that asshole who..."

The aides completed the task by lifting Shirley's head and roughly slipping a pillow under it. Finally, both aides caught sight of Sean in the doorway.

"Sorry, we didn't see you."

Sean was upset, "Do you think you could have someone clean this bathroom?"

"Not my job. The maintenance guy does that."

They both hustled out of the room. Sean moved to Shirley's bedside. "Hi. Ma." He kissed her on the forehead. "How you doin?"

"Lousy. Oh, sweetie, I can't take another day in this god-forsaken place. I got into a big fight with that jerk Batty."

"I heard. What happened at the Bingo Game?"

"I don't want to talk about it." She quickly turned her head away from Sean. "Any luck finding me a new place?"

Sean thought that she was desperately trying to change the subject. "There's a possibility of an opening at St. Joseph's. You are in a good position." He would tell her that she could be moved in a week if all were to go well. But he didn't want to raise her hopes too high. Plus, he was concerned about what Colleen had told him. If she gets on the wrong side of the administration at Winter Hill, he thought they could put a monkey wrench into the move.

Shirley held her good arm to her heart.

"They've got trees, and it's only a short distance to the beach. Edie's there, and her niece, Megan, is one of the nurses. It's got a great view. Right on Quincy Bay. It will be closer to me." Sean had moved to Dorchester since the requirement of the force was for its employees to live within the city limits. "I can get there in fifteen minutes."

"Oh! Oh! Thank God. I can finally get out of here. You did it! I love you. Gimme a smackaroo."

"Don't get your hopes up just yet. There's plenty of paperwork. And I said there is a possibility. It looks good, but not definite."

Sean and Shirley hugged and kissed.

"There is one thing. They won't accept seriously senile or mentally ill patients, so you will need a good report from Mr. Batty."

"My mind is perfectly normal." Shirley's expression turned sour.

"No more threatening to punch Batty. Do you hear me? Please Ma. You got to hold your tongue."

Sean saw this expression before. Shirley was putting on an act of being highly insulted.

"I never threatened to punch Batty! Who told you that?"

"That young nurse." He pointed his finger at the door. "You did. Don't lie."

"All right. So, I did. But I was upset. I wouldn't have actually punched him."

"Be nice to Mr. Batty, and he'll be nice to you. You need a good report to St. Joe's."

"That jerk. Okay, okay, I'll be good. But, you know, just because I complain a lot doesn't make me crazy. There are real problems here."

Sean patted her hand, "I know. But if all goes well, it won't be too long. You just have to behave."

"Promise me. You'll be good."

As Sean walked toward the door, he turned back and warned, "Promise?"

"Promise," Shirley muttered under her breath.

"By the way, I'll be back tomorrow. I have a scheduled family meeting with your newest best friend, Mr. Batty. Just routine, I'm sure."

Bill entered the room as Sean left.

"Hey, lady. You created quite a stir out there today. You've got to cool it."

"Tell me to cool it? You started the goddam fire. This place has gone to hell. If Willy were alive, he'd take care of things."

"Sure, from what you tell me of Willy, he woulda probably beat the shit out of that asshole Batty. Course, then he'd get in trouble. You told me Willy had a pretty bad temper."

"He was a good man, temper or not. Never, ever, ever laid a hand on me. Only wish he hadn't taken his temper out on Sean." Shirley looked off painfully.

"Thought the world of you?" asked Bill.

"Yeah. Maybe he would've thought differently if he knew stuff. I kept things from him our whole marriage."

"I bet nothing would have changed the way he felt about you."

"You don't know my secret."

"Cheated on him?" asked Bill.

"Jesus, no." Shirley shook her head.

"Well then, see. No secret could be that bad. What did you do, rob a bank? Kill someone?' Bill edged closer to her.

"Please." Shirley swished away his voice with her good hand.

"Tell him now. Just picture him on the ceiling and tell him. Then, I promise, he will hear you."

Shirley just looked down at her hands.

"Tell him. Can't be that bad. Now, what's with that shit you pulled in the dining room? You acted crazy. Man, I mean nuts," said Bill.

"That guy scared me. That's all."

"Bullshit. Nelson is a lot scarier than that asshole. The way you handle Nelson. Nelson scares the crap right out of me. That guy, Theodore, no comparison," said Bill.

"Drop it for Christ's sakes. Can't I be scared of someone if I want to be?"

"Fine. But I got to deal with him every day now. So, listen, I'll keep an eye on him for you. Okay?" Bill wandered out of the room.

Everything was still. Millie's bed was empty. Thank God, Shirley thought. Millie was a night owl. She roamed the corridors until the wee hours. Shirley's eyes closed then opened. Light shined from the hallway. There were distant TV noises and chatter in the background.

She saw the image of Willy, dressed in fireman's gear. It appeared on the ceiling tile like clockwork nearly every night before Shirley fell off to sleep. But, tonight, he looked sadder than usual.

"I was thinking. Remember the times I gave you the silent treatment? Especially after your Friday night card games? I used to think if you loved me, you wouldn't have stayed out so late. I got angry cause it made me feel bad about myself. I was selfish, Willy. I should have known that you loved me whether you got drunk as a skunk or not. I took it personally like you were trying to punish me or something. Now I know it had nothing to do with me. I wish I knew that then. Forgive me, huh? Talk to me, Willy. Tell me things will be okay. I needed more time with you. Yeah, sure, we were married so long, but there were things I could never tell you but wanted to. Afraid, I suppose. I so wish you and Sean hadn't waited so long to make up. It pained me so."

She paused and took a deep breath.

"Stop it. Why am I so upset? Thank God, Sean may have found me a new place."

The image of Willy faded away. She could hear the rain pounding on the roof. *Sure as shit*, she would think, buckets would be all over the floor tomorrow. She turned the light off and whispered to herself, "Screw Millie, she would have to fend for herself in the dark. It would serve her right wandering the corridors till who knew when?" Then a flash of lightning startled her. Then the loud boom of thunder. She hated thunder and lightning. It reminded her of that awful night. It reminded her of the man at the bingo game.

Then the voices started again, like every night. She heard them during the day, but it was easier to ignore since many things were distracting her. At night, though, it was harder to ignore. At first, Shirley reported it to the nurses. But it became clear to her that no one would do anything about it. They assured her that there were no voices. They had said it was all in her mind. Sometimes the voices were loud. She thought there was screaming at times, but sometimes she even heard what might have been laughter. It was as if it was in a different room like it was coming maybe from the roof, almost like it was coming from a third floor, but of course, there was no third floor. Then as always, it stopped. At first, Shirley was curious about what exactly the voices were. It reminded her of the time she lived in that god-awful tenement after Willy and her first got married. She used to hear the neighbors on the other side of the firewall fight all the time. So she would take a glass and put it up on the adjoining wall to listen in. The problem with this sound was that she couldn't figure out what the people were saying or where it was coming from.

She stopped telling people about it for fear that the staff would think she was crazy. Then in her mind, the thought occurred to her, who knows? Maybe she was going crazy. At first, it scared her terribly. Now it was just part of this horrible place. It didn't scare her as much anymore.

While she despised this place, she knew how to deal with the miserable aides, that Batty, who she simply referred to as that asshole, and all the poor people, many of whom had lost their minds. She hadn't been this scared for quite some time. Now she was. The guy at the Bingo game scared her more than the voices. It scared her to her core. It took a long time for her to drift off to sleep. If only she could tell Edie. She would be the only person who would understand.

16

E arly the following day, Tommy sat alone by the elevator, as always. Today he was particularly alert. He also seemed a bit more agitated than usual. Suddenly he was startled by something. He rolled up to the wall next to the elevator shaft. He leaned into it and put his ear to the wall. He continued to strain to hear something. He spun around. Then he went to the other side of the elevator wall. With his other ear, he leaned in.

He shook his head. Then he put his hand to his ears.

The rain had stopped late yesterday evening. The maintenance man, Vinny, picked up a bucket of water near Tommy. His back was facing Tommy. Tommy spotted him and started to roll quickly toward him, his stiff foot headed right for his backside. Just in time, Vinny looked around and moved out of the way. Tommy crashed into the bucket.

"Jesus, Mary and Joseph, Tommy." Luckily, Vinnie had a good grip on the bucket. Otherwise, the water would have gone all over the place. Tommy, in a panic, motioned for Vinny to come back to the elevator.

Vinnie asked, "What is it?"

Tommy raced back to the elevator shaft. He motioned for Vinnie to listen to the wall. Tommy put his ear to the wall.

Vinny sighed. He walked to Tommy.

Tommy motioned for him to rush. Then he continued to listen to the wall.

Vinny walked to the elevator wall and put his ear to the wall.

Tommy looked to Vinny for acknowledgment.

"Sure, Tommy. People live in the walls. I'll tell management to have them removed." Vinny walked away.

Tommy continued to listen to the walls.

Martha and Mary, the morning nursing aides, drifted over to Tommy, who was consumed with something in the walls.

Martha snuck up behind Tommy, "Boo!"

Tommy nearly leaped out of the wheelchair if he could, which he couldn't.

"Hey, Mary, you want to have a little fun?"

"Sure." Mary chuckled.

They slowly pulled Tommy away from the wall. Tommy's eyes got even more expansive than they were before. They walked around him. Tommy's mouth opened as if to scream.

"Hey Tommy, want to go for a ride? I hope you don't get dizzy."

Tommy shook his head vigorously. Martha pulled on Tommy's leg, always sticking straight out, and turning him in a circle.

"How fast can you go, Tommy?"

Martha spun Tommy around and around faster and faster.

Mary laughed out loud.

Tommy struggled to speak. Nothing came out.

"What was that? I can't hear you."

They continued to spin him around and around. Finally, the aides poked their faces into Tommy's. "Cat gotcha tongue?"

Out of nowhere, Shirley crashed into Martha's leg.

"Fuck. Watch out, you old bitch. That hurt."

"Stop it right now! I'm reporting you both for patient abuse," yelled Shirley.

Martha stopped twirling Tommy.

"Go ahead. No one will believe you. They all know you've lost your mind."

Mary added, "Yeah, you nutcase."

"You just better leave him alone."

Martha and Mary walked off laughing.

Tommy nodded at Shirley. Even though Tommy couldn't talk, his nod signaled a thank you. Sweat beaded upon his forehead.

Shirley pulled out a napkin from her pocket. She wiped his brow. "I'm so sorry, Tommy. This place changes people."

A tiny tear formed in Tommy's eye.

"You're welcome."

Tommy motioned Shirley to come to the elevator.

"What is it?"

Tommy put his ear to the wall, shook his head, and rolled back to his position, guarding the elevator.

"What were you listening for?"

Tommy shook his head.

"It's gone now?"

Tommy nodded.

Shirley hesitated for a moment. She knew that Tommy was not right, maybe crazy. No way to tell for sure. She never paid much attention to him until now. He was part of the woodwork, a funny, sad elevator guard. "Was it voices?"

Tommy perked up. He nodded. He then went back into whatever state his mind was previously.

Shirley rolled her chair close right up against Tommy's and whispered into his ear. "I hear them too."

Tommy just stared back at the elevator.

That afternoon, Sean, Colleen, Nurse Lauren, and Paul Batty sat stone-faced at the coffee table now turned into a conference room table. Paul spread all kinds of charts and papers on the table. "Mr.

Duffy, your mother is getting worse. She's becoming more and more senile. Almost every night, she talks to herself. Long conversations. I've been here for quite some time and have seen this behavior dozens of times.

Sean shook his head, trying to interrupt. He was not in the least bit convinced.

"What makes it difficult on the family is that the patient can seem perfectly normal one minute, then irrational the next," said Lauren.

Batty chimed in, "Nurse Lauren is correct. Patients are wonderful during the family visit, then as soon as they leave, the behavior changes dramatically. It happens all the time. So you can't judge your mother's behavior on what you witness during your visits."

Lauren added, "It's sad, but your mother's behavior is following that exact pattern."

That's bullshit said Sean in his head voice. "She's just expressing her concerns. That doesn't make her senile. She had a stroke, but her mind is perfect."

Batty responded slow and deliberate, maybe even a little condescending. "Concerns are fine. We take every complaint seriously. But she's making things up that could create a panic situation for all the patients and needless expense for this facility. For example, she claims to see rats. We have a professional extermination service come every week. There are no rats at this facility."

Batty's attitude raised Sean's angst and reinforced for him that neither of them knew what they were talking about.

Sean recalled just yesterday that some creature, a bug, or maybe even a rodent scurried across the bathroom floor. He thought about bringing that situation up but thought better of it. After all, if all goes well, his mother would be out of this facility by the end of the week. He didn't want to create any more issues than he needed to. He struggled not to lose his temper.

"She also imagines that the fire exit doors are locked. That's just not true. She's threatened to report this to the state inspector," said Lauren.

"We spend enough money running this facility without having to prepare for unscheduled state inspections. Enstat runs Winter Hill. They are a premier nursing and rehabilitation corporation. Everything has to be run by the book." Batty stumbled on these words. "I know that Mrs. Duffy wants to be transferred to St. Joseph's. But they also don't take severely senile or Alzheimer's patients. So, they will need a report from us. We must report what we see."

Sean's expression grew intense. "That's ridiculous. I'm a cop. I see lots of senile and Alzheimer's patients. My mother has none of the symptoms."

Colleen looked back at Sean in the direction that neither Batty nor Lauren could see. Then she mouthed, "A cop?"

Sean produced a tiny wink.

Colleen smiled the slight smirk.

Sean nodded.

Lauren's back stiffened. "Yesterday, your mother exhibited extreme behavior. She became hysterical when a new patient threw his bingo cards across the table. She was hardly in any danger. It's things like this that start the steady decline. I'm so sorry."

So sorry, my ass, based on that tone of voice, Sean thought, and looked right back at Lauren.

Paul added more fuel, "The poor man arrived here two days ago. Does that behavior sound rational?"

Sean calmed himself, "You're right. She seems so good when she's with me."

To Sean, Lauren seemed to be enjoying this.

Lauren lectured further, "She wasn't just afraid. She was in a complete state of panic. All the other patients were fine. It's one of the signs." She said in a sort of sing-song way. The word "signs" created the high note of the song.

This situation infuriated Sean. To him, it was so demeaning, like she knew so much better than everyone else.

"While you or I might fear something, when we become senile, every small fear is magnified. I see it every day. Insignificant things became major crises," added Batty.

Butch Donovan walked into the office and sat down.

Batty's eyes widened. "Oh, hello, Mr. Donovan." Batty's neck turned red. "Ah, we are still in the middle of a family meeting. Can you wait outside until we are done?"

Sean noticed something was amiss.

Butch smiled a big broad smile, "Remember, we had an appointment right now, and I don't have much time. But, folks, you don't mind if I wait here?"

Sean could see that Batty was flustered.

"Officer," blurted out Lauren

"Detective," corrected Sean.

Donovan's body language abruptly changed. He backed up a step.

Lauren continued, "Detective, sorry. Please talk some sense into your mother about her complaints. They are unfounded. If they continue, we will have to give a bad recommendation to St. Joseph's."

Sean was aware that the intrusion of Donovan created a heightened awkwardness for everyone and stood up. "I believe we are all done here. Does the situation at the bingo game have to go into the report to St. Joseph's?"

"No real harm was done. We'll hold off. But we can't have any repeat of this kind of thing. You need to talk to her." Sean sensed that Batty was getting impatient. "Sure, Mr. Donovan, we will be done in just a minute. Sorry for being late. I must have missed it on my calendar."

"I will ask Nurse McCarthy to keep a special eye on her this week," said Lauren, who Sean observed also seemed suddenly unnerved by the intruder.

"Thanks for understanding. I'll talk to her." Sean stood up. "Nothing in the report, correct?"

"Not if we don't see a repeat of the situation and no more talk of calling the state inspectors office. Now, I have urgent business with Mr. Donovan."

Sean, Lauren, and Colleen walked out of the conference room.

~

Batty raced over to the door and quickly shut it.

"Paul, your bill is due exactly, fucking now. I don't wait outside of any office. Do I make myself clear? I don't give a shit who is in with you." Butch was not yelling or even using a menacing tone. Instead, he was smiling.

"I need more time." Batty opened his desk drawer and handed Donovan a check. It's a partial payment.

"A check? What do I look like, a check cashing store and a fucking partial payment?"

"I didn't have time to cash it."

"Sorry, since you didn't have time to cash it, the interest just went up. You now owe, let's see, thirty-three thousand. Cash. Now I'm in a great mood today. Since you have a check, I'll assume it won't bounce. That's a good faith effort. But the payment is always in cash. You know that. I'm going to let you off the hook for today. See, I'm a good guy. All you need is thirty-three large by, oh let's say, tomorrow afternoon. No, wait. I can't make it tomorrow. I have some important business. I'm giving you a big break. Let's make it by Thursday. And guess what, since I'm the one who can't make it tomorrow, I won't charge you any more interest. So, see you on Thursday."

Donovan patted Batty on the back and strutted out of Batty's office, passing Sean and Colleen.

"That was strange. Who is that guy?" asked Sean.

"I don't know. He sure made Mr. Batty nervous. I saw him yesterday. Batty said his name was Donovan. Now about your mother."

"I don't know what to think. There is no way she is senile. I've been visiting her since her stroke. She's never shown signs of senility, much less Alzheimer's."

"If you ask me, she's quite the character. I agree. She seems sane to me. When you see her next, ask her about what they said about her talking to herself," said Colleen. "You heard Batty. They won't include the incident today in the report. If all goes well, she'll be at St. Joseph's soon, right?"

"If she makes it. If this incident screws things up for the St. Joseph's move, I don't think my mother will survive here. I didn't tell her the move to St. Joseph's was certain. Good thing. I don't trust that Batty guy." Sean was half talking to Colleen and thinking out loud.

"It's only a little longer," added Colleen.

"What was she so upset about yesterday? I asked her about what happened, and she said she didn't want to talk about it. Some guy upset her. Who is he?" asked Sean.

"Just another of those poor tortured souls that society dumps here," Colleen answered.

"I'll do a background check on him. You, okay?" Boy is she in the wrong business. Sean had been in many contacts with health care workers. Most were compassionate but kept their emotions in check. He felt that this woman would need some hardening to survive in this environment.

"Yeah. I just feel so bad for all these poor folks. Lauren says I'll be sorry if I cater to them. I can't help it," answered Colleen.

"Remember. Compassion with the emotions behind your back," said Sean.

"I'm not sure I will last here. Lauren calls them inmates."

"Yeah, and the staff acts like prison guards," added Sean.

"Oh, so I don't forget. Do you know how Batty spoke about your mother complaining about the fire doors? I hope not." said Colleen.

"Jesus, that would be dangerous. My father was a fireman. If he ever found out that a fire door was locked, he would raise holy shit house hell. Huh. I might want to challenge our friend Batty. These people need to be held accountable."

"I've got to get back to work. We can talk more." Colleen started to rush off.

"How about coffee after work? Just to talk about my mother." For the first time since before the New Year's Eve incident of 2000, as he tended to call it to his friends, he felt a stirring of, what? Relief? It was as if he could talk to this woman about the guilt. He quickly dismissed the thought as crazy. He didn't even know her. These last many years had been dark for him. He worked hard. He caught the bad guys. He was a good, hard-working, empty feeling detective. It pained him to see his mother so helpless and unhappy. He had done a lot of research on St. Joseph's. Getting his mother there would relieve the guilt he felt. Maybe. But maybe sharing the guilt with someone else would be even better.

"Fine. I'll be your spy for your mother for the next couple of days. I'm off at six for my break."

"Yeah, good."

"By the way, the new guy that scared your mother. His name is Theodore Ellis. I'll text you his info, which probably violates all kinds of HIPPA laws. Since you are a cop, right? I'm just doing my civic duty for law and order."

"Yeah."

"So, I'll do the background check on this new guy, our Mr. Ellis. You keep my mother from bossing your boss, and I'll see you at six at Dunkin's for coffee. I'm buying."

Colleen laughed. "Big spender!"

"Yup." That was a good sign.

17

Vinny walked into Paul Batty's office. "Hey, boss. What's going on?"

"The Enstat corporate guys are killing me with their budget cuts. It's looking more like another bad quarter. Well, not a bad quarter as far as profits are concerned. They are making plenty. But the profit projections are behind. Based on their benchmarking, Winter Hill is lagging behind the other properties. They say we must raise more revenue and cut more costs. We have too many Medicaid cases and not enough paying customers. What am I supposed to do, kill off the state cases?"

Paul showed Vinny the report.

Vinny shook his head. "Well, you don't want to lose any more paying customers. I hear that Duffy woman is leaving. She's a pain in the ass."

"Yeah. But she is one of the best paying patients. So, we are doing our best to hang on to her, pain in the ass or not," said Batty.

"You've managed to quiet other pains in the asses before. Right? What about Nelson?" added Vinny

"We have to be careful. Her son is a cop."

"Really?"

"Another bad profit report, and we can all forget raises. Jobs might even go. We just can't afford another state inspection. The state inspection would uncover more than a lack of maintenance. We could get into lots of trouble."

"Ah, sorry, boss, but you could get into lots of trouble. Not we," said Vinny.

"Right. Right. Every time one of those inspectors shows up, it costs me ten grand to fix something. They are the biggest pains in the ass. This Duffy woman has got to be contained. If she figures out how to get to the right person in inspection services, we're screwed."

"Again. You are screwed, not we. Let her go to St. Joseph's. Give her a good report. Fake it if you have to."

"I wish. No, we have to make sure she stays. We just have to be more aggressive in her treatment. That's all."

"What you need to do is to get rid of the non-paying ones."

"Which ones?"

"The real troublemakers, like Bill Bennett. Why is he even here? He should be in a homeless shelter. He and that mangy dog. No money coming in for him. I could give you a list."

"Sure, put a list together," answered Batty.

"So, how's the wife's spending habits going?"

"Not great. As soon as we get ahead, she thinks of something new to buy."

"You know, the corporate guys are sooner or later going to get wise to your little maintenance scam. I can only do so much. Speaking of which, I'm probably due of a little bump in the profits."

"Vinny, you just said they will catch on to us."

"You, not us. Remember? I know nothing. I'm just a lowly maintenance guy. You tell me what to do. You might have to get the maintenance back on track, especially if that crazy Duffy woman makes more waves. But our arrangement would still be in force. Right? As I said, with a little bump."

"Jesus Vinny. That son of a bitch loan shark is looking for his money now. This is not a good time to bring this up."

"As I have been saying. Not my problem, boss. I do the extra maintenance work and keep my mouth shut. Just think about it."

Paul rationalized that no one at Enstat cared about the maintenance work since no one ever showed up to take a look. He reasoned that they wouldn't know that you were supposed to change the HVAC filters every six months. Paul figured that every year would be fine. He also calculated that the fire alarm systems would not have to be checked. Why shouldn't the cleaning service come every other Wednesday, not every week? Who would notice? He kept seeing the landscaping company come every week to trim the bushes and cut the small piece of lawn at the front entrance. Why once a week? He had justified to himself. He could have Vinny clean the bathrooms and do other odd jobs. He figured if things got messy, Vinny could handle things. Vinny never seemed all that busy.

He set up three shell companies, landscaping, maintenance, and a security company to make this plan work. He opened checking accounts in three different banks. Just to be sure, he had mused. He had presented his plan to Enstat. That is, he had presented part of his plan. He argued that having two contracts for each service would improve the quality since each contractor would compete. Competition is always good for business. As far as Enstat was concerned, there were two contractors for landscaping, maintenance, and security inspection. Perfect.

Batty created fake proposals, awarded contracts to his fake companies, issued fake invoices, paid himself for the fake services, and deposited the checks into the fake checking accounts, with a little for Vinny. Batty also justified his financial finagling by committing to himself to document all the embezzled money and someday pay it all off. He told himself that he would repay every single penny.

As Batty began to work the books, he had figured out this scheme that he thought was foolproof for generating a little extra cash on the side. This would be enough to pay off his and Emily's checking account. Then he could start fresh on the credit cards. That is if Emily could keep a lid on the spending.

Now Emily was spending more, and Vinny was getting greedy.

He continued to justify his actions since those bastards at the bank were charging him 18%. He continued to justify. It just wasn't fair.

No sooner had Paul and Emily's checking reserve started to shrink, Emily kicked up the spending. They were now barely living on Batty's legitimate income from the nursing home, plus the embezzled funds. Three months ago, Batty contacted Butch, the loan shark, in a fit of panic. In his warped sense of reality, he figured a quick loan of fifteen grand would fix things.

Fuck, was the only word that came to Batty's mind. Now Butch Donovan was coming back tomorrow. He didn't have the total amount. His partial payment was only seventy-five hundred dollars, which didn't even cover the original fifteen thousand dollars. Now it mushroomed to thirty thousand and raising to more each day. How did it multiply so quickly? He was unnerved and getting desperate.

Batty had been cautious just to skim. Nothing too much. A grand here, a grand there. None of the patients would notice. The staff wouldn't notice. In his justified mind, he believed that the corrupt Enstat was too removed even to care as long as they got their Medicaid payments. He had been careful never to touch the capital funds. These funds were set aside for serious improvements. Enstat carried one hundred thousand dollars in the capital account. Most of it was for smaller projects, like driveway repaving or the heating system. He knew, however, there were thirty-thousand dollars in reserve for the roof replacement. He couldn't keep his mind off that money. That would be enough to get rid of Butch Donovan for good.

He would have to deal with Vinny later.

Since Butch was coming back tomorrow, he had no choice. He wrote a check to a fake roofing company, wrote a check to himself from Enstat for the same amount, plan to drive to the bank and cash the check. It would be tricky to cover that trail. But he would figure out that detail later. Sure, the roof leaked. He swore to himself that he would figure a way to pay it back and have the roof replaced, but for now, he just needed the money fast.

To make matters worse, in his panicked state, he thought about how that crazy old lady, Mrs. Duffy, barged into his office. He couldn't have her call the state. Any sharp-eyed inspector would nose around and notice that maintenance was not done according to the work orders. He needed a plan to keep her quiet. Two years ago, one of the patients, Nelson, complained a lot, the same Nelson, who loved to bother ancient Caroline. The same Caroline, whom Shirley had rescued from the harmless clutches of Nelson. Poor old Nelson had been burned severely in a fire. One of his eyes was missing. But his mind was decent. The facility just upped the medication. A lot. It turned out that Nelson ended up having so many seizures due to the medication that he lost any semblance of reality. Batty rationalized that he was probably better off in, as he liked to call it, in Never, Never Land than having to deal with the scars and a missing eye. Yes, in Batty's mind, he had done Nelson a favor. And in return, Nelson never complained again. So now, he had to deal with another blabber-mouth. He would work that out as well.

Batty decided to "borrow" the thirty-grand to pay Butch Donovan. Tomorrow he would be a free man, free at last of Butch Donovan. Tonight, after work, would be the day that he would finally confront Emily. Now that he would be out from under Butch Donovan's control, he would start fresh. Maybe he might even stop the fake company business after a while and do things right. He planned to create a secret savings account. He would, over time, place money into it. That money would be used to pay back Enstat. He had felt better thinking like that. Then, finally, things would be looking up. He could go back to being a normal person.

Lauren peaked her head into Batty's office. "Everything all right. You seem flustered today? Can I help?"

"No, just that Duffy woman is becoming a big pain the ass. But there is something you can help me with. You manage the patient's cash accounts, right? I was considering how little they use their cash. So how about moving that money into our bank account? In that way, it would be safer and earn a little interest. What's the status of the patients' cash box?"

"Most of the residents are so out of it. They wouldn't even know how to access their money. So, we just keep it in a lockbox in a file drawer behind the nursing station. I have the key."

"Just for curiosity's sake. How much is in there?"

"Not sure. Last time I checked, about eight thousand dollars in small bills. Probably should move it."

"I'll take it from here. Give me the key and the ledger."

Lauren walked into Batty's office and handed him the key.

The office phone rang. Batty motioned to her that it was corporate on the phone

"Yes, sure..."

Lauren nodded and walked away.

Batty further rationalized that patient's money could also come in handy. Of course, he would pay it all back. But there was no hurry since the patients never used it much anyway.

Sean met up with Shirley outside the nursing station. "Hey Ma, I had a long talk with Mr. Batty." Sean wheeled her into her room. He checked out the bathroom. "Good, they cleaned the bathroom. Sean lovingly placed Shirley into her bed, unlike the aides had done the night before.

"I had a family meeting with the staff today. You know, we have this session every couple of weeks."

"I suppose that idiot Batty said I gave him a hard time."

"Here's the situation. St. Joseph's doesn't accept senile patients. So, your acceptance there depends on a mental assessment from guess who?" Sean looked deep into Shirley's eyes.

She looked away. "Batty, right?"

"He told me you are getting, shall we say, difficult mentally, maybe getting worse. If he writes that in his report to St. Josephs, they will not admit you. So you got to behave."

"Do you think I'm losing my mind?"

"No, but it's what they think, not me. Batty and the older nurse told me you talk to yourself every night. Long conversations." Sean locked his eyes on hers.

"So, you do think I'm crazy. You believe that idiot?" Shirley shook her head violently.

"Do you talk to yourself at night?" asked Sean.

"I'm praying. That's all." Shirley couldn't look at Sean.

"Bullshit. You never prayed out loud that I've ever heard. What's that all about?"

Shirley tried to fold her arms, but of course, the left arm was completely dead.

Then Sean laughed.

"What's so funny. I'm mad at you."

"You are talking to Daddy, aren't you?" asked Sean.

Shirley dropped her good arm onto the bed. She turned to Sean and smiled too.

"Yes. I know he's dead, and I am fully aware that dead people don't come alive and talk to people. If I were senile or had Alzheimer's, I wouldn't know I was acting crazy. I mean…"

"Ma, I know what you mean. You are not crazy, senile, or have Alzheimer's."

"I do see him on the ceiling. I'm probably just picturing him in my mind that he's trying to communicate with me."

"That's natural. The problem is that the staff hears you saying stuff, and they are reporting it. It would help if you told them that you heard that they think you are talking to yourself. Which truth be told you are. Tell them you pray to your dead husband and tell them not to eavesdrop on your prayers. Oh, and don't tell them that you have been devout non-practicing Catholic your whole life."

"What do you mean? I used to go to church sometimes, and I follow all the rules" Shirley was relaxing back.

Sean could barely contain his laughter, "When and what rules did you follow?"

"Never to go into a Protestant church. Never read the bible. Don't go to YMCA. You know, a bunch of bible-thumping Protestants runs those places except that nice lady that does bingo. She's probably a Protestant but doesn't act like one. That kind of stuff." She was enjoying herself now.

"Okay. You have got to stop barging in on Mr. Batty. You're making him nervous and drawing attention to yourself."

"What if they are breaking the law?" Shirley was now animated.

"Let it go. If all goes well and you don't get any more bad reports, you might be out of here soon. Just don't cause any more attention to yourself. Please? Just think of how wonderful it will be at St. Joseph's, the beach, Edie?" Sean kissed Shirley and walked backward toward the door. "The smell of the ocean. Maybe fried clams? No Protestants?"

"Before you go. I haven't seen Edie since she was admitted into St. Joseph's. With osteoporosis, can she travel? I'd love to spend some time with her. We need to talk."

"I can get her to visit with you. Maybe tomorrow or the next day. I think a visit with Aunt Edie would be just the right thing for you. She can tell you all about St. Joseph's."

"I'll be good. I got it. Good night. Hey Sean. I'm so proud of you. Love you."

As Sean was about to leave the room, he turned towards Shirley. "Love you too. By the way, I'm having coffee with that young nurse. She's going to watch out for you."

"Be careful."

"Why?"

"She works for them." She pointed towards the nursing station.

"Just for coffee. Nothing else."

18

S hirley's mind raced. They have heard her talking to Willy. Now what? She can't do anything to mess up getting into St. Joseph's. She is afraid to look up at the ceiling now. What if Willy appears? Does she just ignore him? What if he can hear her? If she is silent, maybe he will never come back. She desperately wanted to tell him about her secret. She now wondered how people could have heard her. Are those miserable aides spying on her? Is there some kind of recording device hidden in her room? Are there hidden cameras? Settle down. That's ridiculous. This place is so cheap. They wouldn't invest a cent in any electronic eavesdropping. She relaxed a bit and did not look up at the ceiling, at least not then. She thought that maybe if she just drifted off to sleep, Willy would see her asleep and not be angry.

She couldn't help herself and looked up at the ceiling. There was Willy, just like every other night. He seemed sadder to her. But, of course, Willy never spoke. She so much wanted to speak in a normal voice to him, even if he couldn't talk back. She looked up and then whispered, "They are watching me. So, I can't talk tonight very much."

What if they are just around the corner? Willy just stared back at her with that sad look.

She had an idea.

"Nurse. Nurse." It wasn't exactly a yell, but if someone was just outside her room, that someone would hear and come in. Nothing.

"Nurse. I have a headache. Can you get me an aspirin?" Nothing, no footsteps. All she could hear was the distant sound of TV's and a moan or two from one of the rooms.

"Willy. I will have to whisper from now on."

She took a deep breath. She whispered to the image of Willy. "I've wanted to tell you my secret for a long time. Two weeks before our wedding, Edie and I had gone to the beach."

Then Shirley heard a sound.

It wasn't footsteps exactly. It was a tapping sound, and it was right outside her room. Maybe it was from a walker. She remembered that guy, the one that terrified her, used a walker. She also recalled that the walker had one missing tennis ball on one of its feet. What if it was him? What if he remembered me? What if he heard me starting to tell Willy about what happened behind Hennessey's garage that awful day? Shirley's heart pounded.

The tap, tap, tap sound continued. It wasn't passing by. Whoever it was, it was making circles outside her room. Millie's bed was empty. What if he came into her room? She could scream, but people yell all the time in this place. Maybe no one would come. Did he recognize me?

She grabbed onto the nurse's call button. She pressed it repeatedly.

The tap, tap, tap sound continued.

Now she yelled, "Someone is outside my room. I'm pressing the call button. Please come now."

Tap, tap, tap.

"Goddam you. You are not going to intimidate me. Go away."

Tap, tap, tap.

She picked up her cell phone and dialed Sean. "Jesus, Sean, pick up." Then she heard the recording, "You have reached Detective Duffy. I'm not available right now. Please…" Shirley didn't let the recording continue nor leave a message. She dialed 911.

"911. What's your emergency?" asked the 911 dispatcher.

"I'm a patient at the Winter Hill Nursing Home. Room 207. A man is coming into my room. I believe that he is going to hurt me. Please come quickly."

"Lady. Can't you just call the nurse?"

"I tried, but no one is coming. Maybe the man hurt the nurse. No one is responding to the call button." Shirley glanced up at the ceiling. Willy looked scared.

"Don't worry. The police will come," said the 911 dispatcher. "Is there someone in the room with you?"

"No, please come quickly. My son is Sean Duffy. He's a Boston Cop. Please, I'm afraid."

Tap, tap, tap.

Shirley craned to see if she could see someone. The person was just out of sight. Then she heard a laugh. It was an evil, awful laugh. Did it remind her of the laughter that the rapist used after he came out of the garage? She wasn't sure. She glanced up at the ceiling. Willy was gone.

"Don't leave me. Please."

Tap, tap, tap. Only this time, the tapping got quieter. Then quieter, then stopped altogether.

Sean and Colleen sat across from each other at Dunkin's across the street on Broadway. Sean was excited yet nervous. It had been a while since he was alone with a woman. Why was he feeling this way? He had only met her. He avoided eye contact.

Colleen, on the other hand, was vibrant.

"I'd like to go back to school and earn my bachelor's degree. Then I can take my RN exam. Once I pass, I am out of Winter Hill. If I last that long there," said Colleen.

"That place is bad. I remember when Ma first went there after my father died. It seemed fine. But now. You know, once a person gets placed into a nursing home, it's a bitch to move them. It was close to my mother and father's old house. My mother didn't want to move far from her beloved Somerville, so I didn't think that much about it."

"From what some of the older employees tell me, Enstat will buy a place, then milk it. I don't think anyone from the corporate headquarters has ever even seen it." Colleen was watching Sean's expressions.

"Not surprised." Sean sat on the edge of the seat, still uneasy.

"They tell me the CEO is a bean counter and has no idea about the health care business. I think he came from one of the big accounting firms. I guess making a profit is all that matters. But you know what bothers me more than that?" Colleen looked directly into Sean's eyes, which made him even more uncomfortable.

"What?"

"I can understand that costs have to be closely watched. But, hey, look at me, I can barely pay the rent. But it doesn't cost an extra cent to be kind. I know the patients can be demanding, but the culture there is to treat them like, I don't know, things. It's as though the patients aren't human. It breaks my heart. Someone needs to do something."

Sean scaled back his emotions. "It's just a job. If I took every poor homeless person I find on the street to heart, I could never survive as a cop. So you'll have to get..."

Colleen reached out to Sean's hand. It stiffened.

"Your mother is lucky to have someone like you to care for her. Once they get to a nursing home, it's like they died. But not. Some of those poor souls would be better off dead. Don't you think?"

Sean thought about what his mother said about being careful with Colleen. "I'm not sure about that." Whatever excitement he had, left immediately. Now he wanted to change the subject or maybe just wanted to go. He wasn't sure. "What about you? Your family?" asked Sean.

"My father died four months ago in a nursing home. He was so unhappy. I was the only one to visit him. I came every day. My selfish sister was too busy. It wasn't fair. Thank God he died. He's much better off now."

"Why would you come to work in a nursing home?" Sean was feeling more and more uncomfortable.

"For him. I wanted to make a difference for him and, of course, for them."

Sean's cell phone rang. He glanced at the screen. "It's my mother. I'll call her back in a bit."

"Shouldn't you take it?"

"She'll leave a message if it's urgent, or she'll text me." He glanced at this phone. "Nope, no voice mail or text. Nothing urgent."

Colleen stared off into space. "When I get my RN, I will work in an emergency room. I'd love the action." Colleen leaned into Sean as if to tell him a secret.

"I'm not so sure. I've seen too many messed-up people in the ER." Sean wanted to change the subject. "You said you have a daughter. That must be nice."

"Single parent. I got pregnant. Stupid, careless."

"What about the father?" asked Sean.

"Let's not talk about him."

Sean's phone rang again.

"Your mother?"

Sean stared at the phone. "No. It's work. That's odd. I'm off. Never get a call from dispatch when I'm off duty. Something's up." He answered the call.

"Shit. Thanks, Jack."

"What is it?

"Jack is our dispatcher. Somerville PD called Jack. My mother called 911. She told the 911 dispatcher that her son is a Boston cop, so the Somerville PD called our dispatcher. She claimed a man was trying to attack her." He checked his phone. "Crap. Damn, I should have taken my mother's call. I better get over there and see what happened."

"How about I stay here for a little while. I don't think I want the both of us to walk in at the same time.

All kinds of emotions consumed Sean. This stunt that his mother pulled could completely screw up the St. Joseph's transfer unless she had reason to do it.

He had very mixed feelings about Colleen, particularly from what she said about the patients at the nursing home. Yet, he felt something different being with her at the same time. At least now he had an excuse to leave and regroup his thoughts. So, he put down money and got up to leave.

"How about we meet sometime at my place?" Colleen blurted out.

Sean stood up. What was he feeling? Was he scared, lonely, confused?

"We can go over your mother's charts."

"Are you allowed to take them home?" asked Sean.

"Who will know?"

"Right."

Shirley heard the loud noise of police, with their leather belts and their walkie-talkie squawk boxes. As the police noise got louder, she could hear lots of talking. The police had created a complete uproar among the patients. She now realized that this was not going to go well.

Bill was the first on the scene in his pajamas at the nursing station. His old dog Rudy was by his side. The mobile patients were into the corridor now. Others yelled from their rooms. It was, as Willy used to say often, a clusterfuck. Yes, Shirley thought to herself, this is a complete clusterfuck.

"We got a 911 call from a patient in Room 207," said the Somerville Police Officer.

"That's Shirley Duffy's room," answered Bill.

"Oh no. I'm sorry, Officer. She's getting senile. She doesn't know what she is doing," said Lauren.

Bill just shook his head. "Bullshit. She's fine. Here, I'll show you to her room."

Lauren glared at Bill.

Lauren, Bill, the dog, and the police officer entered Shirley's room.

"A man was going to enter my room. I pulled the nurses' call button, but..." She glared at Lauren. "No one bothered to come to help me. I feared for my life, so I called 911."

"I'll look around." The police officer was not very convinced. He left the room.

"Never call 911. We are going to confiscate your cell phone. Do you know that you upset the entire wing of this facility? If you need help, you call us. It's our responsibility to call the police if that is what's needed. We are running this place, not you. Do you understand me? This situation will not look good in your report to St. Joseph's." Lauren yelled.

"You didn't come when I pressed the call button. You people never do. So what did you expect me to...?"

Lauren barked back. "You imagined you pressed the call button. There was no signal, no light. You imagined the whole thing. There was no man in your room. It's all in your head."

Bill continued to shake his head. "This isn't right."

Aide Martha raced in.

"Hold her down." Lauren pulled out a needle from her pocket.

"What are you doing?" yelled Shirley.

"Doctor left orders that if you got upset, we could give you a shot of something to settle you down. Just relax, don't fight us." Lauren was smirking.

"I don't want a shot. You have no right to force me to take a shot. I'll report you." Shirley tried to fight off Martha and Lauren, but they managed to give her the injection. She continued to battle as Martha held on to her. Slowly, her resistance gave out. She drifted off into a stupor.

Bill repeated, "This isn't right. This is wrong."

Lauren raised her voice. "Tie that mutt up, or I'll have it removed! Return to your room. Everyone go back to your rooms. Nothing is wrong. This was a false alarm."

~

When Sean exited the elevator, Tommy wasn't there. Instead, he rushed to the nursing station. Lauren was busy with paperwork.

"What happened with my mother.

Sean had seen that same condescending expression on her face at the family meeting.

"Absolutely nothing is wrong as we tried to explain to you and I'm so sorry to keep reminding you of this, but your mother is having fits of delusion. She imagined that someone would sneak into her room and hurt her. So instead of pressing the call button, she called 911," said Lauren.

"She tried calling me first," Sean's voice was stern." But I couldn't take it. She wouldn't call me unless she felt she was in real danger. She has never done this before.'

"See, there is always a first time." She said in that same sing-song fashion. The word "first" was the high note in the sing-song. "And I wouldn't recommend you visit her now. We had to give her a mild sedative. She is sleeping soundly."

Then Colleen walked past Sean. She took her place behind the nursing station desk.

Lauren glared at her as she walked by. "Is there anything else?"

"No. I'll talk to my mother tomorrow." Sean gave Colleen a slight glance as he pushed the elevator button.

"You're late. You are entitled to fifteen minutes. I count twenty-two minutes since you left," said Lauren.

"Sorry, it won't happen again. I got sidetracked at the donut shop with a family member of one of the patients."

"We had an incident while you were gone. Maybe if you had been here earlier, we could have avoided it altogether."

"What happened?" Of course, Colleen already knew that Shirley had called 911.

"That Duffy woman called 911. She claimed that someone threatened her or something. People wander all over this floor at all hours.

People forget what rooms they have. It's normal business. She should know better. Unless, of course, she is getting more and more senile, which I believe is the case."

"Why didn't she just press the call button?"

"She claims she did. But she didn't. Although if we went running every time someone pressed the call buttons, we would be doing nothing else. I was working with Nelson at the time. He was having another of his choking fits. I think he does that on purpose, just to get us into his room. Had you been here, maybe you would have heard or seen something," pressed Lauren.

"Nelson is completely out of it. I doubt that he would..."

"I'm taking my break now, my *fifteen-minute* break. Oh, Duffy was very distraught and uncontrollable. We had to give her a sedative. She's comfortable now." Lauren walked toward the elevator, passed Tommy, and pressed the elevator call button. Tommy didn't move, nor did he make any warning gestures to Lauren. Instead, he looked away as Lauren stepped into the elevator and stared squarely into Lauren's eyes as the elevator door was half-closed.

She immediately looked away as the door shut.

Tommy stared at the closed door, rolled to the wall beside the elevator, adjusted himself close to the wall and leaned in and listened.

Colleen examined the nurse's call center board. The call center system was an electronic board, not a modern computer-generated board but an actual board with a series of lights behind the nursing station. Next to each light was a room number, and for rooms with two beds, a bed number. Shirley's room number was 207A. Millie's was 207B. Under each light was a reset button. Colleen also knew that when a patient pressed the call button, the light on the board behind their desk lit up, and a buzzer would go off. Not loud, but loud enough that anyone could hear it from reasonably far away.

If Shirley had pressed the call button, the light should have gone on, and the buzzer sounded. The only way to silence the buzzer and turn off the light was to hit the reset button. When Colleen arrived at the station, Shirley's light was off. One of three things could have happened. Shirley never pressed the call button. Or she pressed the call button, Lauren ignored it, or the call button was not working.

Colleen walked into Shirley's room. Shirley was snoring, and Millie was not in her bed. She pressed Shirley's call button and heard the buzzer in the distance. She walked back to the nursing station. Ahh, the light was on. So she hit the reset button. The light went out, and the buzzer stopped. Everything worked fine. Either Shirley didn't hit the call button, or Lauren ignored it. If Lauren had ignored it while tending to Nelson, she must have reset it. Either Lauren or Shirley was lying. She wondered if any of the patients had heard the buzzer just before the police arrived.

Given how Lauren felt about the patients, she guessed that Lauren was tied up with Nelson, heard the buzzer, and figured that whoever it was could wait. So, what if they had to pee? That was how Colleen figured Lauren was thinking at the time. Then when the police arrived, Lauren saw the light, heard the buzzer, and quickly reset it. Since this was not computer-controlled, there would be no record of when the light went on or when it was reset. Based on what she knew of Shirley, which was not much, she still believed her over Lauren.

The shot knocked Shirley out. Had she been alert, she might have heard the voices again. She had assumed they came from what seemed like above the ceiling, but there are only two floors at Winter Hill. There was no third floor. So, early on, she had assumed that there were people on the roof. But, after several times complaining, she realized that it was fruitless complaining about them. While she had complained to the staff about the voices, she had never brought them up to any other patients except Tommy. And no one had ever mentioned them to her.

While she believed this place was a mess, she firmly believed there was something more. Something strange.

19

TUESDAY LATE PM

Everything about St. Joseph's Nursing and Patient Care Center contrasted with the gloomy Winter Hill facility. It smelled fresh. It was bright and tastefully decorated. Sean approached the receptionist. "I'm here to see Edith Skinner." He hungered to have his mother admitted here.

The woman smiled, stood up, walked around the reception desk. "How are you doing today?"

"Fine."

"Great. Just go right on into the patient's floor. Edie is such a lovely lady. A relative?

"My aunt." Unlike Winter Hill, which had no receptionist he had ever run into, this woman just made him feel welcome. Damn. We got to get her out of that awful place. Instead of feeling better, he felt worse. He worried that something would prevent his mother from transferring to St. Joseph's.

Edie was sitting in the living room area. She smiled a huge grin as Sean approached her. Her health had deteriorated over the last dozen years. While there were no life-threatening issues, her rheumatoid

154

arthritis continued to get worse. She also had advanced-stage osteoporosis. As a result, her bones had become brittle. She had to be careful not to fall or even bump into things. So, her niece, Megan, a nurse at St. Joseph's, convinced her to move there.

"Things aren't so good? Huh."

"Aunt Edie. You are still reading minds?"

"You know better. I can't tell the future, read minds, or talk to dead people. Well, mostly, I can't." She giggled a laugh that Sean remembered from when he was a child. Even though she was old, that sound seemed like it came from a teenager. Sean relaxed. Edie always made him calm.

"So how come you seem always to know things before anyone else?"

"Listen, people say I am a medium. Do you know what that is?

"Sure. A psychic."

"Nope. I've learned that I have a knack for connecting with the energy that other people simply ignore. Many times, I am a conduit to that energy. I feel things. When I empty my mind from my thoughts, energy from others enters."

"So, you do read minds?"

Edie just laughed. "It's all about giving up control, that's all. It just so happens it comes naturally to me. Anyone can be open to the energy around us. That can be both positive love energy and frankly evil and harmful energy. I'm just getting a lot of negative energy from you. So, you just have to trust and let go. It's that simple. Am I a psychic? Well, if so, I never earned a dime from doing it. When I was younger, I was afraid people would make fun of me. So, I more or less kept being a medium to myself.

"Things are not going well. The nursing home administrator and head nurse are giving Ma a hard time. They say she is getting more and more senile. I just don't believe it."

"That's pure crap. Shirley is as sharp as anyone. Just because she talks to Willy doesn't mean a thing." Edie's face wrinkled up in a deep frown.

"How did you know that?"

Edie just smiled. "So you want me to visit her. Right? Of course."

"Are you up for it?

"Yeah. I just have to be careful traveling. My bones are just so fragile. But I know Shirley needs me. So I'm getting that energy from you. It's been a while. Maybe four months?"

"How about Friday, late afternoon?"

"Talk to me. It's more than just your mother. Right?"

"It's this nurse at Winter Hill.

"I would have never placed Shirley there. Do you know that my Buddy died on the site of that place? Go on," pressed Edie.

"I just met her. I was attracted to her immediately. But I'm conflicted."

"You're lonely, and she is attracted to you. Right? Nothing wrong with that. What's the problem?"

"Ma had said be careful because the nurse worked for them, the nursing home staff, the enemy, I suppose. Had she seen something about her that was behind her warning? Her name is Colleen. We had several conversations. I got the impression that she thinks that the patients at the facility would be better off dead. That bothered me."

"Well, if they are treated poorly, I suppose they might be and I don't think patients are treated well."

"Colleen said her father had died in a nursing home. I would have thought that would be the last place she would ever seek to work."

"People like connections. Maybe she needs to make a connection to her father through the nursing home."

"Maybe I'm overthinking? Probably lonely like me," said Sean.

"Good. When I'm there, I'll talk to her. See if I can get vibes.

"What else?" asked Sean.

"You haven't gotten over your relationship with Willy. Right? You feel guilty that you never reconciled until just before he died. You probably never knew how to grieve. Instead of grieving, you just feel guilty. It's not the same thing."

"Probably."

"What I have learned about grieving is this. If you don't grieve soon after a death or trauma, you will bury the pain. But it will never go away. It will come back to haunt you later. The pain is negative energy. It's better to grieve while the hurt is fresh. Imagine you get a wound, like a gunshot. Instead of cutting it out, you leave it in. Then the body covers it with scar tissue and blood vessels. But it is still there, longing to come out of you, the same with grief. You got to get it out of you while it is still fresh. It creates what I call a silent scar. I can almost see that scar."

"See, you are a witch!"

"Okay. Enough. What else is on your mind?"

"Something strange is going on at the nursing home. During our family meeting, this shady guy simply walked into our meeting. Why didn't Batty tell the guy to wait outside his office?"

"Who's Batty, again?" asked Edie.

"He's the administrator."

"Real jerk, right?"

Sean laughed heartily. "Yeah."

"If someone were to walk into a confidential meeting regarding a patient inadvertently, he would have thought the person would have excused himself right away. But, instead, the guy never budged. Batty then abruptly ended the meeting."

"Sean, let me tell you. I was upset when I heard that Shirley was admitted to that place. There is a presence there and I don't like it. You have got to get her out of there. Go on."

"The guy that walked into the office is named Donovan. There must be a million Donovans in the Greater Boston area."

"I'm not getting any kind of feeling about this guy Donovan. You're a police detective. Check him out."

"I'll check with the Somerville Police. Maybe they know something about him. Maybe he's local."

"I'll have a better feel for things when we see Shirley on Friday." Edie was sitting. "I'll have to go in a wheelchair. Damnit. I'm too afraid to walk. No hugging too tight. Okay?"

Driving back from Quincy, all of the emotions hit him. Without warning, a jet fuel of feelings engulfed him. Maybe Edie was right. He kept the scar buried. A deep sob emerged, and his eyes filled with tears. He couldn't see the road clearly and pulled over at the worst possible place on the Southeast Expressway, or the locals called it the Southeast Distressway. It was right at the Savin Hill off-ramp. He partially blocked one of the lanes. The guy behind him had to maneuver his way around him. Sean didn't care that he was blocking traffic. He thought back to that awful day when his father died, and his mother suffered a stroke. Then there had been a whirlwind of things he had to do. It had been entirely up to him to arrange the funeral. At the same time, he had to deal with doctors. His emotions paralyzed him during his father's wake. In his state, there was no time to grieve.

Later, after the months of rehab for his mother, he finally had arranged to get Shirley into a nursing home. He only wished he had consulted Edie. The Winter Hill facility was close to his mother's house, so it made sense. But, back then, there had been no time for guilt either. No grieving time and no guilt time. He had successfully buried the scar. The silent scar.

Sean made a call.

"Hi, Jack. You have buddies over at Somerville PD? Right? Can you ask around about some local hood named Donovan?" He waited. "Yeah, I know. Donovan is a common name." He waited again. "About 6 feet even. Mid-thirties, I'd say, brownish, black hair. He had this crazy 70s style mustache. It reminded me of Will Farrell in that movie about a TV newsman." Sean chuckled. "Anchorman. That was it?' "Thanks, buddy. See what you can find out. A small-time hood. A bookie, maybe?"

He felt better. He flipped on his turn signals. Now he carefully watched for on-coming traffic and darted back onto the expressway. As he approached the Dorchester gas tanks, his cell phone rang. "Hi, Jack. That was fast." He flipped the phone to the speaker setting.

"There is a batch of Donovan's in town. But as soon as I mentioned to Josh, the desk sergeant, the guy looked like Anchorman, and he immediately knew who I was talking about. His name is Dennis Donovan. They call him Butch. You were right—small timer. Basically, a collector for a couple of local sharks in town. Some connection to the old Spring Hill Gang."

"Perfect, Jack. That helps a lot." Sean clicked off the phone, smiled and said out loud. "Ah, so our Mr. Batty probably has a good-sized outstanding loan. I can use this. Blackmail? Never." Now he felt a lot better.

~

Later that night, Colleen reviewed Lauren's task list. She was somewhere on the floor, but Colleen didn't know exactly where. She was startled by the elevator opening. It was way too late for a patient to receive company. Besides Sean, two random visitors, and the YMCA volunteer, no one else had stepped off the elevator since she started two weeks ago.

It was Batty.

"Mr. Batty. It's late. Is everything all right?" asked Colleen.

"I heard about the commotion earlier this evening. Just checking on things," answered Batty.

"All settled. I believe it was a misunderstanding. One of the patients was frightened by someone attempting to enter her room. She called 911."

"Why didn't she press the call button?" asked Batty.

"Well, she claims she did. Maybe she hit the TV remote instead. She had felt threatened."

"It was that Duffy woman. She's losing her mind. A shame, such a shame," said Batty.

"No, I think it was just a mistake. Nothing serious." Colleen was angry but tried not to show it.

"Look, I've got some confidential work to do here." Batty continued, "can you check with the nurse on duty on the first floor? She seemed like she needed some help. I'll be here in case anyone needs anything. I'll call downstairs if I need you. I'll only be a few minutes."

"Sure." The elevator bell rang. Just as she entered the elevator, Colleen looked back, puzzled.

Batty glanced over at the elevator. Tommy was parked across from it, sleeping soundly. Once the elevator door closed, Batty opened the patients' cash box on the bottom shelf of the nursing station desk. He pulled it out and unlocked it. The hoard of cash shocked him. A ledger indicated how much each patient had on hand and a listing of each withdrawal. He scanned the list. He found that Millie Forrester had not withdrawn any money for years. He also knew that the hand-written ledger was the only documentation for any transactions. His mind raced. He thought, lose the ledger, and no one could prove that any money would be missing.

No one in the nursing home could be trusted with credit cards. Each patient could deposit cash in the cash box for perfume, candy, birthday cards, snacks, things that the nursing home didn't provide. There were envelopes stuffed with cash for each patient. Some had no money, particularly the completely out-of-it patients. Once a month, a sundries vendor would come by selling their wares. People would receive their goods from the vendor. The vendor would give a receipt and then go to the nurse, who would withdraw the cash from each patient's account and record the withdrawal in the ledger. Of course, the amount in the ledger was supposed to add up to the cash in each patient's envelope. It was all archaic and subject to the honesty system.

Batty was going to change all that.

He simply took three thousand dollars from Millie's envelope. He then slipped the money into his pocket. He then studied the ledger and searched for the entry for Millie Forrester.

But then the elevator door opened.

"Damn," he would have to finish the ledger later. So he quickly closed the cash box, locked it, stuffed the ledger, and just as the elevator door opened, closed the cash box and put it back where it was.

Colleen walked out of the elevator.

Then Batty looked up. Nelson was standing there watching every move he made; opening the cash box and slipping three thousand dollars into his pocket.

Batty quickly looked away from the gaping Nelson. But, of course, he knew that he was incapable of telling anyone what he had seen. But still, Batty thought. Nelson catching him stuffing money into his pocket unnerved him.

"It was quiet down there. Everyone was asleep." Colleen grabbed Nelson by the arm. "Back to your room. It's very late."

Nelson stared at Batty for a moment, then just walked away.

"Mr. Batty, as I was walking into the elevator, I thought I saw someone in a wheelchair enter the dining room." The dining room was at the far end of the building. "I couldn't tell who it was."

"Huh. I got the impression that Brenda needed some help. Well, thanks anyway. I'm all set here." Batty walked to the elevator and pressed the button. He never gave the person entering the dining room another thought.

20

When Millie heard the noise, maybe footsteps, coming toward the dining room, she quickly wheeled into the kitchen. She had seen Colleen a few minutes earlier and assumed it was her. The door from the dining room to the kitchen was supposed to be locked, but Millie knew that was never the case. The kitchen was one of Millie's favorite places to hang out.

Millie Forrester's dream was to be one of those teachers everyone remembered. She was correct. But for all the wrong reasons. She became a teacher at Southern Junior High School and started by emulating all the teachers she loved when she was in school. Then everything changed.

Those changes came in the form of Patrick Joseph McCabe. McCabe was known to his friends as Paddy. To every kid that passed through Southern Junior High during McCabe's 25 years serving the youth of the City of Somerville, he was known as Bumpy McCabe. McCabe had bumps all over his face. Not tiny pimples, but big bumps, five maybe eight of them. Why would kids be so mean to him behind his back, even the good ones?

Bumpy McCabe was the meanest son of a bitch ever.

Bumpy took Millie under his wing. At first, he taught her how to cope. He had told her that when he had first started teaching (pre-bumps maybe), he too, like her was naïve, idealistic. He would say to her that he also wanted to be loved. Over time, though, he taught her the embezzlement rules, bribery, and intimidation. The only path to survival was to take complete control of the kids. They were the enemy, and she was to be their master, just like him.

Over time, Millie learned the tools only too well. While the kids were punks, they were still just kids, and even the punks dreaded the thought of crossing Mrs. Forester. So, like Bumpy, Millie got an adopted nickname. The kids who, back in 1958, dared to swear called her Miss Fuckster. The good kids called Mrs. F, which was not short for Forester.

During her short-lived idealistic period, she had married young to Andrew Forrester. Two children came quickly. They were raised mainly by Millie's mother, who cared for them while Forrester was working hard to gain the rank of supervisor, and Millie worked just as hard, ruining the lives of every young person who attended her classes. By the time she entered the nursing home, her husband had died, and her sons were the only two people on earth who cared about Millie – barely. They rarely visited. But they did provide spending money for her, money that went into that patient's cash box that Batty violated. While Millie never paid much attention to the money, her oldest son kept track of every cent he gave his mother.

As Millie entered the dark kitchen, her wheelchair ran over something that crunched. Probably a cockroach. Those bastards loved to roam the kitchen just like she did, she thought. She liked to hear the crunching.

The big prize, of course, was the institutional refrigerator. This is what she would raid regularly. She clutched her old satchel.

There were two things that everyone associated with Millie. The old satchel and her penchant for roaming around the corridors naked. Why did she do it? The common perception around the nursing home was that she was crazy or a sexual deviant. To Millie, it was, as she often explained, to get attention. But it was more than that. It was her way of trying to embarrass the staff. She made a point of being naked at the most awkward times. Whenever there was a family day, she would appear nude. Even though family days were not well attended. Millie would roll around naked if a state inspector were to show up by chance. If Lauren treated her poorly, she would time her striptease when Batty and she were together. Over time, though, Millie understood that Lauren learned it was best not to mess with her.

A sudden scurry of a mouse startled her. "Jesus." She made a mental note of where the mouse went. She would try to run over it. She glanced up over the door to the warning sign, which read: "NO PATIENTS ALLOWED BEYOND THIS POINT." She looked up at it and waved it off. Even though the lights were off, there was enough light from the exit sign and the light from under the door to see her way around. Of course, she had been here hundreds of times, so she could find her way around the kitchen blindfolded.

She rummaged through the lower cabinets, stealing sugar, cupcakes, and napkins, and stuffed them into her treasured satchel. This behavior was routine.

It was deadly quiet, except for her wheezing. She bumped into a counter and knocked a pan onto the floor, making a loud bang. Her expression, for a moment, turned to panic. She stopped short in her tracks. She looked back at the door and waited to see if someone was coming. She remained still. Nope. No one would be coming. She began rolling again, continuing her search mission.

She finally arrived at the refrigerator. Her expression now turned bright. She would linger here. She pulled the refrigerator door open. Opening the refrigerator door was the hardest part. She had to put the brake on the wheelchair. She had learned her lesson years ago when she was just an amateur food thief. When she first started raiding the refrigerator, she had pulled on the door without knowing. The suction of the door prevented her from quickly opening it. When it finally opened, the force sent the wheelchair backward, and it came crashing into the metal counter. Her head whipped back and hit the counter. Luckily for her, she wasn't hurt much and, of course, never told a soul. Now she had the process down to a science. She secured her chair, giving herself a little clearance so that when the door opened slightly, she could maneuver her way to open it.

After she succeeded in opening the door, an eerie light splashed across the kitchen, creating a large shadow of Millie in her wheelchair. She stuffed a pudding cup, someone's leftover sandwich, and a nice juicy-looking piece of pie neatly wrapped in plastic into her satchel. She chuckled an evil laugh, thinking that whoever's sandwich it was, would be very upset and of course, that person would blame one of the staff.

Then she felt something. A slight breeze, maybe? She stopped short in her thievery.

An additional light emerged from behind her. She froze. The light slowly disappeared. Someone was in the kitchen. She didn't dare turn around. The light from the refrigerator door was like a spotlight on her. She thought that a staff person would yell at her. She thought maybe she should scream. But, instead, she did nothing.

Then she felt a slow movement of her wheelchair being pulled backward. Her eyes widened, dropped the satchel on the floor and closed her eyes.

~

Wednesday AM

At the nursing home, the highlight of each day was the meals. For many of the patients, waiting to get into the dining room for breakfast, or any meal for that matter was like waiting for the doors to open at a rock concert. This morning was no different.

Once the doors opened, Phyllis and Ruthie raced each other to the dining room for breakfast. They both got to the door simultaneously and got stuck, creating a massive traffic jam for all the patients. No one could pass. Their wheels interlocked.

"Get out of the way. Your wheels are stuck. Move it, lady," yelled Phyllis.

"The Lord's wrath will be upon you, you disciple of the devil. I got here first. You back up!" Ruthie answered back.

"I got here first, you religious nut. So move your righteous ass."

Now others lined up behind them since no one could get into the dining room. Bones, Shirley, and Bill queued up behind Phyllis and Ruthie.

Bones started, "Move it or lose it, you two. I'm starved." He gave them a tug and a push.

Ruthie got free first and raced into the dining room.

"That bitch. Bones, you did that on purpose so that she could get in first," said Phyllis. Phyllis sped into the dining room, following Ruthie close on her heels.

A kitchen aide rolled a large food cart filled with breakfast trays into the dining room between Phyllis and Bones.

Phyllis darted back towards the dining room door, followed by Ruthie right behind. Both screamed. Both crashed into the food cart and knocked it over, sending food and trays and dinnerware all over the corridor. Everyone scattered.

"What the fuck, dude. Holy shit," yelled the kitchen aide.

"Dead, dead. Millie is dead. Oh my God," yelled Phyllis.

"Satan has stripped her of all her clothes. We're all damned. Oh dear Lord, help us and save us in our hour of need."

Lauren rushed over to the mess. "What's going on in here?"

"Hey, nurse lady. It's not my fault. These crazy old bags ran me over," said the terrified kitchen aide. The kitchen aide, who had spent much of the last night smoking dope in his one-room apartment, didn't see dead, naked Millie in the corner of the darkened dining room when he wandered into the kitchen earlier in the morning to prepare for breakfast.

Bones answered, "I heard Phyllis say Millie is dead. I think she's in there."

Lauren ran in to witness Millie, naked and dead in the corner, on the floor. Next to her wheelchair was a pile of clothes. Her head was bloody. "She's cold. Must have happened in the middle of the night." Lauren said.

Paul Batty hurried in.

Shirley was a few feet away, listening in on the conversation. She looked worried. "I'll call the police."

Paul stopped Shirley at the door. "What's going on? Did I hear someone say they were going to call the police?"

"Millie's dead and naked. Look!" Shirley pointed to Millie.

"Gee, that's awful. Why would we call the police?" asked Batty.

"Someone got killed." Shirley turned away from Batty. Then, she added under her breath, "Shit for brains."

"Keep in mind that this is where people go to die. People die here all the time. So we will treat this as routine. The medical examiner will come in, fill out the proper paperwork. Mrs. Forrester will be taken out in an ambulance. Again, routine, normal. No cause for alarm or alert," said Paul without any emotion.

"All her clothes were off. Her head is all bloody." Shirley's eyes got wider.

"First of all. Mrs. Forrester routinely falls out of her wheelchair. She has, or should I say, had a habit of collecting things in her bag. Invariably things fell out. She'd lean over and topple."

Shirley waved her hands. "That's so much crap. But she was naked".

Batty leaned into Shirley's wheelchair. "Mrs. Forrester also liked to parade around naked. Ask anyone. She took her clothes off, probably dropped something, then fell out of her wheelchair, hitting her head on the table or the floor. Then the trauma was too much for her. She's in her eighties."

"Unbelievable."

As Paul and Lauren walked out of the dining room, Bill looked around, took a tablecloth off one of the tables, and gently placed it over Millie's body.

"May God give her peace. She wasn't happy here on earth. I never could figure out how she undressed in that wheelchair. Goddammit, now we'll never get breakfast," said Bones.

"The poor woman was so unhappy. She's now at peace," said Marjorie.

"Maybe you're right. Old Millie was miserable all the time, even to us," said Phyllis.

"Maybe if people had been kinder to her, she wouldn't have been so mean," added Marjorie.

Bill's expression was one of puzzlement.

Marjorie continued, "She's happy now. So let's all be happy for Millie."

Bill answered, "Don't know about that. I still can't figure out how it happened. It wouldn't be the first time she stripped sitting in her wheelchair. Course, mostly, she would kind of roll sorta in slow motion onto the floor. Didn't usually hurt herself. You know what's funny, well not funny. You know what I mean. Her bag isn't here. She never was without that old satchel. She would guard that with her life. Hmm. That's weird. That's where she keeps all her stolen goods."

Marjorie added, "Nothing big. Just stuff. She would sneak in the kitchen and fill that old bag with all kinds of goodies. But, of course, she never shared any of it with us."

Bill kept looking at the pile of Millie's clothes, "You know what's odd? Millie liked to parade around naked, sure. But she did it to bring attention to herself. So why would she strip in the middle of the night? When no one would be looking? Odd."

Tommy wheeled into the room.

Two EMTs arrived. First, they lifted Millie onto the stretcher. Then, they removed the tablecloth and placed a white sheet over her.

Tommy blocked the EMTs from moving out of the dining room. Instead, he motioned to them to come closer to him. Tommy appeared to speak, but no words came. They tried to move him out of the way, but he resisted.

Lauren jerked Tommy's wheelchair out of the way. He shook his head in protest.

The EMTs wheeled her out of the dining room.

Shirley, Bones, and Bill followed the stretcher slowly as if it was a funeral procession. Tommy brought up the rear.

21

Colleen had been on a split shift. She arrived back at 3:00 PM. She walked to the nursing station but then had this creepy feeling like something was wrong. Sure, Tommy was in his usual place keeping guard at the elevator. She figured that now he knew her, he ignored her and would let her pass unencumbered. The typical patients were lining up against the corridor leading from the elevator to the nursing station. Phyllis, Ruthie, Marjorie, Bones, and Bill. She couldn't help but notice that both Shirley and Millie were absent.

Colleen spotted that new guy, Theodore Ellis.

He turned, looked directly into her eyes, and smiled an evil grin. He then walked into his room, aided by his walker, which caught Colleen's eye. She noticed that the walker had a tennis ball attached to one of the walker's feet while the other was bare metal. As he walked, it made an odd sound. A tapping sound.

Phyllis chimed in, "Just so you know. Someone murdered Millie."

"What?" Colleen spun around toward the crowd.

Ruthie added her interpretation, "I don't believe it was murder.

169

Not at least by people of this world. Millie was a sinner. God killed her for her sins."

Bones snapped back. "Ruthie and Phyllis. You old bags are crazy. Millie killed herself. That's what happened. She couldn't stand herself anymore."

Marjorie whispered, "Everyone knows this place is haunted. Right?"

Bones just swiped his hand in the air.

Tommy moved close to Marjorie. He looked her in the eye. Then he nodded, at first slowly, then faster, and faster.

"See, Tommy agrees with me."

Bill spoke out, "Stop it. All of you. We don't know what happened to her, and it certainly wasn't ghosts. You people drive me nuts."

In the meantime, Colleen stood still with an expression of amazement. "Bill, what happened to Millie?"

"They found her dead in the dining room. She was naked. Batty says she fell out of her chair, conked her head on something, and then died. He seems to think this kind of thing happens all the time."

"That's terrible. But I suppose she is in a better place."

Ruthie shook her head. "I doubt it. She went straight to hell."

Lauren handed Colleen some paperwork. "Gotta go. All the orders are here in this pile." She pointed to the stack of papers on the nurse's desk.

"Millie died," whispered Colleen.

"Routine. People die here all the time. This facility is not a goddamn hospital or emergency room where people get better. They come here and die. Deal." She left.

Tommy made a feeble attempt to block her, but she just shoved Tommy's chair aside.

Colleen shifted through some of the papers.

"Jesus." Ellis was right behind her.

Their eyes locked.

"What are you looking at?" snapped Colleen.

Ellis just smiled and nodded.

Then Colleen noticed Ellis's facial expression altered. His eyes blinked quickly. Next, his eyebrows moved up and down. Then, finally, he opened and closed his mouth rapidly and clicked his tongue.

Colleen's jaw dropped, "Christ, Almighty."

~

The Millie situation had shaken Shirley. She usually would linger at the nursing station, but she spent most of the time in her bed today. Millie was a sour old bag, but as a roommate, she was tolerable. She never bothered Shirley. The fact that she had wandered the corridors in the middle of the night created a semi-private room for Shirley.

Colleen walked into Shirley's room and interrupted her musing.

"How are you doing, Mrs. Duffy?"

"It's Shirley," she said with some effort.

Colleen fluffed her pillow.

"You okay? I heard about your roommate, Millie. Were you close?"

"No."

"Sorry to hear that. But it should be a joyful thing for people to die. My father was suffering so badly before he died. So sure, I was sad, but joyful, in a way when he died."

"I don't think she wanted to die."

"No. But if you have faith, life after death will be joyful."

"Well, sorry, but I'm not quite ready to be floating around on clouds, but I've done some things that I don't want to be held accountable for. So no, I'm not ready to die. Sorry. All I want to do is to get to St. Joseph's." Shirley began to breathe heavily.

"You have got to get hold of yourself. You'll be at St. Joseph's soon, I hear. Hang in there. You are so lucky. Poor Millie had no one to visit her. You have Sean."

"I'm not going to make it here. They all think I've lost my mind. They'll give me a bad report. Now that guy is here in this building," said Shirley.

"Who?"

"That guy. Ellis. I'm so afraid of him."

"That fellow Theodore Ellis is harmless. You're letting your imagination run wild. We won't let anything happen to you."

"What about Millie? Who protected her?"

"She fell out of her wheelchair, hit her head, and that's it. She was so miserable here. She's in a better place, a much better place."

"I need to be in a much better place, not this shit hole."

Sean walked off the elevator. Tommy blocked his movement. Sean tried to walk around him, but Tommy continued to block, then moved jerkily. He pointed menacingly at the nursing station. His eyes were wide and terrified.

Sean pushed Tommy's wheelchair out of the way. He opened his mouth to yell, but nothing came out. Sean looked back at Tommy. Then suddenly, Tommy raced toward the nursing station bumping into Sean's leg.

"Tommy. Watch it. What's the matter?"

Tommy pointed rapidly over and over to the nursing station. He violently shook his head. He pointed again. Then Sean placed his hand on his shoulder.

"Take it easy."

Sean pushed Tommy back to his usual position at the elevator entrance. "We need you here to keep the troublemakers out. Right?"

Tommy wheeled up to the wall and put his ear to the elevator shaft. He pointed to the wall. After Sean left, Tommy slowly rolled back to his position outside the elevator. Then he sank into his seat. His head slumped.

Sean walked quickly into Shirley's room. Colleen was still there. Shirley had drifted into a light doze. "How's she doing? My mother looks very tired. Is she all right?" he asked, whispering.

Colleen whispered back. "She's still pretty scared. One of the patients was found dead in the dining room. Just an accident. She's terrified of that new guy. She's also afraid of losing her chance at St. Joseph's

. Calling 911 last night didn't help."

Sean walked to Shirley's bedside.

Shirley came out of her doze.

"Ma. Please don't call 911 again. Just call me.

"Sure, I tried calling you, and it went to voice mail."

"You should have left a message. Stop worrying. There is an advantage to being a cop. I did a thorough background check on that new guy, Ellis. No criminal record, a couple of speeding tickets, widowed with one daughter. Nothing out of the ordinary."

Colleen said, "See, I told you."

"Why does he upset you so?"

"He reminds me of someone." Shirley could not look Sean in the face.

"Who?" asked Sean.

"A long time ago."

"Do you know him? He worked for the power company for years. Do you know anyone at the power company?"

"Everyone knows someone who works for the Edison, but no one I was afraid of."

Sean tried to be reassuring. "See. You're making something out of nothing. He may just remind you of someone. You need to stop thinking about him."

Sean laid his hands on her forehead.

"Can you keep checking on him?" pleaded Shirley.

"Sure. The most important thing is that you get to go to St. Joseph's. So please, please don't do anything that will create problems." He kissed her on the forehead and smiled. "Just act invisible."

"You mean keep my big mouth shut?" Shirley smiled back weakly.

"I didn't say that. But as long as you mentioned it. Yes. Good night." Sean walked out of Shirley's room.

Outside, Sean and Colleen huddled.

"I'm really worried about her," said Sean.

"I'll keep a close eye on her. She'll be fine. That guy is creepy, but he's not the only one in here that should scare her. Maybe you should

173

do a little more research on the guy. Not to change the subject, but you agreed to meet me at my place, remember?

"When can you come?" pushed Colleen.

"You mean to go over my mother's chart, right?"

"Of course. I get off at eight. Tomorrow I have the night shift, so it would have to be tonight or in a couple of days. It's up to you?"

"Yeah, tonight." Sean didn't trust her yet. He liked her, maybe a lot. But he kept thinking something was off, something he couldn't quite put his finger on. He wanted to go to meet with her. He wanted something to happen between them. What was it? He would have to wait and see. In the meantime, he needed her to watch out for his mother. Colleen could do that. He had to be careful. If she thought that the only reason he was interested in her was as a way to keep an eye on his mother, that could backfire. Sean left.

Shortly after he left, Shirley returned to a half-awake and half-asleep state. In this state, she looked up at the ceiling. The image of Willy was there as usual. However, unlike most other times, Willy's face either looked sad or calm. This time Willy's eyes had a look of terror. Was Shirley awake or dreaming? She couldn't tell. Why was Willy looking like that? Then the image of that new guy, Ellis, appeared behind him.

Shirley formed words with her mouth, but no sound came out. She tried to scream. But nothing came. Then that man, that Ellis man, grabbed Willy's fireman's ax and hit him over the head. Willy's head split in two. Blood squirted like water from a firehose all over Ellis. He let out a roaring laugh. Willy's image disappeared. Then Ellis started the facial routine, but it was more exaggerated this time. More terrifying. Then his bloody body lunged at her.

Shirley gasped, still trying to yell.

"Millie didn't just fall off her wheelchair. I broke her neck, just like I'm going to break yours. You teased me. Teasers get their necks broken," said the Ellis vision in a deep devil-like growl.

"Shirley, Shirley, Shirley."

She finally let out a horrible scream.

"Shirley, Shirley, wake up. You're having a nightmare. Wake up. Colleen shook her.

Shirley woke up shaking and crying

"He killed my Willy. Hit him with his ax. That guy did it. He's going to kill me. Where am I? Where's Willy?"

"Shirley. You were screaming. You were having a nightmare.

"No, that guy, that new guy, he killed my Willy. He killed..."

"Your husband died years ago. Remember? Settle down. Bad dream. Just a bad dream."

Shirley settled back to bed. Colleen wiped her brow, puffed her pillow, and held onto her hand. Then she left.

She stared at the ceiling. There was Willy again, only this time, he was fine. No Ellis guy killing him. He was just looking at her. His expression was sorrowful. Shirley wanted to talk to him, but she was afraid if she said anything too loud, the aides or nurses would say she was crazy. So she whispered. "Willy, I have a secret I was never able to tell you. I need to tell you, but I'm afraid. I know you can hear me. I only wish you could speak to me."

Willy nodded as if to understand.

"I've always loved you. I've been faithful to you our entire marriage. You know that, don't you?"

In the years that Shirley communicated with Willy, she never got any feedback. This time was no different. He just nodded but didn't give her any sense that he agreed or disagreed.

"Bill said I should tell you about it. I'm afraid to. I had sort of put it out of my mind for a while, but this new guy brought it all back. It wasn't my fault. I swear."

Then she heard the voices. Were they from the roof? The walls? It was like the migraines that plagued Shirley her whole adult life. They came unexpectedly. They would stay for a while then subside. Once the voices started, Willy would disappear. The voices would continue for maybe an hour, then stop almost on schedule like migraines. Tonight, was no different. She was upset because she thought that perhaps she would tell her story tonight.

Or at least start it. But it was too late. Those voices stopped all that.

Once the voices stopped, she could sleep. Thank God that they didn't go on all night. She often wondered if Willy could hear them too. Since he never spoke to her, she figured she would never know until, of course, she joined him. She had thought a lot about what that might be like, and she didn't like it. She felt as though Willy must be caught into some nether world. She hoped that when she did die, which she was not ready for, Willy and she could then finally go to wherever? Heaven? Together. But not now. That prospect was too scary. For now, getting to St. Joseph's was the next step. She would worry about heaven later. Finally, she drifted off to sleep.

22

Colleen was excited about seeing Sean later, even if it meant they would only go over Sean's mother's chart. When she got excited, she got hungry. She decided she needed a snack from the kitchen.

She walked through the darkened dining room. This is the place where they found Millie. Then Colleen walked into the kitchen. She just stared at the mostly empty cabinets and muttered to herself, "This place is pitiful. I need something to munch on. Cookies, something sweet. Even a half-eaten cupcake would do. C'mon." She wandered over to the industrial refrigerator and opened it. "Oh, wait a minute. There you are! A No Fat Jell-O chocolate pudding. Now, Cool Whip? What a place. No Cool Whip." She scurried around, looking for a plastic spoon in the cabinet. She said, "Ah, there you are," and grabbed the spoon, pulled the foil off the top of the pudding container, and threw it in the trash.

A shadow passed under the door.

"Who is that?"

Tap, tap, tap. Colleen raced toward the door. Then she saw a screwdriver jammed under the door. The door wouldn't budge as she tried to open it. She tried not to panic. What could happen, right? I'm just in a stupid nursing home kitchen. The worse that could happen would be I would be stuck here all night until the kitchen crew arrived. Of course, then she would miss her date with Sean. Was it really a date? She looked around. Sure, there were plenty of kitchen tools. She opened the draw and found a big metal spoon. On her knees, she hammered the screwdriver out from under the door, freeing the door to open.

Then she sprinted out through the dining room into the corridor.

Ellis was walking back to his room. Tap, tap, tap.

Colleen grimaced. "Mr. Ellis. Wait right there!".

He continued to walk.

"I said wait!"

As she caught up to him, he kept walking, ignoring her.

"What were you doing near the kitchen?"

He stopped and looked and moved close to her face.

Colleen could smell his foul breath.

Then his facial expressions became erratic. At first, the eyebrows twitched up and down. Then his ears moved in a rhythm. Then his eyes twitched. Finally, his cheek jumped up and down.

That was the first time Colleen had ever witnessed this extreme form of a facial tic. She had read about facial tics in her nursing program. This was not a case of facial palsy or Bell's palsy due to damaged facial nerves. A facial tic was often associated with anxiety. This, in her mind, was a case of an extreme facial tic. A man with this extreme tic must also have severe anxiety. She shuddered at the thought.

This was also the first time she heard him speak more than just a grunt.

"I bet you didn't know I've been watching your every, every move. I've been watching," said Ellis. He was much too close to her. His teeth were yellow and rotten. Then he licked his lips. That rotted smell continued to ooze out of him.

Colleen gaged.

He licked his lips again.

Colleen backed away from him. "What have you been watching?" demanded Colleen.

"Oh, I won't tell. You were on duty last night, right?"

"So?"

"I watched you the whole time. The whole time." He smiled an evil, awful smile, then walked into his room.

She just stood in place glaring. Then, once he had gone into his room, she turned around.

"Jesus Christ. You scared me, Tommy."

Tommy had wheeled himself over to where Colleen and Ellis were standing. He now was right next to her, motioned to her to come closer, and opened his mouth. Nothing came out. He then abruptly turned and wheeled away, shaking his head.

Colleen checked her watch. Ten minutes left on her shift. Then she would meet Sean in her apartment. The run-in with Ellis shook her. She decided she would check out his room before leaving for the night. Old Rudy, Bill's dog, barked as she walked into the room. Whoever heard of someone having a dog in a nursing home? Bill was sitting on his bed. She was relieved that Ellis was not there.

William James Bennett, Bill, to his friends, was born in Charleston, South Carolina, to Wilma Bennett and his father unknown. Wilma, a local prostitute, and frequent drug user was a bit too careless one night with a john. Usually, she would never have allowed a client to have sex without a condom. However, that one night, she had snorted a day's pay worth of coke and just plain forgot about the condom. The john didn't mind and certainly didn't remind her of her omission. This occasion probably wasn't the first time, but it was the first time she got caught, as she would tell her friends, with her pants down. Abortion wouldn't become legal for several years, and even if it was, she was not about to spend the money to have one. Instead, she would just have the baby and somehow deal with him or her.

Wilma continued to work almost up until the time of delivery.

Then, she casually walked into the Charleston County Baptist Hospital emergency room when it was time. She delivered Bill with little drama. They brought Wilma to a ten-bed ward. She signed off on the birth certificate, named him William James Bennett, after her father. She dressed and promptly walked out the front door. No baby, no hospital bill.

Bill then bounced between foster homes and went to school off and on. By age thirteen, he had had enough of what he called social services ping pong. He, like Wilma, walked out of his latest foster home to make a place for himself in the world. He could read well. He hated math and geography. Bill was tall for thirteen, so getting a job in Charleston wasn't much of a problem, particularly for a skinny black kid willing to work under the table washing dishes, cleaning floors, and stocking shelves. Bill spent those years living in tiny rooms over bars or stores. Then he stumbled upon a traveling carnival. It had set up camp in an empty lot, next to the rail yards outside the city's northern section. He had been walking from his room over the rail-road tracks to Ronnie Mae's Diner, where he had been working as a short-order cook. He never made it to Ronnie Mae's. Like his mother before him, Bill gave no notice, paid no bills, and paid no mind as had been Bill's practice.

Bill became the master of a rusty old Tilt-a-Whirl. He spent the next fifty years as the barker, the operator, the touch-up painter, and the mechanic of that rickety amusement ride. But he loved it. It was home to him. The kids, the music, the screams, even the smell of greasy ozone were all comforting. The soda and popcorn lady, Paulette Beaudine, was his on-and-off lover for much of his carnival career. Did they love each other? Probably. Paulette complained of Bill's, as she would describe it, "his goddam lazy eyes." That meant Bill would, on occasion, get fixated on one of the women passengers on the Tilt-a-Whirl. He would lazily follow her walk as she boarded the ride, then track her movements as she got off. Why she called his eyes lazy, only Paulette knew. Wandering eyes would have been more descriptive. There may also have been times when Bill might have invited one of the objects of his lazy eyes back to the trailer for a quickie. Paulette never had actual proof but suspected he had his ways with many a willing patron of the Tilt-a-Whirl. Yet, despite those occasional indiscretions, they were reasonably committed to each other. So, love? Who's to say?

Both Bill's career and his sexual relationship with Paulette ended abruptly a week after the carnival arrived in Somerville, not far from the Winter Hill Nursing and Rehabilitation Center. The carnival had been set up at an abandoned parking lot on the banks of the Mystic River. In those days, developers had not discovered the appeal of a riverbank for mixed-use housing and retail shops. At that time, the riverbanks were still littered with rusty shopping carts from the defunct Bradlees department store, bald tires, and an occasional urine-stained mattress. The locale was perfect for the carnival. There was plenty of parking. The best part was that the carnival never bothered to get permission to use the property. The only cost was the temporary electric service from the Edison company.

Two days after the carnival set up day, Paulette collapsed. Over the years, Paulette had grown heavier and heavier. She had suffered a massive heart attack. The smoking, the drinking, and the steady diet of junk food had finally caught up with her. The fire department EMTs raced her to the Somerville Hospital emergency room. She was in a severely weakened state. And, of course, Paulette had no medical insurance. After the hospital stabilized her, they sent her to the Winter Hill Nursing and Rehabilitation Center. This situation occurred just after Enstat had taken over.

Bill persuaded the staff at the nursing home to let him stay in her room until she was feeling better. They agreed. Bill also brought along his dog Rudy, who was just a puppy at the time, without their permission. Bill pitched a story that Rudy was Paulette's dog and had no one to care for him when they complained about the dog. The staff reluctantly agreed, but the condition was that he and the dog could only stay until Paulette was feeling better.

Paulette would not be feeling better. Things changed one day after about a month of rehab, which consisted of a nursing aide getting Paulette out of bed for a walk around the floor. After coming back from a smoke on the second-floor deck to their room, Bill noticed that she was not moving, not responsive. He raced to the nursing station. The charge nurse and one of the aides followed Bill into Paulette's room. Paulette was still. Neither the charge nurse nor the nurse's aide paid much attention to Bill, who listened and observed. They examined Paulette and noticed that the inter-venous needle was blue and infected. In a moment of terrible judgment, the nurse told the nurse's aide, "We really blew this one. We should have checked this. In her weakened state, the infection killed her." The nurse caught sight of Bill in that one moment, who began to weep softly. Saying that in front of Bill was the second action she blew severely.

"You killed her. You killed her." Maybe he didn't love her as a wife, but she was all he had. He had pretty much quit his job at the carnival to be with Paulette. So now, all he had was his dog Rudy and colossal leverage over the nursing home.

The nurse, the administrator, the owners also knew it too. So, they cut a deal with Bill. They reluctantly gave him and his puppy Rudy permission to stay at the nursing home for as long as he needed until he could find suitable housing. The time to find suitable housing never came. Bill, who was not sick and not in particular need of nursing care, was a permanent guest of Enstat.

Colleen startled Bill.

"I ain't smokin. That other nurse went through all my stuff and took all my butts. Hey, I know it's bad for me, but what the hell? I'm too old now. If I lived this long smokin, it ain't gonna hurt me much now. Right?"

Colleen was distracted. "Probably not."

"You're the nice nurse. Can you get me some butts? C'mon. I'll die of withdrawal. Please." Colleen knew that Bill was desperate.

"I'm a nurse. I don't think so."

"You came to ask me stuff about my roommate? Huh?"

"Maybe. What's with him?"

"Nothing to tell. Period. My lips are sealed. Zip." Bill tightened his lips. His old brown wrinkled face scrunched up almost in a ball. Then he made that zipping motion across his tensed lips. "He's scaring the piss out of everyone. Even you, I bet. I saw him staring at you. He's the devil. Ruthie, that crazy fanatic bitch is right for the first time in her life. He's the fucking, oops, sorry --- "

"It's okay." Colleen would have laughed if she wasn't so concerned.

"He's the Anti-Christ if ever there was one. Whatever the hell that means. Every time I look at him in bed, his eyes are open, and he's twitching. Something's wrong with him. If it wasn't for Rudy here, I'd be afraid to go to sleep with him in my room. But I ain't giving you no data. Nope. You can torture me. I won't say a word. My lips are sealed."

He made another zipping motion across his mouth.

"I'll get you some cigarettes."

Bill paused for a second. He rubbed his scraggy chin. "Hmm." He made an unzipping motion across his mouth. "What do you want to know?"

"Last night, was he in his bed?" asked Colleen.

"No. He was gone for a while. Then, at about eleven, he got out of bed cause Rudy growled a bit. I looked at the clock. He came back about one-thirty. He was huffing and twitching a lot. I asked him where he went. He told me to go fuck myself. Excuse my language."

"I've heard it before. Go on."

"He was eating from a pudding cup. So, I figure, he must have gone into the kitchen, which we are not supposed to do, but we all do anyway."

Suddenly Colleen stiffened. "Remember you mentioned that Millie's bag was missing. What did it look like?"

"Sure, that disgusting old satchel. Just like Millie." Bill laughed out loud at his humor. Now he whispered, "Well, it ain't missing anymore. He got it. I saw him with it a couple of minutes ago. He stuffed it in his closet. Look."

Colleen opened the closet. There was Millie's satchel.

"Son of a bitch." Colleen just stared into the closet. Then she closed it.

"Now that Millie's gone, we now got rid of one thief for anoth..."

He turned quickly, looked terrified, and then went silent.

"So he... What's the matter?"

Bill pointed to the door. One leg of a walker was at the door. Tap, tap, tap. Ellis was just outside the room, within earshot.

"Ah, that's all. Thanks, nurse, thanks for the ...um , thing there, ah. I'm all set."

He motioned to the door and for her to go.

She nodded. Colleen then made a motion like she was dragging on a cigarette. "I'll get you those things."

Right after she left, Bill laid back in his bed. He had a look of dread. "Rudy, my boy. I need a cigarette real bad. Shit, man."

23

Sean read the address on the text message Colleen had sent him. 158 Winslow Street, Somerville. Sean grew up in Somerville, and he knew it well. But, while Somerville had been going through a nice renaissance lately, with condo conversions and rehabs, sections of Winslow Street, especially the low numbered parts, were still shabby. Drug dealers and hookers still roamed the streets after dark. He hoped that she didn't live in that twelve-family tenement building that the Somerville Police had raided on more than one occasion. But, as he pulled his car closer to 158 Winslow Street, yes, it was that very same tenement. Parking his car on the street in front of the broken-down stoop that faced Winslow Street worried him.

Somerville mainly consisted of two and three-deckers, built in the late 1800s. Most were constructed nicely with some interesting and sometimes even ornate exterior woodwork. This piece of shit building, as Sean had thought about it, was built later, in the 1920s, at the peak of the meatpacking industry takeover of the city. The building was constructed for transients, then, and the tradition continued today.

Sean pulled his newish Dodge Charger around the corner on Bradford Street. Winslow was the main street that ran from

Charlestown through Somerville and terminated at Broadway. His maroon Charger would draw much attention on Winslow Street, especially with the graphic that read Hemi on the side. The wheel rims alone were worth 700 dollars apiece.

The Charger's wheels weren't the only thing he was worried about. This woman he was about to meet on very personal terms made him very nervous. At one point, maybe for just a second, he almost texted a reply to her text that something had come up and he would not be able to meet her. Then, as he turned the engine off on his Charger, he almost did text her. But he didn't.

As he walked around the corner from Bradford Street onto Winslow Street, two Somerville Police cruisers raged by, with sirens blaring and lights flashing.

Colleen lived on the third floor. The building consisted of four three-story sections. Each of the sections had its own entrance. He figured he would have to ring the doorbell to be let in. Not the case. The main door was unlocked. The smell of alcohol, urine, and pot enveloped him when he walked in. Also layered was the smell of food, Indian, Chinese, or Vietnamese, something not familiar to him. Why was she living in such a place? Indeed, she could afford better. It was a twenty-minute walk to the nursing home, but would she dare walk the streets of this neighborhood at night?

He climbed the three-story stairway. There was still time to escape. He could even claim that he had gotten as far as her front door when he got an emergency call from work.

Then he knocked on the door.

Colleen opened the door seconds after he knocked.

Sean's first thought was that Colleen was waiting with her ear leaning on the door.

"Hi. You found my place. I know what you're thinking. It's a pretty bad building in a not-so-great part of town. But it's cheap. Come in."

The apartment was not bad, given what she had to work with. It was a one-bedroom, one-bath place. However, it was not clear to Sean why it was laid out that way. The apartment had a front room, a middle room, one bathroom, and a kitchen all in a row from front to back. A small bedroom was off the middle room to the left. Colleen's bedroom was in the odd middle room, while the small one was for her daughter, Cassidy. That meant no privacy or a door that isolated Colleen's bedroom.

Sean and Colleen settled in the living room in plain sight of Colleen's bed, which must have been a dining room in some weird past.

Colleen introduced Sean to Cassidy, who was curled up on the end of the sofa, playing on her iPad.

"Ma tells me you're a cop," said Cassidy, not looking up from her device. She looked older than an eleven-year-old child.

"A police officer. A detective. Right?" Colleen corrected Cassidy.

"Technically correct. A detective, yes."

"Have you ever been on Cops? You know, the TV show? You know, "Bad, boy, what you gonna do when they come for you, Bad boy, bad boy."

"No." Sean pretty much assumed the girl was making fun of him.

"How come the bad guys never have shirts on? Don't they get cold?"

"I have no idea." Sean now very much wished he had simply walked down the three flights, rescued his Charger, and forgot the whole thing.

"What do you think of her? My mom?" asked Cassidy.

This was embarrassing, thought Sean.

"Time for bed," said Colleen.

"But he didn't answer me!" Sean knew that Cassidy was trying to force the issue.

"Sure. She is very attractive." On rare occasions, Sean had set up a code with his friend Phil to text him or call him at a specific time during a date, just in case he needed an out. So why hadn't he texted Phil?

Cassidy had the most reddish hair he had ever seen. Colleen's hair was light brown. So naturally, or perhaps stupidly, he asked, "So where did you get that red hair? It's nice."

Once the words had escaped his mouth, he fully understood that the hair was not nice, and that the girl probably got teased from the moment she entered kindergarten. Since Colleen's hair was not red, it had to have come from her father, which at this early stage in the relationship, discussion about her father was awkward at best.

Instead, she just answered without any emotion. "My father."

"Of course."

"Time for bed? Are you serious, Ma? It's eight-thirty."

"You know what I mean. Time to go to your room. I have company, and we want some privacy."

The girl slowly got up and, without saying good night or goodbye or nice to meet you walked through the middle room into the bedroom and closed the door. It wasn't a slam per se. But it was loud.

The word privacy hung in Sean's head. The thought of sex was not entirely out of the question as he was driving to Colleen's house. But the layout of this apartment didn't exactly scream privacy. The only way that Cassidy could go to the bathroom was to walk right through Colleen's bedroom.

Colleen's bed continued to stare at him. It was also not made, which was odd given she had time to at least make a halfhearted attempt to pull the comforter up from halfway to the floor. Of course, he thought to himself that the last time he made his bed was sometime in the mid-1990s, but it just didn't feel right. Nothing about this night felt right. He could picture himself in the middle of a hot embrace when Cassidy would walk across the bedroom singing that stupid Cop's song. Oh, he wished that he had talked to Phil.

He felt uncomfortable with Colleen, to begin with. Cassidy didn't help. The lack of privacy didn't help either.

"She's eleven going on twenty-two," said Colleen.

She must have been reading my mind, thought Sean.

"I shouldn't have mentioned her hair. Does she ever see her father?" asked Sean.

"No."

"Sorry. You weren't married? Right?"

"I'd rather not talk about him. Okay?"

That was awkward.

"About your mother. I'm worried about her. Before I left, she had a bad dream. The dream was about her husband, your father. He was a fireman? Right?"

Sean sighed. "Yeah. Naturally, he wanted me to be a fireman. He would have been fine if I chose other professions, like a teacher or a construction worker. I don't know. Other jobs. Being a cop pissed him off. He accused me of being a cop to get back at him. It embarrassed him."

"Wouldn't he be proud of you?"

"No. Being a cop is like playing for the Yankees when you're from Boston. A fireman's son being a cop was a problem. He never got over it."

"I'm sorry. That must have been hard on you."

"She told me that in her dream… Well, she didn't think it was a dream. She said that that new guy, that guy that scared your mother, killed your father with his fire ax," said Colleen.

"Jesus."

"See, these are the things that are working against your mother. The talking to herself, the fainting over nothing, her erratic behavior."

"I'll talk to her tomorrow."

"It's gonna take more than that."

"She's stubborn. But she is not senile. I'm convinced of it."

"Maybe if you can find out something that ties that new guy, Ellis, to your mother. Do you know of any reason why he spooks her so?" asked Colleen.

"Not really."

"Most of the people at Winter Hill are harmless. They are all pretty fragile. But this guy has an aura to him. He's big. I don't see him as fragile. Crazy? Sure. He looked at me today so strange."

"Strange? What kind of strange?" asked Sean

"Evil? Or at least mean. He said he was watching me."

"Watching you? You mean like checking you out?"

"No. Like spying on me. Like he knew something about me. I didn't like it." Colleen shuddered. "I have his chart." She walked over to the dresser in her middle room/bedroom and pulled out a stack of charts.

Sean's first thought was that she indeed had broken some law or rule by taking charts home with her. She must have over a dozen medical charts. What if someone needed one? He thought.

She flipped through the stack and pulled out Ellis's chart. "Theodore Ellis. Last home address. 175 Malden Street, Chelsea. Not from here. Says he lived with his daughter at that address. She is the one who brought him in. Last job was with the Edison."

"I had found that out." Okay, Sean had thought. Now that she had provided pretty much all the information about that guy, and while they hadn't gone over his mother's chart, he wasn't sure there was much more to talk about.

"How about a drink?" asked Colleen.

He figured that the business part of this little get-together was over, at least for now. They were on to personal stuff. No, he wouldn't text Phil to rescue him. "Beer." His mouth had said beer, but in his head, he wanted something much stronger, like a shot of bourbon and a beer.

He watched her walk past her unmade bed down the narrow hall, past the bathroom, and into the kitchen. Then he spotted something on the bedroom dresser that made him do a double-take.

It was a pack of Camels.

She handed him the beer.

"Camels? Don't you think you should switch to filters? Those can't be for you." Sean pointed to the pack of cigarettes, clearly in view.

She chuckled an embarrassed and sexy laugh. "Of course not. I can't believe that I even bought them. They're for one of the patients."

"You're buying cigarettes for the patients? Isn't that a violation of some nurse's oath? Thou shalt not buy butts for sick people or something like that."

"It's a bribe."

"Oh, that's much better. I thought for a moment it was a gift," said Sean.

"I needed some confidential information from old Mr. Bennett. Bill Bennett. So, I bribed him. You cops do it all the time. Informants, right."

"What's going on?"

"It's stupid. Nothing." Now Sean saw that she was upset. His mood changed from wanting to leave in a hurry to wanting to protect her somehow.

"I... I'm just feeling. I don't know. He said he was watching me. That's not all. He sort of threatened me. Well, not threatened exactly, just uncomfortably approached me."

"Why didn't you say something? Maybe something is going on with that guy. Maybe he threatened my mother. If he did, I wonder why she wouldn't tell me. So this guy scares you a lot," said Sean.

"Yes. That's why I asked Mr. Bennett about him, and he wouldn't tell me, so I bribed him with cigarettes. He opened right up. But then, I believe that guy overheard us talking."

"How can I help? He checks out fine. Do you want me to dig a little deeper? I could talk to the daughter."

Then she burst into tears.

"Hey. What's the matter? He's just some creepy senile guy. You people at nursing homes got the pills, the needles. You could turn him into some kind of vegetable." Sean was now feeling better. It was natural that he would want to protect someone who felt threatened. That was his job.

"Stop it. You can't do that." Colleen wiped her nose.

"I don't know. I'm sure that some of the patients get medicated to shut them up," said Sean.

"Maybe. I don't know. You know what? I'm being silly. It's a nursing home. People are senile. Most are sick. It's just an unnatural environment." She chuckled just a bit. "Look at that poor guy Tommy."

"The elevator guard?" Sean felt better.

"Not normal for sure. But harmless."

"Not really. He uses his leg as a weapon." Sean sipped his beer.

His anxiety was beginning to thaw. It was gradually replaced by compassion.

He took her in his arms. As he predicted, she cozied right up to him. He reached for her face and gently pulled her head so that her face was facing his. She moved her face closer to his. Her lips were directly across from his. Her face was still wet from the tears.

Who moved first? Sean didn't quite know. What he did know was that they were kissing now. At first, kind of a light pecking. Then it evolved into passionate kissing. Sean now forgot entirely about Cassidy, the unmade bed, and the possibility of the child catching them. His complete focus was on the kissing. Then the touching.

The sex was fine, normal. There was no Cassidy stomping across from her bedroom, staring at them in bed on her way to the bathroom. No phone calls. Sure, it was awkward. But it was good.

They collapsed into a cozy embrace. Sean's first rational thought was the pack of Camels that Colleen would use to bribe Bill. Then, the thought crossed his mind, not having had sex for quite some time and not having a cigarette since freshman year at college. Camels? Probably not. Plus, he hated cigarette smoke now.

Then a real thought enveloped him. What had he done? There was no going back now. You can't undo having sex. For one thing, he didn't trust her. What was the deal with the father of her child? How was he going to deal with this new complication in his life? Never mind that his mother was going through an emotional roller coaster. Oh yeah. They were going to discuss his mother's situation. When was that going to happen?

He glanced at his watch. It was now ten o'clock.

Colleen became alert. She got dressed.

Sean followed suit. At first, Sean couldn't think of anything to say during that silent period. Now, he said, "we were going to go over my mother's chart. It's getting late."

"Yes. It's getting late."

Sean tried to measure how she reacted to that insensitive and noncommittal comment about getting late and the unsaid words about staying the night. He watched for her reaction.

He got none.

Now he felt uneasy.

Colleen put the final touches on getting her clothes back on. Cassidy walked across the middle room to the bathroom, just like on cue. Then she disappeared into the bathroom. Seconds later, after the sound of flushing, she walked across the room toward her bedroom.

Sean thought that she must have heard the moaning.

Colleen just glared back at her as she almost too slowly walked back to her bedroom.

Sean's heart jumped as Cassidy slammed her bedroom door.

"See. She's driving me crazy with her attitude."

The mood now was utterly broken. Sean thought that was probably for the best.

Colleen had no more weepiness. No tenderness. No emotion. She was now professional.

"I didn't mention something about your mother's case. I wasn't sure that I could tell you since I'm sure the information is confidential. But, if Batty finds out I told you, I would probably get fired. And as you can see, losing my job will not help my already grim financial situation."

"What?"

"I overheard Batty talk to Lauren. You know the charge nurse? My boss?"

"About my mother?"

"Batty was going over the notes for his report to St. Joseph's. I heard him say that he would recommend she not be moved due to her deteriorating mental situation. He mentioned Alzheimer's."

Sean was enraged. "That asshole. I thought he wasn't going to say anything about what happened yesterday or at the bingo game. She doesn't have Alzheimer's. I need to talk to him. Did he send the report?"

"I don't know."

"I'm going to talk to him tomorrow," said Sean.

"You can't say anything about how you found out."

"Don't worry. At our family meeting, there was this guy who interrupted our meeting. I found out who he is, a small-time hood. I'll use that to get some leverage on Batty."

"Alright. Don't you want to check out your mother's chart?"

"No. I've got to resolve this thing with Batty." Sean's mood was now anger. No more worried or awkward. He was enraged. He was also upset at Colleen. Why hadn't she mentioned this earlier?

"It's late. You should be going."

Now what? A good night kiss? A dear John like goodbye. Make-believe we didn't have passionate sex not a half an hour ago. While his mood was angry, he thought that a nice hug and a short kiss would be enough to at least tread water with her. At least until he knew more, Colleen was his only source of factual information into what was going on in that place.

They walked to the door. She opened it for him. He turned and faced her. He pulled her close to him. Did he feel a slight resistance? He wasn't sure. She didn't make a move. Then like he did when they first got entangled, he took her face in both of his hands and kissed her. No real passion. It was enough. Maybe.

Then he left and stood for a second on that third-floor landing. The smell wasn't much better this time, except the cooking smell had dissipated. Instead, the smell of cigarette smoke replaced it. He was glad he hadn't grabbed one of those Camels. As he descended the stairway, he thought about the Charger parked around the corner and those expensive wheels.

The Charger was fine. The wheels were still on. Not much else was fine. His mother was about to be prevented from moving to St. Joseph's. She was terrified of some guy at the nursing home. He just had sex with a woman he only met two days ago that he had some serious reservations about. At least the car was fine.

Now he had to think fast. St. Joseph's wasn't going to hold that room for very long. So he had to stop Batty from sending that report to St. Joseph's.

24

The following day, Tommy was up earlier than usual. Tommy paced around the elevator. Pacing for Tommy was turning in circles in his wheelchair. While he only had one foot to propel him, Tommy was pretty good at navigation since his other foot stuck straight out. This morning he was more agitated than ever. After his encounter with Colleen and Ellis, he had returned to his regular station next to the elevator. As his usual routine, he had listened for the voices. As best as he could, he had leaned toward the wall. For a long time, he had just sat there listening, maybe waiting. Finally, after pacing in circles, now was time for action.

Tommy left his sentinel position. He was going to do some investigation. He rolled down the corridor. The "B" wing. Then he passed the double doors to the screen porch and glanced through the glass-paned doors into the parking lot. The deck was on his left. He rolled by Ruthie and Phyllis's room on his right. Room 205. Then he passed Bill and Ellis's room. Room 202. It was the last room on the "B" wing.

There were only three ways to exit the second floor. The first was the emergency exit at the end of the "B" wing. This exit led to an enclosed staircase that opened to the side of the building. The other exit door was at the opposite end of the building in the dining room. It led to an open metal stairway. That door was not alarmed. It, too, was an emergency exit. The other way out was the elevator, which Tommy routinely guarded.

Tommy moved to the "B" wing exit door. He stared up at the sign that read, "Emergency Exit Only, Alarm Will Sound." Like the exit door at the other end of the building, this door had the standard push bar. The idea would be if someone were trapped or in trouble, all they had to do was to lean up against that push bar, and the door would open. Tommy twisted his wheelchair around with his back to the door. He moved forward about two feet. Then, with a sudden motion, his mobile foot pushed his chair backward, slamming into the push bar.

Nothing. No door opening, no siren. The bar moved, but the door didn't open. So, again, he moved forward. Like before, he pushed with his good foot into the door. Same result. No open door, no alarm. Had the door opened, and the alarm went off, Tommy would have found himself on the landing of the enclosed stairway. Possibly the momentum would have doomed Tommy to a nasty and probably fatal crash two stories down to the ground.

Lauren came running down the corridor. "What are you doing? Don't you know that it's very early in the morning? If you keep this up, I will be forced to restrain you. Do you understand?"

She roughly wheeled him back to the nursing station.

Lauren then got busy with paperwork. Tommy rolled to the elevator, which was just a few feet from the nursing station, where he just parked, sat, waited, and watched.

Shirley was the first to claim her position at the nursing station. Others would trickle in. The morning was the busiest time on the second floor of Winter Hill. Breakfast wouldn't be for half an hour. Within a few minutes of Shirley arriving, the others lined up in their usual places. Colleen and Lauren were engaged behind the desk on the computers. Colleen looked up but did not make eye contact with Shirley.

The chatter among the group gathered around the nursing station was that the nurses were always busy doing some work that didn't involve tending to their needs. They routinely complained to each other that the nurses were not doing any real work. Instead, they believed that the nurses would do anything to get out of interacting with them. On the other hand, many patients believed that the aides all agreed to hide out somewhere. Even though Colleen was new on the job, she suspected that the patients understood that care was a low priority for the staff.

This morning Ruthie and Marjorie lined up on either side of Shirley. Bones and Phyllis took the opposite side of the corridor. Tommy was guarding the elevator.

This morning Bill was missing. So was Ellis.

Then they all heard deep sobbing. Then a moan. Then more sobbing. It was coming from down the corridor, past the elevator.

Bill walked toward the desk. He was carrying the lifeless body of his old dog, Rudy. He struggled to walk. His cane was draped over one arm. The dog's head was dangling freely. Finally, he lost control and dropped the dead dog on the hard tile floor with a sickening thud.

The group at the nursing station moved randomly. There was talking, yelling, and cries of upset.

"The prophecy has come true. Dead animals come flying from above. Revelations 3:17. The end is near. Repent, you sinners. The end is near," yelled Ruthie. Colleen had heard that she was obsessed with the Bible and all things religious. Last week, she checked several of Ruthie's bible citations. None had been accurate.

Ruthie's roommate Phyllis added. "I don't think that's about dead dogs, you religious nut. That's about people running around naked, like poor Millie. God rest her tortured and miserable soul." Colleen also suspected that Phyllis didn't know about the Biblical reference and figured the reference didn't refer to naked people either.

Bones was direct, "First of all, God can't rest Millie's soul. She's burning in hell. Billy, what happened? He sick? He don't look so good."

"He's dead, you idiot. Can't you see his neck is broken? Look, it's like it ain't connected," said Phyllis.

Colleen ran over to Bill.

He wiped his nose. "I was only gone a minute to take a shit. Sorry, a crap. He was sleeping in his usual spot. When I got back, I noticed he was just lying there. Normally as soon as I go near him, his tail would start wagging. Then I noticed his eyes." He sobbed heavily.

Lauren immediately jumped on the house phone. "Please come up here to clean up a dead animal." She took a deep unsympathetic sigh. "Yes, a dead animal. I don't know how. Just get here quick. It will start to smell."

Bill continued to sob. "He was an old slob, but we've been pals for a long time. I don't know, five or six years. He was a stray, you know. We weren't supposed to have pets, but I took care of him. No one ever minded, well, except that bitch, you know who." His eyes darted toward Lauren.

Vinny, the maintenance man, walked in, wearing gloves, came equipped with a cardboard box and a shovel. "Oww wee, who let the dog out! What happened to him? Looks like his neck is broken."

Colleen looked curiously at the dog. Then, finally, she gingerly lifted the dog's head and let it go. Then she glanced toward Shirley.

Shirley was frozen. Her eyes stared straight ahead beyond Vinny, shoveling up the dead Rudy. There was Ellis. He was standing off from the rest of the patients. Then Ellis's facial movements started. His eyes blinked quickly. His eyebrows moved up and down, opened and closed his mouth rapidly, and clicked his tongue.

Ellis smiled at Shirley. Then the facial movement slowed down. Finally, the eyebrows steadied, the ears slowed down, and then it was over.

Shirley snapped out of her trance and looked directly at Ellis.

Colleen observed.

He locked eyes with Shirley with a mean threatening look.

Shirley fainted.

Vinny scooped up Rudy into the box and carried it off. The nursing station group rushed to Shirley, slumped in her chair, her immobile arm dangling alongside.

Marjorie got there first. "Something's happened to Shirley."

Colleen rushed to her. Everyone there moved in unison. Colleen checked her pulse, then raced back to the nursing station. She grabbed smelling salts and carefully placed them under Shirley's nose.

Shirley came to. Ellis was gone.

Colleen rubbed her shoulder. "You left us for a minute."

"I had a bad experience with a dead dog when I was a young woman. It just brought back terrible memories, that's all. Don't say anything to Batty. Please, just say I got sick or something. Don't say I fainted. "

"It was upsetting to all of the patients. So, I fully understand."

"I'm going to talk to Bill a little later. Right now, I'd like to go to my room. With Millie gone, at least I have a little privacy. Until some nut job gets to be my roommate," said Shirley.

Colleen wondered if that new guy was trying to tell Shirley something. Send her a message. She wasn't sure.

Shirley grabbed onto Colleen's sleeve, "Did you see the way he looked at me?"

"Yes."

"Well, if all goes well, I'll be at St. Joseph's by the weekend, Monday at the latest. I suppose I can put up with anything for a couple more days," said Shirley.

Colleen wasn't so sure. She didn't trust that Batty wouldn't ruin her chances to leave.

Colleen was unnerved by the dead dog. She wondered if Ellis was punishing Bill for talking to her. She looked over at Tommy. He, too, looked upset. He waved people to come towards him. Then, he returned to his post at the elevator. His expression was grim. Colleen only wished she could get inside Tommy's brain. She felt that he knew something that the others didn't.

Then the elevator bell rang. The door squeaked open.

It was Sean in a full police uniform.

Tommy spun his chair around and crashed into Sean's leg hard. Then he put a tight grip on Sean's wrist.

"Whoa, that hurt."

Tommy tried to speak. Sean at first gently tried to pry Tommy's hand off his wrist. Hundreds of perps had grabbed Sean, but this grip was one of the most serious. Then Tommy pushed his wheelchair backward, attempting to pull Sean with him. He motioned with his eyes to go with him. Since Tommy only had the use of one hand, he motioned with his head toward the corridor. Sean understood that Tommy needed to have Sean come with him. Except that Tommy couldn't make a sound.

Sean was too much for Tommy. He wrenched his wrist from Tommy's grasp and hurried down the other corridor toward Shirley's room and Batty's office. Tommy crashed into him from behind.

"Stop. I've got to see the administrator. I'll see you later," said Sean as he moved toward Batty's office.

Tommy stopped and turned back toward his post. Then his attention perked up. The elevator chime sounded. He headed to the elevator so as not to miss his next chance.

It was Butch Donovan.

Tommy blocked his path.

"Get the fuck out of my way, retard." Donovan gave Tommy's wheelchair a hard push away from him. Tommy's bad foot, which was in a constant battering ram state, crashed into the other side of the corridor.

Donovan picked up the pace and moved toward Batty's office.

Sean had planned to visit with Shirley before meeting with Batty. He didn't have an appointment, but usually, his uniform tended to supersede those kinds of formalities. As he neared Shirley's room, Donovan briskly walked past him.

The Somerville Police Department had pretty much confirmed that guy that had interrupted their family meeting as a local loan shark collector. Just to be certain, Sean decided to see if he could figure out which car in the parking lot was his and identify the owner. There would be only two cars that stood out: his Charger and this guy's. Colleen didn't have a car. Lauren probably was driving a Civic or Prius. Not sure about Batty. The other workers made very little at the nursing home, so their cars would not stand out. The only problem was that he didn't feel like going through the whole Tommy ordeal again. The only way out was down the fire escape, the one in the dining room. He passed his mother's room into the dining room and spotted a piece of wood next to the door on the floor. He assumed that it was used to keep the fire door open so that one of the staff could sneak outside for a smoke and get back in without causing a fuss. As he walked out onto the outdoor fire escape, he noticed dead butts lying on the rusty landing. He then headed to the parking lot.

Sean smiled to himself. There were only three decent cars in the lot—his Charger for one. First, there was a relatively new Mercedes. That was probably Batty's. It had a Melrose Lion's Club sticker on the rear window. That was not this hood's car. Next, there was a relatively old Camry. That was probably Lauren's. What made him smile was a Cadillac CTS taking up two parking spaces. It was probably a 2018. Naturally, it had chrome wheels. How easy. The license plate read ButchE D12. Sean didn't have to write it down. He quickly called his friend at the Somerville Police to run the plate. The owner, as he suspected, was the very same Dennis Donovan, known by his friends as Butch, who had a substantial rap sheet.

As Sean ended the call with the Somerville Police, Donovan briskly walked to his car. Sean figured that his meeting with Batty was simple. He just needed to collect his cash. Either Batty is lying on the floor in his office with a couple of broken legs, meaning he didn't have the cash, or it was more likely that Batty paid off. Now would be a great time to meet with Mr. Batty unannounced.

To avoid being mauled by Tommy, Sean walked back up the stairwell, avoiding the elevator. Instead, he pushed the piece of wood holding the door open and walked through the dining room into the corridor. As he entered, he heard the elevator bell ring. Sean smiled. Tommy was waiting.

25

The man that exited the elevator was well dressed in a casual way. Fiftyish. Tommy stopped him. The man cleverly skirted by Tommy. He headed to the nursing station.

Before barging in on Batty, Sean decided to check out who this guy was. A visitor? Probably not. Hardly anyone ever came to visit. Another loan shark? An old boyfriend of Colleen? Probably not. Too old. A boyfriend of Lauren? Sean didn't think so. He wandered close enough to hear the guy speak to Lauren.

"Hi. My name is Louis Forrester. My mother Millie Forrester was a patient here."

"Oh, I'm so sorry for your loss. Unfortunately, all of her belongings were shipped."

"Thank you. Well, she was a challenge. Especially as she got older. She told me that she had money in her patients' cash fund. I send her money regularly. She said she was saving for who knows what, but she didn't spend much of it. I'm assuming you kept the cash in a cash box of some kind. She said she had about four thousand dollars the last time we spoke. I'd like to pick that money up. We are in the middle of making funeral arrangements, and every bit helps."

"Correct. Each patient keeps their spending money in our patients' cash box. Only the nurses have access to it."

Lauren bent over the counter and pulled out the patients' cash box. There was Millie's envelope. "Here it is." Lauren then looked puzzled. "There's nothing in her envelope except the ledger of deposits and withdrawals." She handed the ledger to Forrester.

"This shows several deposits over the years, but just a few withdrawals. It shows a balance of over three thousand dollars. Where would the money be? Did the facility have some kind of account that you deposited on behalf of the patients?"

"Probably," answered Lauren.

Sean suspected that maybe Batty had taken the money for payment to the loan shark.

"Well, after your mother died, Mr. Batty must have removed it. So I'm sure you'll get it soon," said Lauren.

"Who's Mr. Batty?" asked Forrester.

"The administrator." She pointed down the corridor to Batty's office.

Forrester handed Lauren a business card. "Please tell him to send the money to me. I'm her only son. I don't think this should go through probate since I'm the person who sent her the money. So how was she at the end?"

"Well, she was not the most pleasant of residents," answered Lauren.

"We were not the least bit close. My mother seemed to get pleasure out of alienating those around her. Well, we will need that money quickly. Please have your administrator call me and let me know when he will send the money." Then Forrester left.

Sean assumed that three thousand dollars was not the total amount that Batty owed. He headed for Shirley's room.

"Sean. Sweetie. I didn't expect you this time of day."

"Ma. You look tired and upset," said Sean.

"I'm not going to make it, Sean. I'm never getting out of this god-forsaken place."

"Don't say that."

"They have more evidence against me. I fainted this morning. Poor Bill found his dog murdered. First Millie, now poor Rudy. I think I'm next."

"C'mon, Ma. Murdered? You can't talk like that. It just gives them more ammunition. You are mentally perfect. But you keep saying stuff that works against you. What about his dog and you fainting?"

"When I was a young woman, I had a terrible experience with a dog, that's all." Shirley just looked away. There was no way she was going to tell Sean about that feeling of when that awful man threw that poor dead, bleeding dog on top of her. She couldn't bear the thought.

"We'll talk about this later. I'm going to meet with Mr. Batty. We have to make sure you get a good report. I want you with me. I want you to bully him. You know. Good cop, me. Bad cop, you."

Shirley perked up. "Sure. I can do that." She immediately put the wheelchair into full motion, almost running over Sean's foot.

Batty's door was open just a crack. Sean could see Batty hunched over his computer screen. Given that Batty did not look injured in any way, he assumed that Batty at least placated the loan shark. He also assumed that given the pattern of loan sharks, this would not be the first time that Batty would have to deal with him.

Shirley blasted in, slamming the door against the wall, followed by Sean.

Batty spun around in his chair. He was sweating profusely. Sean thought that even though Donovan didn't crack a knee or two, he probably unnerved him greatly. Sean had seen the signs a hundred times. Guilty people just can't hide their fear.

"Mr. Batty, I just got a call from the admissions office of St. Joseph's." He lied.

"They say that you told them that my mother might not be accepted because she has dementia."

Shirley crashed into his desk. Batty jumped. "I have never shown any signs of dementia. Sure, I might want to punch you in the nose. Most of the poor sick people in here would love to get a shot at you."

"I did not say or write anything to anyone at St. Joseph's!" Batty was sweating.

"You promised me that you wouldn't report on her incident in the dining room."

"I didn't."

"Well, is this incident documented in her chart? I demand to see your notes. I want to know what you will report to St. Joseph's." Sean was enjoying this. He assumed Batty was now an emotional wreck after the visit with Donovan.

"Those reports and charts are confidential," answered Batty.

Shirley moved toward the desk and bumped into it. She leaned over his desk from her wheelchair.

Sean joined her. He also leaned over the desk, moving as close as he could to Batty's face. "Confidential? I believe that Massachusetts Law states clearly that the patient owns everything in a patient's chart. Nothing can be kept from the patient. And guess what? The patient is sitting right in front of you."

Shirley was pushed tight up against the desk, glaring at Batty.

"Bring me the chart, or I will report you to the Attorney General, who by the way my chief knows personally. If I have to, I'll get a subpoena." Sean was making all this up. Sean didn't know the law about patient confidentiality. He also couldn't quite recall who the Attorney General was. But he had dressed in uniform. He knew that alone would make people nervous, especially guilty people

"I demand you get my mother's chart and show it to your patient."

Batty picked up the phone. "Nurse Lauren, please bring me Mrs. Duffy's chart. I only report what I observe. I don't interpret anything. The facts speak for themselves."

Lauren entered the room and handed the chart to Batty.

"Now give them to my mother," demanded Sean.

"Give me those." Shirley grabbed the charts from Batty. She

opened the thick report. "Sean, the print is too small for me to read these."

Sean then jumped in. "Ma. Do you permit me to read the reports to you?"

"I do," replied Shirley.

Sean read bits and pieces out loud, "Mrs. Duffy shows signs of progressive dementia, most likely leading into Alzheimer's."

"You bastard." Shirley banged into Batty's desk again.

Sean continued reading, "Recent events such as emotional outburst over nothing, continued talking to herself and making false accusations about the conditions of this facility lead us to believe that she is steadily deteriorating emotionally and physically. She even threatened to harm the staff, including the administrator. The nurse on duty documented this."

"Yes, I did threaten to punch you in the nose, but for a perfectly good reason. You are running this place into the ground. I was just venting. I have been kind to these patients, unlike your staff."

"Enough." Sean intervened.

"No. You wrote that stuff in the report to punish me for complaining. Sean, let's write a formal complaint to the state inspector's office and your friend, the Attorney General. I'm sure that I can have many patients sign it." Sean knew that Shirley had made a bit of a leap as far as his friend, the Attorney General. Sean's boss was a friend of the Attorney General, not that he was his friend. But Sean let it go since he felt that Shirley's slight exaggeration was probably lost on what he observed was a completely flustered and now probably paranoid Batty.

"We can have a hoard of state inspectors here in the morning if you want," added Sean.

"Oh. I ran into a guy I've arrested several times. Maybe you know him. Butch Donovan? Nice of Butch visiting a patient. His mother? His father? Who was he visiting? It was great of him to take time off from the loan shark business to visit a sick relative. See, you judge people. I always thought he was a sleaze bag. Maybe not. Who was he visiting?"

Sean had figured that he had done enough.

Batty had gotten the message. "Perhaps the report was in error. I relied heavily on the staff. Sometimes you just can't rely on other people to do the job right."

"So how about you put a call into the administrator's office at St. Joseph's and tell them that you highly recommend my mother to be transferred. Please add that she is a model patient and would be perfect for their facility." Sean was now relaxing.

"I'll make the call, and then you must leave. I'm a very busy man. I cannot devote all my attention to one patient."

Paul dialed the phone.

"Put it on speaker."

Paul grimaced and pressed the speaker button. The phone rang.

"You have reached the admission office of St. Joseph's Nursing Center. Unfortunately, no one is here to take your call. Please leave your name, number, and a short message. Someone will get back to you."

"Leave the message," demanded Sean.

"Yes. Paul Batty at the Winter Hill Nursing and Rehabilitation Center in Somerville. We understand that a Mrs. Shirley Duffy has been tentatively accepted to be transferred from our facility to your facility."

Sean made a circular hand motion as if to say, add more to the message.

"Yes, she shows no signs of dementia. She has been a model patient here. We will miss her cheery mood."

Sean nodded his head in approval.

Batty hung up.

"Now, is that all? Mrs. Duffy, please stop banging the desk." Batty's shoulders slumped.

"Thanks, Mr. Batty. I will follow up with St. Joseph's to ensure your formal written report is accurate. Oh, the next time you run into Mr. Donovan, tell him I said to say hello."

Shirley waved her good hand, "Have a good day, Mr. Batty."

Sean and Shirley left.

Batty waited a bit, then got up and slammed the door. He then slumped in his chair.

~

"What do you have on him?" asked Shirley. "Who's Donovan?"

"I'm a police officer. I have something on everyone."

Loud voices broke the mood.

"What's going on?"

The patients were all gathered around Caroline's room.

Bill yelled, "Why is Nelson sitting on the floor?"

Nelson's walker was on the floor. His head was tilted downward, and his one good eye was wide open.

Bones slowly walked over to Nelson. "Dead. Doesn't move." Bones pushed on his leg. There was no reaction. "Yeah, dead alright. What about what's her name, Caroline. Nelson liked to try to strangle her now and again. Maybe she killed him."

Phyllis jumped in, "Bones, you are as crazy as Nelson. Poor Nelson just wanted to make out with her. He was mostly blind."

"No, you are crazy. I saw Nelson try to strangle her. Well, not really strangle. But, he did put his hands around her neck."

"See. He wanted to kiss her, that's all. The poor man wasn't evil, just had incredibly poor taste," added Phyllis.

Ellis wandered over. He stood looking into the room.

Shirley was still outside of Batty's office. Ellis looked over at her. Then he smiled. Then his facial movements started.

Shirley shook her head, looked down, and headed to her room.

Sean raced over to the crowd. He checked Nelson. No pulse.

Batty joined in. He called the EMTs from his cell phone. "Okay, folks. No panic. Please go to your rooms. Nothing to get concerned about.

Sean cornered Batty. "You need to have the police investigate."

"There isn't anyone in here who would want Mr. Nelson dead, except maybe the Commonwealth of Massachusetts." Batty took a deep breath. "The state paid Nelson's full cost of staying here. He was so fragile. A simple fall would have broken his neck. Please don't mention this to any of the patients. They have enough to worry about. I will mention it to the police."

Sean noticed that Batty was still shaken from his two prior encounters. The one with Donovan and the one with Shirley and him. Sean finally had a chance to look closely at Ellis while he was in the middle of his extreme facial movements. He understood a bit better why this guy terrified his mother. He was creepy. But he felt there had to be more. This was the first time that it occurred to him that his mother was hiding something from him. What was it about this guy that scared her much more than any other patient in this place? After all, he was no creepier than Nelson. The mangled face. The one eye. His mother had told him stories about how she had intervened when he had the urge to touch people. Maybe even hurt people. She had said that Nelson was harmless.

He had mixed feelings about doing any in-depth background on Ellis. His mother would be out of this place in less than a week. Why bother? He glanced over at him again. It was as if this guy knew what Sean was thinking.

Ellis locked eyes with Sean in between one of the facial motions. Ellis smirked.

Sean's heart jumped. He had dealt with a lot of bad people as a policeman. But he was unnerved by this man's expression. It worried him. This guy was scary. He then committed to himself to figure out who this strange person was regardless.

Lauren approached Batty. "We had a visit from a Mr. Forrester. Millie Forrester's son."

Sean was within earshot.

"What did he want?"

"He said that his mother had a pretty large cash account. The ledger shows no withdrawals. So, he was looking for her money. It was about three or four thousand dollars." She handed him the card Forrester gave her. "I told him you would send him the money and please call him to let him know when it will be arriving. He said he needed it for the funeral."

"Sure. I'll send Mr. Forrester the money right away." Batty walked toward his office.

Sean saw him dial his cell phone. He said softly to himself. "He's calling the loan shark."

26

Today was the day for the field trip. Somerville Elder Services now and again would visit the local nursing homes. Sometimes they provided entertainment. Sometimes a little party. Today, Elder Services provided a field trip to Stoneham Zoo to the residents of Winter Hill. The zoo was a half an hour drive from the nursing home. This field trip was not a routine matter. The zoo field trip had been scheduled for over six months. The problem with scheduling something so far in the future for the patients at Winter Hill was that some of them wouldn't survive long enough to take advantage of the adventure, and many wouldn't even remember that it was scheduled. So, when Lauren announced the field trip, the people lined up along the corridor seemed surprised.

That didn't stop them from queuing up at the elevator. Tommy behaved flustered. Many people were coming and going to the elevator.

Elder Services was going to provide the transportation to and from the zoo, and it was rumored that they would provide lunch as well. Lauren peeked out the window and confirmed that the old Ford handicap van was parked at the back entrance pouring a mixture of black and grey smoke out of the early nineties vintage tailpipe.

It took over an hour to get all the patients from the second floor to the main entrance.

Once the travelers were gathered outside, the next step was to load up the old cargo van using the rusty and oil-stained handicap lift. It barely worked. Each time it lifted a patient, the van's engine groaned, and the vehicle lilted sideways.

Two volunteers from Elder Services were the hosts, Tony, the driver, and Louise. Tony was in his late fifties. He wore a tee-shirt that read, "*Somerville Journal 2003 Softball Champs.* Tony was connected with the community newspaper and had played softball on the local team until his knees were too unstable to continue playing. Since that time, he had gained sixty pounds.

Louise was in her mid-fifties. She was not old enough to have been a hippie in the sixties. But her dress, hairstyle, and mannerisms suggested she could have been a product of the sixties

It was time for Shirley to get loaded into the van. Tony operated the lift. He rolled Shirley

onto the shaky paint-chipped lift mechanism that would be at the same height as the van's floor once raised. There were no safety straps or fall protection.

"Hey, Shirl. Looking pretty spiffy. New hairdo. Nice," said Tony. Of course, Shirley knew Tony was making this up since Shirley hadn't changed her hairstyle since entering Winter Hill.

"Thanks, Tony. You are looking pretty good yourself." The last time Shirley saw Tony, he was at least twenty pounds lighter. She knew that and gave him that compliment, nevertheless.

Bones was next in line and fidgeted. "Hurry up. Get her in the van."

Shirley wondered why Bones was always so impatient. It wasn't as if Bones had to get back to some appointment. On the contrary, she mused that his life was consumed by monotony like all at Winter Hill.

Bones feigned coughing. "Jesus Christ. We're all gonna die of smoke poisoning. When was the last time somebody tuned up this beast?"

Ignoring Bones, Tony straightened Shirley on the handicap lift.

"Tony. Be careful. This thing scares the living crap out of me." Shirley, rightfully so, was afraid the lift would collapse and send her wheelchair crashing to the ground.

"Don't worry. Has the Tone ever dropped a pretty lady? I only drop the mean and ugly people."

"Well, we've got our share of them." Shirley surveyed the group heading to the zoo. Ellis was not among the participants. She took a deep breath and muttered, "Thank God," She spoke up, "looks like my favorite mean and ugly one's staying behind."

Tony jumped off the lift, pressed a lever, and the lift began to rise. But, again, the old van leaned to one side, expelling a heavy puff of black smoke out the tailpipe.

Shirley grabbed tightly onto her wheelchair arm with her good hand. "Oh, I hate this. Tony, don't let me fall."

The lift ground to a halt. Tony jumped up and wheeled Shirley into the van. Tony jumped out.

After an hour and a half, the van was loaded up with the patients. Tony secured all the wheelchairs to a metal rack that ran on each side of the van and strapped the others into the jump seats that made up a second and a third row.

Tony put the old van into drive and headed to the zoo.

Tony drove while Louise sat shotgun in the passenger seat. The van would take them through the City of Somerville up to Alewife Brook Parkway, then on to Route 93. The Stoneham Zoo was off exit 34.

Shirley felt that Louise meant well. "Well, we have a treat for you today. We are going to the zoo." Now, most of the group had already been told that the field trip was to the zoo, but that was six months ago. Phyllis didn't quite remember.

"Whoopty do. Why don't you take us to a male strip club? Now that's talking."

Ruthie hadn't said a word to anyone all day up to now. "Sodom and Gomorrah. Never heard of those cities, you evil demon? I'll not go to the strip club. Take me back now!"

Bill winked, then whispered to Shirley, "Yeah, I know we are going to the zoo. I just want to cause a little trouble." He announced to the passengers. "Count me out! If we're going to a strip club, I want women. I don't want to see some white guy's ass. Take me back. No way. No male strip clubs. Hey, there's a great strip club in Arlington. It's right off Arlington Center. Tony, take the first exit off 93 towards Arlington Hight's. I think it's called the Alewife Gentleman's Club. They got burgers and fries and sweet young things."

Marjorie jumped in. "I'll go."

Shirley chimed in, "Don't you fools remember? We are going to the zoo, not a strip club. You people drive me crazy."

Several of the folks sighed a sound of collective disappointment.

Tony laughed out loud, then added more fuel to the fire. "Hey Bill, I'm just about to get on 93. Which exit is that? Is that exit 31?"

Louise gave Tony a dirty look. "No. I never..."

Marjorie added, "I'd rather go to the strip club. I've been to the zoo. I've never seen a male stripper. I've heard they're all gay. But who cares? You can't tell they're gay from looking at them."

"No male strippers! Girls, and more girls," yelled Bill.

Louise leaned over and pressed the van's horn.

"Stop! Stop! Please listen. We are going to the zoo. Plus, I have nice bag lunches."

They all sighed yet another collective sound of disappointment.

She pointed to a cardboard box full of brown paper bags. Louise, clearly flustered, looked around for some support.

Bill added, "What no restaurant! Not even the snack bar for some fries. Shit. This sucks. First, no strippers, then no fries. We might as well be playing bingo."

Louise looked dejected.

Tony leaned over to Louise, "See, I told you so."

∾

The old van loaded up with the patients from Winter Hill entered the Stoneham Zoo. The unloading took as long as the loading. Finally, they gathered around the entrance to the zoo. Louise carefully counted the passengers.

Phyllis jumped in. "What's the matter, lady? You afraid you are going to lose some of us?"

Many nodded their agreement with Phyllis.

After ten minutes of buying tickets, handing them to the Winter Hill residents, going through security, they finally entered the zoo. At one point, they almost didn't make it because Phyllis decided to protest being searched by security.

Shirley took Louise aside after entering the zoo. "Was that really necessary to frisk us with their magic bomb-seeking wand? Do we look like a bunch of terrorists?"

Louise patiently responded, "Well, they have their procedures. We need to follow the rules."

As they walked along together, Louise took on the role of tour guide. It was as if she were speaking to children. "The Bengal Tiger is a native of India. During the latter part of the twentieth century, this being the twenty-first century, you know, the Tiger..."

Her voice droned on and out of earshot. Then, as the group passed the snack bar, Bill moved behind it, motioning to several of the others to join him.

Shirley, Bones, Marjorie, and Phyllis all walked toward the rear of the snack bar.

Tommy stopped, his head moved toward the group, and rolled toward them. He looked around as Phyllis was the last to disappear behind the snack bar. He then wheeled himself back to the snack bar. Finally, he planted himself to the side of the building with his back facing the group, which now formed a circle.

Shirley noticed that Tommy was not going to interfere with their little excursion. "Look, Tommy is going to be our lookout person. Shirley told Bill, "God help anyone who would sneak behind or near the back of the snack bar and listen in on the confidential conversation. Tommy would attack them with his foot!"

Bill bent over, laughing, "Correct. "The only problem is he couldn't warn us." He pulled a pack of Camels out of his pocket. He opened the fresh pack with a flourish. He majestically lit it up. Then as if it was the best thing on earth, took a deep drag, and blew out a huge plume of smoke.

Bones jumped in. "Hey. Hand me over one. Where'd you get those? I thought the Nurse Nazi scooped your whole supply."

Bill grinned widely, "Sources. I got my sources."

Ruthie walked over to Tommy. "What's going on?" She then heard the group and wrinkled her nose. She said to no one, "I smell awful cigarette smoke. Evil habit, invented by the devil himself."

Marjorie pointed to Tommy. "Look, Tommy is standing guard. He's not letting Ruthie pass any further.

Bill handed the cigarette to Shirley. Then, he walked over to Tommy and Ruthie. "What do you want?"

"You are missing the animals. Are you smoking back there? Smoking is the devil's habit. I should report you to Louise."

"Go ahead. No one said we couldn't smoke out here. Do you see any no-smoking signs? We have business to attend to. So if you don't mind, go back to the tour."

"What kind of business?" asked Ruthie.

"None of your business. Just our own private business. Now take off."

Then Shirley rolled over beside Tommy. "Bill. She can stay as long as she doesn't keep talking about her crazy Bible stuff."

Bill looked Ruthie in the eye, "Well?"

"I won't," said Ruthie.

"Okay. Tommy, she can pass."

Tommy rolled aside. Ruthie then joined the group.

Bones jumped in. "That crazy bitch. Ruthie, go join the rest of the crowd. We're having a private meeting."

"Yeah, scram. We're going to worship the devil in a minute," added Phyllis.

On the verge of tears, Ruthie turned her chair around and began to wheel away.

"Let her stay. She promised not to preach to us. We are not going to worship the devil. We just want to talk about Ellis." Shirley wedged herself between Ruthie and the rest of the group.

Meanwhile, Tommy repositioned himself with his back to the group, scanning the zoo for any intruders.

Bones softened, "she can stay as long as we don't hear none of her religious bullshit."

"She promised not to," added Shirley.

"Thanks, Shirley. I'm scared of that Ellis character. He's got the eyes of evil, of the dev... Oops, sorry," said Ruthie. Then she whispered to Shirley, "I think he is the Anti-Christ."

Bones took a deep drag of the cigarette, and while blowing out his smoke, he said, "I heard that."

Ruthie shot back, "I wasn't talking to you."

Bill motioned for the group to gather close. They moved in a neat circle. Bill was at the head. Shirley was by his side.

"We got trouble, and no one at Winter fucking Hill is going to help us."

Marjorie interjected, "Please, your language is shocking me. But if you feel comfortable using it, well, I suppose I will have to listen. I've never said the "F" word in my entire life. But, of course, everyone is saying it now. Even politicians. I bet even teachers say it. When I was in school, only the bad..." She stopped when everyone in the group was staring at her.

"Sorry. Go on," said Marjorie, whose neck turned a bright red.

"Our new guy killed Millie, Nelson, and old Rudy, and I know he wants to kill me," said Shirley.

Bill took another majestic drag of the cigarette.

"I can feel him staring at me. I can't sleep soundly anymore."

The group pulled closer, except for Marjorie, who appeared lost in her thoughts.

Marjorie blurted out, "Well, I suppose I have to get with it. Fuck. There, I've said it. My very first time. Fuck. My second time."

Phyllis was not impressed. "Will you pay attention?"

Marjorie turned her attention to the rest of the people.

Phyllis added, "Bill, the guy is strange, but killing people? And your old dog. That Millie was a pain in the ass, but not enough to get her killed. And poor Nelson never said a bad word about anyone."

Bones added his thoughts, "Nelson never said a word period other than a few grunts. But why would Ellis kill old Rudy?"

Bill punched the wall of the snack bar. "Because he heard me ratting on him to that young nurse."

"What do we do? Go to Batty? He won't do anything, that re-incarnation of Herod," blurted out Ruthie.

Shirley laughed. "Ruthie can't help herself."

Bones shook his head, "Who the fuck is Herod? Herod who? Oh, you mean the guy that killed Christ? But, hey, stay in this century, will you?"

"John the Baptist," snapped back Ruthie.

Shirley interjected, "Enough! Can't go to Batty. Useless as tits on a bull. He'll just tell us we're crazy. Well, in some cases, he's probably right. We are all going crazy. Winter Hill makes us all crazy, right?"

Bill stomped on the cigarette and lit up a new one. Several zoo patrons walked by the snack bar. Tommy glared at them. They picked up their speed and moved on.

"I'm old, and I'm not too afraid of dying, but I sure as hell don't want to die at the hands of a lunatic. He reminds me of something terrible that happened a long time ago. When I was just a young woman. I just worry, which one of us will be next?" Shirley's eyes filled up.

Bones placed his hand on Shirley's shoulder. "I won't let that prick hurt you or any of you. I'll watch for him."

Marjorie jumped in, "I've never said prick before either. So, there I said it. Prick. Yes, that guy is a prick!"

Once more, the group all stared at Marjorie.

"I agreed with you all," said Marjorie.

Bill added. "Have you seen those crazy moves he makes with his face? His eyebrows jump up and down. His ears move. The guy is fucked up."

Bill straightened up as if to take charge. "Okay. We gotta protect each other, especially you, Shirley. Alone we're screwed, but together that son of a bitch can't get to us."

Now Marjorie finally paid attention, "What can we do?" She motioned to the others in wheelchairs. "We can be look-outs. We can scream. Whenever that bastard leaves his room, I can signal you all to be on guard.

Tommy turned around and motioned to the group.

Louise led the remaining patients toward the snack bar. Bill and the rest of the group behind the snack bar stood silent for a moment, hearing Louise provide some additional information about the nearby monkeys.

"Shit. Miss Social Worker is coming. Here's the plan. Whenever we see our friend twitchy acting strange, we tail him. We don't want to let him out of our sight." Bill was now on one knee as if he was a football coach.

"What if we lose him?" asked Marjorie.

Phyllis shook her head, "How can we lose him? We're all stuck in that god-damn hell hole. Where would he go?"

Marjorie agreed, "You do have a point."

Bill took over. "If we do lose him, we'll just have to wait around to see where he went."

Shirley added, "It's at night that scares me. You are all in bed and can't get out without an aide. What then?

"I can get out of bed myself," said Marjorie

"I'll help Phyllis and Ruthie. Bill, you cover Shirley," said Bones.

"Okay, but let's set up some signal. How do we communicate?"

Bill jumped in. "If any of us are in trouble, if that son of a bitch tries anything funny with any of us, just yell for help."

Phyllis was getting into this. "How will we know it's from one of us. Half the people at Winter Hill are yelling for help."

Shirley's face lit up. "Bingo!"

Louise and the rest of the Old People gathered in front of the snack bar. "Oh Tommy, there you are. You missed all the animals. Do I have everyone?"

Bill whispered, "You thought of something?"

Shirley then whispered to the group, "Yup. Just yell Bingo, and we will know it's him."

Bill grabbed his pack of Camels. He pulled out a fresh cigarette and lit it from his old one. He flicked the old one away. "Bingo it is. Now we can't tell anyone else. Agreed? No one. We are now officially the Bingo Gang." Bill motioned to Bones McGraw to take the newly lit cigarette.

Bones took a long drag. "Bingo."

Bones handed the cigarette to Shirley.

She took a small puff. "Bingo." She coughed and handed it to Ruthie.

Ruthie started, "Smoking is against God's Law. The body is the temple of the...Oh, what the hell." She hauled on the cigarette, held it in, and slowly blew it out. Shirley looked at her curiously. She thought she knew exactly how to draw on weed at one point in Ruthie's life. "Bingo." She handed it to her roommate, Phyllis.

She took a long haul. Then, while she blew out the smoke, she softy said, "Bingo." She choked and coughed and laughed and finally handed it to Marjorie.

Marjorie took the tiniest little puff. Shirley laughed to herself since Marjorie did a Bill Clinton by not inhaling and gently blew out barely a trace of smoke. "Bingo. Fucking bingo."

They all giggled quietly. The members of the Bingo Gang put their hands together. "Bingo!" They then high-fived each other.

They walked in silence past Tommy. Marjorie was the last of the Bingo Gang to leave the gang's meeting place. Once they had joined the rest of the Winter Hill patients, Tommy rolled toward the group. Bill patted him on the back. "You done your job well."

Tommy nodded.

27

The place was deadly quiet. Most of the patients on Colleen's floor were still on their outing at the zoo. She was thinking about Sean. What an asshole. He shows up at my place. All he wanted to do was to have sex with me. Then he bails. Doesn't even commit to seeing me. She was upset.

Vinny, the maintenance man, interrupted her musings.

"Hey, Mr. Batty wanted me to do a little construction at the nursing station. He was not satisfied with the security of the patients' cash box. He wanted me to put it in a locking cabinet under the desk. So, I've got to take out the shelves. Then build a box with a door."

"Does he think a patient will steal money from the cash box? We are the only ones allowed behind the nurse's desk. Does he think we would steal money from there?" Colleen was taken aback.

"Hey. I'm the maintenance guy. I just follow orders," answered Vinny. He pulled out the cash strongbox. He then pulled the rest of the paperwork and other junk out from under the desk. "I'll start the demolition of the shelves tomorrow. In the meantime, Mr. Batty's going to store the cash box in this office until I'm done. So, honey, you are my witness that I took the cash box. Didn't open it."

"Yeah, yeah. I see." Colleen was not paying much attention.

"So, I'm not accused of stealing anything. Walk with me to Mr. Batty's office. I'm not taking any chances."

Vinny and Colleen walked to Batty's office. Vinny knocked on the door.

Batty opened it a little too quickly like he expected someone soon. "Oh, Vinny. What do you need?" Colleen noticed that Batty ignored her.

"Like you said. I am starting the renovation of the nurse's desk. So, here is the cash box. The nurse here, what's your name? She walked with me every step of the way, just to make sure no money was missing."

"It's Ms. McCarthy. Mr. Batty. I was with him the whole way. It was never opened."

Batty took the box. He placed it in a drawer. "Thanks, Vinny. We can lock it up in your new cabinet as soon as you are finished. I'm very concerned that it is just too accessible. I will put it in the lockable storage closet every night. It will be safe there."

Vinny and Colleen returned to the nursing station. The distraction from Vinny hardly changed her sour mood about Sean. She was on the day shift and would be leaving by six in the evening.

Back at the nursing station, Vinny did a few measurements, then approached Colleen. "Hey nursey, you sent me an email about the fire protection system? What's that about? It works just fine."

"It's Nurse McCarthy, not nursey. I had a couple of complaints that it's not working properly. So we had a small…"

"A couple of complaints? From the staff?" asked Vinny.

"No. Not from the staff, from the patients. Well, actually from one patient."

"Are you shitting me? From a patient? How would they know anything about the fire protection systems? Look, I'm only one person. Do you know when I started here, they had three mainte-nance men? Last year we were down to two, and now just me. So please don't bring me bullshit work. I have enough to do with real work. The fire protection system is just fine. It's a central system to protect the whole building, set up in various zones. I bet you didn't know that. Also, there is a sophisticated sprinkler system, also set up in zones. Everything is tied into the fire station. Satisfied?"

Colleen didn't want to debate with him. Now she was just angry. "I was going to say before you rudely interrupted me that we had a small fire in one of the patient's rooms and..."

Vinny replied. "If you have a problem, you are supposed to write a work order. I can't take complaints over email. Sorry, procedures. You're new. Didn't anyone train you?"

While Colleen didn't overthink about this complaint, now she was mad enough to make it an issue. "Well, I think this is a major safety issue. What if something..."

"There's nothing wrong with the fire protection system. Period."

"Do you always interrupt people when they are speaking? There was a fire in one of the patient's rooms. Shouldn't it have activated the smoke alarm throughout the floor at least?" Colleen had no idea how smoke detectors worked, but now she wanted to make Vinney look bad. "Aren't there sprinkler heads all over the place? Don't they go off when a fire starts?"

"Would you like to clean up the mess? I certainly don't. Not for a small fire. Besides, if you are talking about that black guy who smokes in his room, we disabled his sprinkler outside his room. This is not the first time we had a small fire in his room."

Now Colleen's anger was replaced by a bit of panic. "So, if there were a real fire in his room, nothing would happen?"

"I gotta go. If you have a problem, fill out a work order. I can't afford to stand here and debate you about what some senile patient thinks." Vinny walked away. "Listen, smoke detectors go off from smoke, sprinklers from heat. A small wastebasket fire wouldn't generate enough heat. You do the nursing stuff and let me handle the technical stuff." Vinny walked around Tommy and pressed the elevator button.

Colleen walked quickly to Bill's room. Ellis was not there. She rummaged through Bill's stuff. Finally, she found a book of matches.

She returned to the nursing station to conduct her own experiment. First, she lit a piece of paper with Bill's matches. Then she stood on a chair under one of the smoke detectors.

But as she suspected, the burning paper did not set the alarm off. If it had, she would jump off the chair and claim that the alarm went off by mistake. Then she would dump the paper somewhere. She was pretty sure that Vinny had turned the whole system off, or at least the section that protected the second floor. She now wondered about the sprinkler system. She didn't dare test a sprinkler since it would douse her and the nurses station if it went off. But she had her doubts. Vinny had said the fire protection system was centrally controlled. That might have meant it could be centrally turned off.

She wasn't sure what to think. Now at least she had some leverage over Vinny and maybe even Batty, which might prove valuable at some time. She wondered if this was Vinny's idea or Batty's.

~

The loading process of getting the zoo's patients into the van was agonizingly long. One patient at a time on the lift. This time there was minimal discussion. The walk in the zoo tired most of the patients. Now they were quiet as the van pulled out of the zoo parking lot.

Louise took Tony aside, "I'm exhausted. At least we don't have to listen to the patients. Most of the group will be dozing."

Not Shirley. She felt better with the support from the Bingo Gang but was still concerned and scared. Marjorie sat next to her.

"Do you feel better?" asked Marjorie.

"Sort of. Thanks for being my friend. Thanks to you and all of the Bingo Gang."

"Thanks? We should be thanking you. You stand up for us all the time. You probably saved old Caroline's life. Nelson would have strangled her. I could never do it. Besides, most people think I'm crazy." Marjorie looked straight ahead.

"First off. Nelson was harmless. I believe that he just wanted to help Caroline. He just didn't know how. Sure, he liked putting his hands around her neck. But he never choked her."

"I guess."

"And another thing. I don't think you are crazy." In Shirley's head voice, the word eccentric came to mind immediately.

"The nurses do. They look at me funny. Sure, I'm eccentric."

Shirley's heart jumped. She thought, Jesus, was she reading my mind?

"Sometimes, I think I am crazy." Marjorie continued to look straight ahead.

"Why is that? What makes you feel that way?" asked Shirley.

"I was barely thirty. I used to visit my Gramma in what they called the rest home. She died there, back in 1958. She didn't die from old age. The place burned down. She died in the fire. So ironically, now I'm in the same place in the same spot. Now they call it a nursing home and rehabilitation center—what a joke. Anyway, I remember Gramma used to act like I do now. Worried about losing her jewelry. Worried about getting lost. I find myself acting the same way."

"There's an old saying that if you think you are crazy, you aren't. Crazy people think they are normal. So that's a good sign."

"I would believe you, but I know there is something wrong with me. That's why I know I am crazy." Shirley believed that Marjorie was deadly serious.

"I agree with you that you might be a little eccentric." Shirley was now able to take a little risk with Marjorie. "But that doesn't mean you are crazy. Look at me. I talk to myself all the time. That asshole, pardon my French, Batty wrote me up because he thinks I have dementia or something."

"I hear voices in the night. At first, I thought it was other patients. I would tell the nurse. They said it was all in my head. My old room-mate, remember Julie Stevens? I told her. She said she never heard any voices. See, I am crazy." Marjorie just looked away.

"What kind of voices?"

"Just people softly speaking. I can't understand what they are saying, but it seems like a group of people. It sounds like it's coming from the roof. Please don't say anything. I don't like talking about this," pleaded Marjorie.

"Just voices?" Shirley was shaken.

"Sometimes laughter. It's hard to tell. I don't know. Why are you asking me this?"

"I hear them too."

Then Marjorie fainted and slumped over in her seat.

It was all Shirley could do to prevent her from cracking her head on the side of the van.

Phyllis noticed first. "Help, help. Something's wrong with Marjorie.

Louise abruptly turned around. "Tony, pull over to the side of the highway.

Tony made a less than subtle turn onto the breakdown lane. The passengers all swayed in unison.

Once the van came to a stop, Louise rushed to Marjorie carrying a first aid kit and placed smelling salts under Marjorie's nose. She came to in a few seconds.

"Everything is fine. Marjorie probably just had a little too much sun. We will be off in a minute." Louise returned to her seat.

Tony pulled the van back onto the highway.

Marjorie and Shirley stayed quiet the rest of the ride back to Winter Hill.

By the time the zoo visitors had returned, it had become nearly dark. That made the unloading process even longer. Once the van was empty, the residents lined up at the elevator in yet another long queue to get back up onto the second floor. As Bones walked past the front door, he bellowed, "Home sweet home. I wish."

Shirley motioned to Marjorie to stay behind at the end of the elevator line.

Marjorie nodded. "Either everyone is lying around here, or just you and I hear the same voices."

"Only us, but I actually believe that Tommy hears voices too. It's hard to tell. Notice how he listens to the walls. I think he hears the voices there. We had a little connection and I think he was trying to tell me that he hears voices." Shirley was deadly serious.

"If we ask around, and no one admits to hearing the voices, then they will think we are both lunatics," said Marjorie.

"We can't tell anyone. And of course, Tommy can't say anything."

"The voices don't happen all the time, usually when it is quiet, and I'm in bed. It was pretty clear that I was the only screwball hearing the voices at one time. Well, now you are the other screwball. Anyway, there was a time when I thought one of the voices was coming from Gramma. You know, she died in the fire. That's why I thought that I was crazy." Marjorie was shaking.

"Same thing. It usually happens when I'm in bed, so we are probably hearing it at the same time," said Shirley

"We are on different corridors, though. I can tell you this. While this scares me, I feel a lot better. Now I know that I'm not crazy. Do you suppose someone is playing tricks on us? Maybe hiding a speaker or something in our rooms?"

"I don't trust those aides, Mary and Martha. I wouldn't put it past them. I can't imagine how they could have done it. But, bless her miserable soul, Millie never heard anything, and she had eagle hearing. She would have said something." Shirley's mind was racing.

"Can I ask you something?" asked Marjorie. "I have a connection with someone who died in the fire. Gramma. Do you know anyone who died in the fire?" asked Marjorie.

Shirley took a long time to answer. Then, finally, her eyes teared up, took a deep, deep breath, and answered.

"Yes."

28

As Colleen blew away the smoke, the elevator bell rang. The doors opened, and the first group of patients paraded out of the stuffed elevator. Immediately, they lined up in their usual position around the nursing station.

"How were the animals? Did you have a good time?" asked Colleen.

Phyllis answered, "Oh, it was a lovely trip. We saw the elephants, lions, tigers, and bears, and no male strippers."

Colleen looked quizzically at the group.

"Stop it, Phyllis. It was fine. We had a fucking good time!" answered Marjorie.

The Bingo Gang all looked at Marjorie at the same time.

"It's the new me!" replied Marjorie.

Ruthie chimed in, "Marjorie fainted. We thought it might be a sign from God."

Bones just shook his head, "You promised. So keep it up, and we'll kick you out of the gang."

Shirley spoke up, "Just a little sun exposure. Marjorie will be just fine. It was a very productive outing."

Bill gave her the thumbs-up sign.

"Where's Ellis? Sulking in his bedroom?"

"I haven't seen him in a while," answered Colleen.

"I wish he would get permanently lost," said Shirley.

Ellis appeared from down the corridor. Colleen and Shirley watched him closely as he approached. He was in the middle of one of his facial movements. The Bingo Gang silently stared as they watched him pass. Then, each one of their heads moved in unison.

They turned as the elevator chime sounded. Tommy rolled out, followed by a group of patients. He solemnly rolled out of the way to let the group pass, then moved to his usual position guarding the elevator. Shirley and Marjorie glanced over at him. Then, for maybe the first time, Tommy looked deeply into Shirley's eyes, then to Marjorie's.

Shirley thought that she saw a sign of understanding and perhaps humanness. She nodded at him. He continued to look at her, then turned his attention to what she figured was his mission after a second or so. Guarding.

"Well, I'm glad you all had a great time at the zoo. I'll see you all tomorrow." Colleen raced toward the elevator.

The zoo excursion had exhausted Shirley. She went to bed just after dinner. While very tired, she felt better. The formation of the Bingo Gang gave her at least some sense of safety. She wondered when her beloved Willy would appear on the ceiling. She would tell him about the gang and the voices. Only very quietly. Her musings were interrupted by Marjorie, who shuffled into Shirley's room.

"Do we need to talk about the voices?" asked Marjorie?

"I've heard of people who share the same kind of vision or dream. So I think you, Tommy, and I are experiencing some kind of shared memory. I don't believe in spirits or ghosts. It's the only explanation." said Shirley.

"I told you, my grandmother died in the fire at the old rest home. I feel so guilty for not visiting her on the night she died. I often wonder if it is her talking."

"Guilt will do funny things in our heads. Maybe Tommy is carrying guilt as well," said Shirley. "I heard someone say that guilt is like a silent scar. I know that sounds funny cause scars don't make noises. But it sure is a scar on your soul. You hearing the voices and maybe Tommy too is a sort of comfort. Either all three of us are crazy, or we are all okay," Shirley gently touched Marjorie's hand.

"You are right. You are fucking right!" yelled Marjorie.

Both Marjorie and Shirley burst into wonderful, cleansing laughter.

"Fucking A," Shirley responded.

Sean walked in. "Did I hear two old ladies swearing their asses off?"

"Not us. Sean, this is my friend Marjorie. She had a breakthrough today. She learned how to say the f word."

"Thank you, Sean, for visiting your mother. She's a good person. I'm envious. I rarely see my son. Take good care of her." Marjorie walked out of the room, turned, and blew Sean and Shirley a kiss.

"How's it going with the young nurse? I think her shift ended at six. Did you see her?"

"No. She had left before I came in." Sean knew that Colleen's shift ended at six o'clock and frankly didn't want to run into her. It was awkward now. He wasn't sure what to do or think about her.

"We still have to make sure that you are cleared for St. Joseph's. If all goes well, and Ma, you don't go causing trouble, we should be good to go as soon as Monday."

"Monday? That still seems like a long time off. That guy. You know that guy I told you about makes me very nervous. I told you he reminds me of a guy that scared me when I was younger. The guy was a mechanic. He worked on the fire engines."

"I have some good news for you. I did a little checking on your evil guy. It turns out he worked for the power company. Climbed poles and stuff, I'm assuming. He lived in Everett. You told me he was an auto mechanic in Somerville. Right. He's not your guy."

"Are you sure? They both did the same kind of thing he does with his face. You know, blinking his eyes, moving his eyebrows, that kind of thing."

"Lots of people have nervous facial tics. So you gotta stop worrying about him. Sure, he's creepy. But Ma, face it. He's not the only creepy one in here."

One of the things that always puzzled Sean was what his father had told him before he died. Willy said something about beating the shit out of a guy, almost killing him. He did this because of something he did to his mother. Willy had pointed to his eyes and then to his eyebrows. He was trying to tell Sean that the guy he almost killed did something funny with his eyes. His mother had an issue with a guy who did the same thing. Coincidence? Probably. He would not mention this to his mother. Sean was still convinced that this guy at the nursing home was not someone she knew from years back. But still? His father must have been incensed to almost kill a man over something to do with his mother. Once she got to the new nursing home, he would probe her. Now was not the right time. He needed to get her settled down.

"Can you dig a little deeper?"

"Sure. We'll talk later about what that guy did to you years ago."

Shirley turned away. Then she looked up at the ceiling.

"Let's say he threatened me. Real bad."

"Later. Okay?" said Sean.

"Just do a little more digging. Please."

"I have his old address. He lived with his daughter. If you want, I'll go visit with her."

"Yes. Please."

"Done. Do me a favor. Forget about that guy. Just keep thinking about St. Joseph's. You will be looking out onto the beach from your window. We can take walks. You can dip your toes into the freezing cold water. I'll get some fried clams at Sullivan's in Southie. We can eat them on the beach." Sean had wished it was going to be as easy as that. Unfortunately, there were still a lot of obstacles to overcome.

"I need some peace about that guy. Please keep checking."

"Fine." Sean hugged and kissed his mother and left.

Sean wondered what would happen if and when Shirley mentioned to Colleen that her son had visited with her after she had gone off her shift. Would this be the final straw in this short-lived relationship? Yet, when he thought about her, he still felt attracted to her. That was complicating his thought process.

As he walked to his car, he thought that an unannounced visit might at least be a way of keeping his options open. After all, Colleen lived just a few minutes away. He could use some excuse why he came later than usual to the nursing home. That was it. He decided. He would drop in. He would sort of make up to her, although he hadn't done anything wrong. He just felt that it was uncomfortable the last time he left her. Maybe he was the problem. His resolve strengthened. He would drive over to that crappy apartment building, put his Charger in jeopardy, and visit with her.

Again, he parked his car on the side street. It wasn't quite as dark as the first time. The apartment building looked better in the dark. But, unlike the last time he came here, this time he was firm. He would walk up those crappy stairs and knock on the door. He was determined today to set things right.

He knocked on the door. He almost said, "Boston Police, open up." In those few seconds, he wasn't quite sure what to expect. He knew that Colleen probably had been home from work for no more than an hour. He wondered if she would answer and sheepishly say that she was expecting someone. Maybe she would be in pajamas. Didn't matter. He was determined.

To his surprise, none of those things happened. Instead, Cassidy answered the door, which he thought odd since an eleven-year-old shouldn't open the door to just anyone.

"My mother's not here," Cassidy said with a sour expression.

"When will she be home?"

"Who knows?" Cassidy said casually.

"Is there someone with you?" asked Sean.

"You mean like a babysitter? Cassidy returned the volley.

"No. Of course not. You're what, eleven? I just figured you shouldn't be left alone in this..."

"Neighborhood? I can take care of myself. Do you want to wait? She will probably be home soon. My grandmother watches me when my mother stays out late. So, I figure she will be home soon."

She let Sean in.

Sean was now not so sure this was a good idea. It was almost seven o'clock, and he knew that Colleen had left work at six. It was just a fifteen-minute walk from the nursing home to the apartment. He wondered what she was doing.

He sat down on the very same couch where they had sex. That made him feel odd.

"Does your mother leave you alone very often?" This was a bad idea. What if Colleen never shows up? How long should he stay?

"Sometimes."

It was clear to Sean that Cassidy was in no mood for small talk. But he decided to persist. "Do you see your father very often?"

"He's dead," said Cassidy without an ounce of emotion.

"Oh, I'm so sorry. When did your father die?"

"Right after I was born. My mother said he was a real prick."

Sean was hardly a prude. On the contrary, his language was often offensive. But hearing that eleven-year-old girl say the word "prick" like it was nothing shook him. Now he wanted to hear more.

"Why do you say that?" asked Sean. He half expected the girl to say something like, "He screwed my mother over." He braced himself.

Instead, Cassidy softened a little, "He treated my mother bad."

She should have said "badly," but he was no expert on the English language. Besides, if he did develop a relationship with Colleen for some reason, he would have to win over this child. "How?"

"How what?" Cassidy continued to work on her iPad.

"How did he mistreat your mother." He wanted to ask her how her father died.

"You ask her. She was there. I wasn't."

"How did he die?"

"My mother killed him," Cassidy replied as if it was an answer to what grade she got on her book report.

"What?"

"Just kidding. Maybe. I don't know. He died in college or something. I just like to think that Mom killed him cause he treated her like crap."

~

The door opened. Colleen walked in. She had a take-out bag of Burger King food. She handed Cassidy the Burger King bag. "Please eat this in your room. We need private time."

Cassidy slowly walked to her bedroom and slammed the door. This time it was a real slam. The creaky apartment shook.

Sean thought he heard a couple of magnetic things fall off the refrigerator door in the kitchen.

"Eleven and going on twenty-five," Colleen repeated. Then, finally, she slumped into the chair. "What am I doing wrong?"

"She will grow out of it.".

"So why are you here?" said Colleen. She looked away. Her lips were barely opened when she said that.

"I think I gave you the wrong impression after last night."

"That's not one of the bullshit things guys say, is it? Waiting long?"

"No."

"I know what you are thinking. I shouldn't have left my kid alone." Colleen turned toward Sean, just a little close.

Sean could smell her. It was nice. He didn't want to talk about Cassidy, his mother, her dead ex-boyfriend. He pulled her close to him. He could smell her perfume. It was mixed with some kind of medical smell and just a hint of Burger King fries. It was all fine.

They kissed.

"I'm sorry about last night. Let's start over."

"Okay. Sure."

He kissed her gently goodnight and left. It was later than he thought. He raced down the three flights of stairs, out the front stoop, walked quickly around the corner to the side street where he parked his precious Charger. It sat there with four flat tires. Four slashed flat tires. He knew that Colleen had not been happy with him. She didn't seem surprised that he was in the apartment. Maybe she saw his car. It was obvious. Could she have slashed his tires? He figured that if someone wanted to do him harm, they would have stolen his wheels, not slashed his tires.

<h1 style="text-align:center">29</h1>

"I'm home." Paul Batty made every attempt to sound cheery when he entered the house. Even though he was deeply in debt to a loan shark, he was an embezzler and was in fear of getting caught. Emily raced to him as he entered the doorway. She gave him a big hug.

"Wow, you're in a great mood." Batty knew when Emily was in a great mood that usually was not good news for him.

"You know that I've been checking Zillow for the last couple of weeks. Just to check."

"Sure, you were looking for something a little bigger in Melrose." Batty didn't like the sound of this line of conversation. "Frankly, it's just the two of us. We don't need more space. Do we?"

"It's not the space, Paul. It's the, I don't know, the look."

"What look?" asked Batty.

"The 50's look. Anyway. I found the perfect house. Perfect. Perfect. Perfect." Emily was beaming.

"Great. What street is it on? How far away from here?"

"It's not in Melrose. I told you the other day. Remember when Carl and Mary came over. I saw Mary looking the house over. I was embarrassed. Guess where the perfect house is." Batty had seen this expression on Emily's face many times. He knew he had to be careful. One wrong move, one wrong grimace, or negative comment would send Emily crashing into an angry mess.

"Stoneham? Medford?"

"No. Medford? Are you kidding me? Winchester. I've always dreamt of living in Winchester."

Batty never recalled Emily ever mentioning Winchester. He would have to gently figure out a way of postponing any thought of buying a new house without creating a week-long silent treatment. That was often followed by hours of him begging forgiveness. Then giving in to her whims. Batty was struggling to keep his emotions in check.

"Remember Lori, my best friend from college?"

Batty wracked his brain. He dated Emily while in college and didn't recall any best friend named Lori. "I think so."

"Well, she and her new husband just moved from Melrose to Winchester. She just posted some great pictures on Facebook. Winchester has a much better school system. But, you know, when the time comes. It's just more professional."

Elite. That was the word Emily wanted to say.

"The house is only a mile from downtown, near route nine. So, it would be about the same commuting time for you."

"Route nine, huh? Not too close. You know the noise?"

"No. Not that close. What made this house a real steal was that it needs a lot of work. But it was in the right neighborhood. The price was reduced from 1.5 million to only 1.25. So even though it is not much bigger than our house, it had a much stronger resale value. I fear that given the housing market; someone will grab it out from under us."

"Sure, the housing market is strong. But..."

"So. This is my surprise. I put in a bid." Emily was almost jumping up and down. Her whole body was shaking. "I made an executive decision. I know you will love it."

"Don't I need to sign something? It will be in both of our names."

"Yeah, sure. It was one of those Docu-sign things. I just logged onto your email and signed it for you. It's official. We are moving to Winchester! We have enough for the down payment."

"We will clear at least two hundred and fifty thousand, easy for this house. We can always get a loan for the renovations, which shouldn't be more than fifty to one hundred thousand dollars. Plus, wouldn't it be fun to have projects to work on?"

As soon as Emily mentioned the word loan, he immediately pictured Butch Donovan. His heart was sinking fast. Paul had failed to tell Emily that he had taken out an equity loan on the Melrose house four months ago. He, like Emily, had forged the Docu-sign forms. As a result, the house was leveraged up to the current market value.

"When can you see the new house?"

"Soon. I'm pretty busy at work. Maybe this weekend."

"Can't you take time off work tomorrow?"

"Way too much to do tomorrow. It's Friday. Our busiest day."

Emily was disappointed but not deterred.

"Saturday, for sure, " demanded Emily.

"Saturday," said Batty with a fake smile.

It was a bit early for Shirley to go to sleep. If she fell asleep now, she would wake up in the middle of the night and have difficulty getting back to sleep. It was also a little early for Willy to appear on the ceiling. She needed to tell him about going to St. Joseph's. Then she heard the voices.

Suddenly, Tommy rolled into her room, and tears were streaming down his cheek. Finally, he moved to her bed.

"You are hearing this too, aren't you?

Tommy didn't answer. He couldn't.

Shirley put her hand on his.

His tears continued.

Then Marjorie came in. "Are you hearing them now?"

"Yes. What does it mean?"

Marjorie placed her hand on top of Shirley's and Tommy's. "It means that we are not crazy! Tommy, you understand?"

They stayed until the voices faded away.

"Whenever we hear the voices, let's get together. It feels so much safer and better.

Tommy rolled out of Shirley's room without looking back. Marjorie patted Shirley's hand. "Now we got to protect you from that monster, that twitching monster. We can now that we have the gang. The Bingo Gang."

They laughed as Marjorie left.

Willy appeared on the ceiling a few minutes later.

"Willy, I have to whisper. The staff thinks I'm going nuts cause I'm talking to myself. My friends are going to protect me. Sean is working hard to get me the hell out of here. But I still need to tell you my secret."

Willy looked down at Shirley with so much compassion.

"I don't think you would have loved me like you did if you knew my secret. I just couldn't. Soon maybe." Her eyes were drooping. She needed to sleep.

Willy faded from the ceiling.

She drifted into one of the more peaceful periods of sleep than she had in months. Unfortunately, it would be her last peaceful sleep at the Winter Hill Nursing and Rehabilitation Center.

Batty could not sleep. Once he had confirmed that Emily was sound asleep, he decided to pay the nursing home a visit. If Emily found him gone for some reason, he would say he got a call from Vinny, who had gotten a call from the charge nurse that there was a leak or flood or something at the nursing home, and he had to go there. But, of course, he wouldn't want to wake her.

Batty was a wreck on the drive from Melrose to Somerville. It was well after eleven PM. He almost near ran a stop sign on Main Street in

Medford. Good thing Medford was a dry town, meaning no one could buy alcohol there. It wouldn't have as many police patrolling the area.

Batty was plotting his next move. He had begun to incubate a plan to free him from his burdensome debts. The plan would also rid him of the embarrassment of going to jail for embezzlement.

He had two problems, not counting Emily. The first was that he had to pay back Millie's money from the cash fund to her family, who in his mind didn't give a goddam about her until she died. The second was the thirty thousand dollars he "borrowed" from the Winter Hill capital improvement account. He hadn't thought about it then, but his other problem was that he had fudged the books to look like he was doing more maintenance and repair than was being done. And Vinny was also in on this scheme.

He thought it was a brilliant plan.

Why he hadn't thought of it before was beyond him. He could kill two birds with one stone. It all centered on the business office on the first floor of the nursing home. To call it a business office was a bit of a stretch. It was just a closet with a computer, a printer, and file cabinets. The computer was also a server. The facility used accounting software designed specifically for nursing homes. The software system was called MediCalc. MediCalc was a product built by two brothers in Saugus in 2008 that was supposed to serve the entire community of nursing homes. The two brothers sold exactly ten copies of the software product. That was it. They collected a few thousand dollars a month on software maintenance. It was just enough to keep the brothers in business. When there was a bug or issue, the users called customer service. In reality, customer service was either Don or Joel, one of the two brothers. Enstat abandoned the brothers years ago. They standardized on a Bay State Software System but figured that converting from MediCalc to Bay State was an expense they would rather avoid. So, they allowed Winter Hill to stay on MediCalc as long as the two brothers were still in business.

Paul Batty knew enough about MediCalc to adjust the books not to attract attention. As long as Winter Hill was making a decent profit, Enstat didn't dig much. The problem for Batty was that the thirty thousand dollars was too big a gap to be able to hide.

Batty knew that his plan was brilliant because the brothers didn't have much of a backup and recovery data plan. Unlike the Bay State system, MediCalc ran a system synchronization routine only once every other week. In other words, the only record of the thirty thousand dollars that Batty had "borrowed" was contained on the hard drive in the business office. The thirty thousand dollars was moved on the books four days ago. The last synchronization was twelve days ago. Synchronization was a term the brothers used for backing up the hard drive. The next scheduled backup would happen in two days. So Batty would plan to ruin the hard drive so that the record of the missing thirty thousand dollars would not be recorded as part of the backup plan. While it wouldn't be a permanent fix, it would certainly buy him a lot more time. He figured that Enstat's accountants would take a long time to reconstruct the accounts. Even then, the chaos caused by the destroyed files would create enough confusion that maybe it would never be figured out. That was his hope anyway.

On his way from Melrose to Somerville, the plan took hold. A recent mishap had inspired him. Batty had this habit of putting his iPhone in his shirt pocket. He had done this for years with no problem. The other day, while going to the bathroom, he had to blow his nose. When he finished, he pulled out the Kleenex from his pocket, then dropped it. He bent over to pick it up. As he leaned over to pick up the Kleenex, his iPhone fell out of his shirt pocket into the urine-contaminated toilet. He quickly retrieved the phone and wiped it off. It was too late. The phone was completely dead. Naturally, he never backed up his phone. All his contacts, pictures, everything was drowned in a sea of urine.

This misfortune had inspired him. All he had to do was soak the computer and destroy Winter Hill's computer system's hard drive before the next backup. Water will kill a hard drive just like it killed his iPhone. So he figured the simplest way to drown the computer was to have the sprinkler system go off in the business office. A ruined hard drive meant that the records of the last two weeks would be gone. Perfect.

That meant that he would have to do it tonight or tomorrow night at the latest.

It would be a small fire. He would bring the patients' cash box and the only record of deposits and withdrawals into the business office. Then create a small wastepaper basket fire. It would generate enough heat to set the sprinkler system off. It would drown out the fire and conveniently the computer's hard drive. Sure, he would have to deal with some water damage to the other areas of the building, mainly in the rehab area, which no one used anyway. He would then be in the clear. Of course, he would be around to make sure the fire would be quickly extinguished. He even thought maybe he would even be a hero. He would be the guy that put out the fire. He liked that. In fact, he loved the plan. He felt better. He would have to figure out a way to invalidate the purchase and sale agreement on the house in Winchester. But, he thought, first things first. He needed to destroy the hard drive.

Just to make sure, he would have to ruin the hard drive in advance of the fire. So he would have to pour as much water on the computer before the fire.

That was the plan. Go to his office. Bring the patients' cash box to the business office. Vinny and that young nurse were the only people who knew that he had taken the cash box from the nursing station to his office. He would just say that he thought the cash box would be safer in the business office if anyone questioned him. Besides, no one was going to question him. It was just going to be a little fire. He kept saying to himself over and over again, no big deal.

He worked it out in his mind that one of the crazy patients was wandering around, probably that black guy, who always caused fires and was snooping around in the business office. Since the guy was senile anyway, he would flick an ash into the wastepaper basket, which Batty would make sure was full of paper. Then the fire would trigger the sprinkler system, which would douse the computer. After that, he would be free. Well, except for Emily.

He would never have to face Butch Donovan again.

Then he spotted a 7 Eleven, a couple of miles from the Winter Hill. It was just after eleven o'clock, and he wondered why they kept that name. He pulled into the tiny parking lot. He would buy a pack of cigarettes. He wondered if the store had video cameras. If, for some reason, someone would suspect that the fire was a setup, his face could be recorded buying a pack of what? Marlboro's, Winston's? Camels? That might raise a suspicion that the little fire might be intentional.

One other distraction that generated some anxiety was that he didn't know what brand of cigarette the black guy smoked. What if the arson people investigated? What if they found a Marlboro when the black guy smoked Lucky's or something? He started to worry. Then he quickly dismissed his worry as paranoia. It was only going to be a small fire, then a big splash that would ruin the computer. No arson investigation. He was being silly.

Batty did spot the video camera at the 7 Eleven. He made sure his face was turned away, just in case. Then he made a decision. He bought a pack of Merit 100s, the brand he used to smoke in college. He made sure the clerk gave him a pack of matches
. After he made his purchase, continuously looking guilty, he raced out of the 7 Eleven to the Winter Hill.

30

When Batty arrived on the second floor, Lauren was half asleep at the nursing station. "Paul. Why are you here?"

"Those guys at corporate need a stupid report tomorrow. I couldn't sleep, so I thought I would do it now. Things quiet?"

"Yeah"

"Okay. I'll be in my office. I feel uncomfortable with the patient's cash box in my office. So I'm moving it to the business office, in case anyone is looking for it," said Paul.

"Sure."

Paul's office was at the end of the A-wing on the second floor, directly across from Shirley's room. He went to his office. Took the cash box. He had to pass by the nursing station to get to the elevator. "Heading to the business office." He told Lauren.

She grunted in return.

The elevator came right away. Batty pressed the first-floor button. Tommy was dozing a few feet away. The door opened to the deadly quiet first floor, he rushed out of the elevator and passed the still empty first-floor nursing station

He muttered, "Where is the nurse on duty? Who cares?" She wasn't there. He opened the double doors to the rehab rooms and entered the tiny business office. There was the computer humming. Not for long. He hurried to find papers to stuff into the wastepaper basket, filled it with plenty of fuel and spoke to himself, "Not too much. Don't want to burn the place down. Just enough smoke to set off the sprinkler."

He planned to return to his office to ensure Lauren would witness that he was in his office. But instead, he went back to the second floor and passed Lauren. "I just put the patients' cash box in the business office. It should be fine there."

Lauren yawned and just nodded.

Batty then walked to his office. He looked confused. He continued talking to himself, "Let's see. Now back downstairs to drown the computer. I've got to avoid walking by Lauren again. Shit. Great. The outside fire stairs." He was sweating now. "I'll have to open the outside door." This was a risk since a police car, or fire engine could be speeding by, and the noise would bellow throughout the building by opening the door. If Lauren somehow caught him taking the fire escape, she could wonder why he just didn't take the elevator to get to the first floor. This door had no alarm.

He was a wreck. No choice, he thought.

He opened the fire door. Once outside, he eased it almost closed. As Sean had done earlier, he stuffed that little piece of wood between the door and the door jam. If Lauren caught him outside, he would say that he just needed a little air and didn't want to bother anyone. It didn't matter. There was no police car or sirens. He made sure the wood piece was firmly in place to ensure the door didn't close since the door automatically locked from the outside.

It worked. Now Batty walked around to the front entrance to let himself in again. This was nowhere as simple as he thought it was going to be. Thankfully for him, the first-floor charge nurse was still amongst the missing. He made a mental note to check on where she had been. For now, that was a blessing.

～

Bill rested on his bed, looking at the TV.

Lying on his bed, Ellis stared at the wall as if deep in thought. He was fully dressed.

Bill shut the TV off with the remote and turned to his side. His eyes were heavy. He opened them wide. Then his eyes closed, then opened. His body jumped, his eyes closed, and his breathing was now regular.

Ellis looked over at Bill and smiled.

The corridor was empty. The only sounds were a TV from a distant room and water dripping into a bucket.

Lauren flipped through a magazine. She locked on to the clock. "Christ, it's not even midnight yet."

Ellis walked over to Bill's bed and leaned over into the bed. Ellis nodded. He pulled open his storage cabinet and pulled out Millie's old satchel. He stopped and looked over to Bill, who didn't move. Ellis took a big, deep smell of Millie's satchel. Then put it back into the storage cabinet.

Bill was snoring. Ellis smiled.

Ellis and Bill shared room 202, the furthest room on the second floor from the nursing station of the B wing. Winter Hill Nursing and Rehabilitation Center had two floors. Each floor had just two wings, the A-wing and the B-wing. The first floor consisted of the lobby, where the original owners had spared no expense. The lobby walls were covered with actual cherry wood paneling. On one side of the lobby was a beautiful matching cherry wood nursing station that doubled as a reception desk. The furniture in the lobby had been expensive in its day. Now it just looked dated and worn out. Occasionally patients would linger there, but since most of the residents were on the second floor, there wasn't much activity in the lobby. Since there were no rules or curfews, patients could roam around.

Ellis left his room, turned, then lumbered to the elevator, his walker making an odd sound of tap, tap, tap from the one foot covered with a tennis ball and the other bare metal. So every movement of the walker made a sound. He took the elevator to the lobby.

The original idea of the facility was to offer all kinds of rehabilitation services. The A-wing of the first floor, which was to the left of the lobby, consisted of two large rehabilitation rooms, the business office, and the electrical room. These rooms were directly below the dining room and the kitchen, the same kitchen where Millie had died.

There was no nurse at the cherry wood nursing station, which was to the left of the elevator. On either side of the lobby, there were double doors. The B-wing had six rooms to Ellis's left, numbered 101 to 106, three on one side of the corridor and three on the other. He walked down the B wing corridor. Two women shared Room 103, which was under his room.

He poked his head into Room 103 and walked in. The orientation of the beds, the TV, and the little side tables was the same as his room. So, he moved directly to the storage cabinets.

There was plenty of light from the parking lot to see the unmistakable silhouette of a purse owned by one of the residents.

The original idea of the first-floor layout of rooms on the B-wing was for short time patients. They would be younger people whose stay at the facility was strictly for rehabilitation. That stopped ten years before. The facility was now exclusively occupied by people waiting to die. The residents of room 103 were Barbara Parrish and Joyce George, both in their 90's.

Barbara had left her purse on the roller table instead of putting it in the storage cabinet.

Ellis grabbed it.

It wouldn't have made a difference had she put it in the storage cabinet. Ellis would have stolen it, either way. So then, to make things even easier for him, Barbara had the bed closest to the door.

He took a deep whiff of her purse, then slipped it under his arm. In Somerville, hardly anyone ever called it a purse unless they talked about some small change purse with that little clip on the top. In Somerville, all purses were called pocketbooks. What Barbara would most likely say in the morning was, "who stole my pockabook." That's how people in Somerville pronounced pocketbook.

Ellis planned to slip back to his room and stash the pocketbook in his storage cabinet alongside Millie's old satchel.

Then he heard a noise and moved to the sound.

~

When Batty turned the light on in the rehab area, he was startled by an awful scouring sound. Cockroaches. For a moment, he felt a little guilt. He recalled what that pain in the ass Duffy woman had complained about. Bugs, or was it rats? Anyway, after this situation was to be over, he would increase the cycle of pest maintenance. He told himself after this little affair, he would begin to run this place much better. No more cutting back on maintenance. Screw those corporate assholes.

His mind raced. Maybe when he was in the clear, he would confront Emily and stop her crazy spending. All of this was her fault. He wouldn't have had to deal with Butch Donovan. Unlike Donovan, he was basically a good, honest guy. Sure, it was Emily's fault. But, once this was fixed, things were going to get better. He knew it.

Now he had to find a bucket. He would need a fair amount of water to ruin the computer. Why hadn't he thought of this before? The supply room was on the second floor. He had never been inside it, but he assumed there were plenty of buckets in there. After all, the ceiling was constantly leaking. There were buckets always on the floor. He should have thought of that when he was on the second floor. It was too late now. He noticed a plant in a big planter.

He took the plant into the business office. He removed the plant from the big vase. Damn, there was a couple of holes in the bottom. He would have to stuff some paper towels in it to keep the water inside it. Why hadn't he thought of a bucket? The bathroom was on the other side of the business office. He would have to fill the bucket quietly, then douse the computer, then start the fire, then race back to his office. Back at his office, he would smell the smoke, race down, and save the nursing home.

Not so fast. After Batty filled the planter with water, he turned around and walked right into Ellis.

"Jesus Christ." Batty jumped. The planter was now leaking water all over Batty's shoes. His perfect plan was crumbling before his very eyes. "Why aren't you in your room?"

Ellis just smiled. Then his eyes blinked quickly, and his eyebrows moved up and down. He opened and closed his mouth rapidly and clicked his tongue.

Batty stared at him in horror.

Ellis turned around and walked through the double doors into the first-floor lobby. He hit the button for the elevator, then the elevator came, the door opened, and he walked in. His facial movements continued.

Batty just stared, shaken.

Ellis had Barbara's pocketbook in plain view. After the doors closed, Ellis pushed the pocketbook into his face and took a deep, deep whiff.

That was it for Batty's plan for the night. No drowned computer. No fire. He was crushed. He had to clean up the water on the floor. He had to sneak back up the fire escape and return to his office. Then he had to put the plant back together.

Ellis had shaken him. If he even could talk, which Batty had no idea about, he witnessed Batty being on the first floor when he was supposed to be on the second floor. How could he explain that he had a leaking plant bucket in his arms in the middle of the night? His only hope would be if there were some kind of investigation and if Ellis would even volunteer information for some reason, no one would believe him.

Batty fixed the plant. Then he made his way up the fire escape. Thank God, he thought, the fire door was not fully shut. Once inside the dining room, he kicked the wooden piece to the side and gently closed the door. Thankfully for him, Broadway was quiet, with no police cars or fire engine noises entering the building. He returned to the safety of his office. The scheme would have to wait until tomorrow. Only this time, he would plan things out a bit better. He started to feel calmer. Okay, this was a test run. He would need a bucket. He would have to figure out a better way of covering his tracks. "Yeah," he muttered, "It was going to work." But he lost a day. The two brothers at MediCalc would be accessing the computer the day after tomorrow.

He had to do the deed tomorrow.

PART III

THE SCARS HEALED

<h1 align="center">31</h1>

"Quiet night?" Colleen's shift started at 6:00 AM. Lauren was ready to leave that very instant.

"Yes." She picked up her stuff and was at the elevator. Tommy moved out of the way to let her pass once the elevator door opened. "Oh, Paul was here late last night. He moved the patients' cash box to the business office, just in case you needed it. Not that anyone ever needs it." She entered the elevator without saying another word.

Tommy shook his head. While Tommy couldn't talk, Colleen knew his expressions were explicit. Tommy didn't like Lauren.

Colleen was still mad at Sean, despite the impromptu visit and attempting to make up. Maybe she would get over it. But she had her doubts about him. So, she would ride it out for a while and see how things went.

However, she did not have doubts about the Winter Hill Nursing and Rehabilitation Center. It was terrible. Forget about the building, the services, the cleanliness, or the bugs. Yes, she had seen the bugs but kept her mouth shut.

The one thing she was sure about was that these patients were treated horribly. And that continued to bother her. Every time she saw the way Lauren treated them, she thought back to her father in that nursing home in Arlington. They were all the same. The nurses, the aides. They would talk to each other while putting the patients to bed like they were cleaning shelves at Dunkin. It reminded her of a couple of days ago at the Star Market when the cashier talked to her friend, the bagger. The cashier continued to brag about how she was making out with her boyfriend the night before. It was as if the girls had no idea that real live people were right in front of them. It was as if they were unaware that they were dealing with real people, with real feelings, that got hurt. Hurt a lot. Like how Serj, the now-dead father of Cassidy, didn't give a goddam good shit about his baby and the lives he shattered. Not just hers, but her mother and father.

She had wanted to scream at the cashier. Now she wanted to scream at Lauren, Batty, and Vinny.

That's how everyone around here treats the patients. That's what killed her father. Not the lousy liver or senility. It was the cruel treatment. She hated them all for it. It was a blessing that her father died. A true blessing from God himself. As much as she missed him, she was glad he didn't have to be treated like that. If she could have, she would have put him out of his misery. She only wished she had done that.

Bam.

Her thoughts were interrupted by a loud crash. It sounded like a body landing on the floor, coming from room 208. Room 208 was diagonally across from the nursing station and next to Shirley's room. That was Caroline's room.

Colleen raced into room 208. Martha and Mary were there.

Martha said, "We were moving the patient out of bed and into her wheelchair when I slipped on the hard floor. Mary couldn't catch her, and she fell. I don't think she got hurt."

Colleen had just been thinking about the careless cashier and bagger not paying any attention to her. She figured that Martha and Mary were probably embroiled in some personal conversation. Unfortunately, they weren't paying attention and lost their grip on Caroline's near lifeless body. "What's the patient's name?"

"Room 208," answered Mary.

"I didn't ask what her room number is. What is the patient's name? Mary?"

"I don't know."

"Martha?"

"Me either."

"Well, maybe if you took a little time even to know the patient's name, you would pay better attention to her."

Mary jumped in, "She's fine. Didn't hit her head or anything." Then the two picked her up and placed her into her wheelchair.

"I'll have to submit a report." Colleen was enraged.

"Nothing happened."

"You dropped her on the floor."

"No, we didn't. She slid off the chair and onto the floor. We didn't drop her." Martha came to Mary's defense. "We've got it covered. No report is needed. You're new. These people are like dead weight. Or like dead fish." Mary laughed out loud.

"Don't. Not for a minute, laugh about this. I'm filling out a report." Colleen raced out of the room and bumped into a disheveled Paul Batty. Batty was heading into his office diagonally across the corridor from Caroline's room.

Batty hadn't had much sleep. By the time he arrived home, it was close to 3:00 AM. The run-in with Ellis had utterly unnerved him. Even though he had told himself that he had executed a perfect trial run, by the time he snuck into bed, he wasn't at all at peace with this plan. For the rest of the night, he continued to run various scenarios in his mind of how he could pull off this plan. Would it be better to do the fire during dinner, when none of the patients would be inclined to wander around? How would he get the buckets into the business office without arousing suspicion? Then he discounted that idea since he wouldn't know who to pin on putting the cigarette butt into the trashcan. Finally, he was distraught and exhausted.

"What's the problem?" he asked as he ran into Colleen.

"The aides. That's the problem. They dropped one of the patients on the floor. We should file a report."

"Did you witness this?" Batty did not want to deal with this. He just wanted to hide into his friendly, cozy, secluded office and work out the finer details of his plan to avoid prison and never, ever have to deal with Butch Donovan again.

"No, but I heard a loud bang. Then I saw Caroline on the floor."

"Look. It was probably an accident. The aides have a lot to deal with. So you don't need to file a report. End of story. Understand!"

"Mr. Batty. She is not dead! The staff needs to be more careful. Goddamn it. Treat them like real people." Colleen turned from Batty, face red, and ran to the nursing station.

Batty yelled down the corridor at her. "No report needed. Maybe you should think of another career." Batty went into his office. The last thing he wanted to deal with was an emotional nurse and anyone investigating. He just had too many things on his mind.

Now it was Emily. The thought of confronting her during this period of personal stress bothered him greatly. Maybe the best thing to do was get the money he needed for the deposit on the house. He knew there were a lot of contingencies outlined in the standard real estate purchase and sales agreement. So, at least for now, he would put down the deposit on the new house, then figure out how to get out of the sale. But to do that, he would need more money.

He would call Butch Donovan.

Regardless of the intricate details of the plan, there would be no choice but to carry out his plan tonight, probably after dinner, but not too late. He would ask Butch to help him since this probably was a two-person job anyway.

He called Butch. He would be there at seven tonight, with ten thousand dollars in cash, just enough for the deposit on the house. Batty decided to visit the first floor to get a better feel for pulling off his plan. As he walked by Colleen at the nursing station, he stared straight ahead. He made a mental note that he would fire her when this whole thing blew over. As he passed the nursing station to the elevator, he had to work his way by Tommy, in his usual position. Batty had no time for him. "Out of the way."

Tommy didn't budge. If there was such an expression as "fuck you," Tommy wore it, and Batty understood. He pushed him out of the way and pressed the elevator button. Batty got a severe anxiety attack on the short trip down the elevator. Maybe it was the lack of sleep.

Again, there was no one at the first-floor reception desk. What the hell. Again, like last night, it was probably better. The business office was empty. Right next to the business office was the utility closet. He had never paid it much attention. Now he was curious about it. He opened the door. There was an electrical panel buzzing away, boxes with some kind of spare parts, a couple of packages of light bulbs, and two buckets. And in the corner, a fire extinguisher.

The anxiety attack settled down. This could work. He would douse the computer. Make sure that the hard drive was no good. Then he would return to his office. He would call to make sure his receptionist was nowhere to be found. Donovan would drop the lighted cigarette into the wastepaper basket, text him then leave by the front door. Batty would smell the smoke and run downstairs, put the fire out with the fire extinguisher after the sprinkler went off. Then he would be the hero. He would have removed all the cash from the cash box and make sure that fire burned what was inside.

He thought the plan would work. He returned to the second floor, eked his way around Tommy, and returned to his office.

Then all hell broke loose.

"Bingo. Bingo. Bingo."

Phyllis was the first to figure out what was going on. Someone from the Bingo Gang was crying out for help. One of her favorite movies was *West Side Story*. In the opening sequence, one of the gang members from one of the gangs, called the Jets, was getting beaten up by the rival gang. The poor kid screamed out, "Jets. Jets". Then the Jets gang members came running from all directions to save the kid. The call to action of Bingo reminded her of the scene from *West Side Story*. After all, she was a member of the Bingo Gang, and one of the gang members was in trouble. The only problem was that Phyllis couldn't walk, never mind run. It was still before breakfast. She wasn't sure who from the gang was up from bed. She spun around and raced her wheelchair over to her roommate, Ruthie.

"Quick. Get out of bed. Someone from the gang is in trouble." Luckily, Ruthie was mobile enough to move from her bed into her wheelchair.

"C'mon. I think it's coming from Shirley's room. Phyllis and Ruthie had rooms on the Broadway side of the building. Directly across from her room was the second-floor deck. She spotted Bill and Bones sharing a cigarette on the deck as she left the room. She wheeled across the corridor and banged on one of the glass panes on the door.

Bill opened the door.

"Bingo. Bingo. Bingo." The screaming continued.

"Hear that?" yelled Phyllis.

Bones joined in. "What is that?

"Are you an idiot? We made a pact, remember? When someone is in trouble, they yell 'Bingo. So get your ass in gear," bellowed Phyllis.

Meanwhile, Ruthie was out of bed. "Jesus, lead us into the battle between good and evil."

The four gang members raced as quickly as possible, given their disabilities, down the B-wing. Then, finally, they passed the Tommy-less elevator.

"Where's Tommy?" Bones looked back and forth.

They passed the empty nursing station.

Then they saw Tommy leaving Room 208. He waved his good arm in the motion to come quickly.

Room 208 was Caroline's room.

Batty and Colleen stood silently just inside the door. Shirley was crying.

Caroline was lying on the floor. Her head dipped in a pool of blood.

She was dead.

Bones and Bill walked over to Shirley.

"She was murdered!" yelled Shirley. "He is going to kill us all."

Batty sighed.

"The aides dropped her not an hour ago. The aides denied it, but I didn't believe them. She hit her head and lost consciousness. She slipped out of her chair onto the floor. She was barely alive," said Colleen.

"You people don't get it. She was killed, just like Bill's dog Rudy and Nelson. It's a pattern," said Shirley.

Batty yelled. "Everyone, leave this room. Now. You, call one of the aides and call Vinny to clean up the floor." Then, he commanded Colleen, "and don't make up situations you did not witness. I plan to talk with you later."

"Clean up? Are you serious? Destroy evidence. This is a crime scene," blasted Shirley.

"No. Mrs. Duffy. This is a normal occurrence at a nursing home. Now either go back to your room or get ready for breakfast."

Shirley turned around, leaned over her wheelchair, and tried to pat Caroline on the head. But it was too far a reach. She turned her chair around and slowly and reverently rolled out the door.

Phyllis looked away.

Ellis appeared. He smiled, took his index finger and middle finger, pointed them at his eyes, and then pointed at Shirley, Phyllis, and Ruthie. He repeated the gesture.

Shirley hurled her wheelchair directly at him. "Bastard."

Ellis easily avoided her.

Batty yelled, "Stop this now. Would you like me to write this tendency towards violence in my report to St. Joseph's?" He stormed out of the room and walked with his head down across the corridor to his office. He entered it and banged the door shut. The whole corridor shook.

Bill and Bones and the rest of the Bingo Gang walked out of Room 208.

"I'm starved. How long to breakfast?" Bones headed to the nursing station to hang out.

Tommy rolled back to his perch next to the elevator.

By this time, Marjorie had made it outside Caroline's room.

"Where were you?" Phyllis chided Marjorie.

"I heard a noise, but I didn't know what it was." Marjorie's room was at the far end of the B-wing. "By the time I figured out what was going on, it was all over."

"Well, next time, lady, pay attention. Caroline was murdered," replied Phyllis.

"Jesus." Marjorie immediately realized that Ruthie was listening. "Sorry, Ruthie. I wasn't exactly taking the name of our Lord and Savior in vain. I was praying for Caroline's soul sort of."

"Doesn't matter. We are all going to be murdered." Ruthie rolled away, heading to the nursing station.

"Phyllis, Caroline was murdered. Monday, I am supposed to be leaving. I don't think I will make it," said Shirley

"Your son is a cop, right. Can't he arrest that twitching son of a bitch?" asked Phyllis.

"We need evidence."

They both rolled silently away.

32

Shirley called Sean, "I found poor old Caroline lying on the floor. Dead. Blood was everywhere. Then Ellis looked at me and pointed to me like I was going to be next. Sean, I'm convinced that Ellis killed her. Batty doesn't do anything. Can you get me out of here? Please?"

"Ma. Maybe we can do something over the weekend. I'll be by later today."

"I panicked and tried to ram Ellis with my wheelchair," added Shirley.

"In front of Batty?"

"Yeah."

"Shit. I really wished you hadn't done that. Well, we still have a lot on Mr. Batty. Please don't do anything like that again. Please."

Sean needed to do something soon. So, he called into the station to tell the on-call Sergeant that he needed to take a sick day or personal day to take care of a family matter. But, before he headed to St. Joseph's to pick up his aunt Edie, he needed to learn more about Colleen and maybe a bit more about Ellis.

He dropped into Somerville City Hall to check out who was listed on the birth certificate for Cassidy McCarthy. City Hall was located right next to Somerville High, where he graduated. He hadn't passed by his old school in some time. While he had some good times there, it also reminded him of the tensions with his father that simmered during his high school days. He also knew how upset these tensions made his mother. Maybe he could have been less of a pain in the ass. He wasn't sure. Maybe his father wasn't all to blame, his father was dead now, and his mother was in distress. It was his job to help her out.

While at City Hall, he also wanted to find out if Theodore Ellis was born in Somerville, just to make sure.

The city clerk confirmed that there was no record of Ellis being born or living in Somerville either. He knew that all records before the '70s were manual and not consistently accurate.

This just didn't add up in this mind. He would still follow up.

He found the birth certificate for Cassidy McCarthy. She was born to Colleen McCarthy and a Serj Sarkissian. Serj's address was 4 Douglas Ave in Somerville. He found the current residents at 4 Douglas Ave were Kohar and Zareh Sarkissian. Probably Serj's parents. He also checked out Serj's death certificate. The cause of death was listed as an accident involving an automobile, but not an automobile accident. Odd, he thought.

He decided to pay the Sarkissian's a visit. 4 Douglas Ave was on the corner of Edgar Ave., a rather steep hill right off Main Street, near Paul Revere Park. Sean was a bit apprehensive about making a cold visit. First, he had no jurisdiction in Somerville. Second, he didn't want to tell these poor people even why he was bringing up something as painful as the death of their son. Was he taking advantage of being a police officer? He was also concerned about discovering something terrible, something awful.

There were no parking spots on the little side street of Douglas Ave. So, he had to park on steep Edgar Ave, some ways down the hill, and pull his front tires (his brand-new front tires) toward the curb like it says to do in the Registry of Motor Vehicle drivers handbook, which he had not looked at in twenty years. He labored up the hill and turned left onto Douglas Ave. There were half a dozen three-deckers jammed onto that little street. This part of the city was often called Armenia Town though many Armenians had fled to more spacious communities. Not the Sarkissians. He should have checked to make sure that Kohar and Zareh were parents and not siblings. Screw it.

Sean was a little out of breath by the time he reached the front porch of 4 Douglas Ave. He opened the front door and entered a little hallway with a large staircase facing him on the left. His luck, he thought, the couple lived on the third floor. To his left was his salvation. The Sarkissian's lived on the first floor. There were three doorbells with handwritten labels next to each. He decided to knock as most good police officers would.

Mrs. Sarkissian opened the door a crack keeping the chain lock engaged.

"Yes?" An older attractive woman peeked through the crack.

Sean flashed his Boston Police badge. "Mrs. Sarkissian?"

She nodded.

Sean hurried his speech to avoid spooking poor Mrs. Sarkissian. "Detective Sean Duffy with the Boston Police. Nothing to be concerned about. I just want to ask you some questions about your son, Serj."

"My son Serj died eleven years ago. What is this about?"

"I know. I met his daughter, Cassidy, and her mother. I have a couple of questions. This will take just a minute."

"I have never seen my granddaughter since the accident. Her mother has never allowed us to see her."

"Why is that?"

"You'll have to ask that McCarthy woman. We have never done anything to her. We continue to grieve over our son. He wasn't perfect, but he had a good heart. So what did you want to know?"

"Well. Her mother is a nurse at the Winter Hill Nursing Home. You know. On Broadway."

"I know it. Not far from here. You said you are a Boston Police Officer." Mrs. Sarkissian queried him. She had a slight accent.

Sean was not sure how to approach this. "My mother is at Winter Hill and…."

"I see. And you are wondering if she is the person she appears to be. Is that it?"

"Well. Yes."

"Oh, she is sweet as pie when you first meet her. When Serj started dating her, we were thrilled. Such a lovely, sweet girl at first. Pretty. Shy. Or so we thought. Then Serj started to get a different picture. She was fine one minute. Then she got crazy the next. She accused him of cheating, of having sex with other girls. Serj broke it off. By then, she was pregnant. I asked him. He never cheated on her. While she was pregnant, she continued to call him all the time. By then, he had a new girlfriend."

"Did she leave him alone then?"

"No. Didn't matter. She continued to call," said the woman.

"So, would you say she harassed him?"

"Let me guess. You met this lovely, sweet girl while visiting your mother at the nursing home. Then you got involved. Like Serj, you started to see something that disturbed you. Am I close?"

"Something like that," answered Sean.

"So, this isn't official police business, is it?"

"No. I'm sorry, I shouldn't have disturbed you. I'll go." Sean backed away from the door.

"What do you want to know?" Mrs. Sarkissian continued to talk through the tiny opening in the door.

"How did your son die? The report said it was an accident."

The poor woman gave out a deep sigh.

Sean now could smell something cooking. Like stew. For some reason, it made him sad. Even though his home life wasn't perfect, there were good times as well. Birthdays and Sunday dinners at home. What would those Sunday dinners be like at the Sarkissian's after their son had been taken at such a young age? Would the couple spend the rest of their lives sad, grieving, eating their stew that was now cooking, not saying a word? Sean wished that he had dropped the whole Colleen thing. It was over.

"I don't know exactly. On Saturday, June 23rd at 11:12 in the morning. See, you remember tiny details," said Mrs. Sarkissian.

This didn't make Sean feel any better.

"My son came storming into the house. He had parked his old Plymouth around the corner on Edgar Ave. But, as usual, there were no parking spots on this little street."

"I know. I had to park down the hill."

"Then you see how steep it is. Someone had slashed one of his tires."

Fuck, was the first word that entered Sean's head voice.

"I peeked out the side window that looks over Edgar Avenue. She was standing right next to his car. She was standing there with the baby in a carriage. My son…"

She stopped.

Sean thought the pause was long, but it was probably not more than a couple of seconds. He wished he hadn't disturbed that poor woman. Maybe she hadn't thought about her son. But, unfortunately, he had dragged up his memory. He felt more and more guilty.

"Serj screamed at us. 'She did it. That bitch. I know she did.' Why she was there, we don't know. Maybe to gloat. Maybe she slashed his tire. Who knows?"

"Slashed his tire?" Sean was unnerved. All he could think about was his four slashed tires from last night.

"My son raced back outside to change the tire. The next thing I know is that she and her baby came banging on my door yelling that the car fell on top of him while he was changing the tire." Poor Mrs. Sarkissian filled up. Tears poured out of her sad eyes.

"I'm sorry for bringing this up." Sean wanted to run.

She collected herself. "He should never have jacked the car up on such a grade. The police said the emergency brake was set, but you know, in an old car, the emergency brakes never hold."

"Yes, I know. I've had my share of old cars." Sean thought that was a stupid thing to say.

"What we never figured out was why he was under the car. If the brake failed and the car rolled forward off the jack, it should have just dropped down on the rim. Why was he so far under the car?"

"What do you really think happened?" asked Sean.

"She was harassing him and yelling at him because she had to take care of the baby. So he probably told her off. But then, I shouldn't even think this."

"What?"

"She pushed him under the car, causing the car to roll off the jack. I shouldn't have said that. Of course, we have no way of knowing. But I bet she upset him. Then he lost concentration. I just don't know."

"You blame her?"

"Yes. Either directly or indirectly. I'm pretty sure she slashed his tire. If she didn't do that, he would still be alive today. I know that."

"Thanks. I'm sorry that I had to bring this up."

"Don't get involved with that woman. This is a warning from a mother. A mother knows. We have instincts."

Sean thanked her and left. He trekked down the Edgar Ave. grade. With a car jacked up, it wouldn't take much to push someone under the car and set the car rolling until it fell. He shuddered. He wondered if Cassidy was right when she said that her mother had killed her father. Would Colleen have implied that to her daughter? Jesus. Sean had witnessed Colleen's changing moods, but murder? Would that put his mother in jeopardy? Maybe everyone at the nursing home. Crazy. Crazy thoughts. Sure, Serj's mother was devastated by the death of her son. But it made sense that the car would be unstable jacked up on such a steep grade as Edgar Ave. It was stupid to change a tire on a steep grade. Doesn't every owner's manual warn you to always use a jack on level ground? He needed to get his head on straight.

Yet?

Then Mrs. Sarkissian's words echoed in his brain. Mothers have instincts. His mother had strong instincts. She had such a strong intuition. She could meet a person and know that person's character immediately, just by spending a few minutes with that person. He committed to himself to put those crazy thoughts about Colleen out of his head and focus on his mother's strong intuition about that guy at the nursing home. He needed to concentrate on getting answers on Ellis.

Now he headed to St. Joseph's to pick up his Aunt Edie. Then, he mused, maybe she could fill in the blanks with her, as she would say, her enhanced intuition.

33

Shirley didn't join the rest of the Bingo Gang at the nursing station. She stayed behind just outside Caroline's room. The pitiful thing was just lying there. While alive, even though Caroline was virtually unaware of anything, Shirley thought that she could understand her. She would tell her little stories about her life. She could tell her anything. Shirley laughed and whispered to herself, "She could certainly keep a secret." Now she was murdered. And worse, no one was going to do anything about it.

The relative silence of the A-wing was utterly disrupted. The EMTs had arrived with the sterile stretchers to take Caroline away. There would be no autopsy, no collection of evidence.

"Shit," muttered Shirley. Martha and Mary arrived on the scene as well.

Colleen, as ordered, had called the aides to help with the cleanup. The aides were only responsible for stripping the bed and emptying Caroline's storage closet. After that, they packaged all her stuff. It was as if she was never there. Then Vinny came in with this pail and bucket of water.

Shirley had had enough. She rolled back into her room.

～

Colleen gave the aides their instructions. She stood and watched for a few minutes, then walked back toward the nursing station.

Then she stopped.

She heard the laughter.

She walked toward Room 208, stopped, and listened. Vinny, Martha, and Mary were in the room.

"We can't have dogs in a nursing home. The mangy mutt was shitting all over the parking lot. Was it my job to clean up the dog's shit and piss? I had to put a stop to it. Someone was bound to step in the shit, get it on their shoe and track it all over the place. The dog was half dead anyway."

"This patient was a pain the ass. But, yeah, she was not half dead. She was mostly dead. I heard that in a movie!"

Vinny, Martha, and Mary laughed out loud

Colleen stormed into the room. "You have no respect for the dead. She was a human being with a heart and a soul. Thank God she is in a better place. You people should be ashamed of yourselves."

Vinny was the first to respond, "Hey Nursey. Go fuck yourself. Why don't you complain to Mr. Batty? Just so you know. He's going to fire you very soon anyway. Complain all you want. You are fucking history."

Mary piled on. "What a pussy you are. Go back to wherever you came from. Complain to Batty about us? Don't you know that we give Paul whatever he wants every Tuesday? Do you think he is going to fire us? Fuck off."

"You'll be sorry." Colleen stormed off. She was consumed with rage.

～

"Where is Shirley?" asked Marjorie. "She missed breakfast."

"Marjorie, please go check on her. I'm worried about her," said Phyllis.

Marjorie knocked on Shirley's door, even though she could see Shirley just sitting in her wheelchair looking down at the floor.

"I was proud of you for trying to run down that awful murderer, whatever his name is." Marjorie sat on Shirley's bed.

"I don't feel like talking. Sorry. Did you draw the short straw?" asked Shirley.

"I guess you could say that. I was volunteered, but I didn't mind. I wanted to talk to you about this morning, and you know, about the voices."

"I'm so sad. I had such high hopes of getting out of here. Don't get me wrong. I love all of you. But this place. I just can't stand it and with that guy here. I feel we are all doomed. We are all going to die, like poor Caroline."

"We don't know what happened to her. I heard rumors that the aides dropped her. Maybe that killed her."

"I don't see how she would have fallen out of her chair without some help. Anyway, I tried to ram into Ellis, or whatever his real name is. So now Batty will write that in the report to St. Joseph's. They will never take me now."

"You don't know that. Didn't you say that your son was helping you?"

"Yes. But it is probably too late."

"My son Benny has not visited me since… I don't even remember. He lives in Pawtucket. He's an accountant. He keeps saying he will come to visit, but he is always busy with clients, and his car is old and a hundred other excuses. It's only about 80 miles from here to Pawtucket. He could have made an effort." Marjorie gazed off into space.

"I'm sorry. You said you wanted to talk about the voices."

"Well, we know that Tommy hears them too. There are two explanations. The first is that all three of us have shared, I don't know, experiences. Sometimes people can transmit ideas to other people. So, the three of us are having the same dream at the same time."

Shirley gave Marjorie a doubtful expression. "I find that hard to believe. What's the second explanation?"

"Oh. Ghosts. Spirits that got trapped in here and can't get out? Since you, Tommy, and I all have connections to the fire at the old rest home, the spirits are trying to communicate with us."

"You believe that?"

"I do. I believe that one of the spirits is my grandma. She wants to communicate with me. Maybe if she could, she could escape the sort of never-never land she exists in."

"I see my Willy every night on the ceiling. But I always figured he was just in my imagination. So why do the other ghosts make noises, and Willy is silent? See, I don't buy it. Like you said in the van the other day. Maybe we are all just crazy. Maybe that's what happens when you get old and are trapped in this god-forsaken place. It's no wonder we are all hearing voices."

Sean sat in a padded chair overlooking an ornate fireplace at St. Joseph's next to Edie. His mind was racing. The visit with the Sarkissians exhausted him emotionally. He just felt guilty dragging up the memory of that poor woman's son. Now he didn't know what to think about Colleen. Should he be concerned not just about that Ellis character, but about Colleen as well? Sean planned to get Shirley out on Monday, even if St. Joseph's wasn't quite ready. Maybe Edie could even spend most of Saturday with her.

"Sean, you look awful," said Edie. "I'm sensing your love life is not going well. Correct?"

"That's why I love you so much. You don't beat around the bush. I told you about the nurse at Winter Hill."

"Things got too far, too fast. Right?"

"Sex before really knowing a person. I know. I should know better."

"You are too hard on yourself. Now settle down. What happened?" asked Edie.

"First, I'm mad at myself for being so weak. Then I found out my tires were slashed. I assumed it was Colleen's way of getting back at me. It took me two hours to get home. I had to wait for the tow truck, which took forever, particularly at that time of night. Then I had to have my car towed to some local Somerville tire shop. The shop was closed. I had to fill out a form and drop my keys into the night drop-off."

"Isn't that a little extreme to slash your tires? Do you think she really did that?"

"Well, she apparently slashed her old boyfriend's tires. So yes."

"Wait. You are a detective, right detective? You were in a bad part of town. I know the area. There are gangs of teenagers who key cars and slash tires for fun. Did you even think about investigating?"

"No. I assumed."

"Take it slow. Be kind to yourself. Now, what's going on with Shirley?"

"I'm planning to move her on Monday, regardless of whether they will take her in here. I fear that something will happen over the weekend. She seems to be more and more upset."

"I can stay over tonight, then leave late on Saturday," offered Edie.

"That would be great. Talk to her. Calm her down," said Sean.

"You need to calm down too. And just take it slow with the nurse. When I meet her, I'll see what kind of feelings I get from her. All I'm getting from you is stress. Take me to see my cousin."

Sean helped Edie out of the Charger and into a wheelchair. Even though she could walk, she was always in danger of falling or even banging into something. Her bones were so fragile that even the slightest bump could break a bone. They entered the Winter Hill Nursing and Rehabilitation Center. Edie glanced at the sign with the missing "r."

"Not a good sign." Edie took a deep breath. "I feel my Buddy's spirit here. But there is evil here. It's strong. I feel a terrible sense of tragedy. We have got to get Shirley out of here. Soon."

"Maybe tomorrow, then. Instead of Monday," said Sean.

"Yes. Tomorrow is better than Monday. I can't pinpoint the evil. It's not coming from one place. It's all around this building. I'm concerned."

Sean and Edie walked off the elevator. No Tommy. Then he heard the breakfast noise. It was a low din of people talking, forks touching dishes, spoons stirring coffee. Then the smell hit him. It was not like the beautiful smell of freshly brewed coffee, donuts, and breakfast bagels of Dunkin or Dunks, as the locals called it. Instead, it was an institutional smell. No bacon. No fresh coffee. It was a mixture of cleaning fluid and warmed-over oatmeal.

The dining room was at the end of the A-wing. Tommy would be there. There was no crowd hanging around the nursing station, which was just to the right of the elevator. He knew Colleen would be at the nursing station.

"Hi, Colleen. This is my Aunt Edie," said Sean as he walked by.

Colleen nodded.

"It was nice last night. I'm glad you came by."

"It was until I left."

"What happened after you left? "Asked Colleen.

"Someone slashed all four of my tires."

"Well, the neighborhood isn't that great. You said so yourself."

"Why would someone slash my tires rather than steal my wheels? Those wheels go for at least seven hundred bucks a pop."

"Maybe you took someone's parking spot. They get pretty mad about that." Colleen looked directly into Sean's eyes.

"There was plenty of parking spots when I got there. I don't think so. It seemed like it was …"

Edie intervened, "Sean tells me that there is an empty bed next to his mother. Is it alright if I stay the night with her?"

"I'm sure that will be just fine. But frankly, it's best if you just stay. I won't say a word to anyone. I doubt anyone will notice."

"Great. C'mon Sean, let's go see Shirley."

As Sean pushed Edie's wheelchair away, she whispered into Sean's ear, "You were going to accuse her of slashing your tires. Right?"

"Yes."

"Don't. I'm not getting any particular feelings from her. I do feel that she has some anger, but not from you. It seems it is more like something built up over time. It's hard to tell. But there are terrible vibes coming from all over this floor. Sean, I'm frightened. I also know that Buddy is here. Close by. I wouldn't have expected his spirit to linger here this long. Before they built this place, I used to visit the empty lot. His spirit lingered there. But then, when they started digging and building, I stopped going. I never had the heart to visit. Let's go see Shirley. Make plans to get her the hell out of here. Fast."

~

Shirley sat silently in her wheelchair.

Sean walked in. Edie was waiting outside the room. "Hi, Ma. Are you alright?"

"No. He's going to kill me. All of us. I'm not going to make it out of here alive."

"Why would you say that?"

"That man I told you about. He killed Caroline this morning. We all know it. She was found dead, lying in a pool of blood. Then he motioned to me like I was going to be next. Please help me." Shirley was ashen white.

"Ma. You can't know that. I already checked that guy out. He's old, probably just senile. There was nothing in his background that would even hint at violence. People fall all the time here. You can't know that she was murdered." Sean wasn't sure himself. Edie's words echoed through his brain.

"It's not just me. Many of us here, well, not real sick ones, believe it. Some are a little crazy. Anyway. We just know. First Millie, then Bill's dog Rudy, then Nelson. Now Caroline. The guy has only been here a couple of days, and since he came, we've had all of these murders. You're a cop. Don't you think that's more than a coincidence?" asked Shirley.

"You are leaving on Monday. Maybe even sooner. Period. You have got to settle down. No one is going to kill you. Now, I have a surprise for you."

"What?"

"Edie? Come on in." Sean called for Edie.

Edie, in a wheelchair, sped into Shirley's room. "Jesus, Mary, and Joseph. Edie!"

They embraced the best they could, considering they both were in wheelchairs.

"Edie is going the spend the night here. I cleared it with the nurse. So she can sleep in Millie's bed."

"It's too dangerous. People are dying. That man might go after you, Edie. You can't protect yourself."

"What man?"

"The man who..." Shirley blurted out, then burst into a horrible spasm of tears and agonizing crying.

"Who what?" Sean's eyes widen.

"The man from the beach? I know." Edie, as best as she could, put her arm around Shirley. "You've kept this inside for such a long time. Sean, something happened when she was twenty. We were at the beach, and a man was apparently stalking us. I left. Oh, I regret it terribly. I left her alone on the beach. I felt it as I was leaving. I felt the evil. But I was too frightened about getting caught in a thunderstorm. Back then, I didn't trust my strong intuition gifts. I tried to ignore them. Now I accept that they are there."

"It's him. I know it. Now he is killing people."

"We don't know that. I've checked him out," said Sean.

"He had this dog. A beagle." Shirley choked on the words. "This man killed my friend Bill's dog yesterday. It's the same man. Please believe me."

"Ma. What did he do to you?"

"Sean. The dog's neck was broken. How could that be an accident?" Shirley took a deep breath. "Plus, he does this thing with his face."

"What thing?"

"His eyebrows go up and down. His ears move. I can't. I can't even talk about it. This guy, this Theodore Ellis, does the exact same thing. It terrifies me."

"Ma. Lots of people have these kinds of…I don't know. Palsy. The guy is probably eighty years old. it could be a result of just old age."

"Please. Don't patronize me. It's the same thing. I know it. Sean, you are my only hope. No one in here is going to do a damn thing. That Batty idiot is useless. The charge nurse Lauren is a mean bitch. Those aides are terrible. The only decent one here is that new young nurse. Although, I don't trust anyone who works here. Ellis pointed right at me while I was near poor dead Caroline. Like saying, 'you're next.' I tried to run into him with my wheelchair. I know. I shouldn't have done it, but I had to do something."

"Doesn't matter. You are getting out of here. I don't think Batty will say anything. Now you have got to settle down. Look, I've taken some time off today. I'll do more background on this Ellis guy. Meanwhile, do not provoke him or cause any more trouble. Please. Now that Edie is here, she will keep a watch."

"Thank God, Edie."

"Did he try to hurt you, this guy from the beach? Goddamn it, what did he do to you?"

"It's the same man that is killing people here and Bill's dog."

"Sean. Your mother can't talk about it. See what you can find more about this guy Ellis. Then maybe figure out who the person was from the beach," said Edie. "Once we know that he's dead or in prison or something, Shirley can relax more. Right now, she is convinced that beach man and Ellis are the same person."

"It was a long time ago. But I'll try. I'll see if I can find out who he is. What do you know about him?" asked Sean.

Shirley was trying to catch her breath.

"I know this is extremely hard for you. Like Aunt Edie said, if we can find out who he is, then we can put to rest your fears about this Ellis character."

"Unless it's the same person." Shirley could barely get this out. "I don't know much. He was about the same height as Ellis. Same build. It was a long time ago. But I remember that facial thing he did."

"What about a name? Where he lived. Anything?" probed Sean.

"No name. All I know is that he worked at the Hennessey's garage on Vernon Street. He did work on the fire engines every so often. That's where he saw me first. But, Sean, I can't do this. It brings up horrible memories."

"Shirley. We've got to find out soon." Edie looked up at Sean with a frightened expression. He forced you into his car. Correct?"

"Not exactly. That's why I'm so guilty. It was pouring. Thunder and lightning. If I weren't so afraid of the storm, I never would have gotten into his car."

"It was not your fault! Dammit! The bastard. I should have warned you. I felt the evil, but then I walked away." Edie was now crying.

Sean jumped in. "Okay. What kind of car?"

"Jesus Sean. It was over fifty years ago. I have no idea. All I know was that it was dark red and smelled bad."

"So it probably wasn't new. Two-door or four?"

"Four, because he put the dog in the back seat by opening the back door." Shirley rubbed her eyes.

"So nothing else about the car. No car make nameplates on the dashboard?"

"I don't remember. Dammit." Shirley continued to sniffle.

Sean stood up. "Ma. I'm so sorry about what happened to you. I wish I had known." He hugged her and held on for several seconds.

Shirley grabbed onto his hand. "Thanks for all you do for me."

"One thing. Did Dad know?"

"God, no. I've wanted to tell him for so long but just couldn't. I've been guilty about it for our whole marriage."

"Okay. So all we know is that the guy was about six feet tall, has or had a pronounced facial palsy, drove a late model dark red four-door sedan. Was a mechanic and worked at a garage on Vernon Street. Not much to go by. But something." Sean rubbed his chin.

"Now go. Hurry," said Shirley.

"Nothing else? Edie will be with you." Sean walked toward the door.

"There was one thing I just remembered. It is probably nothing."

Sean walked back into the room.

"He was very proud of the car. He wanted to show it off to me. He said the car was the same one that was in a movie."

"What movie?"

"He mentioned the name. Something about a rebel, I think."

Sean checked his phone. "I'll check 50's movies with the word rebel in the title." He looked up. "The movie *Rebel Without a Cause* immediately came up."

"I think that was it. I'm sure that was it."

"Now I'm searching for Cars from *Rebel Without a Cause*. Yup, here it is. It's a 1949 Mercury Coupe." Sean showed Shirley and Edie the picture of the car.

Edie answered first. "Yes, it looked a lot like that car."

"It sure did look like that, except with four doors. The back looked a little different but very similar."

Sean smiled. "Well, we have something more to go on. Our guy drove a late forties era dark red Mercury."

Sean left Shirley's room. Edie followed him.

"I don't know if that guy is the same person, but we have got to get her out of here. Maybe even today. Do what you can to find out about this Ellis guy. My feelings are so strong."

34

Despite complaining all the time, Vinny Calderone liked his job at the nursing home. Outside of work, he would refer to himself as the Maintenance Manager or Maintenance Supervisor. Once, he even toyed with calling himself the Vice President of Operations and Maintenance. There used to be three maintenance people, so technically, he could have been a supervisor at one time. Now there was only him. The reason Vinny liked his job was because he had lots of free time, despite the desperate maintenance needs of the nursing home and because of the leverage he had over Batty.

The maintenance shed was in the far corner of the parking lot. It contained power tools, lawn equipment, the snowblower, and gardening equipment. Vinny told his friends that he had a man cave at work and was free to putter around and even bragged that he was building a workbench for his house during his spare time.

Vinny did not own a smartphone. Instead, he owned an old flip phone. While it worked, he rarely used it. Today it was sitting at the nursing station being charged. It didn't matter to Vinny because he had a walkie-talkie strapped to his belt in a big leather holster. If he needed to communicate with someone at work, he used the walkie-talkie, and his voice sounded at each of the three central walkie-talkie stations. One was on the first-floor nursing station, which hardly was ever staffed, one in Batty's office and the third at the central control unit on the second-floor nursing station desk. The central control unit was sitting next to Vinny's charging flip phone.

The control unit dated back to the late eighties. It stayed on all the time, day, and night, just in case of an emergency. The system was designed for three maintenance workers. But now there was just Vinny, so the other two units were spares tucked into their charging slots. They hadn't been used for years. A red light on the unit's base right next to the power toggle switch shone brightly.

Vinny swallowed the last of his submarine sandwich and washed it down with a large swallow of soda. He had decided to do a little sanding of the top portion of his workbench. He checked his watch. It was a little after one o'clock.

Since the sander was loud, he didn't hear the hammering. Then he noticed something out of place. He had left the maintenance shed at quarter to noon to go to the local sandwich shop for his lunch. He returned about 12:15 PM. So, he had only been gone for just about half an hour. He noticed the gas-powered leaf blower was missing. He knew it was on the second shelf from the bottom right next to the lawnmower. The gas can also was gone. "What the hell?" he muttered out loud. Someone had taken it. While the equipment was not his, he took care of the nursing home's tools like they were. Further, he and only he was authorized to use the leaf blower. Usually, the shed would always have been locked. But he was only gone for half an hour? And he didn't lock it. Someone must have slipped in while he was getting his lunch, he thought. Who?

He turned off the sander. That's when he heard the leaf blower. It was coming from right outside the shed door. Vinny jumped out of his stool and yanked at the door. It didn't budge. "Who's out there? What's up against the door? Open this goddam door. Now." He banged on the door. "I'll kick your ass" Open the door."

He pulled his walkie-talkie out of its holster. He clicked on the call button.

Silence.

"You have got to be kidding me." He checked the battery. It was fully charged. He had used the walkie-talkie many times from the shed. It always worked. The only way that it wouldn't work was if someone turned off the central control station at the second-floor nursing station. Now he was in full panic mode. He needed to get out. Surely someone would notice he had been missing. Wouldn't they?

He saw exhaust smoke from the leaf blower. It was coming in from under the door. But, all he could hear was the sound of that blower, the one that was missing from the second shelf from the bottom right next to the lawnmower.

He started choking. The exhaust smoke quickly filled the shed. He started to feel light-headed and became disoriented.

Then the leaf blower stopped. As Vinny sat on the floor, he heard the sound of nails being pulled out of wood. Then he heard wood dropping to the ground. It took a few minutes to clear his dizziness. He stumbled out. He saw several two-by-fours lying on the ground with nails driven into them. He turned and saw a piece of paper nailed to the door that read in scribbled handwriting: Dog Killer. By then, whoever had done this to him was gone. Then he looked up onto the deck.

Tommy was watching.

Colleen walked casually over to the walkie-talking central station. Then, she flipped on the on-off switch and walked away. The red light on the control station turned on.

Bill joined the group at his usual position.

The elevator door opened. Only this time, Tommy was not right at the entrance. Vinny, white-faced and still coughing, walked briskly to the nursing station. He stared at the walkie-talking central console. "Who the fuck turned this off?"

Colleen answered. "It's on, isn't it?"

"Someone turned it off. Then they must have turned it back on. Someone trapped me in the maintenance shed. Someone tried to kill me."

"You look fine to me," Bill jumped in.

"Kill you? Who would want to do that?" asked Colleen in a sing-song voice. "What have you done to deserve that?"

"Yeah. What have you done?" Bill gave Vinny a menacing look.

Colleen added, "I've been here the whole time. No one from this floor has left the building."

"I'm going to report this to Batty. You all will be in trouble."

"I have no idea what you are talking about. You're the maintenance man. You are supposed to make sure that everything is working. Maybe you need to do your job and check things out."

"Fuck you," answered Vinny, still coughing and choking.

Tommy moved right up to the nursing station and stopped. He pointed to his ears, pointed to the deck door, spun around, and turned his ramrod leg toward Vinny. Then he picked up speed and headed directly for him.

"Jesus, watch out!" Vinny jumped out of the way.

Tommy slowed down and then rolled past the nursing station and stopped.

Colleen went back to doing some paperwork. She looked up.

Marjorie stood next to Tommy. Shirley and Edie joined him.

"What's with Tommy?" asked Colleen.

"He knows something. We just don't know what," said Marjorie.

"If only he could talk," added Shirley.

Bill slowly walked up to Colleen. He grinned widely and winked. Colleen winked back.

Time was running out for Paul Batty. The computer system would be backed up tomorrow morning at seven o'clock. If he didn't destroy the computer tonight, he was bound to be found out about the missing money. He dialed Butch Donovan

"I need ten thousand dollars tonight. Is that something you can do? Great. Come by about six-thirty tonight? Perfect. Oh, and I need a favor. I need to start a tiny fire in the business office. All I need you to do is pour a couple of buckets of water on the computer, then start a fire in the wastepaper basket. Five hundred bucks? Butch, it will take you less than five minutes. Okay fine. I know. You only get a small percent for all the work you do. Just add the five hundred to the ten thousand."

As soon as he hung up with Donovan, his cell phone rang. It was Emily. He put the phone on speaker. "Don't forget. Sometime today, please withdraw the money for the deposit on OUR NEW DREAM HOUSE." Emily yelled into the phone. Batty sighed. "And more great news. Jordan's Furniture had a huge sale only at their Natick location for dining room sets. Some of them were thirty to forty percent off. So, I bought a brand-new dining room set. The old one just won't fit in the new house. It was only thirty-four hundred dollars. While I was there, I figured that the matching hutch would go great as well. That piece was not on sale but was only two thousand dollars, give or take a few hundred dollars, not counting the sales tax. Imagine for just a little over five thousand dollars, we would have one of the best dining room sets in all of Winchester."

Batty just listened.

"Aren't you excited?"

"Very much. Sorry, someone is at my office door. See you tonight. I'll have the money. Love you." Batty clicked off the phone.

Batty thought back to the five hundred bucks he would have to pay Donovan for a five-minute job. But he needed to avoid the situation that happened last night. This needed to go smoothly. Batty figured the best time to do the little project was right after dinner. Most of the patients would all be tucked away in bed, and the others, like that Duffy woman, would at least be in her room.

Butch would meet Donovan at his office after dinner. First, Batty managed to secure four empty water buckets. That was easy since it hadn't rained since Monday. Vinny had stored the buckets in a closet on the second floor next to the nursing station. During lunch, Batty took the buckets from the closet, filled them with water, and brought them one by one downstairs to the utility closet, which was next to the business office.

By the time lunch was over and the patients began assuming their regular locations throughout the second floor, Batty's master plan was in place. He had four buckets filled with water in the utility closet. The only thing left to do was have Butch Donovan go down to the first floor after giving him five hundred dollars.

In his mind, the plan was perfect. Butch would drop into the electrical room. Then he would take the water buckets into the computer room. He reminded himself to tell Butch to close the main doors from the lobby that led into the rehab area and the office just in case someone was in the lobby. He would also make sure that the person that staffed the first-floor nursing station was on break. That would be easy since she was always somewhere else. Finally, it dawned on him that he should check out her work habits. Later. Butch would pour water all over the computer. Then once the water ruined the computer, Butch would drop a lighted cigarette into the wastepaper basket.

Once the sprinklers went off and people started to smell smoke, Batty would run down with the fire extinguisher and put out the fire. He would be a goddamn hero. He would make sure he put out the fire with the fire extinguisher.

Batty took a deep breath. He thought to himself. It will be all over tonight. After hardly any sleep last night, he would sleep soundly tonight.

35

S ean was conflicted. He had no logical reason to investigate Ellis further. The guy didn't have any apparent connection to a long since closed repair garage. He had retired from the power company in the late 1980s. What were the odds that some guy who did something to his mother fifty or so years ago would show up in the same nursing home as his mother's? He had needed to get his head together after the upsetting knowledge about Colleen's dead boyfriend. Even though he had asked for the day off, he had decided to go to the station and do some paperwork. He figured that would take his mind off Colleen and his mother. It didn't work.

"I thought you took today off." Carlos, one of the other detectives, distracted him.

"Yeah. Got a lot on my mind."

"Sex or money?" asked Carlos.

"No. It's my mother. Well, sex too. I met this woman."

"See, it's always about sex. What about her. She nice?"

"Attractive, articulate, great lover, but..."

"There is always a but. What is it? Smokes. Does drugs. Has a jealous husband?"

"Nope. The only problem is that she may have killed her ex-boyfriend and probably slashed my tires. Other than that. Perfect," said Sean.

"Are you shitting me? You are shitting me, right." Carlos was laughing out loud. "Christ, you broke up with the last girlfriend cause she was too something. I forgot. Was it clingy or not affectionate? You have graduated, my friend."

"It's not funny," said Sean.

"You're screwed. If you break up with her, she kills you. If you stay with her, she kills you anyway," said Carlos. "Where did you meet this nutcase?"

"She's a nurse at my mother's nursing home."

"Not the one where the patients are dying off one by one?" Carlos's demeanor changed.

"Yes. Look, patients die at nursing homes all the time. My mother thinks some guy who hurt her years ago is now one of the patients. So, I am getting her out of there. Soon. Monday at the latest."

"So your mother is being stalked by some maybe attacker and is being nursed by a boyfriend killer? Now I understand why you are so distracted. Get her the hell out of there. Did the nurse really kill her boyfriend?"

"I don't know. The boyfriend's mother thinks so. And the nurse's daughter thinks she did. It was an accident. The guy was crushed changing a tire, and…."

"You had sex already, right?"

"Yeah."

"Then you tried to cool it? She was pissed and slashed your tires. My advice is to get your mother the hell out of that nursing home, and then you won't have to run into the nurse ever again. She sounds like bad news. But what do I know? I'm on wife number two. If I were you, I'd do a complete background check on this guy in the nursing home and find out as much as you can about the guy in your mother's past. Then you can convince her the two are not the same person. Good luck," said Carlos as he left the detective's room.

Carlos was right. Maybe Colleen was capable of doing something to the patients at the nursing home. Maybe even his mother. After all, he angered her. He supposed that he did take advantage of her sexually. No, wait. She wanted it just as bad. Maybe in her warped mind, she wouldn't see it that way. Damn. He kept looking at a piece of paper and couldn't read a goddam word.

Sean knew that Ellis was married in Everett and had one daughter. He also knew that he had been living with his daughter just before entering the nursing home. Her name was Julie Marsh. Not much to go on.

He decided to visit Ellis's daughter in Everett.

Now it was dinner time. Was it too late to visit a perfect stranger, flashing a Boston cop badge for the second time in less than a day in a city where he had no jurisdiction? He was now in Dorchester. Driving across Boston during rush hour was a slow process. He wouldn't get to her house until about six. He resisted the urge to forget the whole thing. The only good thing about going to Everett was that he would be on the right side of Boston to link up with his mother and Edie. He figured Colleen would not be working the night shift. That was a plus.

He would spend a couple of minutes with the daughter and hopefully confirm that this Ellis character was not the same man that hurt his mother. Then he would explain to her that her intuition was not correct and figure out what to do to Batty or threaten him again so that he doesn't mess up his mother's move to St. Joseph's. As far as Colleen was concerned, he would take Carlos's advice. Once his mother moved to St Joseph's, there would be no need to go anywhere near the old nursing home or Somerville, for that matter.

Everett was located just over the Mystic River from Somerville. Julie Marsh lived in a two-family on Clinton Street, next to a small red brick beat-up manufacturing building. The house had the classic aluminum siding that suffocated any semblance of architectural features that the house might have had when it was built in the late 1890s. As he entered the front door, he inhaled a strong smell of old cigarette smoke blended with... What? Sean couldn't quite place the other smell. Old carpets? Cat urine? The tiny front hall consisted of a stairway on the left rising straight up to the second floor, then abruptly turned to the right. The top two stairs were sharply angled.

At the top of that turn was a door. Sean imagined that a person opening that door, who might have been half-drunk, could lose footing and fall down the stairway. The very left of that top stair was a triangle-shaped step with hardly any tread at the far end.

He stood on the awkward top step, eight inches below the door. He imagined that if Julie Marsh had wanted to, it would not be too challenging for her to kick him, and it would have sent Sean sprawling down that stairway, which was all wood.

He knocked hard on the door. After all, it was just a bit past six o'clock. If he were advising a woman, it would be not to open the door.

"Who is it?" A muffled voice emerged from behind the door.

"Boston Police. No emergency."

She opened the door.

Sean was a little surprised. He knew that this woman had lived in Everett for years. Why would she open the door for a Boston police officer? Maybe people don't know the rules. He was relieved. The top of the stairs had no railing to hold on to. So, he needed to get into the house.

Once Julie Marsh opened the door, Sean got the full smell of the place. He confirmed that one of the smells was stale cigarette smoke, and the other was kitty litter that hadn't been changed in a while. Two cats stood between Marsh's legs.

"This is about your father. May I come in? It will only take a few minutes."

Julie motioned for him to come in. She lit up a cigarette. "What has he done?"

"Nothing. Nothing." Fortunately for Sean, she didn't invite him into the living room, which was to the right of the front entryway. There were two additional cats curled in cat balls on either end. Sean moved a short distance to the right of the open door to prevent any sudden fall down those awful stairs.

Julie looked to be in her mid-fifties. She was hardened. Thin. Her face was wrinkled. Sean had seen so many women who had that same general look. Someone who had a hard life. Someone who drank a lot and didn't eat a lot. She also looked sad. Real sad. Sean had bet this woman had had plenty of heartaches. He didn't want to stare into the apartment. But he snuck a glance. There were laundry baskets, newspapers, and dinner plates littering the room. "This is not a police matter. It's personal. My mother and your father are both at the same nursing home."

"Is he causing some kind of problem with your mother?"

"No. Not at all. It's just that she is terrified of him, and I don't exactly know why. So I thought you might be able to help me understand him a little better so I could kind of relieve her fears," said Sean.

"I'm afraid the more she knows of him, the worse she's going to feel. He's a miserable bastard." Julie made a half-hearted attempt to blow her smoke away from Sean's face. "He used to berate my mother for years before she died."

"Your mother put up with it? If this is hard for you, I…"

"Doesn't matter now. Ma's gone, and now he's over there."

"I'm sorry. He was violent? Did he ever attack other women?"

"Not that I know of. He knew how to manipulate my mother."

"I know this is a stupid question, but why didn't your mother leave him?"

"Why didn't she leave my father? She didn't love him. To protect me, probably. Maybe she was afraid he'd hurt her if she left. Who knows why people do things?"

"After your mother died, he moved in with you. Why did you let him?"

"It's complicated. After all, he is my father. I supposed I felt sorry for him." She walked into the cat-infested living room. She flicked her ashes near an ashtray but missed. Most of the ashes ended up on the beat-up coffee table. The two greeting cats leaped up to join the other cats on the sofa.

"So, he got sick, and you got him into Winter Hill?".

"He's sick alright, but not physically. Don't let the walker fool you. He's strong. I tricked him into going to the nursing home."

She took a deep drag and turned to Sean. "He's losing what's left of his mind."

"Senile? asked Sean. He was getting a little concerned. Even if he wasn't the guy that hurt his mother, he could be dangerous.

"No. Crazy. It was getting concerning. He was getting erratic. Punched the walls. Yelled for no reason. So, I had a doctor say he was getting Alzheimer's. He wrote up a slip. Did all the paperwork. I told Dad that I had to visit a friend at the nursing home the next day. Dropped him off and haven't been back since."

"Does Winter Hill know about his behavior?"

"You know. I told them, but I got the feeling they didn't give a rat's ass. The union's medical retirement plan would pay for his bills, so they took him. Own him now. I'm off the hook."

Sean shook his head. "I understand."

"And there's no way that he's ever coming back. I'm moving soon and not leaving a forwarding address. I frankly don't want to know how they treat him." Julie grabbed hold of the front door. Sean knew it was a kind of message that people send when they want you to leave.

But Sean needed a bit more information. He figured this would be his last chance and moved toward the door. "What's with his facial movement? That funny motion with his eyes and eyebrows."

Julie let go of the door, walked into the living room, and slumped on the sofa, scattering the cats. "It's like a god-damn signal. It happens when he's thinking, plotting. When he got outraged and waited for Ma to come home, that movement thing would go crazy. You didn't go near him when he was doing that."

"You said you felt sorry for him. Why?"

"He had a tough life."

"Bad childhood?" asked Sean.

"His father died when Dad turned sixteen. He then lived with his mother until she died when he was in his twenties. I never knew her."

"Thanks for taking the time with me. I should go."

Sean walked toward the door.

Julie got up and followed him. Two of the cats walked with her. Then the cats returned to the sofa.

He took a step onto that dangerous top step then turned around. "He worked for the Edison, right?"

"Worked for the Edison Company for years. But, hey, tell your mother to stay away from him, will you?"

Sean's heart was heavy. For two reasons. Twice in one day, he had brought up hurtful memories to two perfect strangers for his self-centered reasons. The second reason was that he never got solid answers to his questions. His visit to Ellis's daughter only confirmed that Ellis was crazy and may be dangerous. All that meant was that he had to get his mother away from him.

Sean pulled over next to the Mount Vernon Café. He needed a drink. The Mount Vernon was the same restaurant where his mother and father had their wedding reception. He glanced over at the restaurant. The owners had kept all kinds of old pictures, including pictures of his parents.

Pictures? Sean felt like a fool. What kind of detective was he? All this stress of his mother and the uncertainty of Colleen had clouded his judgment. Old pictures. That's what he needed. If Ellis's daughter had a picture of when Ellis was young, in his twenties, that would undoubtedly help confirm or not that this was the man who was at the beach. Edie also saw him. He would have to go back to the daughter's house.

36

The quietest time of the day at Winter Hill was right after dinner. Most of the patients got sleepy after stuffing themselves with the institutional food in the dining room.

Bones McGraw was back in his room, getting into his pajamas. He peed and farted a couple of times and carefully placed his walker next to the bed. Then, he hopped into bed, turned on the TV with the remote, and was snoring within seconds.

Marjorie carefully placed her necklace and earrings on the end table. She would not fall asleep for quite some time. As usual, she would hear the voices in an hour or so. Maybe she would change her routine and visit with Shirley. After a visit with Shirley and together listening for the voices, she hoped she would fall asleep. She feared that some night they would not stop. Even though she had been hearing them for a while, they always upset her. Once they had stopped for the night, she felt relieved. She knew, though, that like when a migraine subsides, they come back sooner or later. She climbed into bed, not sure what exactly to do.

Ruthie was already in bed. Martha, the aide, had carelessly lifted her out of her wheelchair and into bed. Ruthie read a page from the

Bible and muttered some prayers. Her roommate, Phyllis, stared at the TV.

Bill was sound asleep. The bed next to his was empty. Ellis was somewhere else.

Tommy was in his usual spot guarding the elevator. He, too, was waiting for the voices.

Lauren, the charge nurse, was behind the desk, doing some sort of paperwork.

Shirley was in her bed.

Edie was reading a book in what used to be Millie's bed.

Shirley was staring at the ceiling, waiting for her beloved Willy to appear. She wondered what would happen when she did see Willy, with Edie right next to her. Would she be silent, or would she assume that Edie would understand? She wasn't sure. She hoped and wished that this time he would say something to her. But she also didn't hold out hopes. She wondered if Sean would visit. She knew that when Willy's image would vanish, she would hear the voices.

Butch Donovan strutted up to the elevator. There was no one at the first-floor reception/nursing station. He thought that was a good sign. He wasn't sure he wanted to get involved in this dousing the computer with the water situation. When he had thrown out the number of five hundred dollars to Batty, he had fully expected Batty to balk and to offer a lower number at least. Instead, much to Butch's surprise, he caved in immediately. The guy just accepted his first offer. What a pussy.

When Donovan walked off the elevator, Tommy intercepted him. Butch pushed him quickly out of the way. Tommy made Butch feel creepy. Butch quickly walked past the nursing station to Batty's office.

"Hey, Paul." Butch pulled out a large envelope from his leather jacket pocket. "Ten grand, my friend. I kept the five hundred for the computer job. Same terms and conditions."

"This is cash. I sort of thought it would be a cashier's check," said Batty. "I didn't count on cash.

"What do I look like a Pay-Day Loan Store?"

"It's okay. I'll deal." Donovan noticed that Batty's body was in a knot.

"Was there someone at the reception desk?" asked Batty.

"Nope. All clear.

"There are four buckets of water in the electrical room. All you have to do is drop a lit cigarette into the wastepaper basket, the one next to the computer. I've stuffed it full of papers. Then when the paper catches on fire, pour the water on top of the computer. Then leave."

"I don't smoke. I don't carry cigarettes."

"I thought of everything" Batty handed Butch the pack of cigarettes and a butane lighter. "Just get the cigarette lit. You don't even have to drag on it."

"Fine. Fine. Sorry, but I'm gonna need a hundred more," Butch, noticing Batty was nervous, figured he could squeeze a bit more out of him.

"Didn't we agree on five hundred?" At this point, Donovan could tell Batty was desperate.

"I didn't know I would have to smoke a cigarette. That's worth at least a hundred bucks."

"But you don't have to drag. Never mind." Batty pulled some twenties out of his pocket and handed the money to Donovan. "Please hurry."

Butch quickly walked past the nursing station.

Lauren looked up and gave him a quizzical look.

Tommy blocked his way. For the second time, Donovan pushed him out of the way. He hit the elevator call button, stepped aboard, and headed to the first floor.

The reception desk on the first floor was still empty. The patients on the first floor were all tucked neatly away in bed. He opened the double doors to the rehab wing. Then, as directed by Batty, he closed the double doors, just in case the reception person came back to work. Donovan took the water buckets out of the electrical room into the computer room.

He tried lighting up the cigarette. It wouldn't catch. Fuck. He would have to drag on the goddamn cigarette. "Should have asked Batty for a full grand," he said out loud. He took a drag. Then he coughed.

"Yuck." Then he threw the butt into the trash can and waited. A tiny flame started. He glanced up at the sprinkler head. He had to hurry. He picked up the first bucket of water and splashed it on the computer. The screen saver picture lit up from the slight movement of the mouse from the water. The screen saver displayed a picture of the Winter Hill Nursing and Rehabilitation Center front lobby. Butch laughed at the picture. He figured it must have been taken in the eighties. The screen saver then cycled to the exterior of the building, which looked a lot different from what the building looks like now. Even the front sign had the now missing "r" in the right place. Donovan chuckled to himself at the image. He toyed with the idea of forgetting the whole thing. Then he figured that if he did, he might lose additional revenue from Batty, who for all he knew might end up in jail. Better to keep the money flowing.

No luck. The computer was still working.

He needed more leverage. "Have to get higher up to splash the fucking thing," he said out loud. He needed a ladder or something. Looked around. The only thing high enough to climb on was the computer chair. He tested it to see if it was strong enough to hold him. However, it was a nineteen-nineties era swivel office chair. One that had only four wheels. New office chairs all had five wheels for greater stability. He rocked the old chair. To him, it seemed fine. This one would have to do.

Donovan stood awkwardly on the chair. It was not steady. He leaned forward to pick up a full water bucket. The sideways motion created a torque that pushed the chair backward. With the weight of the bucket pulling him down, in combination with the chair moving backward, Donovan went tumbling. He slid onto the computer table, knocking a stack of computer manuals into the burning basket. He

295

then bounced off the desk onto the basket, knocking it over. Donovan hit the tile floor hard, rendering him unconscious. The computer manuals then caught on fire, and so did Donovan's suit, which was one he got during a two-for-one sale at Target.

No smoke alarm sounded. Sprinkler heads have a tiny glass tube filled with red glycerin-like material. When the heat reaches about 140 degrees, the glass tube bursts allowing the water to flow from the sprinkler head. The glass tube burst soon after Donovan fell off the office chair. Since Vinny had shut off the main control valve, there was very little water pressure in the sprinkler pipe to the sprinkler system, so some water squirted out of the sprinkler head, but not nearly enough to even reach the fire. It just dribbled on the computer desk.

∼

Sean raced up Ellis's daughter's stairs. He never even thought about how dangerous the half-assed stairway was. He knocked hard on the door. "It's the Boston cop again."

She opened the door.

"That was fast. Did he finally do something?" asked Julie.

"No. I forgot to ask you one more thing. If you're too upset, I'll come back later."

"What's the difference?" She was smoking. The cats were still in the same position on the sofa from when he was there the last time.

"I never thought to ask, but do you have any pictures of your father, when he was younger, say in his twenties?"

"Why do you ask?"

"My mother ran into a man a long time ago. I just want to make sure that your father was not that man."

Julie interrupted. "Why, what did the man do to your mother?"

"I'm not sure myself. My mother was vague. All I know was that it was traumatic. I want to make sure that your father is not that guy. It isn't very likely. But my mother is very old and probably a bit paranoid." Sean felt bad betraying his mother.

"I have an old photo album in my closet. I haven't looked at it for a long time. It's buried under stuff. I'd have to check for any old pictures. Do you mind waiting?"

"No. While I'm waiting, I'll make a quick call."

Julie headed into the bedroom. "It's here somewhere," said Julie.

Sean dialed. "Hi, Edie. How are things going? Quiet. Great. I'm in Everett. As long as things are quiet, I'll head over there in the morning. Thanks so much for watching out for my mother. Any bad feelings? Still huh. Well, if anything happens, call me immediately."

Sean was still standing on that awkward, angled front step. He had to hold on to the wall since there was no railing to keep himself from falling backward.

"Your father worked for the Edison Company. Did he climb poles?"

"No. He fixed stuff at the plant. Why?" asked Julie from the bedroom.

"Plant? What plant? Didn't you say he was a lineman?" asked Sean.

"You know the plant. The Mystic Power Plant. Right here in Everett. He fixed pumps and valves and shit. He hated heights. He would never climb a ladder, never mind a pole. He was a mechanic." Julie walked out of the bedroom with two old photo albums under her arm.

"Mechanic? You mean like an auto mechanic?" asked Sean. "Can I come in?"

Julie nodded. "A mechanic, fixed things. He started as a car mechanic. When he was in his twenties. That was until he got beat up so bad he almost died. That was before he met Mom. What's this all about?"

Sean ignored her question. "What happened? Who beat him up?"

"Dad never told me the story. Mom did. No one ever found out who the man was or why he beat up Dad. He was in the hospital for a long time. Never returned to the garage. The only thing I know is that guy that did it to him wore some kind of uniform."

"Like a soldier?"

"Not sure."

"A fireman?" Sean was very concerned.

"Sorry."

"Do you know the name of the garage?"

"No," said Julie

"Where was it?"

"Could have been in Chelsea or Somerville. He was born in Brockton, then moved up here. Lived in Chelsea and Somerville for a while. Lots of pictures of when I was a baby. My father took the pictures, so he was hardly in any of them. Oh, here is one of him at my high school graduation."

Sean glanced at the picture. This picture might be fine, but not ideal. "Anything earlier." Julie flipped through the first album. "Not really." She threw the album onto the sofa. The cats jumped off and scattered. She carefully thumbed the pages. "Oh, here is one." She pulled the picture out of the album. "This looks like maybe a picture of him in high school."

Sean stared at the picture. "This looks like the Somerville High front door. It was torn down, but I remember it from when I was a kid."

"Could be. I don't know. He never talked much about his growing up. At least not to me."

"Anything that shows him a little older?"

She continued to flip. "How about this one." She pulled the picture out of the album and handed it to Sean. He stared at the photo. It showed Ellis leaning on the backside of a dark-colored car. The picture was black and white. He flipped the photo. Handwritten on the back was "1956."

It was the car that caught his attention. The fact that the man was leaning on the car strongly suggested it was his. Not some stranger's. It was a four-door sedan since he could see the rear door handle. One of the taillights was visible. It wasn't like the 1949 car in *Rebel Without a Cause*, but the roofline was similar, almost identical.

"What are you staring at?" asked Julie.

Sean's attention was distracted. "It's the car. I like old cars. Just wondering what make it is."

"I have no idea."

"Can I borrow this picture? I promise to give it back to you."

"Take it. Keep it. Anything else?" Julie lit up another cigarette. The cats regrouped on the sofa.

"No. Thanks so much," answered Sean.

"Listen. Do me a favor. Don't say anything to my father about talking to me. Okay?"

Sean walked down the stairs. At the bottom of the stairs, he continued to examine the car in the picture. It was not exactly the same as the car in the movie, but it was close. The picture was black and white so that it could be maroon. On his phone, he looked up early model Mercuries. The 1950 was the same as the 1949. Then he flipped to the 1951. It looked almost identical to the 1949 except for the taillights. The front was the same, but the 51 had little fins with the taillights sticking up. The car Ellis was leaning on was a 1951 Mercury four-door sedan.

His heart jumped. A squirt of adrenaline rushed into his stomach. His mind raced back to the day his father tried to tell him about killing a man. It was Ellis. Now he knew. His mother was right. The man who did something terrible to his mother was Ellis. But his father knew about it somehow and she never knew that his father had known about it all along. He would find the right time to tell her. In the meantime, he needed to get her away from Ellis. He texted Edie. "Changed my mind. I'll be over to see you and Ma. See you in less than an hour."

37

Batty was biting his fingernails on his left hand. The right-hand nails were all down to the quicks. It shouldn't have taken this long, he had thought. Now he was convinced that Butch had stiffed him out of six hundred bucks. He should never have trusted him. First, he thought that Butch probably took the elevator down to the first floor. Then he pictured him laughing to himself. Then Butch would feel the wad of cash in his pocket. Finally, Batty pictured Butch strolling out the front door. He knew that he had no leverage with Donovan. What was he going to do? Sue him for failure to perform a little minor arson job? Now he was out six hundred bucks for nothing. Plus, the computer would be backed up tomorrow. He would be screwed. He would have to do the job himself.

Then he smelled a faint smell of smoke. Yet, there was no alarm. Whenever the sprinkler system went off, it should have sounded the fire alarm. It was an integrated system. No alarm sounded. The computer room was directly under the rooms across the hall from his office. Maybe smoke was leaking up through the floors across the hall and into his office. It was still very faint. He decided it was time to investigate. He grabbed the fire extinguisher.

As he walked toward the nursing station, Ellis passed him. Batty should have stopped him and asked him where he was going. Batty's office was the last room at the end of the A-wing on the parking lot side of the building. The only rooms beyond his office were the dining room and kitchen, which theoretically was off-limits to patients except during meals. So the only place Ellis could go was either into his office, which Batty had locked, the staff break room, which was also locked, or the staff bathroom, which wouldn't make sense since each of the patients' rooms had bathrooms. The only other place Ellis could go would be into Room 208, which was now vacant due to the recent death of Caroline, or Room 209, which was Shirley's room.

Batty didn't do anything since he had more pressing things to do.

As Tommy had discovered a couple of days earlier, not only had Vinny disabled the smoke detection and sprinkler systems, but he had locked the exit door, the one located at the end of the B-wing on the second floor. Whenever someone would open the exit door, a very annoying alarm would go off. Batty was sick and tired of these alarms going off at least twice a day. Batty had asked Vinny to install a lock right after the fire marshal had done the annual inspection.

Batty walked past Lauren carrying the fire extinguisher. "Do you smell smoke?"

"Yeah. It's faint," said Lauren, who was reading a magazine.

"I'll check it out." He wanted to show Lauren that he was brave by showing her the fire extinguisher. He would need a witness to his bravery after putting out the fire.

Batty walked quickly by Tommy, who let him pass without much fuss. While in the elevator, Batty read the warning sign. DO NOT USE THE ELEVATOR IN THE EVENT OF A FIRE. Ironic, he thought. When Batty arrived on the first floor, the smoke was more intense. As usual, there was no one at the reception desk or no one from the B-wing in the lobby. As planned, the double doors separating the rehabilitation area, the computer, and the electrical room from the rest of the building were closed.

Lauren smelled the smoke much stronger now. The nursing station was next to the elevator machine room next to the elevator shaft. Since the elevator shaft and the machine room were two stories, they acted as chimneys. Even though the fire itself was still confined to the rehabilitation area and computer room, these shafts sucked the smoke from the relatively sealed areas up into the second floor. She started to get nervous.

She walked past the elevator. At this time of night, Tommy was usually comatose. But, tonight, he was moving back and forth around the elevator door. Lauren could tell that he, too, smelled smoke.

Tommy rolled sideways up to the elevator door, and as best he could, he leaned down toward the bottom of the door. Then he backed away and then pulled forward.

It was clear to Lauren that Tommy, like her, was nervous.

She stopped at the elevator. She intended to go to the first floor and find Batty. However, she decided not to use the elevator since she smelled smoke. She wasn't about to be caught in an elevator during a fire. She wasn't exactly sure why that wasn't a good idea, but every elevator she had ever been in had strictly warned against riding in elevators during a fire.

She wasn't going to take any chances. The stairway at the end of the B-wing would be the most responsible route to the first floor and to Batty. She pushed the panic bar of the emergency exit door. She knew that it would sound an alarm, but maybe this was an emergency after all.

She pushed the bar. The door didn't open, and she tried it again. It was locked. Being a stickler for rules, she got furious. An emergency exit door with a panic bar should never be locked. She would have to complain vehemently to Batty. Maybe Vinny should be disciplined. That was his job.

The only other way out was the emergency exit door that led to the fire escape on the opposite side of the building on the far side of the dining room.

The smell of smoke was getting stronger. Her heart rate was getting faster. She walked past Tommy and the elevator, hesitating for a moment. It sure would be easier taking the elevator. Tommy was now in a bit of a frenzy. He pushed up against Lauren and motioned a warning to her. She made a split-second decision not to use the elevator. She pushed Tommy out of the way and headed to the dining room.

~

Edie and Shirley could smell smoke as well. Shirley was in her bed, staring at the ceiling, waiting for Willy to appear. So it was about that time.

"Do you smell that?" asked Edie. Edie's text message notification sounded. "Just got a text from Sean. He's in Everett, heading over here. ETA in less than an hour." Edie typed a reply into her phone.

"Good. Smells like smoke, not strong, but still," said Shirley.

"I'm going to investigate." Edie got out of bed and left the room. She did not use her wheelchair.

Shirley could hear Edie's footsteps fade. Then Shirley heard the sound. Tap. Tap. Tap. She had heard that sound before. It was the sound of a walker with one of the tennis ball feet missing. The only one in the building with a walker like that was Ellis.

That man who coaxed her into his car turned her from a carefree, sharp, young woman to a more serious one. He had injected her with a lifetime of guilt and shame. He created her silent scar. Sure, she had buried it. She had a good life with Willy, but it was always there. At times, it was stronger and at other times less so. But it had colored her. Her relationship with Willy was wonderful. But he was certainly not perfect. She would be angry with him. She had intended to give him a hard time during those times, mainly when he came home drunk in the middle of the night. But her guilt and shame inhibited her ability to be angry with him and tell him just what she thought. So instead, she would hold back because she was not perfect. How could she criticize him when she had that dark secret, that silent scar? He couldn't hold it over her head because he never knew about it. But she did. She held that shame over her head. Sure, her life had been okay, fine, maybe even great at times. But that awful day after the beach behind Hennessy's garage changed everything. That was a million years ago.

Now he was back. She was sure of it.

Ellis walked into her room.

She hit the nurse's call button. Since her room was at the far end of the A-wing and on the opposite side of the nursing station, she could barely hear the little ring it made.

She didn't know that Lauren, who was on duty that night, was just as panic-stricken as Shirley was but for very different reasons. Shirley knew the call button drill. You press it. A board behind the nurse buzzes. The light above the room numbers shines. The buzzer sounds until the nurse acknowledges the call. That signifies that at least the nurse knows you want attention. Then, within a few minutes, the nurse or aide shows up often longer. In this case, the buzzer continued, which meant that the nurse was not at the station. She was either helping some other patient in the bathroom or wrapped up with something else.

Ellis stood in her room, glaring. No one had acknowledged her call for help. And Edie was now somewhere else.

Shirley's other option was to dial 911 on the landline phone provided by the facility or use her cell phone to call for help. She already had been badly burnt by calling 911 the other night. She could call her son, but he was driving from Everett to here. She knew it would take him at least half an hour to get there.

She decided to take matters into her own hands. She had had enough of all those years of guilt and shame. She had modified her behavior because of that monster. So, despite her handicap, she was going to fight.

"I know you," said Ellis. "Remember me?" He was smiling. He slowly walked towards her bed.

Shirley's wheelchair was parked next to her bed, tucked beside her moveable bed table. Shirley planned to get into the wheelchair, speed toward him, push him out of the way, and then escape into the corridor.

It was a bad plan.

First, Shirley had no use of her left hand and left foot. Second, she had never been able to get out of bed and into the wheelchair without help from at least one aide.

She figured she would employ the element of surprise. She turned sideways and gripped the arm of the wheelchair with her good right hand. She pulled herself toward the wheelchair and attempted to angle herself off the bed and plop into the waiting wheelchair. It didn't work. The wheelchair simply rolled out of the way. Shirley tumbled onto the floor. Luckily, she broke her fall by holding on to the wheelchair. But now, all her leverage was gone.

The sudden motion startled Ellis.

She had no idea that she could move so fast like a fish on the smooth bare floor. But she could. Within a few seconds, she had reached Ellis's walker. First, she yanked it out from under him. Then with only her good right hand, she pulled his leg toward her.

He lost his balance and fell on his back. Unfortunately for Shirley, he didn't hit his head on the floor. "Holy fuck." Ellis squirmed toward her.

Shirley fish moved toward the corridor, hoping he would be sufficiently stunned to let her pass.

Instead, he gained his composure a lot sooner. He rolled off his back and moved on top of Shirley. He turned her over onto her back.

His face was directly facing hers.

She couldn't move. "You son of a bitch. You raped me and left me."

"Rape? Are you kidding me? You asked for it. You loved it. They always do, just like all the others. They tease, they show off their bodies. Like you did at the beach. You cunts are all the same. I bet you want it now. That's why you pulled me on the floor."

It was clear now that Shirley was not the only rape victim. Somehow that made her feel just a little better. If he had a habit of attacking women, then maybe in the future, if there were a future, she wouldn't carry as much guilt. Then the thought left her.

It was his breath.

Only this time, it was free from alcohol, but she remembered it. It was the smell. She pushed her head away. Was he going to try to kiss her again, like the last time?

Since he was lying flat on top of her, she couldn't move, but neither could he do much. He made a feeble attempt of trying to pull off her pajamas. Then his eyes blinked quickly. His eyebrows moved up and down. He opened and closed his mouth rapidly and clicked his tongue.

She closed her eyes and shook back and forth. Then, she listened for the nurse's call button in her panic and upset. It was still buzzing. A few minutes earlier, she had seen a nurse rush by her room into the dining room. The nurse that everyone called the bitch.

Ellis reached down to Shirley's crotch.

That was it for Shirley. Then it dawned on her. This time she was not alone. Not alone in the front seat of that car that looked like the one in that movie. Not alone like in the back alley behind Hennessey's garage. Forget the nurse. She screamed as loud as she could. "BINGO! BINGO! BINGO!

"Stop that." Ellis was confused. "Why are you yelling that? Stop."

She persisted, 'BINGO! BINGO! BINGO!

Bones appeared in an instant. Well, in a Bingo Gang instant, which was a bit longer than a mere instant. But at least he arrived before Ellis could do any more harm. First, he had smelled the smoke. That had awakened him. Then, while sniffing around at the elevator door, he heard the scream. He also noticed that the nurse's call light was buzzing. It was Room 209, Shirley's room.

Bones had yelled back to the gang to meet at Shirley's room. She was in trouble. He rushed to Room 209 as fast as his old legs could carry him.

Bones pulled Ellis off Shirley. Bill joined in. Ruthie rolled up and hit Ellis lightly over the head with her Bible. Marjorie and Phyllis watched. Even Tommy rolled up, leaving his elevator station.

Marjorie undid her pearl necklace. She wrapped it around Ellis's neck and pulled it tight.

Phyllis banged into him with her wheelchair.

Ruthie yelled, "Take that, you demon! The Bingo Gang strikes back."

Shirley sat up, on the one hand, slowly forming a fist. She landed a solid punch across his jaw. "That hurt. Damn."

The Bingo Gang cheered.

"What the fuck were you doing, you cocksucker?" yelled Bones.

"That's a horrible word to say, Bones!" Ruthie looked around. "Well, it is. I'm not even sure I know what it means."

"Which one, Ruthie? Fuck or cocksucker." Bones answered back.

Marjorie helped Shirley pull away from the stunned Ellis. She leaned up against the door. "I tried to tackle him. He almost got away."

Bill wanted some answers. He held a bedpan in a threatening manner over his head. "You hurt Millie, then Nelson, then poor Caroline. Confess, or I'll destroy you!"

"I never touched them. I never hurt that woman. I followed her in the kitchen. But then she wanted to make out with me. She took her clothes off but then fell to the floor. That was it. I don't know what happened to the rest of them." Bones kept him down on the floor.

"You're lying."

The gang all joined in, "Confess. Confess."

"Nope. I never laid a hand on any of them. Let me go."

"You're lying. I'll kick the living shit out of you. Confess you bastard." Bill was deadly serious.

Bill crashed the bedpan over his head.

38

Batty approached the double doors, which it so happened were fire doors. They had provided a seal between the rehabilitation area and the rest of the building. Opening the double doors would create a perfect oxygen hit to the now-developing fire.

Batty, in one quick motion, opened the doors and raced in. The burst of oxygen fed the fire. Within seconds, the flames entirely consumed Batty. His motion accelerated the fire tenfold. Sadly, he didn't die instantly. He lasted a few seconds but was unable to utter a scream. His final thought wasn't of Emily or the debt that he was in but of a kind of wonder. His last thought was, "What the hell happened to the sprinkler system?"

The fire had been building quickly. Until Batty fed it, it still had been confined to the tiny computer room but still had been generating a fair amount of smoke and heat. The wall separating the computer room and the adjacent electrical room suddenly vanished. The electrical panel fed from an underground conduit and cable from Edison Vault SV127 under the sidewalk on Broadway was getting a little soft. Before Batty fed the fire with fresh oxygen, the lights and power had still been on.

The fire was like a living organism, hungry for the dual food of oxygen and combustible materials. The fancy sofa in the waiting area was its next victim. It was heavily padded with foam. The sofa frames were all wood and they were covered with cloth. So the sofa was a perfect meal for the adolescent fire. The curtains satisfied the fire's unquenchable appetite. The cherry wood reception desk that was hardly ever occupied provided a slow-burning and intense platform for the fire's march to the B-wing of the first floor and then to the second floor.

The windows in the rehabilitation section of the first floor exploded outward with a deafening roar. This sent smoke and flames shooting outside. The sound was so loud that customers buying alcohol from the Paul Revere Liquor and Wine store on the corner of Main Street and Edgar Ave, not far from where his car had crushed Serj, could hear the sound. Then, the fire roared its most immense fury.

Then the lights went out.

The heat immediately grew tenfold, and the electrical panel melted into one big molten metal pile. It created a substantial short circuit. Since the main breaker was just one big piece of molten plastic and metal, there was no fuse to stop the steady flow of electric current coming from the Edison transformer in the underground electrical vault. As a result, the high voltage fuses on the transformer blew, shutting power to the nursing home and the whole block along Broadway and several side streets.

That's when the screaming began from Rooms 101 through 106 on the first floor of the B- wing. But, unlike the voices that Tommy, Shirley, and Marjorie heard every night, these voices were from real people.

This fire was serious.

It grew from infancy in the tiny wastebasket, from a toddler in the computer room to an adolescent that captured the electrical room to a full-fledged adult.

The window explosion happened simultaneously as Bill hit Ellis with the bedpan. It was as if Bill, by hitting Ellis, had started a chain reaction.

~

The only light came from a couple of emergency lights and the red exit light.

Lauren had heard Shirley yelling Bingo as she pushed on the bar to the door that led to the fire escape. She opened the door while ignoring Shirley's screams. She didn't know that the old metal fire escape was blazing hot. She stepped out onto the metal landing, severely burning her shoes and then her foot. She fell back into the dining room and screamed. The door closed.

She jumped to her feet. What she saw horrified her. The floor on the far corner of the dining room just melted away. The computer room, where the fire had started, was directly under the dining room. After the lights went out, the only light came from the exit light. The lights in the parking lot were out as well. The whole section of Sycamore Street was utterly dark. The dining room was lit bright again, only this time by the flames shooting through the floor joists. She knew that it wouldn't be long before more of the floor would melt away. Then the joists would burn up, and the whole floor would collapse.

She had to get out.

She took one of the heavy chairs in the dining room and threw it through the kitchen window with all her strength. Then, without thinking, she vaulted herself through the ragged wood and glass window into the pitch-black parking lot.

She landed upright, but she crushed both knees and hips. She collapsed not five feet from the burning building. She then crawled on those shattered knees as far away from the building into the pitch-black parking lot as she could before she fainted.

She left over a dozen patients behind without even thinking about it.

~

Traffic on Broadway had slowed to a crawl. Still, no one had called the Somerville Fire Department since everyone who looked on figured that someone else would call it in. Most people would assume that there was a direct line from the fire detection system to the firehouse. While that was true, most people would not have believed that Vinny would have disabled the system.

One observant commuter who watched the flames erupt from the left side of the building spotted two patients exiting the building on the far right. That would be from the B-wing on the first floor. Luckily for the first-floor residents, Vinny hadn't bothered to install locks on the exit door leading to the stairwell. The two people were in pajamas, coughing and gasping. It turns out that the two ladies were Barbara Parrish and Joyce George. Ellis had stolen Barbara's pocketbook the night before. Barbara never noticed that her prized possession was missing. Later, she would figure it was lost in the fire, which would be true, except it would burn from inside Ellis's storage unit, not from her room.

The commuter, a hero, named Randy Frantz, saved eight lives this night.

He worked as an X-Ray technician at the Somerville Hospital. After his shift had ended, he had driven from the hospital down Central Street and taken a right onto Broadway, just a couple of blocks from the nursing home, which would be on his right. His usual plan was to head to I-93, face the nightmare traffic on the Southeast Expressway, agonize over to the left at the Braintree split to Route 3, and take exit 17 to his home off Union Street in Braintree. He had been doing this same route virtually on autopilot for the last fifteen years.

Randy would never be the same again. That drive would never be routine again.

Randy pulled the car over, just several feet from the end of the building on Broadway. He raced into the building. The smoke on the B-wing was heavy but tolerable. He had grabbed a stack of Burger King napkins in his glove box doused them with water from his water bottle. He placed them over his mouth. He could feel the heat coming from the A-wing. In a split second, he wondered why the fire department wasn't already on the scene. He even thought it might be prudent to call them. He had left his cell phone in the car. There wasn't time. Then the thought left him immediately.

His only thought was to get the people out fast.

Room 101 had two wheelchairs, each one near each bed. The closest rooms to the lobby were 101 and 104. He could tell those rooms were the most at risk since he saw the flames shooting out of the A-wing. So rather than take one patient out at a time, he decided to load up a single wheelchair with as many people as possible, just to get them out.

One man was yelling, "We can't walk."

"Hurry, just lay on top of each other in the wheelchair. We got to get out fast."

He stacked two people from Room 101 and one from Room 104. "Hold your breath. Don't breathe deep. I'll get you out."

He pushed them through the exit door and out into the sidewalk. "Don't breathe until we get far enough away from the building. The air even outside was thick with smoke. He unstacked them and laid them on the concrete. He raced back in.

Two men from 105 could use their walkers to get moving. They were disoriented. "This way. Follow me." He was able to direct them to the exit. He then stacked the remaining patient in Room 104, a terrified frail woman who looked over ninety years old, and two little men from Room 103. He had to remove the lady from Room 104 from the wheelchair, restack the guys and then put the little old lady on top. He was afraid the two guys from Room 103 would crush her. That exercise nearly killed him. He worked frantically and got all three outside. Finally, nearly exhausted and now feeling intense pain from smoke inhalation, he staggered back into the building. This time, barely able to breathe, he stacked the remaining two patients from Room 106, which thankfully was right next to the exit door.

"I've got you. You will be safe." Then, he could get them out onto the sidewalk using all the strength and willpower in him.

That's when he heard the fire engines.

All he could say was, "thank you, dear Jesus." He dropped to the sidewalk and sat amongst the survivors of the first-floor B-wing. All alive. He sobbed and sobbed.

~

Right after the lights went out, Edie called 911. "The smoke is getting pretty thick."

The dispatcher told her that the fire department was either on their way or already there.

"Oh, and don't panic," said the dispatcher over Edie's speakerphone.

"Great," answered Edie.

Edie was slow to react to the Bingo call to action of the Bingo gang and showed up after Bill had hit Ellis over the head with the bedpan.

Once Edie saw Ellis, she whispered to Shirley. "I'm sure that's the man I saw at Revere Beach. It looks like the group took care of him."

"I knew it all along. It was that crazy facial motion," said Shirley.

Once part of the floor melted away in the dining room, smoke poured into the second floor. Luckily, Lauren had closed the dining-room door behind her. But the smoke was coming into the A-wing under the door. The red exit door sign provided just enough light for the group to see the smoke coming from under the door. "

"Who's got a cell phone?" asked Edie. "Use it as a flashlight."

"How?" asked Marjorie.

Phyllis jumped in. "Just swipe from the bottom. How long have you had an iPhone?"

"Never mind that. We've got to get out of here. That smoke is getting worse," pleaded Shirley.

There were eight other patients on the second floor, not counting the Bingo Gang. All of them are trapped.

"We've got to get out of here. The smoke is coming from the dining room or the kitchen. We can't use the elevator. The only way out is the emergency exit down the hall." Bones explained.

Tommy went nuts. He shook his head back and forth. Then he drove his wheelchair from one side of the corridor to the other.

"What are you doing, you maniac," yelled Bones. "We can't waste time dodging you. We gotta get out of here."

Tommy was moving fast back and forth. Since it was dark., no one could be sure exactly where he was at any given time. So he effectively blocked any move toward the locked exit.

39

Then time seemed to stand still. Edie sat down on the floor. The smoke seemed to slow down. Bill, Bones, just stood standing. Ruthie and Phyllis sat still in their wheelchairs.

"What's happening?" asked a confused Marjorie. "Are we dead?"

"I don't know," answered Shirley.

Tommy rolled to a stop. But he was still moving his body and fully aware.

"Form a circle around me," said Edie.

"Do you hear voices, Edie?" asked Marjorie.

"No. But I can feel a presence. I am a medium. People on the other side don't speak to me. But they can communicate with me. Not with voices, but with thoughts. In my thoughts."

"Who are they?" asked Marjorie.

Phyllis jumped in. "What's going on? We have got to get out of here."

Edie said, "We will. This will only take a minute. I sense that spirits need to communicate something to each of you, Tommy, Marjorie, and Shirley. And me. Something important. But they seem happy. Happy to be able to tell you what they have wanted to for a long time. But they cannot communicate directly with you."

"Did Shirley tell you we all hear voices? Are we hearing the same voices at the same time?" asked Marjorie.

"I don't think so. I think that each of you is hearing your own thoughts. Not real voices. But, they can use me as the conduit to tell you what they want you to hear. But again, not through audible voices."

"Sure spirits are happy while we get toasted to death." Phyllis was heading into the darkness.

Bones pulled her back. "Wait. We are a team. We go together. Give her a minute."

"I feel my Buddy so strong."

Ruthie jumped in. "I'm dead. I know I am. And I am in hell? See, that's what I get for not praying more."

"Shut up, Ruthie. You are not dead. You are simply an idiot," yelled Phyllis.

"Let's hold hands. The three of you."

"Shirley, I promised you that I would never tell anyone about what happened to you after I left the beach. Well, I broke that promise."

"Edie. No. I was so ashamed. How could you?"

"I told Buddy. But I made him promise never to tell a living soul. I was so upset. I had to tell someone. I'm sensing from Buddy that he broke his promise too. I'm getting a strong feeling that he told Willy."

"What? When?"

"I don't know exactly. I'm getting a sense from Buddy that he wants you to know that Willy knew all along. I'm guessing it didn't make any difference. He loved you and never, ever blamed you."

"How do you know?"

"I just do. Trust Buddy. Trust me. I get the feeling that Buddy is also waiting for me. And that I will be with him soon. As I said, it's not a voice, just my thoughts, but they are not my thoughts. They are Buddy's. Now he has left. I believe he has gone to the light and he is happy. I just know that."

"Willy knew all along. So why didn't he tell me?" pleaded Shirley.

"You'll have to ask him when you two meet up again."

"Edie, I feel so relieved. All these years of hiding cause I was too ashamed to tell Willy. And it didn't matter to him. So I can die happy."

"Jesus, Mary, and Joseph, Shirley. I'm not ready to die now. We have got to get the fuck out of here." Bones was yelling. "The goddam smoke is getting much stronger."

"Marjorie. I'm now getting strong thoughts from someone real close to you. I believe it's a woman. I'm getting a feeling about a birthday card. Not a store-bought one. But a homemade one. Do you know what that means?"

Marjorie put her head down and wept. "Yes. It was my birthday. I arrived home. Phil had arranged a big surprise birthday party for me. I never got to visit my Gramma. It was the first time I missed seeing her in I don't know how long. I've never gotten over it. I feel so guilty. She died in the fire. I never saw her again."

"I'm getting an image of an old woman giving you a piece of paper. She has a big smile. She is so happy and grateful to you. Of course, she is not saying this. But I feel she is begging you to heal that scar, that guilt. I get the thoughts that she wanted you to know. She loves you more than you will ever know."

Marjorie stopped crying and hugged Shirley. "I can now die happy."

"Stop this talk of dying. I am not ready to die. C'mon. I'm choking." Bones was now coughing.

"Okay, just one more thing. Tommy. A chorus of people invading my thoughts, trying to tell you something. I'm getting a word, something like a protector, a guardian like a guardian angel. I get the feeling that you made their life better. I'm not sure how. I'm getting a strong sense of a string of words, something like, 'thank you, dear Tommy. You were our salvation, something like that."

Tommy was deathly still. Tears flowed down his cheeks.

"Great, no more talk of dying happy. Now let's roll." Bones was taking charge.

The dining room door exploded open and simply disintegrated. Flames shot into the A-wing within ten feet of the assembled Bingo

Gang. A massive cloud of toxic thick black smoke poured into the corridor.

"Everyone get on the floor. That's the only safe place for now. We have to move fast." Bones was taking command. He dropped to the floor.

Ruthie and Phyllis slipped out of their wheelchairs onto the floor, Bill and Bones dropped, and Edie slid onto her stomach.

"We have to slide on the floor to the exit. That's the only way out," commanded Bones.

Tommy did not get out of his wheelchair. Instead, he raced away from the crowd, past the break room, the nursing station, and the elevator to the door to the outside deck.

"Tommy, you'll die if you stay in your chair. You have to get low on the floor." yelled Bones.

It was too late. Tommy had disappeared into the darkness.

The gang had decided to form a human train. The idea was that each person would hold onto another person's legs to make sure no one would be left behind. After all, a proper gang hangs together. Bones was the engine, Marjorie was next, followed by Bill, Edie, and Ruthie. Shirley was the caboose.

The train was in motion. Slow-motion. It had moved only a couple of feet outside of Room 209 when it came to a sudden stop.

Ellis grabbed onto Shirley's leg and yanked her back to him.

Shirley lost the grip of Ruthie's leg.

Ellis was pulling her closer and closer to him.

The smoke was dropping nearer to the floor. Flames were shooting up to the roof through the dining room floor. Most of the floor of the dining room was gone. Only joists remained. The joists were black and glowing.

The floor of the corridor was quickly disappearing, leaving gaping holes. Flames were getting closer.

"BINGO! BINGO! He's got me. He's pulling me back," yelled Shirley.

Ruthie let go of Bill's leg. She stood up straight. Now Ruthie had been confined in a wheelchair for years. This amazed the gang and even her.

"Ruthie, what are you doing? Get down. You'll die from the smoke." Bill yelled.

"What the fuck is going on.? We gotta move." Bones begged.

Ruthie, in one continuous motion, fell on top of Ellis.

Shirley freed herself. "C'mon, Ruthie." Shirley squirmed like a fish to Bill and held on to his ankle. "Ruthie, grab my ankle. Let's go. Now."

"No. I'm gonna sit right here on top of that devil. I'll be reading him passages from Luke. That will be punishment enough for him. Go, I'm so ready to meet Jesus. Go. I'm not moving."

"Move it. Move it," Bones yelled.

The human train started up again.

Shirley looked back. Ruthie was still on top of Ellis. Ellis was so stunned he couldn't figure out what had happened. Within seconds, the floor melted. Ruthie and Ellis just disappeared onto the first floor. Shirley thought she heard a faint, "Praise Jesus."

The floor was now getting hot.

Shirley could see open joists. The floor was melting toward the gang. "Pick it up, gang, or we will be exiting the building through the floor."

Tommy had reached the door to the deck. He knew that it opened outward. It was also locked. However, it was not a fire door but a standard wooden door with a large glass insert. He rammed himself into the glass. Nothing happened. He looked behind him. Ruthie and Phyllis's room 205 was opposite the deck door. The door to Room 205 was open. He backed into the room as far as he could. Then like something out of *Fast and Furious*, he put his wheelchair into gear and headed directly into the glass part of the door, his ram of a leg and foot sticking straight out, heading for the glass.

CRASH. The window of the door shattered. The good news was that he had created an escape route. The bad news was that oxygen accelerated the fire. Also, while the door window was now broken, the door was still locked. It would be challenging for the old folks to climb through the opening.

He repeated his move. He once again backed into Room 205 and once more accelerated into the door. This time he angled toward the wooden frame. BAM. The door flew open. The structure had been weakened by the loss of glass and was no match for Tommy's ram-like leg.

The residents of Rooms 203, 204, and 207 crawled on the floor onto the deck. The smoke was not as bad since these rooms were farther away from the fire.

The Somerville Fire Department was now fully on the scene. They were fighting the fire from the parking lot, Sycamore Street, and Broadway. On his mother's side, Willy's second cousin, Dickie Skinner, a recent addition to the Somerville Fire department, spotted a group of people on the outside deck. He quickly alerted his captain. They rushed two ladders up to the deck. The deck was wood, so they had to hurry.

Dickie was on the deck. He helped the choking patients down the ladders.

By this time, the human train had reached the nursing station. Next, they had to pass the elevator to reach the deck.

"Hurry. Go to the deck. Hurry. It's close." yelled Tommy. His voice was high-pitched.

The former residents of the second floor B-wing were carried down to safety by then.

Tommy yelled to Dickie Skinner. "There are people inside. Now! Get them out."

Dickie ran into the B-wing. "Sam. We got more inside. Fast. Give me a hand. Sam Thomas, a young black man from Medford, ran in to help Dickie. Sam and Dickie pulled the surviving members of the Bingo Gang to the deck's safety, down the ladders, and onto the parking lot. Tommy was the last one rescued.

"Get this guy to a paramedic. His leg is bleeding badly." Tommy's battering ram leg was pretty cut up.

Finally, minus Ruthie, the Bingo Gang gathered safely in the parking lot. The EMTs worked on them. They were mostly alright.

Bones started, "Holy fuck. Did you hear Tommy speak? Was it me, or did he tell us to go to the deck? His voice sounded like a little kid. Am I the only one who heard him?"

"I heard him too. Funny, he has a high-pitched voice. I would have thought it would be like a growl. But, instead, he sounded like a teenager before their voice changed." Bill added.

"Anyone got a smoke?" asked Bones.

"A smoke? Are you kidding me? Haven't you had enough smoke to last you a lifetime?" Phyllis just shook her head.

"A lifetime may not be that long, lady. Bill, you got a smoke?"

Bill handed him one. They both lit up.

The Winter Hill Nursing and Rehabilitation Center was now entirely on fire. The roof collapsed onto the second floor and then onto the first. It howled in pain. It groaned in agony. Then as if it suddenly lost its life, it moaned its last miserable breath. Finally, the building fell into itself. It was over. It was no more. No more institutional food. No more miserable aides who were not in the building during the fire. No more Paul Batty, no more Vinny, and no more loan shark, Butch Donovan. Sadly, no more Ruthie.

40

By the time Sean had exited the highway, he had heard over the police radio that the Winter Hill Nursing and Rehabilitation Center had burned to the ground. The reports were that many of the patients had escaped, but at least four people were unaccounted for and feared dead.

Sean did the math in his head. About a dozen people on the first floor and maybe twenty on the second. So that was about thirty-two patients, plus the night shift staff, which was only a couple. So that meant that no more than forty, maybe fewer, people were there during the fire. So the odds were not that bad that his mother had survived.

He pulled into the back parking lot while the EMTs were triaging. The building was gone and was now just a pile of smoldering rubble.

He spotted Shirley, ran towards her, kissed, and hugged her. This was the first time since he got into that awful argument with his father that he sobbed. Then, an EMT propped her up on the back of an ambulance.

"I'm fine. Just a little smoke in my lungs. Ruthie died. The others are okay." Shirley took a deep breath. "I'm assuming that awful man died too."

"You were right. He was the guy from the beach. I should have trusted your intuition. I spoke to his daughter. He was a mechanic at a garage that did maintenance work on the fire engines. She told me that some man in a uniform beat him up so bad he almost died. Before Dad died, he tried telling me that he almost killed a man. That was right after you got married. That man was Ellis."

"Daddy beat that awful man up so bad he almost died?

"Yes. He didn't tell me any of the details. It was just before Dad died," said Sean.

"Edie was the only person who knew about what happened to me. She had promised me that she wouldn't tell anyone. But she broke her promise and told her boyfriend, Buddy. Buddy and your dad were best friends. He was his best man. Wow, so he beat up that awful man, huh. Good for him. If only he had told me."

"I guess he wanted to protect you. But it sounds like you found out that Dad knew about it already. How did you find out?" asked Sean

"Edie kind of helped me along the way."

"Edie just knows things. Did she have one of her feelings?"

"Yeah. One of those feelings. That miserable bastard showed up a couple of days ago. He did this weird thing with his face, like a nervous twitch. Moved his ears, his eyebrows, his forehead. That's when I knew."

"His daughter told me about it."

"He did that same thing with his face the night he..." Shirley welled up.

"It's okay, Ma. You don't have to talk about it.

"You know, Sean, aside from almost being burned alive, being attacked by a sicko maniac, and losing poor Ruthie, I had one of the best nights since I lost your father."

Sean laughed out loud, "What?"

"I feel more peace now than I have for, I don't know, sixty years. I am truly a happy woman. Someday, I'll explain it. Plus, you wouldn't believe me if I told you. Edie called my guilt the silent scar. Well, guess what? It's gone." Then Shirley's tears flowed from her reddened eyes.

She began to moan, first softly, then louder, then louder. Her whole body shook, and she cried and cried so hard.

Sean knelt by her side and held her. "Are you okay?"

After a bit, her crying subsided. "Yes. I am so, so okay. Do you know what it feels like to be truly cleansed of guilt and shame? That's what I am feeling. Now you too need to heal your guilt. You have done so much for me. Thanks. I love you so much."

Edie walked slowly over to Sean and Shirley, careful not to lose her balance. "Willy is not sad anymore."

"Thanks Edie. You have been a blessing to me."

"I'm guessing that all your records, reports, and charts are gone. I checked yesterday at St. Joseph's. They had not received any reports from Winter Hill, good or bad. All they received was the glowing voice mail from Mr. Batty, which was a result of our little blackmail scheme."

Shirley just laughed a huge cleansing laugh. "We did an excellent job of good cop, bad cop or maybe just bad cop, bad cop."

"The St. Joseph's people said they were looking forward to your arrival."

The remaining Bingo Gang gathered around Shirley, except Tommy. The EMTs were still working on him.

Andy Buckley, the fire captain, joined in. "Sean. I haven't seen you since you were a teenager. I worked under your father when I first joined the department. What are you doing here?"

"My mother was in there." Sean pointed to the rubble.

"Shirley, right?" He took hold of Shirley's good hand. "I had no idea you were a patient here. It must have been awful. Thank God you got out alive."

"I had lots of help. So you knew my husband?"

"Willy was a good man. He taught me a lot. But I remember that all he could talk about was his Shirley. Shirley, this. Shirley that. I am so glad you made it out. This could have been even worse than it was."

"He was a fine man," said Shirley. Then she became distracted. She spotted Tommy who was rolling toward her. She pointed to him. "There he is!"

Everyone from the Bingo Gang to the others on the B-Wing, let out a huge cheer. They chanted, "Hero. Hero. Hero. Tommy's our man. Hero." Tommy just waved. For the first time in the years that Tommy was at Winter Hill, he smiled.

"Ma. You are coming home with me tonight until your room is ready at… Say it with me."

They both yelled at the same time, "St. Joseph's!"

The Bingo Gang cheered.

Sean pushed Shirley in one of the borrowed wheelchairs toward his Charger.

"Wow. Nice car."

Sean carefully lifted her out of her wheelchair into the back seat. He got her strapped in. Then he loaded the wheelchair into the trunk.

She was smiling broadly. Then her mood took a serious turn. "Do you still see that young nurse?"

"It wasn't her shift. Right?" asked Sean.

"No. I saw the charge nurse."

"Yeah, the one who kept telling me you were losing your mind."

"I saw her just before the lights went out. I wonder if she made it out alive," said Shirley.

Sean started the engine, put it in gear, and checked the rearview mirror. Colleen walked toward the car. Sean shifted the car back into park. "Speaking of the young nurse. Her name is Colleen. It looks like she wants to talk to me. Sit tight. I'll be there in a minute." Sean got out of the car and approached Colleen.

"Looks like I'm out of a job. Thank God your mother made it out alive. I heard about the fire. I could smell the smoke from my apartment. I had to see it for myself. I suspected they monkeyed around with the sprinklers and alarms. Bastards."

"Well, the arson folks will figure that out. Right now, I'm going to take care of my mother. What are you going to do?"

"I don't know. No more nursing homes for me!"

"Look about the other night. I..."

"I've got issues. I know that. I did that to your car. Your tires. I get so enraged at times that I do things that I shouldn't. I got a text from Cassidy's grandmother. It was nasty. It said some cop was investigating the death of her son. That was you. Wasn't it?"

"Yeah."

"I didn't push Serj under the car. But I was yelling and screaming at him and calling him every name in the book. Finally, he got so angry. He moved quickly, then..."

"He shouldn't have changed the tire on such a hill. It wasn't your fault."

"It was my fault. But I never intended for him to die."

"What now?"

"When I got the text from Mrs. Sarkissian, I got so mad, I started to throw things around the house. Then Cassidy asked me what the matter was. I told her that you were spying on me. And I was mad. Then she blurted out. Don't kill him like you killed my father."

"You don't have to do this," said Sean.

"I realized that I've got to get help. Do you know that I was so mad about the maintenance man-killing that poor old man's dog? I wanted to punish him. So I enlisted the old man, and we plotted to punish him. But see, that was wrong."

"Well, if he were the one who turned off the sprinkler, he would get in a lot of trouble, probably go to jail."

"I'm not going to say anything about it. I need to focus on myself. But once I settled down, I realized you saw something in me that wasn't right."

"I also saw a lot in you that was very good. So I was attracted to that part of you."

"I will go to therapy. Then, who knows. Maybe was see where things go. Plus, I owe you a set of tires."

"Forget about the tires. Okay?"

Colleen kissed Sean on the cheek and peeked inside the Charger. "Ms. Duffy. I'm so glad you are okay and away from this dreadful, hateful place." She then walked away.

Sean jumped into the car.

"Now, let's get some fried clams and fries. Almost dying makes me starved." Shirley let out a big sigh.

The Boston Globe ran a front-page story, below the fold, about the fire. The story stayed close to the facts. The Boston Herald, which had a tabloid format, used the entire front page with a color picture of the building still in flames collapsing. The headlines read, NURSING HOME NIGHTMARE. Both papers reported that arson was probably not suspected, although they noted that the fire marshal still had several questions left unanswered. They wrote that three bodies had been recovered.

The state and Enstat had a problem. They had several nursing home patients without places to stay. They found one or two beds here and there throughout the Boston area, at least temporarily. Shirley's bed was available at St. Joseph's to move in immediately. They also had three vacant beds customarily reserved for rehab patients. Marjorie and Bill were transported to St. Joseph's from an uncomfortable night's stay at the Somerville Hospital Emergency Room.

The arson squad did not know that Butch Donovan's car was still there and would remain there for quite some time until the investigators figured out why Butch would have been at the place where the fire originated. The other cars were Lauren's Civic and Batty's Mercedes. The police towed Batty's car to his home in Melrose. Emily traded in the leased base model Mercedes for the latest Porsche Panamera three weeks later.

41

Sean and Shirley spent the evening at Sullivan's, a popular take-out stand along the shore in South Boston. They ordered hot dogs, fried clams, and fries. Shirley hadn't tasted fried clams since before Willy died. Then she settled for the night in Sean's apartment. Willy did not appear in the ceiling. There were no voices in her head. She had spent much of her adult life with a cloud of guilt and shame hanging over her. It wasn't like she thought about it every day, but it was always there in the background, coloring what joys she did have. She regretted that it took so long for her to free herself of it. This night was perhaps the most peaceful one she had experienced since Ellis had attacked her.

St. Joseph's was on Shore Avenue in Quincy, just a block from Quincy Bay. Today the sun was shining. There was an armada of sailboats in the harbor. Unlike her street view from Winter Hill, Shirley had a full view of the harbor. Also, unlike at Winter Hill, the windows opened. She sat in her room and took a deep breath of fresh sea air.

Life was now perfect. Marjorie, Edie, and Bill were there for company. She would make new friends. And whenever that time comes, would join Willy, and not worry about telling him her secret. She wheeled closer to the window. She just stared at the bay. She wondered whether Willy would appear on the ceiling ever again. She thought not. Maybe the reason Willy appeared on her ceiling was his way of trying to tell her that he knew her secret. Maybe he had wanted to tell her before but just never could. She felt that Willy could now rest. She could finally breathe fully. Her guilt, her silent scar, was gone.

Her mood was interrupted by a nurse. "Mrs. Duffy. Welcome. I will be your weekday nurse. I'm Beth. The nursing station is just down the hall. Of course, you have the call button. But we will be checking in on you regularly. You will love the night nurse. She is like a stand-up comedian. She loves to gather the patients and tell jokes. Her name is Francesca. I'll be back later for your turn-down service."

Marjorie poked her nose into Shirley's room. "Smell that air."

Shirley twirled her wheelchair around from the open window. "Hi, Marjorie. Are you sure we didn't die? And this is heaven? I haven't had a turn-down service since the night Willy, and I celebrated our twenty-fifth. That was at the Statler in downtown."

"I know. It's wonderful. Both Bill and I are here only temporarily. But I talked to Benny. He's coming up from Rhode Island tomorrow and will try to get me in permanently. How much you want to bet that Bill will finagle his way into staying permanently here as well."

"Where is Bill? I haven't seen him since the fire," said Shirley.

"Where else? In the dining room across the hall, scrounging for a snack."

"What happened to us during the fire? Was it real or some simultaneous dream? I still can't figure it out," said Marjorie.

"Who knows? All I know, it was something we both needed before we die," said Shirley.

"See you tonight at dinner."

"Heaven. Yes." The sea breeze washed over her relaxed face. She closed her eyes, turned her wheelchair back toward the window, fell into an easy doze, and snored lightly.

Then she suddenly awoke and opened her eyes. It was all black. All she could smell was laundry detergent. She realized that she was unable to breathe. Her good hand instinctively rose to her face. She felt a hand. It was pressing on what she now knew was a pillow, hard against her face. She knew that it would not be long before losing consciousness and then dying. After all, she went through, surviving the fire and surviving that awful man, she wasn't ready to give up yet.

In a split second, she devised a plan. No, goddamit, she would not die. She dropped her good hand to the side of the wheelchair and let it hang limp. Then, in a split second, she grabbed onto the wheel. With all her might, she thrust it backward. It ran over something. A foot?

"Shit." It came from a muffled voice.

Shirley then pushed the wheel forward, then back again to create a circular motion.

The pillow dropped, and she looked up.

It was Ellis. What? With everything in her. She rammed the chair into his legs, throwing him off balance. His walker went flying. Then Shirley saw him regain himself. Ellis thrust the pillow again toward Shirley's face.

Then Shirley yelled. BINGO. BINGO. BINGO.

This sound caused Ellis to hesitate for a moment.

BOING. It was Bill, armed once again with a bedpan. He hit Ellis on the head, and Ellis dropped to his knees. Marjorie ran into Shirley's room.

Shirley was gasping for breath, but not so much that she didn't ram into Ellis's ribs.

Beth ran into the room.

"I thought Ellis died in the fire. We saw him fall through the floor with poor Ruthie on top of him," said Marjorie.

Beth added. "They brought him in this morning. He apparently fell on some rehab cushions and ran out the side door. The EMTs took him to Central Hospital. He was released with only minor cuts and bruises this morning and suffered some smoke inhalation. We had an extra bed here. So they brought him here not an hour ago. What was he doing?"

"He held a pillow over my face."

"I'm so sorry," said Beth. "No one told us that he was a problem. Unfortunately, we have not heard from the staff at Winter Hill."

Within a few minutes, two members of the Quincy Police Department entered the room.

Bill stepped in front of them as they walked into the room. "She was yelling for help." He never disclosed their secret code for danger. "I ran into her room. I just happened to have a bedpan in my hand. See, I was planning to take a shit."

The police officer never asked him why he needed a bedpan if he could walk around without the aid of a wheelchair or even a walker?

"Then I saw him holding a pillow over Shirley's face. He was trying to kill her. So I did the first thing that came into my mind. Hit him with the bedpan."

"I dozed off. Then I couldn't breathe. I managed to push my wheelchair into his legs. Then Bill conked him. He saved my life."

The policeman was able to revive Ellis. They sat him up.

"What were you doing?" the policeman asked.

"Nothing. I was just visiting my friend. I had helped her out at the old nursing home before the fire."

"He's no friend of mine," said Shirley.

Bill stepped in. "That's bullshit."

Sean, who hadn't been more than a couple of miles from St. Joseph's, again had on the scanner that there was some problem at St. Joseph's. This night was the second in a row that his mother was in the middle of a crisis. He took the first exit off the highway and raced back to St. Joseph's.

By the time Sean arrived, Ellis had walked out of St. Joseph's in handcuffs.

"Ma, are you okay?"

"Sure as shit. Almost dying two days in a row is good for you. I'm fine. Bill, here saved my life." She wheeled over to Bill and pulled him down to her. "See, it's good to have friends and sometimes good to be in a gang."

Sean just shook his head.

The cops loaded Ellis into the Quincy police cruiser.

Sean kissed his mother goodbye. "Ma, please, no more drama, at least for one night."

St. Joseph's was a converted mansion. Unlike the Winter Hill Rest Home and the Winter Hill Nursing and Rehabilitation Center, it was renovated with care, using the latest building standards and technology. Yet, it still retained the charm of an old New England structure. The most prominent feature was a wraparound porch in the front and side of the building. Even though the building was a block removed from Quincy Bay, there was a nice ocean view from the porch. And on a quiet night, you could hear the waves splashing on the shore. Tonight, was that night.

The patients had a wonderful dinner. Marjorie had said good night to Bill and Shirley.

Edie walked into Shirley's room.

"What a disaster! I was so much at peace during breakfast. Then something hit me. They must have brought him in after breakfast. What was he thinking?" asked Edie.

"Maybe he believes that I can prove he raped me. Or maybe he is just crazy. Who knows? We have Bill as a witness to attempted murder, so ..."

"You are all set. Ellis will never get back into St. Joseph's. He will end up in an institution."

"Edie. I'm a little shaken. Still, I feel so free. Let's go outside."

Shirley wheeled herself out onto the porch.

Edie followed her.

Shirley just stared for several minutes at the sea. They was no more staring at the ceiling. Shirley closed her eyes. She could smell the ocean, hear the gentle sound of the waves splashing onto the shore, and felt extreme peace and joy. Sure, it would be wonderful if she could share this with Willy. That would come soon.

"Hey, lady. You want company?" It was Bill.

She grabbed onto his leathery hands. "Sit. Sit.'

"I'll leave you two." Edie left.

Bill pulled up a rocking chair. "Look, the moon is nearly full. The nuts will all be out."

"The nuts have already been out." Shirley just stared ahead. "It's wonderful, isn't it?"

"I'm gonna figure out how I can stay here. Maybe claim that I'm your bodyguard." Bill also stared ahead at the now dark ocean.

"Well, you saved my life. That should count for something."

"Yup. Too bad Bones, Phyllis, and Tommy are somewhere else."

"Yeah. Didn't Tommy speak? I heard him, "said Shirley.

"You know, Ellis didn't kill my dog Rudy," said Bill.

"Sure he did. He murdered Millie, Caroline, and probably Nelson. And Rudy.

What are you saying?"

"Nope. That young nurse overheard Vinny, that asshole mainte-nance guy telling the aides that he got rid of him. Vinny killed Rudy. He didn't want to deal with dog shit. He was dog shit himself. She's the one who got me my smokes."

"Huh. What about Millie? She was murdered."

"Probably not. While Ellis was lying on the floor, he said that he followed her into the kitchen as she was looking for food, like we all liked to do."

"I never did."

"And wanted to, you know, get friendly? You know what I mean? Then things got complicated."

"How? I didn't hear him say that."

"Well, you were pretty preoccupied. Anyway. Millie took her clothes off like she liked to do. But in the process of fooling around, she fell off her wheelchair, hit her head, and died."

"What about Caroline and Nelson?" asked Shirley.

"The aides did it. Well, they dropped her on the floor. They didn't give a shit. That probably did it. Who knows about Nelson? He was on his deathbed anyway. They drugged the living shit out of him."

"Well, that bastard, Vinny. I hope he gets his."

"Funny you should ask. We scared the living crap out of him between the nurse and me. We trapped him in the tool shed. I nailed the door shut with some two-by-fours. Then I ran the leaf blower and blew smoke under the door." Bill laughed heartily. "I spotted Tommy watching from the deck." Bill could hardly contain himself. "That young nurse turned the walkie-talkie off!"

"Bill, you could have killed him."

"Nah. I turned off the leaf blower. I pulled the boards off the door then hightailed back into the building. Boy, Vinny was pissed. Taught that prick a lesson."

Shirley planted a kiss on Bill's cheek. "You are a hot ticket."

"I don't know the rules around here. But I am going to partake." Bill pulled out a pack of cigarettes, the very same pack that that nurse Colleen had given him, not a couple of nights ago. He lit up. Then blew out a massive flow of smoke. "Ah."

Shirley had to give up smoking after her stroke. However, one could make a convincing argument that the years of Merit 100s may have contributed to her stroke. "Hand me one of those."

Bill was more than eager to comply. He handed her a fresh cigarette.

Shirley gently placed the cigarette lovingly between her lips.

Bill lit the match.

Shirley took a deep drag and blew it out. "Heaven. Now I am in heaven."

Bill followed up, "Fuck the cancer. We are too old for cancer anyway."

Shirley took another long drag. "Fuck the cancer."

EPILOGUE

Eventually, the arson squad concluded that the fire was accidental. The squad determined that the fire's origin was in the computer room. It found evidence of a cigarette in the wastepaper basket. It speculated that a patient perhaps was poking around the computer room and dropped a cigarette butt into a wastebasket. It also assumed that a visitor, namely a shady character named Butch Donovan, must have smelled smoke, and tried to put the fire out with a water bucket, in fact, four water buckets. They then speculated that he was overcome with smoke and fell to the floor, hitting his head on the computer desk. They never quite figured out why such a shady character was in the nursing home, to begin with—perhaps visiting some long-lost relative. No one bothered to try to make that connection.

They also determined that the real unsung hero was the administrator Paul Batty. According to the nurse on duty Lauren Morehead, it appeared that Batty had smelled smoke and armed with a fire extinguisher, went to investigate. His body was found right outside the computer room with the extinguisher at his side. Apparently, they reported that the fire consumed him before he could put out the fire. Morehead said that she also tried to rescue the patients by attempting to flee out the exit door in the dining room. She claimed that the fire had made the metal fire escape too hot and then stated that the fire had engulfed the entire dining room and kitchen area. She testified that she tried to leave the dining room area, but her floor was giving away. Her only escape was to jump out the window. She was expected to make a full recovery. Later, she decided to abandon her nursing career and is now trying to sell her story of courage during the tragic fire to a literary agent. So far, she has been unsuccessful.

Emily, the widow of the unsung hero, mourned for her husband, Paul Batty. She did collect the life insurance on Paul and was able to buy the Winchester home with cash from the insurance. Emily never revealed to anyone why the home equity account was completely drained. She figured why not let dead dogs lie. It didn't matter. The insurance windfall was unexpected. Her mourning lasted exactly four months. She remarried at an elegant ceremony at the Mystic River Boat Club.

Investigators never figured out why the sprinkler systems or the integrated alarm systems malfunctioned. The fire destroyed any definitive clues. Instead, they determined that Enstat was criminally negligent for allowing a lock to be installed on the emergency exit door. The fine effectively put Enstat out of business. Enstat fired Vinny immediately after the investigators issued their report.

Ellis's criminal case was straightforward. Several of the patients at the nursing home, including Bones McGraw, Bill, Phyllis, Marjorie, and Shirley, issued a statement to the effect that patient Theodore Ellis had a history of violence and that a long time ago, he had raped Shirley. Sean provided evidence gleaned from Ellis's daughter. Bill testified that he witnessed Ellis placing a pillow over Shirley's face. The eyewitness testimony of both Shirley and Bill was enough to convict him of attempted murder. The rape charge was too old to have any real bearing. Ellis was sentenced to ten years at Massachusetts Correctional Institution at Norfolk, a medium-security prison in Norfolk, Massachusetts.

Colleen sought therapy for her urges of rage. Sean and Colleen failed to meet again.

Tommy never spoke another word. He stopped acting as a guard and ended up in a pleasant facility in the western part of Massachusetts. He died shortly after that. He had taken on too much smoke in the fire. His lungs had given out, and his heroics had done him in. He died with a smile on his face.

Sean went to work on behalf of the rest of the Bingo Gang. He arranged for Phyllis and Bones to be placed in St Joseph's.

Not entirely, but the Bingo Gang was now back in action.

Edie stays busy performing psychic readings for the patients at St. Joseph's.

Early in 2020, the St. Joseph's administrator was highly concerned about the impact of COVID-19 on nursing homes. She quickly instituted strict rules about hand washing, mask-wearing, and distancing. To this day, no patients or staff member has been infected by the virus.

ABOUT THE AUTHOR

Meehan is a marketer for a software company. And a storyteller. He's published three full-length books about the software. The books tell stories of how companies can use the software to help their business. Meehan authored dozens of articles and blogs and is a sought-after public speaker. He has traveled around the globe, entertaining audiences with stories and insights.

ALSO BY B. J. MEEHAN

Lifethreat

Getting Over Getting Fired

Made in the USA
Las Vegas, NV
27 January 2024

84929677R00204